# TRUST AND TREACHERY

*Dianna Louise Lund*

ISBN: 154263248X
ISBN 13: 9781542632485
Library of Congress Control Number: 2017900946
CreateSpace Independent Publishing Platform
North Charleston, South Carolina

## CHAPTER 1

# SUNDAY, JANUARY 20, 1793

"Death! Death! Death!"

Henri LeBeau's words chilled the air of the Rouen wineshop. It was a poor place to escape the cold. The small fire in the tiny grate seemed to shiver rather than burn as pale winter light filtered through one grimy window over two scarred tables, a few chairs, and the battered board that served as a counter.

"Death to all enemies of the Republic!" LeBeau's eyes swept the room. His smoldering glare fell first on the two men sitting across the table from him and then on the wineshop owner, Rene Dubois, hovering behind them. Francois Meunier and Yves Michel shifted uneasily in their seats, but neither they nor Dubois dared to disagree with their friend.

Nodding his head which seemed to balance precariously atop his skinny neck, LeBeau repeated, "Death!" before he stared at the back of the solitary customer hunched over the counter.

Meunier opened his mouth, shut it, and then finally said, "But Henri, I heard –"

"Death to the Anglais!" LeBeau's hand slammed down on the table as he rose so suddenly that his chair tumbled backward.

Meunier grabbed the chipped tumbler in front of him, but Michel's beefy hand was slower. The dockman's glass tipped. Sour burgundy spilled across the table and then dripped onto the floor like blood.

Immediately Dubois, thin as the wine he served, bustled over to the counter and grabbed a dirty rag.

The customer at the counter turned and leaned against it, one elbow resting on the well-scrubbed surface. His face was shuttered, blank as he watched Dubois use his rag to mop up the spill. He lifted the glass in his hand to his lips, only a slight whitening about the knuckles at odds with his relaxed stance.

"Sit, sit," said Dubois, righting LeBeau's chair. "And enough talk of death, Henri! It's hard enough to make a living without…" Dubois glanced back at the customer standing at the counter. He put a hand on LeBeau's shoulder. "Enough."

LeBeau shook his head in reluctant agreement, his attention, like Dubois', now drawn to the tall man standing a few feet away.

"Seen you today," LeBeau said, his lips pursed in concentration. "Near the river." The man's black hair, straight nose, pronounced cheekbones, and dark blue eyes were no more unusual than the frayed clothing on his lean frame.

Le Beau's frown deepened. "With a cart and a horse." His head jerked towards the window and then back again. No cart was in the street outside.

"And at the market?" The man's question was its own answer. He took another sip of wine. "Not every week, but ..."

"You're a ragman," blurted out Michel in sudden recognition. "Bought a shirt from you last spring."

"That's me. Richard Verinder, ragman. Buying here, selling there. Never long in one place. I like to keep on the move." Verinder threw out the unnecessary information with a crooked smile.

"And you was 'round the houses near the river this morning. Me and Henri seen you while we was unloading a barge, didn't we?" Michel turned to his friend to confirm the memory. But LeBeau said nothing, his zealot's eyes narrowed and suspicious.

"I was there." Verinder swallowed the last of the wine in his glass and shrugged, pushing away the memory of what he'd learned just before making his last sale of the day. "Doing a bit of buying. Some selling, too."

"So where's your cart, Verinder?" LeBeau demanded.

"*Le Cheval Noir.*"

"The Noir?" LeBeau repeated, his disbelieving voice rasping over the syllables. The inn a few streets away was not the sort of place a ragman would stay.

"It's too cold to sleep outside. Cart's in the stable. And I'm in the cart."

"Under the rags," Dubois guessed at once.

Verinder saw the fiery dockhand's wariness begin to evaporate. Some of his own tension eased. "It's a place to sleep. A good one when it's full as it is now. *Le Guillotine* has put whole wardrobes on the market in Paris. Come to the square tomorrow and see. Plenty of warm winter cloaks. All with more than one tear, but yours for a coin or two." Verinder picked up the cap he'd laid on the counter a half hour before and limped toward the door.

His awkward gait once again made him the center of attention.

"Your right leg?" LeBeau questioned, his eyes locked in wary misgiving on the ragman.

"A lucky shot by a gamekeeper years ago," Verinder replied evenly, the familiar lie coming easily to his lips. Dubois pulled out a chair from the wineshop's only other table and motioned toward it.

"Lucky!" Michel exclaimed, his large burly frame rocking in disagreement as Verinder sat in the empty chair next to his.

"He's alive, isn't he?" Meunier snorted in disgust. "Didn't stay 'round afterwards either, I bet." The stocky man looked at Verinder and waited for some sign that he was right.

Verinder bent to put his cap on the table, his face momentarily hidden as he said, "Didn't want to push my luck."

"Something like that give anyone a reason to stay on the move." Meunier raised arms that easily wielded a blacksmith's hammer and drove one fist into his palm. "And to hate aristos and them as worked for 'em."

The others growled in agreement.

"You said Paris. Been there recently?" asked Michel

"Yes," said Verinder. "A few days ago."

"They say after Capet shakes hands with *Le Guillotine* tomorrow, the *Anglais* will declare war." Dubois looked questioningly at Verinder as he spoke, then walked around the table, pushed the wineshop's remaining chair into the circle, and sat down heavily.

"Paris is full of the same rumors," Verinder agreed.

"These *Anglais,* pah!" shouted LeBeau, "Always the English. What business of theirs what we do here in France?"

Meunier, Michel, and Dubois sighed almost in unison. LeBeau's question was one they'd heard daily for weeks.

"And we have these meddling English here in Rouen, Verinder." LeBeau leaned toward the ragman, the muscles in his neck straining with emotion. "Yes, here in Rouen," he repeated, looking at his three friends for confirmation.

"Henri, we've…" Dubois pleaded to no avail.

"The doctor's wife and niece. They are English!" LeBeau's voice rose to an angry shout.

"But," said Dubois, "you know the niece was born here, and her aunt has lived in Rouen for years. The committee has already examined their papers. And Docteur Mansard is a good man. He treated *ma petit* Lucette when she broke her arm. Madame

Mansard sent a custard. And her niece Élisabeth made a rag doll for Lucette."

"Citizeness Mansard," stressed Le Beau," and her niece are English!" He spat the word out like a curse. "We should go to the house. Drag them before the committee again. They are enemies of the Revolution!"

"They say if war is declared, all the English will be arrested," added Michel. "What are they saying in Paris?"

As four pairs of eyes shifted to mark the ragman's reply, Verinder said simply, "The same."

"And none of it matters, Henri," Meunier said patiently. "As I've been trying to tell you, the good doctor's wife will be leaving Rouen before she can be arrested. She has a fever. She'll be gone soon. In a coffin."

"The spotted fever?" Verinder asked, his words tinged with alarm.

"No," answered Meunier. "At least, I don't think so. Why? Have you heard anything?"

"Rumors," Verinder answered. "A ragman hears things." He shrugged before adding, "These days you can't be too careful. Besides, if he's a doctor, well..."

The dread of typhoid hung unspoken over the men. Michel was the first to break the silence. "The ragman's right, you know, about being careful."

"This doctor – Mansard, you said? Would he be the one living in Rue Orbe near the *Cheval Noir*?" wondered Verinder aloud.

"No, that's Berthold, the chemist. Mansard lives in Rue St. Vivian," answered Dubois. "Why?"

Verinder rubbed his chin. "Mansard's wife's dying. Perhaps she's already dead. After a death, there are usually bargains to be had by the ragman."

"No! You wouldn't. You said yourself the house may not be safe!" Dubois stared in disbelief.

"Besides that harridan who lives with them won't let you in the door," said LeBeau venomously, looking at Verinder's patched and shabby dress.

"Fever on one side of the door, and me on the other," replied Verinder. "I've made plenty of bargains while standing outside and even better ones after saying I'll be forced to boil the clothes before I can sell them." Verinder stood; and then picking up his cap, he settled it on his head.

"You'll be thrown off the steps," said Dubois.

"Come to my wagon tomorrow and find out," invited Verinder as he turned to leave.

"I will," promised Dubois. "My wife'll want one of those cloaks!"

"I'll save the best for you!" called Verinder from the doorway.

Minutes later Verinder stood at the rear door of a nearby *boulangerie.* Inside, the proprietor and his son were setting up for the next day's bread making. The younger man's flour-covered hand pointed to a pile of leftovers. Verinder dropped a coin on the counter and took a small loaf. Once outside the bakery, Verinder broke the loaf in two and jammed half in a pocket. With one shoulder leaning against the front wall of the shop, he munched on the stale bread and casually scanned the street. None of the three men from the wine shop was in sight.

After finishing his meager meal and taking a final look up and down the street, he headed for the Rue St. Vivian.

The pale winter sunlight was fading quickly by the time Verinder found Docteur Mansard's house. The modest, half-timbered residence stood on a quiet street, a small sign stating the owner's occupation near the front door. Out of it came a gray-haired woman. She moved purposefully down the street, her grim face set in concentration. She passed Verinder without even seeing him.

The harridan LeBeau spoke of, Verinder guessed. Off on an errand. Good, he thought. Then moving quickly towards the back, Verinder rapped three times on the rear door. When no one answered, he knocked again.

A moment later, a petite woman answered. Her brown tresses had escaped their coiled braid and straggled about her round, plain face. Her cheeks were wet with recent tears, and she wiped still more tears from her dark gray eyes with the back of her hand.

The doctor's niece, Verinder recognized immediately. Élisabeth, he added silently. And she's been crying. So Meunier was right. Out of respect, he removed his cap and shoved it into his only empty pocket.

"I'm sorry about your aunt," Verinder said simply.

"Aunt Claire? She only..." Elizabeth stated incoherently. She stared at Verinder, who stood in the doorway and regarded her with sympathy. "Who are you?" she demanded

"A friend. You must trust me. May I come in?" Verinder asked even as he hurried inside and shut the door behind him.

Though the intensity of his gaze and voice seemed oddly comforting and sincere, Elizabeth frowned at Verinder, angry with herself for not stopping the tall, tattered stranger from entering the house.

Verinder saw that Elizabeth was suspicious, yet there was no time for social niceties. "You are Docteur Mansard's niece, an Englishwoman," he stated rather than queried, his rôle as a rag-man momentarily shed as another better-known rôle was taken up.

"And you are…?" Elizabeth moved forward, pushing Verinder back toward the door.

But instead of answering her question, Verinder asked one of his own. "Is your uncle in the house?"

"He is, and Matiaz will be back soon," Elizabeth said before demanding for the third time, "Who are you? Tell me or leave."

Verinder backed against the door, preventing Elizabeth from opening it. "I'm a friend. A friend who knows you're not safe."

"Your name, friend. Now. Or it will be you who's not safe."

"Louis XVI will be sent to the guillotine tomorrow," Verinder began quickly.

"All of France knows this." Elizabeth stared at Verinder and then crossed her arms.

"In a day or two, England will declare war on France, or France may even declare war on England. Whatever happens, English people in France will be arrested or worse. There's already ugly talk in Rouen. One firebrand seems to have a private grudge against the English. Against you and your aunt," Verinder emphasized. "He could easily stir up a crowd. He'd like nothing more than to march at the head of a mob and attack this house. Today it's wineshop threats - death to the *Anglais.* Tomorrow he may decide to go to the Committee."

Elizabeth's arms fell to her sides. "I've heard the talk."

"So have I," added her uncle, walking into the hallway. "And your warning." Docteur Mansard's shoulders sagged, and he shook his head as he looked at Verinder and said, "You're right - Élisabeth is not safe here. I should have taken her to Le Havre months ago, but my wife..." Here the doctor's voice broke, and he was unable to continue.

"Uncle Léon," Elizabeth said gently, putting a hand on the doctor's arm. "You have been all that is good. I could not have asked for a better uncle." Then she turned to Verinder and explained, "My aunt has been ill these many months. Uncle has been so worried about her that his time has been filled with tending to his patients and to her. Then Aunt Claire caught a fever. Uncle tried, but she was already so weak. An hour ago, she..." Elizabeth bit her lip. Her fresh tears mingled with those of Docteur Mansard as she clung to her uncle's arm.

Verinder hated the need for haste that made him appear to disregard their grief. "Mademoiselle Élisabeth, I regret Madame Mansard's passing, but I must impress upon you the urgency of your own situation."

Docteur Mansard wiped his eyes with his handkerchief and then folded it methodically before replacing it in a pocket. He turned to Elizabeth and stated, "He's right. You must go back to England." Looking at Verinder, he continued, "But I cannot leave. Not now. My wife..." Mansard paused and swallowed before finishing, "She deserves a proper burial."

"And she will have it. Uncle. I'll leave afterwards, in a few days," Elizabeth soothed, bending slightly over the doctor as he tried to control his tears.

"It may be too late."

Verinder's calm words brought Elizabeth's eyes back to his face. She scowled, angry that a stranger had laid an additional burden on her grieving uncle. "And why should we trust you?" stormed Elizabeth. "We don't even know your name!"

Verinder did not reply immediately. Years of command had accustomed him to making quick decisions. Decisions upon which his own life and the lives of others depended. Leave now. You've already stayed too long. This was the obvious decision. And it was one he couldn't make. But to offer his help, to share the secret of his name would put his life in her hands.

And her life in mine.

"I am Richard Verinder, a poor French citizen and itinerant rag dealer." Then, his decision made, Verinder answered the question Elizabeth had asked several times, adding in English, "And I am Richard Sinclair Verinder," now giving his name its Anglicized pronunciation, "an Englishman heading for Le Havre and a ship back to England." He did not add either of his two titles. One would only add more fear to an already dangerous situation. And the other was so new that it had an air of unreality about it. "*Pardonez-moi* for my bluntness" he said, returning to the safer French, "but to stay here long will endanger the success of the business entrusted to me." Verinder noted the appraising look in Elizabeth's eyes and the stunned one on her uncle's face.

"Though," Verinder hurried on, "you, Docteur Mansard, need to remain here in Rouen, for the safety of all in your house, your niece," Verinder paused invitingly.

"Citizeness Laurence," Elizabeth supplied.

"Citizeness Laurence," Verinder noted, "must return to England. At once. With me."

Docteur Mansard drew in his breath with a hiss. "With you?"

"With me. In the cart." Verinder looked directly at Elizabeth and added, "Where you'll be safer than in this house."

Verinder watched deliberation chase shock from Elizabeth's face, then saw her angle a glance at Mansard and realize that staying was not an option. Finally, she said, "And how are you going to explain the presence of a woman at your side. No doubt you have a regular route and customers who know you."

Verinder nodded approvingly. "Have you some old clothes?" he asked looking at Elizabeth's simple blue gown.

"You mean, do I have clothes that make me look like the companion of a ragman? *Oui*."

"Have you skill with your needle?"

"Yes, but..." Elizabeth began in a puzzled voice before understanding came. "Mending tears, replacing buttons, patching seams. It is work I do often. The ragman's seamstress."

"Yes."

"*Une cousine*, like our Matiaz, perhaps?"

"No, not a cousin. If this is to work – and our lives depend upon it – you must be thought to be my wife." The final word came as a surprise even to Verinder. But once it was said, he realized Elizabeth would be safe playing no other rôle.

"Your wife! But..." Docteur Mansard looked in dismayed astonishment at Elizabeth, who pursed her lips and said nothing.

Yet it was Elizabeth whom Verinder addressed, his eyes locked on hers. "Citizeness Verinder will be safe. From everyone." After Elizabeth nodded, Verinder rushed on, convincing himself as well as his listeners of the wisdom of his decision as he spoke. "For some time, I have talked vaguely of a serving woman I want to marry." Verinder allowed himself a wry smile at this revelation. "She's been my excuse to stay away from, from..."

"Entanglements?" Elizabeth supplied.

"*Mai oui.* Entanglements." Good, Verinder thought. She is thinking rather than becoming hysterical.

"So, no one along your route will be surprised to see her at your side." Elizabeth pictured herself riding on a wagon with a man she did not know. "To see me at your side."

"That's right. A relative, a cousin, when I have never mentioned one before, might raise suspicions. Business has been good lately so I can afford a wife. Especially one who is good with her needle. *Le Guillotine* has given us ragmen much cast off clothing to choose from," he ended bitterly.

"And given me little choice, it seems." Elizabeth pushed aside her doubts with a shake of her shoulders and sighed. "I imagine that cast-off clothes would be your only reason for coming to a house like this one, wouldn't it?"

"*Certainement.*"

Elizabeth glanced at her uncle. Both thought of the dresses Claire Mansard would never wear again. Take them. The words formed soundlessly on the doctor's lips.

"There are some upstairs," Elizabeth choked out. "I'll bring them down." With that, she hurried from the hall. A moment later her feet could be heard on the steps.

Docteur Mansard shook the image of his dead wife's clothes from his head and turned to Verinder. "English! I never would have believed it. Your French is as good as mine, but then so is Élisabeth's. And her papers say she was born here in Rouen as, indeed, she was. Thank God."

"Was that how you met your wife?"

"Yes. Yes, it was." Docteur Mansard smiled at the memory. "I was called to attend to the wife of an English gentleman. Élisabeth's mother. Her sister Claire was traveling with them, and…" He bit his lip, remembering the woman he had loved for thirty-two years. "We never had children of our own so when Élisabeth came to Rouen, it was, it was…" Mansard found he could not continue so instead he said, "You will keep her safe, out of danger?"

"I will, and remember that there is much more danger if she stays here, especially after war is declared," replied Verinder.

"War." The doctor shook his head sadly. "It will come whether we want it to or not. But by then, Élisabeth will be safe in England." He looked at Verinder and repeated, "She'll be safe. That's all that matters now. Though she won't be happy to return to her brother in Hampshire. To Gideon Laurence. They are…" Mansard shrugged. "Nothing alike. And there was some disagreement. About what, I do not know. But it was why Élisabeth came here to live with us. Her brother..." Mansard hesitated. "I met him once. He is a proud man. Not an easy man. Perhaps you have such a brother?"

"He's dead," said Verinder woodenly, her mind suddenly wrenched back to what he'd learned hours earlier. "Edward," his voice stumbled over the name. "I saw…"

His tone brought the sharp eyes of the man of medicine upon him. "You saw something today?"

"Yes, I..." A muddy alley near the Seine took shape as Verinder spoke, his grief forming into words for the first time. "A London newspaper. Packing from goods smuggled up the river perhaps. I was going 'round the houses there, buying, selling as I always do, and it was patching a hole in a window." Once again, he saw the pealing green paint on the door next to the broken window. "I raised my hand to knock, and there was Edward's obituary." The terrible moment of discovery replayed itself in his memory. The words of the black-edged notice seen by the merest coincidence were now engraved on his heart. How he had managed to deal with the woman who came to the door, Verinder would never know. Somehow a transaction was made. The next thing he remembered was unharnessing his cart at the *Cheval Noir.*

"*Votre frere, no,*" Mansard inquired, "he must have been important to warrant a notice in a London paper."

"The Earl of Rossbury." Was the Earl of Rossbury. And my only brother. Verinder closed his eyes and saw his brother's face. A face drawn with pain when he'd gone to Earl's Wood Park before returning to France on his latest assignment. How like Edward to minimize his illness, Verinder thought. I should have known! I should have been there!

"Ah, so your nephew..."

"My brother never married."

Docteur Mansard's eyes widened in shock. "Aristocrats..." he began fearfully.

"I know what happens to aristocrats in France," said Verinder in a level tone. "But your niece will be the wife of an ordinary ragman. She will be safer with me than with you in Rouen."

"Yes, Élisabeth will be safer with you," Docteur Mansard reminded himself. There was no time to say more, for Elizabeth could be heard descending the stairs.

Verinder did not need to hear Mansard's promise of silence. He could see it in the doctor's nearly imperceptible nod. Mansard will say nothing, Verinder told himself. Not even to his niece. It's too dangerous.

Elizabeth reentered the hall, a bundle of clothes in her arms, just as Docteur Mansard grasped Verinder's hand.

Something's passed between them, Elizabeth decided. Probably Uncle Léon's need to be assured that I'll be safe. Safe. That's what I thought I'd be when I came to Rouen. Instead... She looked at Verinder and her uncle who had both turned towards her. Safety seemed an odd thing to associate with a ragman met less than a half hour earlier. Verinder, she thought, could have done nothing, said nothing after hearing about us. Instead he is jeopardizing his own safety by taking me with him. Yes, I'll be safe with him.

Keeping her thoughts to herself and offering the clothes bundle to Verinder, Elizabeth explained, "Most of these are Aunt Claire's but a few are mine. I tied them up in an old dress. You'll find my needles and threads in a work basket in the center."

"Good," said Verinder, taking the bulky load from her hands, which were somewhat work-reddened and chapped.

Elizabeth saw Verinder's gaze shift to her hands and his nod of approval. "No one would mistake these hands for those of a lady."

"When we've time, I'll debate that point with you. But I've stayed here too long already, and you need to know what to do tomorrow."

"Tomorrow!" Docteur Mansard exclaimed. "So soon?" His lips trembled as he extended a shaking hand towards his niece.

"Yes, tomorrow, Uncle. He must leave after the market, just as he always does. Am I right?" Elizabeth gripped Mansard's hand and turned to Verinder.

"*Oui.* But first I must be at the market. Several people expect to see me there. I'll close, as usual, by late morning. Then I'll leave Rouen by the Le Havre road. You must be on it, and you must leave the house before dawn. That firebrand I mentioned. I don't trust him. I hinted that the fever mentioned when Madame Mansard was spoken of might be something far worse, but how long his fear of the spotted fever will keep him away, who can say?"

"Long enough," Docteur Mansard said, a hint of resolution now in his voice. "I will see to that. Within the hour, my neighbors will know that Élisabeth is worn out from nursing my wife and down with the fever herself. My cousin Matiaz has already gone for Fr. Clément. That is, Citizen Clement. He works for Reynaud the undertaker. With a little help from Matiaz and Clement, I believe I can arrange Élisabeth's death."

"And if I spread a few rumors tomorrow, I think you'll find no one will want to approach your niece's coffin, much less look inside," added Verinder.

"An early start then for me tomorrow. Before our neighbors are stirring," Elizabeth concluded. "They must not see a dead woman leave the house."

"Where will you go? If you should be seen..." Docteur Mansard worried aloud.

"To the cathedral." Elizabeth pictured the Gothic church in the center of Rouen and began to trace the route that would take her there from the Rue St. Vivian.

"The cathedral? Are you sure?" asked Verinder. Churches were no longer places of safety since the Revolution had made the practice of religion dangerous.

"Since the Civil Constitution, Notre Dame is empty. And it is not in the part of Rouen where we are known. According to Matiaz, only a few older women spend any time there now. And most of them simply want a place to rest out of the cold, away from work or demanding husbands. I can sit there, just another tired woman needing some quiet. Then after the sun has risen, I'll leave and start walking west. If I put two or three more pieces of tattered clothing into my basket, I can pull them out so that that it appears that I've been doing some buying. Then when the ragman stops his cart to pick up the rag woman who has been out collecting castoffs to be mended and sold while he has been selling others at the market, no one will give them a second glance."

Holding the clothes bundle with his left arm, Verinder said, "You're right. It will work." And then extending his hand towards Elizabeth, he added, "All will be well. You have my word."

Impulsively Elizabeth took Verinder's offered hand in both of hers. The warmth of his grasp and the admiration gleaming in his eyes brought color to the cheeks that she had thought too old to blush. To cover her confusion, Elizabeth said, "A bargain then as our lives are in one another's hands."

"And our honor," added Verinder, knowing both Mansard and Elizabeth would understand what he meant. "Until tomorrow then, Mlle Laurence. Docteur Mansard, my condolences. I must go." Immediately Verinder reached for the door and lifted the latch. Then he was gone, the door closing behind him.

Neither uncle nor niece said a word for a moment. Mansard noted the color in Elizabeth's face and speculated on what lay ahead for her in England.

Her voice interrupted his reverie. "Uncle Léon, we've work to do."

"That we have, my dear." The doctor added, "And *adieux* to be said."

"Yes, and *adieux* to be said." Both, Elizabeth knew, were thinking of the woman lying upstairs.

## CHAPTER 2

# MONDAY, JANUARY 21, 1793

Hours before the sky lightened, Elizabeth prepared to leave the house on Rue St Vivian for the last time. She and her uncle had talked long into the night and said their good-byes before retiring for a few hours of sleep.

So it was Matiaz who went with Elizabeth to the door. "My prayers will be with you. Send him word somehow when you are safe. He will fret for you otherwise." Elizabeth nodded, and the two women clasped each other in a warm embrace. Then Matiaz dropped some coins into the large, cloth-covered market basket Elizabeth carried. "You may need these." Neither spoke as the older woman opened the door. Then as Elizabeth murmured, "*Merci, Matiaz,*" the door closed behind her.

The wintry air was frigid. Elizabeth stepped out briskly to keep herself warm. Leaving Rue St. Vivian behind, she sighed in relief. No light had shone in a neighbor's window. No door had opened unexpectedly.

For some time, Elizabeth saw no one. Then as she neared the old town, one or two pedestrians frequented the narrow streets. I am Madame Élisabeth Verinder, Elizabeth repeated silently as she headed for the Cathedral de Notre-Dame. The wife of a ragman. A mender of clothes.

A large puddle lay ahead of her. From the opposite direction, a young *travailleur,* shoulders hunched against the cold, hands in his pockets, stepped onto the narrow path around the puddle. The workman elbowed past her without even a polite *Bon jour, Citizeness.*

Good, thought Elizabeth picturing what the laborer might have seen if he'd bothered to look. A nobody. A shapeless woman in stout shoes, a thick kerchief, heavy mitts, and a shabby cloak. A nobody. A safe nobody.

And Gideon. What would he think? The question surfaced unbidden. My brother, Elizabeth concluded, would be scandalized. Both by my appearance and my behaviour.

For years, Elizabeth had put her past into a closet in her mind and refused to talk about it. Now with her return to England only days away, the memories crept out. Memories of Hopeden Hall. Her brother Gideon. And their nearest neighbor Sir Augustus Tremaine.

Tremaine was Gideon's closest friend. He was also a man whose emotionless pleasantries made Elizabeth feel like a thing, not a person. Yet despite her lack of encouragement, Tremaine had proposed – and been refused. A few days later he had found Elizabeth alone on one of her long rambles. His violent advances had left Elizabeth bruised, torn, and profoundly shaken, Gideon's smiling reaction to her condition only making the situation worse. Afterwards being in any room with Sir Augustus was a chilling horror. Marriage to him was unthinkable. Something Elizabeth made clear when Tremaine proposed again.

Yet Gideon continued to invite Sir Augustus to dine with them. Often. And the baronet seemed to know where Elizabeth was going whenever she left Hopeden. His cold appraising eyes followed her everywhere. Soon Elizabeth stepped outside her brother's house only in the company of her niece Emma.

Tremaine prided himself on being a man who always got what he wanted. And he wanted her. Intended, she feared, to have her. Perhaps even with Gideon's help.

Only in distance, Elizabeth decided, was there real safety. And no one she knew lived farther from Hopeden than her Aunt Claire who, a generation earlier, had stunned the family by marrying Léon Mansard. Though the Morestones had never forgiven their daughter, Elizabeth's mother Anne had written regularly to her sister. A correspondence Elizabeth continued after her mother's death. When a friend sought Elizabeth's companionship on a journey to Paris with her husband, Elizabeth immediately wrote to the Mansards. Her request for a visit brought a joyful reply.

Her brother's reaction was rage. "Travel! To France! You're mad, Elizabeth! You will learn nothing in Mansard's house except disobedience and loose behaviour. I'll not have it!" His anger, however, did not stop Elizabeth from leaving.

I only intended to stay in Rouen for a few months, she recalled. But Aunt Claire and Uncle Léon immediately made me part of their lives, and there was always some reason to stay just a few weeks longer. Then Aunt Claire's illness made leaving impossible.

Elizabeth's recollections brought her to the great west door of Notre-Dame. The sky was still dark as she stepped inside. The vast emptiness of the nave warned her that the Revolution had turned worship into an act of treason. Elizabeth groped her way forward, the darkness within blacker than the pre-dawn sky outside. She stepped around a woman sleeping on the floor and inched cautiously towards the Lady Chapel. There the tomb of the d'Amboise cardinals, a Renaissance masterpiece, reminded her forcibly of Claire Mansard's death. Elizabeth moved towards a stone seat carved into the wall. I'll be safe here, she thought, until it's time to leave.

At midmorning, René Dubois admired the green cloak he had purchased from the itinerant rag dealer.

"My wife can mend these tears," he said while standing near the back of Verinder's cart. "If you find another garment like this, save it for me. I'll buy it when I see you again."

"A gown to match the cloak perhaps? Well, I'll see what I can do," replied Verinder. "I'm always glad to make a sale."

Dubois spotted Henri LeBeau in the crowd milling about the nearby stalls. "Henri!" he cried. "Henri LeBeau!" he called while waving the cloak like a signal flag.

After his lanky friend reached Verinder's cart, Dubois flourished the cloak for LeBeau's inspection. "It is a fine cloak, is it not? Sophie will be admired when she wears it," ventured Dubois, seeking confirmation that his recent purchase had been a good one.

"Yes, yes, a fine cloak," admitted LeBeau. Then nudging the wine shop owner with an elbow, he added, "The cloak is to keep Sophie warm so Sophie will keep you warm, eh, René?"

After the two men had laughed together at this remark, LeBeau continued, "Well, Docteur Mansard will no longer have any one to keep him warm at night." He paused, inviting the question he knew would follow.

"Why? What have you heard?" asked Verinder.

"I happened to pass *la maison d' le docteur* this morning and saw Reynaud, who makes *les cercueils*, coming away from the house. Reynaud told me that Docteur Mansard has ordered a coffin for his wife. To be delivered this afternoon. And Mansard's niece is sick with the fever that took his wife. Reynaud talked to Mansard in the hall. The doctor, he thinks, is worried about the infection spreading."

Dubois, recalling what Verinder had said the previous day, asked, "It's not the spotted fever, is it?"

"Don't know about that," LeBeau said. "But Docteur Mansard will be better off without those *Anglaise* just as France will be better off without Capet!" His voice rose to a shout as he pronounced the hated king's name.

People nearby growled in agreement, a few cheering in anticipation of the guillotine's next victim. Verinder said nothing and turned instead to a plump woman, a child's hand held in each of hers, who asked, "Got anything for either of them?"

The morning hours passed slowly for Elizabeth. She remained in the darkness of the Lady Chapel, watchful and still. She pulled her cloak tightly about her for warmth. And wished she had something to do other than think.

Sad and happy thoughts about the uncle she had learned to love and would probably never see again. The uncle who would miss his wife but who had already decided to invite a nephew and his wife to live with him. A nephew who wanted to study medicine. They'll come, Elizabeth was certain, and breathe new life into doctor's home.

My home for the last five years. And home is now... Where?

With Gideon at Hopeden again? Tremaine's calculating face loomed before her, and she shivered as she recalled his touch. But perhaps he has married. If I knew... If there were some way to find out, somewhere to go first. I could, I could, what? An idea began to form and slowly take shape amid the chapel's dark shadows.

Finally, light from the cathedral's open door began to filter into the interior of the building. "Time to leave," Elizabeth sighed thankfully.

Once outside, Elizabeth settled her cloak about her shoulders and then began to walk west. I've plenty of time to reach the Le Havre road before the market closes. That's where Verinder will be. My husband! Elizabeth reminded herself with a start. For all the days between here and England. How many days will that be? Four? Five? Days. And nights.

It will never work. The thought kept pace with Elizabeth's steps. It will never work. Never work. Elizabeth's heart pounded with the same rhythm. Never work. Never work. Then she stopped. Uncovered the basket and dug out the old shirt and two faded skirts she'd buried at the bottom. "It must work." She whispered the words aloud as she put the old clothes over the top of the basket. "It must."

"All will be well. You have my word." Verinder's promise of the previous day repeated itself in Elizabeth's memory. You have my word. That's what he said. And I believe him.

All will be well, Elizabeth repeated. All will be well. With a mental shake, she added, But it won't be if you stand here all day. Then, the sun at her back, she set off once more.

Two hours later Verinder drove his cart down the familiar Rouen street that became the road to Le Havre. He scanned the faces of the people on it as he searched for the woman he'd promised to help. Near the outskirts of the town, Verinder saw Elizabeth in an open doorway, talking to a tired-looking woman balancing a baby on one hip. At almost the same moment, Elizabeth glimpsed Verinder, the cart moving steadily towards her.

"Here comes my husband now," Elizabeth said. "Late as usual."

"Aren't they always?" answered the woman as she turned to go inside.

"Where have you been?" demanded Elizabeth. "I have all of this," she pointed to her small bundle of old clothes. "And the basket. It's heavy! You are never around when I need help. You've been ogling some young girl at a wine shop after the market, haven't you?"

Their only audience was a stoop-shouldered man pushing a barrow.

Understanding immediately what Elizabeth was doing, Verinder retorted, "Sales at the market were brisk. I was open a full half hour later than usual."

As soon as he stopped the cart, Elizabeth lifted the bundle of clothes. She thrust it at Verinder and ordered, "Take this." Next, putting the basket's handle over her left arm and lifting her skirts so that she could secure a foothold, she scrambled up the side of the cart. Then she planted herself on the backless seat and asked suspiciously, "If business was so good, where's the money?"

The old man grinned his pleasure at this interesting sideshow and offered, "A good beating is what she needs!"

"Keep your opinion to yourself, Citizen!" Elizabeth yelled down while shaking her fist at the advice giver. "Get this cart moving," she told Verinder, "or I'll take the lines myself!"

Verinder replied abjectly, "*Tout de suite, ma petit cheri*," twitched the reins, and felt the cart rumble forward. The old man simply shook his head and pushed the barrow toward Rouen.

A quarter of an hour later Rouen was behind them. With no one in sight. Elizabeth whispered, "*Pardonnez moi.* I behaved badly back there. The ragman doesn't deserve to have a shrewish wife. I promise you she was left behind in Rouen and will not appear again."

"No apologies needed. Even though you made me feel like a perfect milksop!" Verinder smiled to show that he saw the humor in the situation. "You played your part well. However, I am happy that you plan to behave better in the future!" Scanning the road ahead and behind, he noted with satisfaction the absence of other travelers.

Watching him and guessing that times when the road was empty were few, Elizabeth observed, "You want to tell me what to do. Don't worry about offending me. You can tell me your plans as bluntly as you like. I know that our safety depends on doing what you say."

"*Merci.* You're right. It does. But I have only a few instructions for you. First, *Français* always. Even when we are alone as we are now. Never use one word of English or show that you understand it."

After Elizabeth nodded her agreement, Verinder continued. "Second, we will say nothing about our real lives – even to each other. We are Richard and Élisabeth Verinder, the ragman and his wife. The less we know of one another, the easier the deception will be. After we reach the coast of England, there will be time to say whatever needs to be said." Verinder paused and stared sightlessly at something beyond the immediate horizon.

"*Oui,*" said Elizabeth, "there will be time then."

"However," Verinder added, "if there's anything about you that I would be expected to know, tell me now. My own slight limp you will ignore. Everyone on my route knows about the gamekeeper's lucky shot that left me with a broken leg. Badly set. Healed poorly." He shrugged.

Once again, the lie came easily. It was what Verinder always said in France when people asked about his leg. Something no one who knew him in England ever mentioned. Even after nearly twelve years, the truth was painful. Yorktown. His men suffering through the long siege. His unit's futile attempt to cover the failed retreat across the river. The musket shot that nearly killed him. No, it was not something to be spoken about. Not here. Not in England.

"That can't -" Elizabeth stopped. Nothing about our real lives. That's what he said. So, ignoring what she knew to be a lie, she began again. "Anything that a husband would be expected to know..." she thought aloud. "My manners. Especially at table. They are not those of Madame Verinder."

"Your manners," Verinder replied, "need not concern you. Someone who worked as a seamstress in a grand house would have learned her manners there."

"And," Elizabeth admitted with a grimace, "I suffer from *mal de mer.* In fact, the channel crossing from Dover to Calais when I came to France was quite unpleasant."

"I'm sorry about that. The crossing I hope to make at week's end from Le Havre will, no doubt, be equally as unpleasant. I'll do all I can to help you when the time comes."

Once again scanning the still empty road, Verinder hurried on. "Third, do not offer any information about your past as a seamstress. Say that it is too painful to talk about. Your French, your dress, your appearance, even your hands – none of these will betray you. The only thing that will is saying too much."

"I understand," Elizabeth said slowly. "I am to be Madame Verinder. To assume the rôle as an actress would. To pretend that this journey to Le Havre is an elaborate theatrical production in which you and I are the principal players."

"*Exactement!*" replied Verinder. "And last, you must trust me. Trust me when I say that for Madame Verinder, this journey will not be as dangerous as you may fear. For who will remark a rag dealer and his wife making their rounds? Trust me also when I say that I have made the journey before and know every step of the way. And last, trust me when I say that," he paused, searching for words that would not offend, "though our audience sees us as husband and wife, I shall have a care for your reputation."

Hearing Verinder put one of her unvoiced fears into words brought the flush of embarrassment to Elizabeth's cheeks. She could think of no reply.

Seeing the blush and another cart coming towards them, Verinder cursed his blundering stupidity. "I am afraid we start

Act One here." Pummeling his brain for a topic to help Elizabeth begin, he asked, "What's in the basket?"

Elizabeth took a deep breath and answered, "While you were selling from the cart, I bought two meat pies for our dinner as well as a loaf of bread, some cheese, and some dried apples." Elizabeth had reorganized the basket during her long wait in the cathedral and blessed Matiaz and her uncle for each item they'd placed there. "How well did we do at the market?"

"We did well, though not everyone who stopped at our cart bought something. One of them was that man I told you about yesterday. The one I met at the wineshop." Verinder waited for a moment, knowing Elizabeth would remember the man he'd described as a firebrand. He sensed Elizabeth's tension and continued, "According to him, there may be fever in Rouen. He said it has already carried off a doctor's wife. Her niece is also sick and not expected to live. It's a good thing that we have left Rouen behind us, no?

"Yes." Elizabeth's face paled. "A good thing," she whispered as an involuntary shiver shook her body.

"You're cold." Verinder reached behind him and grabbed a torn cloak. "Use this as a lap robe. And let's eat those pies. It's been hours since breakfast, and I'm hungry."

Later, after their meal, Verinder described the customers he'd dealt with that morning, starting with the first one of the day. Before long Elizabeth was asking questions and adding her own comments to Verinder's. As he neared the end of the list, Verinder was pleased to see that food and talk of ordinary things had restored the color to Elizabeth's face.

By the time the final customer's haggling had been discussed, Elizabeth felt she could no longer hold her head up - the strain of months of nursing, the early morning, and the deception like a weight too heavy to carry all taking their toll. I shall close my eyes for a moment, she thought, and think of nothing at all.

Moments later, Verinder realized that Elizabeth was asleep. Carefully sliding closer to her so that her head could rest against him, he kept the horse moving west.

Verinder's drive through the Forest de Roumare was uneventful. On a cold, winter afternoon, few were abroad. The passage of a ragman was such a familiar sight that none of those they passed did more than raise a hand in greeting. After the clumsy vehicle bumped over one particularly bad rut, Elizabeth woke. The fading light pointed to an early twilight, the sun nearing the horizon as the woods of oaks, beeches, and hornbeams were left behind.

Both admired the late afternoon view of the Seine Valley spread out before them. Then Verinder said, "My destination is the farm of Guillaume and Charlotte Martin and their children Paul and Jeanette. It is on the other side of St. Martin de Boscherville. In exchange for some garments for the children, we can stay snug in their barn. We will manage our own supper."

Elizabeth realized that Verinder's chatter was anything but idle. As the ragman's wife, she would be expected to know his habits. Consequently, she listened carefully and repeated the names of the Martins to herself as Verinder spoke.

The small village with its Norman Romanesque church, formerly a Benedictine abbey, was soon passed. Minutes later, two farm buildings could be seen to their right.

Verinder turned the horse onto the farm track. Immediately Elizabeth saw a long, thatched roofed building. It was made of cob and pisé, evidently the living quarters and cow shed. Next to it was a similar but smaller building. Into it, a boy about eight years old led a dappled mare, her head drooping.

When the boy heard the cart approach, he looked over his shoulder. Suddenly he dropped the horse's halter and ran towards the cart. "Richard!" he shouted. "You're back! Wait 'til you see the work we've done on the dovecote! What have you brought me this time?" Meanwhile, the boy's horse plodded into the barn.

As soon as Verinder had stopped the cart, he jumped down and scooped the lad into his arms. "Paul," he laughed, "you have grown again. But what makes you think I have anything for you?" he teased.

Charlotte Martin stood in the doorway of the farmhouse, one arm shading her eyes from the nearly setting sun, a toddler clinging to her skirt. Having heard her son's shouts, she had come outside to welcome the visitor. "Paul," she remonstrated, "where are your manners? Apologize at once."

"*Pardon*," said the boy disconsolately as Verinder set him on his feet. Then he looked beyond his friend, the ragman, to his cart, and to the unfamiliar woman on the seat.

Immediately Verinder said, "This is my wife. Élisabeth. We've been able to marry at last."

Elizabeth put her lap robe cloak aside and clambered to the ground. "Madame Martin," she said, "it is good of you to allow us to stay the night here." She was relieved to hear how ordinary her voice sounded.

"Richard," whispered Paul, "did you really bring me nothing?"

Before his mother could interject an angry retort, Verinder said, "We shall see. But first you have a horse to tend to and so do I. We must hurry if you plan to show me the dovecote before dark."

With these words, Verinder gave the boy a friendly push that sent him running into the barn. Walking to the side of the cart, Verinder removed a small bundle of clothes and Elizabeth's workbasket. Elizabeth, seeing Verinder's slightly halting stride as he moved to her side, was thankful he had warned her. As Verinder handed her the basket and clothes, the fleeting pressure of his hand on her arm sent a silent message of encouragement. "You will want these." Then he led the horse and cart towards the barn door.

"Come into the house," offered Charlotte Martin, "and warm yourself."

"*Merci*," replied Elizabeth before she followed the younger woman, the child still clinging to her, into the farmhouse.

Madame Martin pointed to a low stool near the hearth. "You may sit there."

After Elizabeth settled herself, she placed her workbasket and the clothes by her side. At the top was a child's blouse. One sleeve dangled by a few threads from the armhole. Realizing the blouse was meant for the Martin's daughter, Elizabeth opened the workbasket, selected a needle and thread, and began to mend the blouse.

"That's a fine work basket," commented Charlotte, busy with preparations for her evening meal

Too fine for a rag woman perhaps, Elizabeth feared. Then with sudden inspiration, she said, "It was a gift." She gave the farm wife what she hoped would pass as a sly, knowing look. "From my former employers."

"I'm sure you needed it more than they did." Charlotte's wooden spoon vigorously stirred a pot on the hearth. "Verinder told us you were a seamstress. Mended garments will fetch a higher price at the market than torn ones."

"We hope so," replied Elizabeth. She looked up from her work to find the dark eyes of the Martins' four-year-old daughter, still hiding behind her mother, upon her.

Elizabeth smiled. "Jeanette, would you like to see what is in my workbasket?"

Although the child nodded, she remained where she was. Her mother remarked, "We see few strangers here. Jeanette is shy, not like Paul." Then she asked, "Was the Rouen market good today?"

"My husband," Elizabeth began, the two words feeling odd to her, "told me business was brisk. I was not there myself. Since this trip was my first visit to Rouen, he said I might visit the cathedral so I did. It is a fine building."

"You will do well together. A ragman needs a wife though I do not know whether I would like a wandering life myself. Still it's bound to be better than sewing for some demanding aristo, eh?" Charlotte Martin did not wait for an answer to her question and continued, "And Verinder has never seemed like one who would beat his wife when he is angry so, no doubt, you are luckier than most. But you have only been married a little while, right?" She paused only long enough to see Elizabeth's nod and then added, "So I could be wrong. You can tell me if I am after your next trip from Rouen. Still," she concluded with a sigh, "life is hard for everyone now, no matter what they do."

"That is true," agreed Elizabeth, thankful that Charlotte Martin seemed content to do most of the talking. Then she put in the last stitch and stuck the needle in her basket's needle cushion. She held up the blouse. "Hmm, this looks as if it would fit a little girl," she said as she looked once more at Jeanette.

"Well, Jeanette," encouraged the child's mother, "if you want it, you must speak to Madame Verinder."

After gazing at her mother and then at Elizabeth, the child stepped hesitantly over to Elizabeth's stool. Her right hand touched the blouse as her eyes seemed to inquire whether Elizabeth really intended to give it to her.

"Shall we see how it looks?" asked Elizabeth. She offered the blouse to Jeanette who put up her hands to hold the garment against her tiny chest. "I think it looks fine, don't you, Jeanette?"

The girl did not answer but continued to gaze at Elizabeth who felt as if she would melt in the child's dark eyes. If I had married... Elizabeth banished the thought and replied as if Jeanette had spoken, "I am glad that you agree. But I can see that you also think that it needs...” Elizabeth trailed off as she moved the bundle of children's garments onto her lap. She rummaged through them. “This!” She lifted a dark blue pinafore marred by a long, jagged rent in the back.

“For me?” Jeanette questioned. The child's hand reached out to stroke the dress that was only slightly too big for her.

“Yes, for you,” agreed Elizabeth. “Shall I mend it for you?”

“Mend it now.” Jeanette handed Elizabeth her needle cushion.

“If you come back very often, she will soon be as bad as her brother,” laughed Charlotte.

“Verinder put aside all these items for your children. It's little enough payment for a roof over our heads and for stabling the horse.”

Jeanette crept close to Elizabeth, her small body pressed against Elizabeth's side. Charlotte Martin, seeing her daughter content and knowing she would have less mending to do than usual, was thankful that the ragman had brought his wife to the farm. And since she did not often have the company of another woman who seemed as willing to listen as Madame Verinder, Charlotte Martin decided to share the story of her husband's minor triumph. “Let me tell you about our dovecote,” she began as she continued preparing the evening meal.

Twenty minutes later Mme Martin had finished her narrative and was stirring a kettle of soup hanging over the fire. As she watched, Elizabeth slipped the mended pinafore over Jeanette's head. At the same time, the door of the farmhouse opened to admit Guillaume Martin. The farmer carried a lantern and was obviously near the end of a conversation begun earlier. With him were his son and Verinder.

“So,” concluded Martin, “there's the dovecote, we've now been allowed to build. Eventually we'll enlarge it. It'll supply a bit of meat for the pot. Without the tax to the lord and the tithe to the church, we may even be able to buy this farm. That is, if the next grain harvest is good and what we make from the spinning stays the same."

Jeanette, hearing her father's voice, had turned to face the door. When he had finished speaking, she marched toward him in her new pinafore. "Papa, look!"

Paul, who had been told that a wool jacket, albeit rather frayed and missing a button, awaited him inside, spotted the bundle of clothes at Elizabeth's side, and ran toward it.

Hoisting his daughter into his arms, Martin told Verinder, "You are good to the children. You always bring more than you need to."

"Things like these," Verinder pointed to the small heap of clothes Paul, now wearing the promised jacket, sifted through, "never bring much at the market. And, as you can see," he motioned toward Elizabeth who was putting her needle cushion into her work basket, "business has been good."

"If you can afford to marry, business must be good." Then looking at Elizabeth for the first time, Martin added, "We had heard about you. Verinder's mysterious seamstress. But we wondered whether you were real or only a story to keep Verinder here out of trouble. I'm glad he was telling the truth! And you must start saving children's clothes," he said, after Elizabeth rose and moved to Verinder's side. "Perhaps soon you will need them for your own family."

"You may be right," replied Verinder, looking at the farmhouse table where Charlotte was beginning to set out her meal. "But now I think we must leave you to your supper."

Martin handed Verinder the lantern. "We'll say good-bye in the morning." Then he opened the door so his visitors could leave.

When the door had closed behind them, the only light was that from the lantern. Verinder and Elizabeth silently picked their way across the farmyard and entered the barn. Verinder said, "Right." Veering in that direction, Elizabeth saw a lively fire blazing on the hearth at the far end of the building.

"At one time," Verinder began conversationally, "this was the only building on the farm. Guillaume Martin's great-grandparents lived here. When times were good, the owner provided materials for a new farmhouse. This building then became the barn or byre. When Martin's parents were alive and the family was larger, the Martins lived here. But after his parents died, he tore down the wall dividing the living quarters from stable area to make the barn larger. Yet the hearth remains, and fortunately for us the chimney draws well."

Elizabeth saw that a pot of water was heating on the hearth and asked, "Can we use that water to wash before we eat?" The events of the day had made her feel more than a bit grimy.

"Find the big bowl in the box over there while I draw another bucket of water from the well," Verinder answered. He grabbed a pail and the lantern. He hesitated, wanting to tell Elizabeth how well she was doing. But the habit of keeping his feelings to himself was long engrained. And the memory of another woman's mocking laughter and sarcastic 'I already know!' kept the words locked in his mind. He turned away silently and hurried out.

While Verinder was gone, Elizabeth found the bowl, a badly chipped basin that appeared to be someone's cast off. Using a couple of tattered shirts to protect her hands, she lifted the boiling pot and poured some water from it into the bowl. Next with a knife found in the box, she sliced the bread and cheese. She placed the slices on the cloth from her market basket. Looking at the arrangement with satisfaction, Elizabeth heard Verinder return to the byre. "Supper in a few minutes," she announced as Verinder began to pour a little cold water into the hot water in the bowl.

After washing her travel-stained hands and face, Elizabeth returned to Verinder's box. There she unearthed a small porcelain bowl, its loveliness marred only by the thumb-sized piece missing from the lip. Elizabeth turned to Verinder, a question in her eyes. Drying his hands on a rough cloth, water dripping from his hair, Verinder said, "Yes, it is Sèvres. Perhaps thirty years old, I think. I saw it at the stall next to mine in Amiens and convinced myself it would be useful. I prefer not to think about what may have brought it to that particular stall."

The pain reflected in his face made Elizabeth put aside any other questions though more than a few were forming in her mind. Instead she busied herself with cutting some of her dried apples and putting them into the bowl. After adding barely enough hot water to cover the apples, she topped the bowl with the lid from the pot.

"What are you concocting for our supper?" Verinder inquired.

"Something edible, I hope," Elizabeth replied. "Everything, such as it is, is ready though."

Verinder fished a cup, two battered spoons, and a bent toasting fork out of the box. Then turning the box on its side, Verinder said, "This is the most comfortable seat in the house."

"Not to mention, it's the only seat in the house." Elizabeth's lips twitched in a smile.

"Water to drink. And the bread and cheese is already sliced, I see," said Verinder. He gave Elizabeth the cup and indicated that he would use the ladle in the pail. "If the cook is prepared to take the advice of the seasoned traveler, I will show you how to make both a bit more appetizing."

"Have not I, as your wife, vowed to obey you in all things?"

The mirth evident in Elizabeth's voice made Verinder decide to answer in the same vein. "But, of course! So observe carefully as I wield *la fourchette*." Placing a slice of bread near the hearthstone to heat and a chunk of cheese on the fork, he held the cheese over the fire. Before long, it began to sag a little. He dropped the melted cheese onto the warm bread and spread it with a spoon. "Ah, a masterpiece!" he noted, looking at his creation. "The first one is for you. The next one you must do yourself."

"This is good. In fact, it is very good," Elizabeth observed after her first bite. While Verinder held the fork over the flames a second time, she remarked, "You are an expert with the toasting fork."

"My brother and I sat before many a fire..." Verinder's statement remained unfinished as he bent over to smooth the melted cheese atop the bread.

For a few minutes the two ate in silence broken only by the occasional stampings and soft snufflings of the horses stabled nearby. That the brother Verinder had mentioned was part of his real life seemed obvious. Why he was a subject that produced pain, Elizabeth did not know although thoughts of her own brother were certainly not a cause of gladness. As she picked up the fork and speared a piece of cheese, she remarked, "Paul likes you. His face lit up as soon as he saw you."

"Yes, Paul and I are friends. He is like..." Verinder paused, thinking that Paul reminded him of his own son Simon at the same age. He continued, "He is full of energy and always cheerful and eager to help."

Elizabeth pretended not to notice that Verinder's sentence had ended differently than he originally intended. Instead she said, "We must buy some more food tomorrow. And that reminds me," she remarked as she pulled the coins Matiaz had given her from the bottom of her basket, "to ask where you would like me to put these."

His left eyebrow lifted in surprise. "A corner of our box would be a good place."

As Elizabeth did so, she inquired, "What is our destination tomorrow?"

Finishing his first slice of bread and cheese and reaching for the toasting fork, Verinder answered, "Caudebec-en-Caux if we are lucky. Martin thinks there will be rain, perhaps sleet, tomorrow and so do I. If the road becomes too muddy, we can take refuge in St Wandrille."

Their talk of what the next day might hold brought them to the end of the bread and cheese. Elizabeth then lifted the lid from the bowl and used her spoon to mash and stir the contents, one third of which she poured into her cup. The remainder she offered to Verinder.

"This smells good," he said. Sampling the mixture, he added, "And it tastes good, too."

"I am glad you like it. You see, you are not the only expert in this family," Elizabeth replied. "It needs some spices though."

"On a cold night, you made something warming from some dry apple slices. I am not about to complain about the lack of cinnamon or nutmeg!"

When the simple meal was over and both had drunk their fill of water, Verinder said, "I want to take another look at Angélique. She is a most important partner in our business."

Elizabeth began to gather the dishes they had used. "While you do, I can clear this up."

After making sure the mare had sufficient fodder and was tethered securely in her stall, Verinder drew her another pail of water from the well. Then he ran his hands down her legs. Grateful to feel no sore spots or swellings, he returned to the hearthside. All traces of the meal had disappeared. A covered pot stood near the fire Elizabeth had already banked, and Elizabeth was mending a skirt found in the wagon.

"You are an admirable wife," he observed. "I could ask for none better to accompany me on my rounds."

"Thank you, husband," Elizabeth replied, glancing up at him with a smile. The intensity of his gaze surprised her. "How is Angélique?"

"She is fine for the night. And we too should be thinking of sleep. It has been a long day, and you look tired. I will make up some beds while you finish that mending." And as he spoke, Verinder formed two straw piles not far from the hearth. At the top of each pile, he laid a shabby blanket. These he covered with cloaks and skirts from the back of the cart

The beds made, Verinder realized that Elizabeth needed some privacy before retiring. "I'll draw a fresh pail of water," he said. "Then it will be ready in the morning. I won't be too long." Once again, he went out into the night with the pail.

When Verinder returned, Elizabeth lay on the straw bed farthest from the hearth, her own cloak and a pile of old clothes over her.

"Sleep well, Élisabeth," he said as he extinguished the light in the lantern.

"And you, Richard," Elizabeth whispered in return.

Something nameless and terrible chased her. Cold and frightened, Elizabeth knew she had to keep running. If the faceless terror behind her caught her, something too horrible for words would occur. But her spent legs seemed unable to move. Her exhausted body was on the verge of collapse as unseen quicksand slowed her feet and made each step an effort. Then something from the darkness behind her reached towards her.

"Don't," she screamed. "Don't!" Suddenly her cries were silenced by a firm kiss, her mouth covered by lips at first insistent and then gentle. Lips caressed her own with such sweet passion that a strange lightheadedness made her feel as if she were drowning in the embrace. As Elizabeth awoke, her heart pounded as though she'd been in a race. Her breath coming in short gasps, Verinder's lips released hers.

No sound from the house, Verinder noticed with relief, as he tried to steady his breathing and understand his reaction to what had happened.

The glow from the embers of the banked fire allowed both Verinder and Elizabeth to see the barest outline of the other. Each attempted to read in the other's face the answers to the questions that crowded their thoughts. As the end of the nightmare faded from her consciousness, Elizabeth heard herself cry out and realized her screams had been in English. Verinder had kissed her to smother her words.

Verinder, while trying to calm the trembling of his hands on Elizabeth's shoulders, said, "It was only a nightmare. Everything's all right."

"Yes, only a nighmare," Elizabeth whispered. Verinder's glittering, unreadable eyes were close to her own. She felt his warm breath on her face and his fingers pressing into the skin beneath the thin cotton of her chemise. A shiver born at first of desire became a shudder as the immodesty of her behaviour became apparent. Then after Verinder removed his hands from her shoulders and moved away, Elizabeth's teeth began to chatter with cold. She had kicked aside her coverings as she'd run from the faceless tormentor of her nightmare.

"You are cold," Verinder said unnecessarily as he heaped the blanket and cloak over Elizabeth's shivering body."

"I, I sh-shall b, be fine in a mm, mo-ment," Elizabeth stuttered, trying to still her shaking. Instead of a reply, she heard Verinder's movements. The rustlings of straw and the swishing and thumping of blankets.

Moments later, Verinder returned to her side. Without a word, he lifted her into his arms and laid her on the blanket-covered straw bed he'd made. Elizabeth was so cold by now that the impropriety of the entire situation seemed far less important than the return of warmth to her body. Trust me, Verinder had told her earlier. And although this night was like no other in her life, Elizabeth believed she could trust this man who held not only her honour but also her life in his hands.

"Lie on your left side," Verinder ordered as he methodically piled clothing over her. When he was satisfied that the bed was as warm as he could make it, Verinder carefully lifted the coverings and eased himself under the mound next to her. "Move closer to me," he suggested calmly while his breathing continued its erratic rhythm. "You'll be warmer if you do."

Edging towards Verinder and feeling the warmth from his body pulling her like a magnet, Elizabeth cradled herself against Verinder's back, her cheek resting below his left shoulder.

"Try putting your right arm around me," Verinder offered, his voice husky with emotion he could not disguise.

When her arm tentatively crept over his chest, his right hand immediately captured hers. Verinder's steady heartbeat and the heat from his body filled her with a peaceful lassitude. Elizabeth, feeling safe and warm, snuggled closer.

Finally, hearing her even breathing, Verinder whispered, "Beth?" Hearing nothing in reply, he smiled. Images of Elizabeth scrolled across his inner vision. Elizabeth looking at Jeanette Martin with longing as she slipped the mended pinafore over the child's head. Elizabeth smiling as she mashed apples. Elizabeth quietly making herself useful after their simple supper. Then another image overshadowed these – Elizabeth's lips soft and yielding under his own.

Emotions Verinder thought he had buried after Sarah's betrayal emerged and then blurred into a kaleidoscope of images. The faces of his dead brother Edward and of his son Simon. The grounds at Earl's Wood Park. The medals on his dress uniform hanging in Rossbury House in London. They all reminded him of responsibilities waiting for him across the Channel.

Even more immediate were the responsibilities of the journey to Le Havre. And I'll need to keep my wits about me if I am to conclude it safely.

No, Verinder amended, if <u>we</u> are to conclude it safely. Cheered by the plural and lulled by Elizabeth's soft breath on his back and her trusting hand still in his, Verinder slept.

## CHAPTER 3

# TUESDAY, JANUARY 22, 1793

Some instinct warned Verinder of a watching presence even before he heard the whispers.

"They're still asleep."

"But *Maman* told us to give them the milk."

"Maybe we should just leave it here."

"But what if Richard trips over the bowl?"

At the same time, Verinder felt Elizabeth stirring, the pre-dawn light and the Martin children's whispers combining to awaken her. She stretched, then stiffened as she realized they were not alone.

"Good morning, Richard," Elizabeth said, hoping her voice sounded like that of a newly-wed wife.

"Good morning, *ma petite.*" Verinder rolled over to face her and gave her a chaste kiss on the forehead as he touched her face with his left hand.

"You're awake!" chorused Paul and Jeanette.

Verinder and Elizabeth turned to look at the children. "*Maman* told us to give you this milk for your breakfast," Paul said and held a bowl forward.

"Thank your mother for us," replied Verinder.

"You won't forget to say good-bye, will you?" inquired Paul anxiously.

"No, I won't forget," answered Verinder.

"Good!" Paul grinned. He set the bowl of milk on the up-ended box near the banked fire and grabbed his sister's hand. "Come on, Jeanette. We need to tell Papa breakfast is ready."

After the two children left, Verinder said, "Stay under the blankets where it's warm for a few more minutes while I stoke up the fire." As he spoke, he pulled on his shirt and shoes.

"Thank you," Elizabeth said, knowing that Verinder was giving her time to dress. "It is definitely more than a bit cold this morning." She watched him add fuel to the fire. "While you see to Angélique, I'll prepare our breakfast."

"*Bon.* The earlier we start on our way, the better," he replied. "I won't be long."

By the time Verinder returned, Elizabeth had dressed and almost completed the rebraiding of her hair.

"Breakfast should be ready soon," she observed. Seeing his left eyebrow raise in what she already recognized as a sign of inquiry, she continued, "Just porridge, I'm afraid. We've only a bit of the loaf left, and I want to save that and the last of the cheese for our mid-day meal. But," she assured him, "there's plenty in the pot. Last night I put the grain in with some water to soak. Starting the day with something hot seemed one way to keep off the cold--at least for a while."

"Too bad it won't keep out the damp. Rain is definitely on the way." Verinder picked up a blanket and began to fold it.

Elizabeth grabbed the other end. After the blanket became a square of material, Elizabeth stepped towards Verinder to give him the two corners she held, and their hands touched. Seeing her blush at the contact, Verinder remarked, "We're behaving like newly-weds, Madame Verinder, but then that is exactly what we are."

Her eyes flew to his face and saw approval there. "Being a," Elizabeth paused, "wife for the first time is difficult. I..."

He interrupted, "No one expects you to be a seasoned matron. You are doing well. Very well." He considered adding more but instead said lightly, "Now when do we eat? I'm hungry, and even porridge and milk sounds like a feast."

"Your wish is my command," Elizabeth laughed, picking up his mood and a ladle for the porridge at the same time.

Less than an hour later they had packed the cart, harnessed Angélique to it, relayed their thanks to the Martins, and said good-bye. Verinder turned Angelique onto the main road and immediately fell silent, his lips in a tight, thin line, his eyes bleak.

It's that promise he was forced to make to Paul, Elizabeth thought. The promise to return to the farm after the next trip to Rouen. The promise he can't keep.

Finally, when Duclair was in sight, Verinder said, "The Martins are the only people with children I ever stay with. Madame Martin happened to overhear me making inquiries in Boscherville on my first trip through, and..." As what had happened next was apparent, there was no need to finish the explanation.

"Someday you may be able to..." Elizabeth began comfortingly but unconvincingly.

"Someday is far too long when you are Paul's age!"

Then to add to the gloom, the rain Guillaume Martin had predicted began to fall.

Elizabeth grabbed the boat tarp Verinder had readied and pulled it over their heads. But the tarp provided little protection, and Duclair and the River Austreberthe were crossed in wet misery.

Not far beyond Duclair, the road forked. Verinder turned right.

"Business should be good in Le Havre," Verinder said, "so we'll bypass Jumièges and cross the promontory here." Then with a glimmer of a smile, he added, "You can see the abbey – and it is impressive – on our next trip."

"I shall hold you to those words," Elizabeth replied lightly, touching his arm briefly.

When Verinder did not respond, Elizabeth realized, He is still thinking about the lie he told Paul. His honour is important to him. And that lie... She glanced at Verinder now staring straight ahead at the road. That lie and all the others. Whatever he's doing in France, he's paying dearly for it. And the last thing he needs now is my chatter. Or questions.

However, their mutual silence as the cart headed towards Yainville was a companionable one. Later when the track they followed rejoined the main river road, Verinder turned the cart north and headed for Le Trait, the square church tower of Yainville left behind them.

Because the rain continued to pelt down unrelentingly, neither wanted to stop for a mid-day meal. Instead, Elizabeth hoisted her market basket to her lap and then handed Verinder a hunk of bread topped with a bit of cheese. "Not as appetizing as what you made for us last evening, is it?"

"No, it isn't," Verinder answered after his first bite. "But it's much better than nothing."

Sensing that conversation might now be welcome, Elizabeth asked, "Where are we?"

"When we turned back onto the main road, Yainville was behind us. Up ahead – that's the parish church of Le Trait. You can just see it through this heavy mist," he noted ironically. "Next comes Caudebequet with the Abbey of St-Wandrille to its north. You have heard his story, no doubt."

"Yes, I have, though it is not a popular one at present." She lowered her voice although they were alone on the road. "King Dagobert and the count turned monk – not figures of respect today. The abbey has no monks now, does it?'

"None. The Revolution has seen to that." Elizabeth's sigh prompted him to inquire, "You were wondering about the guest house, weren't you?"

"I did wonder where we'd stay tonight. You mentioned St-Wandrille yesterday."

Looking at Elizabeth, Verinder saw how wet and bedraggled she was. "Please accept my apologies. I have been lost in thought all morning. You are wet and probably as happy with me as a raw recruit with his sergeant major on a forced march."

"That sums it up fairly well!"

"Well, if you can bear to miss St-Wandrille, I feel we should press on beyond Caudebecquet to Caudebec-en-Caux. A buyer with a much larger and more varied inventory than ours is often away from Le Havre on business. When I last saw him, he said he might be starting such a journey on either the twenty-sixth or seventh. I do not want to miss him."

Elizabeth nodded her understanding. "Then you must do whatever needs to be done to bring us there by Friday."

"And," Verinder continued, "I happen to know that Caudebec has a small inn. A modest place. I haven't stayed there. But I'm sure we'll find a hot meal and a fire. And it's a place where a rag-man with a new wife might stay. Especially on a wet evening." He looked up at the sky, which showed no sign of lightening. "We shall both be well and truly soaked before we arrive, but..." He shrugged and then turned to see Elizabeth's reaction.

"You are right, of course. On to Caudebec-en-Caux," Elizabeth agreed while giving him her brightest smile. "I can always see St-Wandrille on our next trip, *oui*?"

"*Absolument*!" Verinder rejoined. And please God, that next trip is not one taken under guard later this week.

The afternoon was drawing to a close when Verinder and Elizabeth entered Caudebec's inn. Their entrance drew the attention of the innkeeper and two others, their conversation halting as they stared at the new arrivals. Hoping to dry her sodden clothes, Elizabeth sought the fire while Verinder limped towards the innkeeper.

"Good afternoon, Citizen," began Verinder. "Have you a room where my wife and I can spend the night?"

"Yes," replied the innkeeper, his gaze taking in the appearance of the stranger before him, doubt forming about his ability to pay.

Before Verinder could speak, one of the other men said, "You're a ragman, aren't you?" Without waiting for Verinder's confirmation, he turned to the innkeeper and said, "You remember him, Ridoubet? Comes through here after Rouen on his rounds." Seeing recognition on the innkeeper's face, the man continued, "He sold my wife this shirt." The man, a sandy-haired fellow of medium height, glanced down at the garment he wore. "She bought it the last time he came through."

"You're right," grinned Verinder. "But I don't remember the shirt."

"And I don't remember your wife."

"That's because we've only been married a few weeks."

"Congratulations, Citizen!"

"I don't know, Justin," interjected Ridoubet, glancing over at Elizabeth. "Just because your Céline is a gem..." He broke off as a short woman with an angry face burst through the curtain covering a doorway behind him.

"Thérèse," the innkeeper said at once. "This good citizen wants a room for tonight."

Eyeing first her husband and then Verinder with suspicion, the innkeeper's wife asked bluntly, "Can you pay?'

"Madame Ridoubet, I can," replied Verinder evenly.

"Suppose you expect something to eat, too."

"Yes, and stabling for our horse."

The seeing Elizabeth sitting by the fire, Madame Ridoubet glared at Verinder.

"My wife," Verinder explained, feeling a bit like a guilty schoolboy standing before an angry headmaster.

"She looks soaked to the skin!" accused Madame Ridoubet.

"Madame, the rain..." began Verinder before Elizabeth's coughing interrupted him.

As Verinder hurried to her side, he heard Madame Ridoubet's voice behind him.

"Men! You're all alike! Kept the poor woman out in a winter rain all day and went about your business as usual. She's probably caught her death of cold."

In the moment Verinder had with Elizabeth before Madame Ridoubet pushed him aside, he noted the laughter in her face. Elizabeth's coughing, he then realized, was a cover for the giggles she could scarcely conceal.

"Poor lamb," cooed Madame Ridoubet. "Do you have any dry clothes?"

"In the cart," Elizabeth replied, her renewed coughing causing Madame Ridoubet's eyes to narrow.

"Bring in those dry clothes after you see to your horse, Ragman," demanded Madame Ridoubet.

"I will." Verinder headed for the door.

Satisfied that her orders would be obeyed, Madame Ridoubet turned to Elizabeth. "Come into the kitchen. I've a big fire there, and we can get some of these wet clothes off you. Supper is only a vegetable ragout. But it's hearty. I put some meat gravy in it. That'll warm you up."

While Madame Ridoubet hustled Elizabeth through the curtained doorway, the three remaining in the room heard her say again, "Men! They're all alike!"

"Sometimes women can be the very devil," whispered Ridoubet to Justin when he was finally able to finish the sentence he had started five minutes earlier.

With wary looks at the curtain, both men nodded.

In Rouen, René Dubois also thought of the woman who labored on the other side of the curtain behind him. His wife Sophie had been pleased with her new cloak. Very pleased. He smiled at the memory.

His musing was interrupted when Henri LeBeau came through the door of the wine shop and stepped up to the counter, a scowl on his face. Dubois set a measure of wine before him. "What has happened. You look upset. Have you had bad news?"

"You could call it that," muttered LeBeau. He glanced around the shop and saw François Meunier sitting in a corner with two others. "Meunier!" LeBeau motioned the other man towards the counter and then tapped the side of his nose with his forefinger.

Leaving his other friends at the table, Meunier immediately joined the two at the counter, a question in his eyes.

"I've had a letter," Le Beau announced, drawing a folded paper from his pocket

"A letter!" his friends chorused in surprise, for letters were something completely unknown to any of them.

"Took me a while to find someone to read it to me. It's from my sister Constance in Le Havre. It seems Tellier, her husband, has died." Seeing Dubois and Meunier's sympathetic looks at this sad news, LeBeau growled, "Don't feel sorry for him. He was a stupid fisherman. Didn't even have his own boat. Constance never should have married that scum."

"And you must go to Le Havre to console your sister, no?" asked Dubois.

"I need to go to Le Havre all right. But not to console Constance. The man Tellier worked for … Armand Bertaux. A widower. Owns two or three fishing boats. Had his eye on Constance for some time. Wasn't man enough to do anything about it while Tellier was around, of course. Met him once. Knew right away that if anything happened to Tellier, Bertaux would bide his time and then make Constance an offer she couldn't refuse."

"Couldn't refuse," gasped Meunier. "You mean he would force her into becoming his…" He lowered his voice. "His kept woman?"

"No, you fool," continued LeBeau. "He'll offer to marry her. He's no children of his own, and Constance has those two brats of Tellier's. Spoils 'em both. Kept 'em at home when they could've been earning. Only let Guy go out with his father the last two years, and he's twelve! And Delphine at ten is still at home with her though Constance brags about how good she is with the baking."

"But, but," Dubois said, failing to understand the source of LeBeau's anger. "If this Bertaux marries your sister and makes her children his heirs, doesn't that take her off your hands?"

"Letting Constance marry Bertaux is the problem!" yelled LeBeau. "Always knew Tellier'd die before Constance, her being only half his age. And I figured Constance and those two of Tellier's would come to live with me. I've plenty of room for all of them. That hovel I live in could use a woman's hand."

"You're right about that," noted Meunier. "You never seem to cook or clean. And as for mending..." He looked at a long tear in LeBeau's jacket and shrugged.

"Exactly!" exclaimed LeBeau. "Constance could take care of all that. The boulangerie would take on Delphine. And Guy could work with me down at the river. Three of us earning. Things'd be good."

"But," asked Dubois, "why would your sister come live with you if this Armand Bertaux-"

"Because I'm her older brother, that's why!" interrupted LeBeau. "I'm the one who put food on the table after our father died. Besides I'm head of the family now. She'll do what I tell her to. I don't care what Bertaux says. A man like that – fair to everyone, the men on his boats told me. Bah! I don't believe it! There's a bad smell about this whole thing, and it's not just those fish he catches. But poor dumb Constance'll never see it 'til it's too late. This letter," he waved a paper taken from his pocket. "I bet he wrote it. Constance can't read or write. And it didn't come from Guy, no matter what the signature says. Only a word about Tellier's death. Then on and on about Bertaux's kindness. How good he is. How kind he is. Seems he's even raised Guy's wage. Hah! No one's that good. Someday Constance'll thank me for saving her from that man's clutches."

"But what if he has already…" Dubois began.

LeBeau snorted impatiently. "Not him. He'll wait until summer. Then he'll ask. I know his type. And his so-called kindness is no more than paper, I tell you." He waved the letter in anger. "So I'm going to Le Havre before that snake can strike."

"To Le Havre? Now?" Dubois shook his head in disbelief.

"By barge?" asked Meunier.

"No," replied LeBeau. "Borrowed a horse. Called in a small debt," he smirked. "Leaving early tomorrow. If I push the nag, I'll reach Le Havre on Friday morning."

"But you'll have to ride after dark to do that," said Meunier.

"So what? You and I have worked longer hours than that when a barge needs unloading."

"But, LeBeau," put in Dubois, "people say there are bands of thieves who might..."

"Pah! They don't scare me. I also borrowed these." He pulled back his jacket to reveal two pistols, one stuck in either side of the waistband of his trousers.

"*Mon dieu*!" exclaimed Meunier.

"Don't worry about me, my friends. Worry about anyone who tries to bother me between here and Le Havre! With any luck, I can buy a cart cheap, load Constance and her brats and belongings onto it, and be back here in Rouen by the middle of next week. Might even be able to trade some of Constance's household belongings for a cart. After all, she won't need them once she is living with me." LeBeau grinned.

"Of course, of course. That goes without saying," agreed Dubois, glad that the LeBeau had not asked to borrow money. "Still it is a long journey to make alone, and your sister isn't even expecting you."

"You're right. She's not expecting me. And her surprise will work in my favor."

"Don't run into any surprises yourself, LeBeau, on your way to Le Havre," said Meunier.

"Don't worry," replied LeBeau. "I won't."

Richard Verinder reentered the inn at Caudebec-en-Caux some thirty minutes after he left it to care for Angélique. In his arms was a large bundle.

After he looked askance at Ridoubet, the innkeeper disappeared behind the curtain. A moment later Thérèse Ridoubet appeared. Holding out her arms, she ordered, "Give me those clothes, Citizen. Your wife is in the kitchen. You can take your other things up to your room." She nodded towards the stairs at the back of the inn's common room. "First door you come to. Can't miss it."

"*Merci*, Madame Ridoubet," Verinder said while handing over Elizabeth's things.

"Humph!" sniffed the innkeeper's wife. "Don't thank me. Your wife says you kept driving in the rain this afternoon because you wanted her to have a fireside, a hot meal, and a warm bed at day's end." Her tone of voice implied that she suspected that Elizabeth had simply been trying to make the man standing before her look good.

"That's true, Madame Ridoubet," said Verinder. "We are but recently wed. And while I am used to sleeping rough, my wife is not. I wanted her to have comfortable lodgings tonight. And I remembered the inn here in Caudebec. This is a place I have heard others speak well of."

"Humph!" sniffed Madame Ridoubet again, mollified by Verinder's praise. "Well, you'll get nothing fancy here. But the room and the bed are clean. And supper will be ready when you are. I can serve you over there." She pointed to a table by the fire.

"Thank you again, Madame Ridoubet," acknowledged Verinder. "I..."

Interrupting, the innkeeper's wife grunted, "Just don't keep us waiting!" Then she disappeared behind the curtain with Elizabeth's dry clothes.

A quarter of an hour later Elizabeth, wearing one of her two spare dresses, her nearly dry clothes hanging over her arm, entered the common room from the kitchen. Seeing Verinder talking to four men near the fire, she mounted the stairs, found the room Madame Ridoubet had told her was theirs, laid her clothes across the back of the only chair, and returned to the ground floor.

As Elizabeth neared Verinder's side, one man in the quartet around him confirmed, "Then you will set up your cart tomorrow morning so that our wives can look over your goods."

"Yes, I will. Though we can stay no longer than two hours. We want to reach St-Maurice-d'Etelan before dark. Their market is on Thursday. I usually do a good business there. But, if something your wife wants," he noted, looking around the circle of men which had now grown to six, "needs a small repair, my wife will mend it before we leave."

As the men were exclaiming over this offer, Madame Ridoubet, a tray laden with dishes in her hands, pushed through the circle to the table. "That's right! Give the poor woman some more work to do." She set out two bowls full of ragout, a quarter of a loaf, and two small tankards from which steam rose tantalizingly. "If you become tired or cold tomorrow," she said to Elizabeth, "you just come into the kitchen with me. And you lot," the innkeeper's wife addressed the six villagers, "put in your orders at the counter and let Madame Verinder eat her supper in peace."

The men around Verinder trailed over to the counter. Behind it the innkeeper fussed with glasses. Then one of them called cheekily, "Thérèse, any of that," pointing to the tankards on Verinder's table, "left?"

"It's Madame Ridoubet to you, Rudolphe. Unless you want me to entertain your friends here with stories about your sniveling cradle days!"

And when the youth had the grace to look abashed, Madame Ridoubet relented slightly, "Now stoke up the fire a bit for me, Rudolphe. And get that lazy husband of mine to set out some tankards. There should be enough for you all."

While the six were sipping the hot liquid from their tankards, the outside door opened to admit a stranger. The tall, dark-haired and dark-browed newcomer walked to the counter. "I want your best room for the night."

"It's taken."

The stranger glanced at the tattered looking couple near the fire. "Well, they can..."

"It's taken," repeated Madame Ridoubet. "But we've another room. It's small. But I think you'll find it satisfactory. Payment in advance," she finished firmly.

The stranger set two coins on the counter. "That ought to be enough for supper and stabling as well." Madame Ridoubet nodded and disappeared behind the curtain. "That little oaf outside said he'd see to my horse," he told the room at large.

Neither Verinder nor any of the room's other occupants told him that the oaf was the Ridoubet's intensely shy son.

Moving the room's only other table closer to the fire, the stranger took off his wet cloak and hat. He laid the cloak over the back of a chair and his hat on the seat to dry.

Verinder and Elizabeth continued to eat their meal in silence. Meanwhile, the men at the counter waited for the explosion that would come when Madame Ridoubet reentered the room.

But as the innkeeper's wife returned with the stranger's meal, he turned his back to the fire and shook his head. "You all ought to be celebrating. Citizen Capet is dead!"

Madame Ridoubet stood rooted to the floor. For once she was speechless. Ridoubet seized the tray from his wife's hands. Then the innkeeper hurried to the stranger's side and began serving him.

"What's this you say? The kin-, er, Citizen Capet dead? We heard that the Assembly had, had… But we did not know if the sentence…" He glanced around the room, hoping someone else would speak. Then he pulled the tray to his chest like a shield and said, "Tell us what you know about this thing, Monsieur, er, Citizen...?"

"Rovault. Jacques Rovault," the newcomer replied around a mouthful of food.

"He's come from Paris!" Rudolphe guessed before adding, "Haven't you?"

Happy to have ten other people waiting for his every word, Rovault swallowed another bite of ragout. "Not bad, Citizeness, not bad at all," he said before answering Rudolphe's question.

"Yes, I was there until yesterday morning. Business matters, you know."

"Let the man eat," Madame Ridoubet interjected. "He'll tell us in his own good time." Her sarcasm was lost on most of those in the room. However, Verinder sensed she was angry over Rovault's comment about the ragout which both he and Elizabeth had found delicious. He also sensed that the situation was dangerous. Yet to leave the room before Rovault gave his news would only raise suspicions. So he and Elizabeth were forced to remain and to hear the man out. Giving her hand another surreptitious squeeze, Verinder then tore off a piece of bread and sopped up the last of the gravy in his bowl with it.

Yet one of those in the inn did run out the door, undoubtedly to fetch someone else. Seeing the man leave and guessing why, Rovault chewed slowly. The others in the room watched him and whispered among themselves.

Within minutes, the man who had left returned with a woman. Verinder recognized him as the villager who had congratulated him earlier. The woman had to be his wife Céline. Rovault put down his spoon and pushed his bowl away to indicate that he was ready to tell his tale.

Noting that Rovault had left a small portion of his ragout in his bowl, Madame Ridoubet glared. Her husband hissed, "Shh, shh," an unnecessary action since the room was already quiet.

"As I said earlier, business took me to Paris. That business is as a member of the Jacobin Society in Le Havre." He paused, looking around the room at the eyes fixed on him.

"While I was in Paris, the voting on Capet's execution occurred. The motion for reprieve was, of course, denied," he added as if he had been an integral part of the deliberations. "Capet was taken from Temple and sent to the guillotine at the Place de la Révolution on the twenty-first."

"That was yesterday," noted Madame Ridoubet.

"Yes, it was," agreed Rovault.

"You said you left Paris yesterday morning. So you did not see Capet on the scaffold?"

"No," blustered Rovault. "But you can take my word for it that Citizen Capet has been separated from his head! No last-minute appeal would have allowed nor even heard."

Verinder remained silent. He knew Rovault's announcement of Louis XVI's death was true. And once the news reached England... He willed the others to ask Rovault questions and Elizabeth to say nothing.

"What will happen next?" gasped Ridoubet.

"What are they saying in Paris?" asked Rudolphe.

Rovault's voice over-rode these questions and others to which he did not know the answers. "The Assembly will make its pronouncements. All in good time, Citizens. For now, all of us must beware of the enemies of the Republic who surround us."

"Enemies?" repeated a startled Céline, unaware that she had spoken aloud.

"Yes, enemies!" exhorted Rovault. "France has many enemies. Some right here among us. They will be rooted out." He smiled and nodded. "We will root them all out and send them to shake hands with Madame Guillotine. Them and the rest of Capet's tainted line. That Austrian woman Capet called wife and their litter of brats must be next."

"Next?" Rudolpe echoed.

"Yes, they'll be next." Rouvault nodded, his eyes shining with satisfaction. "And I plan to be in Paris for that. To see Little Capet and Madame Guillotine meet." He laughed grotesquely. "Oh yes, I'll be there to see that whole Capet brood shaved very close!"

"...children!" whispered Elizabeth involuntarily into the hush fallen after Rovault's last statement, her eyes filling with tears.

"Yes, children, Citizeness," snarled Rovault. He rounded on Elizabeth immediately. "Capet's children! Do you want to see your countrymen killed in an uprising to try to put one of them in Capet's place?" he shouted without waiting for an answer. "Are you perhaps a secret Royalist? Well, are you? Are those tears for Capet's whelps?" He had risen from his seat and stood over Elizabeth. His finger stabbed towards her with each question.

"The tears are for my children," Elizabeth cried out at once. The danger she was in made the lies spring to life almost without thought. "The children I may never have because aristos kept me slaving over their carelessly ripped shirts. And their torn flounces. And their unraveled laces. Aristos forbid me to marry! And now, now, it may be too late for me. Too late for children." Then putting her head in her hands, she sobbed loudly.

Elizabeth prayed she had not overplayed the only rôle that might extricate her from the results of her emotional reaction to Rovault's invective. Prayed no one would recognize that her tears were born of fear, not regret. Then she felt a woman's arm about her shoulders.

"See what you've done now," scolded the innkeeper's wife. She looked at Rovault with contempt. "You're not a father. I can see that plainly enough."

With no more questions coming from anyone at the inn, Rovault fumed. He was furious with the woman who had stolen the center of his stage.

"There, there," comforted Madame Ridoubet. She patted Elizabeth's back gently. "You have your man now." She smiled in Verinder's direction while he, feeling some of the tension drain from his body, nodded. "You're still young enough to see babes of your own in your arms."

"That's right," agreed Ridoubet. "Thérèse here was..." His wife's glare silenced him.

"Babes you'll want to keep safe from the Republic's enemies," Rouvault said before Madame Ridoubet could reply. "And France has even more enemies than before now that Capet's been given what he deserves. The talk in Paris was of war and..."

"War! oh no!" squeaked Céline. "They wouldn't take you, would they, Justin?" she asked her husband.

Her face hidden as her head rested on her folded arms, Elizabeth feared the direction this new turn of conversation was taking. She leapt to her feet so quickly that she overturned her chair. Then dashing a hand across her face as if to wipe away her tears, she shouted, "So we must all be one. United in our love of France and our countrymen!"

Everyone, including Verinder, stared at her as if she had just gone mad. With ideas tumbling through her mind, Elizabeth chose the first one that came into focus. Before her courage failed her, she began to sing. It was a song she had heard often in Rouen in the past months.

*"Allons, enfants de la Patrie,*
*La jour de gloire est arrivé!"*

Verinder, as astonished as the others in the room, had the presence of mind to stand. The others stared and then stood also, even Rovault, in admiring attention.

Elizabeth's *La Marseillaise* captivated the small audience. The song made her the center of attention, a place she wanted to avoid. But its power was shifting the emotions of those present to less dangerous ground.

*"Aux armes, citoyens!*
*Formez vos bataillons!*
*Marchons! Marchons!*
*Qu'un sang impur abreuve nos sillons!"*

The fervor of Elizabeth's stirring rendition of the six-month-old call to arms was contagious. Exactly as she prayed it would be. When the last line had been sung, the small group erupted into cheers and applause.

*"Vive la France!"* shouted Rudolphe.

"*Vive la Republic!*" echoed Justin, not to be outdone.

"Citizeness," admired Rovault, his eyes shining with appreciation of the patriotic spirit of *La Marseillaise.* "I should like to hear your story for you seem a true daughter of the Revolution."

"Oh, I... It's nothing very special, you know," Elizabeth replied weakly. She looked at Verinder who had warned her the previous day about saying too much.

Two steps brought him to her side. Putting his left arm about Elizabeth's shoulders, Verinder felt her lean against him.

"Citizen Rovault," Verinder began, "my wife is tired as you can see." Hearing these words, Elizabeth allowed her body to lean even further into Verinder's and her shoulders to sag as if with fatigue. "We have had a long, wet journey today, and..."

"The poor lamb belongs in bed," finished Madame Ridoubet. "As do some of the rest of us as well." Turning to Verinder, she ordered, "You take her up right now. She needs her rest." Then being practical, she added, "You can go through the kitchen first. There's hot water in the kettle and a basin. And outside... Well, go on with you both."

Verinder nodded solemnly and moved toward the kitchen.

"Céline," called Madame Ridoubet as she began to gather bowls and utensils from the two tables. "Could you help me carry these dirty dishes to the kitchen?"

"Of course, Thérèse," agreed her friend. She was eager to escape the prying questions of Rovault who frightened her with his talk of the guillotine and war.

Two of the men also left, an early work schedule calling them to their own homes and beds. The others clustered about Rovault to gain more details about the exciting events taking place in Paris.

Ten minutes later after the door of Madame Ridoubet's best room had closed behind them, Elizabeth began to apologize. "I'm sorry..."

"You were wonderful," Verinder whispered.

"No, I wasn't. Just very frightened."

"So was I."

"Truly?"

"Yes."

"We seemed so close to..." Elizabeth left her real fear unspoken, the sharp blade of the guillotine menacingly close in the darkness of the room.

"Shh, no more. The walls..."

Verinder's unfinished warning about the thinness of the walls forced Elizabeth to consider the man who would sleep on the other side of one of them. She shuddered.

To give her something else to think about, Verinder pointed out in a voice she could scarcely hear, "As you can see, there is but one bed. I can sleep on the floor."

"No," Elizabeth replied in a voice that matched his. "No, I..." she hesitated. "Remember this morning." The faces of the two children were sharp in her memory

"I do," Verinder recalled with a smile Elizabeth could not see, his memory harking back to an earlier time in the morning hours than hers. "And you're right."

"If you… That is, your back..." Elizabeth's words stumbled out uncertainly. "It was warm. And safe."

"I understand. I, too..." Unable to continue his sentence, aware of an emotion that was very different from what he felt in the common room downstairs, Verinder asked instead, "What side of the bed do you prefer?"

"The same as last night," Elizabeth replied. "That is, over here," she gestured to the left.

"It's so dark that..."

"Yes, I see," she said, knowing he was referring to the conventions of modesty that seemed inconsequential in this place. "Or rather I don't see."

"I remember noticing a candle on a table earlier. Don't move. I'll try to find it."

"There's no need. I have undressed in the dark before. I can manage."

Silence followed as both readied themselves for sleep. Verinder heard blankets shifted as Elizabeth eased under them. Then he carefully stretched out on the right side of the bed and drew his half of the bedclothes over his tall frame. As soon as he had done so, her arm stole over his back and curled around his chest. He put his hand over hers to show that her nearness was not intrusive.

"Good night, Richard," Elizabeth whispered into the darkness.

"Sleep well, Élisabeth," Verinder replied, the contentment he felt surprising him as he recalled the dangers of the evening. Then to reassure her that their fearful journey would not last forever, he added, "By Friday, we should reach Le Havre."

"Yes," Elizabeth breathed, "Le Havre."

Safety, both thought before they slept, lay only three days away.

## CHAPTER 4

# WEDNESDAY, JANUARY 23, 1793

Verinder stepped through the curtain dividing the Caudebec inn's public room from its kitchen. Elizabeth's market basket lay on the big, well scrubbed table in the centre of the room. Into it Madame Ridoubet was packing several items.

"This," Elizabeth put two coins on the table, "should pay for our breakfast and the food you have given us."

"Too much." Madame Ridoubet pushed one coin towards Elizabeth.

"Ridoubet said I could come in," interrupted Verinder, standing cap in hand, near the doorway.

"Humph" was Madame Ridoubet's only reply as she scanned Verinder's feet. When she saw that his shoes had carried no mud from the inn yard into the kitchen, she nodded with approval.

Verinder, seeing her inspection, grinned.

"Your wife has warmed herself by the fire," commented Madame Ridoubet. "Take care she stays that way today."

"I intend to," replied Verinder.

"And now you are on your way to St Maurice d' Etelan, *non*?"

"That's right," replied Verinder. The three walked out of the kitchen into the public room and toward the door. Nearby,

Ridoubet and his son were talking. "We should arrive well before dark."

"*Bon.* After dark," observed Madame Ridoubet with a disdainful huff, "there are men abroad. Men you wouldn't want your wife to meet. But I needn't remind you. You have traveled the road before." Seeing Verinder's nod of agreement, she continued, "And you will stay for the market tomorrow morning, of course."

"I usually do quite well there," Verinder said.

"You are not staying at the inn, I hope! Those Fouchets!" She sniffed dismissively. "They know nothing about running an inn. The food is oversalted. The rooms are..." She paused in her torrent of abuse and ended darkly, "Madame Verinder should not stay in such filth!"

"She is right, you know," the innkeeper added.

"Of course, I am right!" Madame Ridoubet glared at her husband.

"In St Maurice I sometimes stay with Madame Duval. She has heard about my wife and will be glad to meet her," replied Verinder. He drew Elizabeth to his right side. She moved unhesitatingly into the half circle created by his arm. Verinder remembered a beautiful golden haired woman who shrugged away from a similar gesture and then abruptly returned his attention to the conversation.

"Ah, the widow Duval," began Madame Ridoubet.

"Her son is the blacksmith. He's nice," interrupted her normally silent son.

"That's right, Étienne," agreed Madame Ridoubet. She smiled at the boy now standing by her side.

"Is Duval a friend of yours?" Elizabeth asked.

"Yes," Étienne replied. "Yes, he is. We even have the same name."

"Would you like us to deliver a message from you?"

"Oh, yes," Étienne answered. "Tell him, tell him..." He hesitated, and for once Madame Ridoubet did not interrupt. She had never heard her son address so many words to a stranger before. "Tell him I remember what he said," the boy finally stammered.

"We will," Elizabeth assured him. "I'll tie a knot in the corner of this cloth over my basket." Elizabeth fitted action to words. "Now I shall be certain to remember."

Because her eyes were on young Étienne, Elizabeth did not see Madame Ridoubet's swift look of appreciation. "You will be warm and well-fed with Madame Duval. What is more," the innkeeper's wife added, thinking of her other guest of the previous evening, "you won't have to mix with self-important fools there."

"Not like some we could name," inserted Ridoubet. "Right, Thérèse?'

"You've changed your tune," accused his wife. "You seemed to think Citizen high-and-mighty Rovault was worth listening to last night!"

"That was before..." Ridoubet looked at his son and left his sentence unfinished. Étienne would not profit by a reminder of Rovault's scornful words upon his departure. "We do not need customers like him!"

"And should he or any of his kind return," said Madame Ridoubet. "Well, they'll wish they hadn't!"

"Rovault could be a dangerous enemy," Verinder observed.

"Pah! He is nothing but a puffed up nobody trying to sound more important than he is," argued Madame Ridoubet.

"Yes," agreed Verinder. "But men like Rovault are still dangerous. In Paris," he stopped, uncertain now how to give his warning without appearing to know too much.

"What about Paris?" asked the innkeeper and his wife in unison.

"A rag man travels. He sees and hears what people, at times, do not intend him to see and hear. In Paris, some men, much like Rovault, are powerful. And those who disagree with them..." Verinder shrugged.

The look the Ridoubets exchanged told Verinder they understood.

Still, Ridoubet protested. "But we have rights now. The Revolution came, and now we have rights," he repeated.

"I hear little about rights," observed Verinder. "But I do hear ugly talk. Ugly talk about Madame Guillotine and war. The Rovaults of France seem to care only for their rights. The rest of us must protect ours as best we can."

"Huh!" grunted Madame Ridoubet. "Well, one thing's certain - talk won't bake the bread or make the soup. Be off with you and leave me to my work!"

"Perhaps we'll see you when you travel this way again?" asked the innkeeper. He opened the door.

"Perhaps," agreed Verinder as he guided Elizabeth into the inn yard.

Later that morning Henri LeBeau whistled tunelessly to himself as he urged his borrowed horse along the road Verinder and Elizabeth had traveled only a day earlier.

Won't Constance be surprised to see me Friday morning! Le Beau chuckled aloud. The idea of grabbing his sister and her two children out from under Bertaux's nose pleased him. He saw the shabby rooms he lived in transformed by his sister. Saw the small luxuries he could afford when three wage packets came into his hands weekly. And since I am the head of the family, they will all do as I say. No doubt about that.

And no doubt about those two *Anglaise* back in Rouen. One dead. The other good as. Le Beau smiled as he recalled what he had learned early that same morning as he detoured past Docteur Mansard's house on his way to collect his mount. The doctor's niece was near death, a neighbor had told him. The fever that had claimed Madame Mansard was ravaging the woman who nursed her.

We need no *Anglaise* in France. None, Le Beau told himself as his horse continued westward.

That afternoon at the forge in St Maurice d' Etelan, Étienne Duval gave a final tap of his hammer on a wagon axle. The repair complete, the blacksmith, a short barrel-chested man with close cropped black hair and massive arms, wiped his hands on the leather apron he wore and turned at the sound of approaching wheels.

"Ragman, you're back," he called out as soon as he saw Verinder's cart.

"Yes, I'm back," Verinder acknowledged. He climbed down from the cart. "And this time, my wife is with me."

"It's about time you were wed," Duval grinned. "*Ma mere* doubted whether the seamstress you talked about was real."

"She is real," Verinder replied with a warm glance in Elizabeth's direction. "Her mending helped us make some sales this morning at Caudebec-en-Caux."

"And your hope is to do the same at the market here tomorrow, *non*?"

"*Mais oui*."

"And to leave the cart and horse here overnight?"

"Right again."

"Then let's get her unhitched and inside," said Duval.

After Elizabeth clambered down from the driver's bench, Duval began, "Well, Madame..." He hesitated, the ragman's name forgotten.

"Verinder," Elizabeth supplied as the two men led Angélique inside.

"That's right. I remember now," continued the blacksmith. "My mother will be happy to see you, Madame Verinder."

The two men began the unhitching process, and Duval rattled on. "She's the village matchmaker. A real mother hen. Always trying to pair everyone off."

"Not like Madame Ridoubet then, is she, Richard?" asked Elizabeth, happy to find Verinder's first name slipped from her mouth so easily. "I can't imagine her urging anyone to marry!"

"Ah, the formidable Madame Ridoubet!" interjected Duval. "But," he added thoughtfully while pitching some straw into a stall, "a mother hen, nonetheless. Maybe you weren't there long enough to find out."

"Oh, I think we were there long enough to see her true colors," observed Verinder. He looked pointedly at Elizabeth before drawing a bucket of water from the trough near the anvil.

The blacksmith laughed aloud and then nudged Verinder good-humoredly. "I see how it was. I bet you felt the bite of Madame Ridoubet's sharp tongue, Ragman!"

"I did," admitted Verinder. "And it sounds like you've been bitten, too."

"I won't deny it," Duval rejoined. "But I like Madame Ridoubet. She's, she's..." he paused and ended simply, "she's a good woman." He motioned to Verinder, and the two men pushed the cart into a corner.

"A woman whose son thinks well of you," Elizabeth stated.

"Étienne?" asked Duval. Seeing Elizabeth's nod, he asked, "How is he?" He tossed a ragged horse blanket to Verinder. "You can put this over her. Might keep her a bit warmer tonight."

"Étienne told me to say that he has not forgotten what you said," related Elizabeth.

"Good lad!" smiled Duval. He leaned on the side of the stall and watched Verinder rubbing Angélique down. "Met him when I went to Caudebec to repair some equipment. Customer made it worth my while to set up a temporary forge there. The boy..." He rubbed his chin, remembering. "We have the same name, you know. Étienne's small for his age and needs a bit of confidence. So I told him about another puny little fellow people were always saying wasn't strong enough to do anything. Me!" He grinned at their expressions of surprise.

"*Oui,* it is true. But old Vinçart, the blacksmith. He gave me a chance." He sighed, remembering the boy he had once been. "And later gave me his daughter, too! And now," he spread his arms wide as he looked about his forge. "Well, you can see for yourselves."

"No wonder Étienne calls you friend," remarked Elizabeth.

"My wife will be calling me something far worse if I stay here talking much longer!" the smith said.

"Don't let us keep you. Angélique has all she needs," observed Verinder. "Thanks to your help." He grabbed a small bundle and the workbasket from the cart and handed the basket to Elizabeth. "I'll come back for the cart before the market."

"I'll be here," said Duval while the three walked towards the big double doors at the front of the forge. "Tell *ma mere,* I'll see her tomorrow."

"We will," called Verinder as Duval, having closed the doors, hurried off.

While Elizabeth and Verinder picked their way down the muddy street, Verinder recalled the confession Elizabeth made when the road was free of travelers.

"We've both discovered I have little aptitude for acting," Elizabeth had told him. "I tend to wear my emotions, right here." She had pointed to her sleeve. "I was able to salvage last night's careless slip. But next time..."

Just then two horsemen had appeared so Verinder had not been able to tell her that being able to hide falseness behind a mask of apparent honesty was not a virtue. If I did, she wouldn't believe me. She knows it's something I've grown too good at doing. Something many of us are too good at doing. He saw Sarah's wide-eyed and open face and pushed the memory away.

Sometime I must tell Elizabeth... Verinder wasn't sure of what he wanted to tell her. But he was sure that the time for telling her was not now. Think about the present, he reminded himself. There'll be no time in the future if you don't.

The pair reached a corner. Verinder pointed and said, "The house is down this lane." He squeezed Elizabeth's arm with his left hand and motioned back towards the forge with his right. "That was well done. You have made another friend."

"Thank you for..." Elizabeth began with a grateful look. "I..." Unable to complete her thought aloud, she said, "It is hard to believe Duval was ever a quiet boy like Étienne Ridoubet."

"Impossible you mean," replied Verinder. "I think part of his past has been reinvented in his imagination. Though there is no denying his lack of inches."

"He more than makes up for those with..." Elizabeth began.

"Words!" finished Verinder. "When you meet the widow Duval, you'll see his mentor." He grinned in anticipation. "For despite what he says now, our blacksmith was no withdrawn and shy youth."

"Nevertheless, letting Étienne think so was kind."

"Yes, it was." And because the Duval door was nearing, Verinder stated, "Exactly as the widow Duval is. You won't be able to say more than two words. Her late husband, her children, her grandchildren. You will know them all tonight. And we shall tell her of our plans for the future."

"The future?" Elizabeth questioned with a puzzled look at his face.

"A married man should not be on the roads with his wife at his side. It is time I settled down," Verinder said. The shadow of another idea flitted quickly across his mind. "It's time I started a shop in town. A ragman may do well there. Especially if his wife is a seamstress. Traveling in all weathers is for bachelors and younger men than I."

"The future," Elizabeth noted, "is a safer subject than the past."

Verinder shook away the faces Elizabeth's words had brought to his mind's eye and rapped on the door. Almost immediately it was opened by a woman whose height and width seemed to be about equal.

"Ragman!" Madame Duval exclaimed loudly. Then smiling hugely to reveal a number of gaps in her teeth, she looked at Elizabeth expectantly. "And who is this?"

After Verinder's introduction, Elizabeth was nearly smothered against the widow's large bosom. Tonight, both thought as they went inside, we remain safe.

Hours later Henri LeBeau sat near the fire at the Ridoubets' inn in Caudebec-en-Caux. He thought about his sister and her children and money he would have after they came to Rouen. Behind him, he was dimly aware, the innkeeper was talking to two of his friends.

Rudolphe nodded towards the stranger. "Another customer tonight, eh Ridoubet?"

"That's right," said Ridoubet. "Name's LeBeau. He's from Rouen. Says he's going to Le Havre on business."

"Le Havre?" repeated Justin. "Just like..." No one wanted to mention Rouvault's name.

"He's from Rouen, you say," said Rudolphe instead. "Maybe he has heard more about the, about the..."

Rudolphe's unfinished statement hung in the silence at the counter. Finally, Ridoubet shrugged and said, "Ask him."

Rudolphe shot back, "I will!"

Sauntering over to the fireside and seating himself, Rudolphe felt the eyes of his two friends on his back. "Citizen LeBeau of

Rouen, I believe?" he asked the man now nearly dozing next to the hearth.

"Yes." LeBeau eyed Rudophe suspiciously.

"I wondered," began Rudolphe, trying to find the right words. "That is, we thought since you are from Rouen… Well, last night a citizen from Le Havre..."

"From Le Havre, you say?" LeBeau demanded. "Citizen Bertaux?"

Quailing under LeBeau's angry look, Rudolphe stammered, "No, no. It was Citizen Rovault. A member of the Jacobins there."

"A Jacobin? A patriot then!" insisted LeBeau.

"It is as you say," gabbled Rudolphe. "This patriot. Rovault. He had come from Paris. He told us that Citizen Capet was... He said that Citizen Capet is..."

"Capet is dead! All France knows this," finished LeBeau. "What else did he say? Was he present in Paris for the execution?"

"No, Citizen, he was not," answered Rudolphe. He looked toward those near the counter. "We thought that you, being from Rouen, might...?" His unstated question was plain and brought Justin over to the fireside. Ridoubet cast a leery glance at the curtain behind the counter before following him.

"I know only what I heard in Rouen before leaving this morning. Capet shook hands with Madame Guillotine on Monday. We are well rid of him!" LeBeau's drowsiness was forgotten in his hatred of the dead king.

"Citizen Rovault," remembered Justin, "said there would be war with England. He said the family of Capet would, would..." The sharp blade of the guillotine seemed to flash before him. He gulped and said, "Would follow him."

"It will be so, Citizens," replied LeBeau. "Capet's death is only the beginning."

"That's what Citizen Rovault said," observed Rudolphe.

"He is right!" declared LeBeau. "And better days are ahead for France!"

"Just like *La Marsellaise* says!" exclaimed Justin.

*"La Marsellaise?"* repeated LeBeau, sounding puzzled.

"We heard it last night," said Rudolphe. "Sung by the ragman's wife."

"The ragman's wife?"

"Yes, Madame Verinder," said Rudolphe. "She stood – right over there." He pointed to the spot. "And sang. It was beautiful. We all thought so." He looked at his friends who nodded to confirm his words. "Even Citizen Rovault was impressed."

"Madame Verinder, you say?" asked LeBeau. Verinder! The name of the ragman he'd met in René Dubois' shop and at the Rouen market. But, he thought, Verinder has no wife.

"The wife of the ragman. She has a fine voice. We all stood up to hear her." Rudolphe began to hum a bit of the tune.

"I'd like to meet her," said LeBeau.

"Perhaps you will. The ragman is on his way to Le Havre. Tomorrow he will be at the market in St Maurice d' Etelan."

"Really?"

"It is as he says, Citizen," nodded Justin sagely.

"Well, perhaps I'll hear the good Madame Verinder's voice myself." LeBeau knew could reach St Maurice before the end of the morning. "But," he added to hide his interest in the ragman, "I'd also like to meet this citizen from Le Havre. Rovault, did you say?"

"That's right," agreed Rudolphe.

"He'd been to Paris, you said. Perhaps you can tell me what he told you?" inquired LeBeau.

"Certainly!" said Rudolphe. "We were all here," he motioned towards his two friends. "The three of us, well, we can tell you what Citizen Rovault told us."

"*Bon*," replied LeBeau.

And while the men from Caudebec told him of Rovault, LeBeau allowed his mind to drift to the more interesting story of the ragman.

And his wife! LeBeau thought to himself. Who is she? he wondered. And why is the ragman keeping her a secret? Only enemies of France have secrets. I'll get to the bottom of this one, he considered smugly. There may even be something in it for me. As he pictured himself denouncing the pair to the local committee, a smile curled about his lips.

## CHAPTER 5

# THURSDAY, JANUARY 25, 1793

"He's not the same man!"

The widow Duval pointed an accusing finger at Verinder.

Elizabeth, restitching a ripped seam, stabbed a finger with her needle. She kept her eyes lowered, her heart beating a tattoo in her throat as she sat on the back of the cart.

Verinder finished rearranging clothes on a board atop two boxes that served as his stall. He looked up to see Madame Duval glaring at him, another woman at her side.

Attracted by the widow's loud voice, those in the St Maurice market moved towards her.

"Look at him, Marie," continued Madame Duval. "He's changed. He's not Verinder the ragman. I knew it at once last night."

"Madame Duval," began Verinder. He knew the widow well and guessed what was in her mind. "Have you brought your friend to my cart to find a bargain?"

Madame Duval glanced around to be sure she had the attention of the small crowd. "No, I have not, Ragman. I brought her to see," she paused, "a married man!"

Laughing hugely at her own jest, Madame Duval waddled behind the stall. Her elbow jabbed Verinder's ribs. Then her arm circled Elizabeth, who had risen from her seat at the rear of the cart. Meanwhile, the citizens of St Maurice laughed with the widow, a few pointing at the blushing cheeks of the ragman's wife.

"Yes, the ragman is a married man." Madame Duval's chins wobbled as she nodded. "And I tell you, citizens, he is a new man. A man with plans for the future."

"We all know what they are!" called out a farmer. He looked at his obviously pregnant wife and then at Elizabeth.

Another burst of laughter greeted this sally.

Putting swollen hands on her ample hips, Madame Duval retorted, "Those may be your plans, Gustave Monteaux. But Verinder here has bigger plans."

Not to be outdone, Monteaux countered, "I'd say my plans were big." He peered roguishly at his wife. "Wouldn't you agree, Jeanette?"

"Gustave," Jeanette Monteaux hissed. "Not here! Or when we get home, I'll be giving you some big..."

Voices from the crowd asked, "A big what, Citizeness?" "I'd like some of that!" "Care to share your plans?" Others simply hooted and guffawed, all enjoying the unexpected pleasure of this small sideshow.

"Well, Madame Duval," asked Monteaux. "Are you going to tell us what the ragman's big plans are?"

"A shop of his own, that's what! In Le Havre." Madame Duval made the announcement as if the idea were hers. "Says traveling about is no life for a married man especially in winter."

"Why didn't you say so earlier?" asked Monteaux.

"Does that mean he won't be returning to St Maurice?" A woman trailed by four small children squeezed forward through the crowd.

"I'm afraid it does," responded Madame Duval. "So if it's a bargain you're looking for..."

At once three people jostled each other to reach the front of the stall. "Told him I'd get a crowd here today," the widow Duval whispered to Elizabeth.

Verinder served customer after customer. With their well-worn coins, he also received words of congratulation and wishes of *bonne chance.*

With a cheery wave over the customers' heads, the widow caught Verinder's eye and shouted, "I'm good for business!"

The need to deal with a customer's question kept Verinder from replying. When he looked up again, Madame Duval was gone.

Three quarters of an hour later, Verinder and Elizabeth lifted the last box onto the cart.

"Wait!" Madame Duval puffed her way towards them, a covered basket on each arm.

"Had to come back to say good-bye," the widow said, breathing hard. "Hope you didn't mind my little joke earlier this morning." She set the baskets on the back of the cart.

"*Pas de tout,*" Verinder said at once.

"*Bien.*" Madame Duval uncovered her two baskets. "Have you anything to put this into? Thought you could use it. Étienne said you'd be sleeping rough, somewhere between Lillebonne and Tancarville."

Elizabeth looked at the baskets filled with food and then at Verinder before replying, "*Certainement.* I have a basket of my own." She began to put the food from the widow's baskets into her larger one.

"We cannot take all of this from you." Verinder pulled some coins from his purse.

"*Non, non,*" Madame Duval said. "Call this a wedding gift. Or a farewell present. For I doubt I'll be seeing either of you again."

"But Madame Duval," remonstrated Verinder, "we owe you a commission. Do we not, Élisabeth?"

"*Mais oui,*" Elizabeth replied. "Of course, we do."

"A commission?"

"Yes, your little drama this morning was good for business." Verinder jingled his coin purse.

"We did much better than we thought," improvised Elizabeth.

"*Vraiment,*" said Verinder. "So this," he dropped some coins into one of the empty baskets Elizabeth passed to him, "is really yours. You earned it twice over." Then he slipped the handle of the basket over Madame Duval's arm.

"If you say so." Madame Duval looked at the coins in the bottom of the basket.

"We do say so." Elizabeth covered her bulging market basket with a cloth.

"You two make a lovely couple," Madame Duval observed with pleasure. "You work well together. You'll make that shop of yours a success, I know." Her gap-toothed grin was wide as she continued, "And perhaps I'll get Étienne to take me to Le Havre. I've a fancy to look at the sea before I die." Her smile seemed to become even wider, if such an occurrence were possible. "I'll find that shop of yours. And I bet I find more than the pair of you living behind it!"

Miles away, Henri LeBeau led his limping horse down the road towards St Maurice. The horse had cast a shoe shortly before he reached Villequier. There he had been told the closest forge was in St Maurice d' Etelan.

Blasted horse! LeBeau swore under his breath though there was no one on the road to hear his curses. I'll never be in time for the market.

Maybe, LeBeau told himself, the ragman and this wife of his will spend another night in St Maurice. People love to talk, he reminded himself. With any luck, I'll learn something. And even if I don't, I'll have a surprise or two for that pig Bertaux. If I continue today and ride late, I can still reach Constance's home by tomorrow.

He quickened his pace.

Early that afternoon Elizabeth tidied away the remains of a mid-day meal. Once more they'd eaten while the cart continued its slow progress west.

Drawing a ragged cloak more closely over her legs, Elizabeth thought about the past two days. He's on guard. Always. Elizabeth stole a look at Verinder. Without me, he would be less conspicuous. In less danger.

Elizabeth shook her head. Jacques Rovault's angry accusation and even Madame Duval's teasing one made the danger seem very real, very close. As if danger were following them.

Verinder marked Elizabeth's slanted glance and the shake of her head and cast a quick look behind them. The road was empty of other travelers. "Only a few more days," he said quietly. "Le Havre tomorrow. And then, with luck, a ship to England the next day."

"England," Elizabeth whispered. The place she had left years earlier. To stay safe! She shivered.

"My back feels frozen, and yours must be the same," Verinder said at once. "If you put the boat tarp over our shoulders, I think we'll both be warmer."

Moments later, they huddled beneath the big tarp. "It's colder today than yesterday," Elizabeth observed, sliding closer to Verinder.

"It is," agreed Verinder. "Sleet and a hard frost later I'm afraid." Seeing Elizabeth's anxious scanning of the sky, he continued, "Don't worry. We'll reach those abandoned buildings I told you about before dark. Tonight we'll be safe from questions, I promise you. Trust me."

Verinder felt Elizabeth's nod on his shoulder. The seeing another cart trundling towards them, he said, "And a fire and supper before too much longer."

That afternoon, a foot sore Henri LeBeau led his horse to Étienne Duval's forge at St Maurice d' Etelan.

After Duval examined the mare, he announced, "Only needs a new shoe."

Sitting on a barrel, LeBeau rested his feet while Duval used his bellows on the fire.

"Hoped to see a friend at the market today," LeBeau said idly.

"Oh?" asked Duval. He wiped the sweat from his forehead with a sooty hand that left his face grimier than before. "Who's that?"

"Verinder, the ragman," LeBeau answered. "*Le connaissez-vous?*"

"After today, everyone in St Maurice knows the ragman," grinned Duval.

"Sounds like a good story," said LeBeau.

"*Oui, certainement.*" Duval continued working the bellows as he began, "It was all my mother's idea."

Duval spun out the events of the morning, ending his story only when the metal on the fire was red hot. "We all had a good laugh, I can tell you that!"

"*Bien sûr.* Verinder and his wife laughed, too, no doubt."

"He did." Duval picked up the mare's hoof and looked at it again. "But Madame Verinder, she blushed like any lately wed wife would."

"I haven't seen her yet," said LeBeau. "Verinder's last visit to Rouen came when I was away. What's she like?"

"Madame Verinder? Élisabeth, I believe is her name," replied the blacksmith as he grasped a lump of hot metal from the fire with his tongs.

"*C'est vrai, Élisabeth.*" Élisabeth? Élisabeth? LeBeau repeated. He gasped aloud. And then closed his mouth quickly. Élisabeth! That's the name of Docteur Mansard's *Anglaise* niece! LeBeau's eyes glittered. The blacksmith loves to talk, he realized. Let's see how much this fool will tell me. "Before they married, Madame Verinder worked as a..."

"Seamstress. Does beautiful needlework. Made repairs on many of the things Verinder sold this morning."

LeBeau vaguely remembered that the doctor's niece had a reputation as a needlewoman. That's right! Dubois said she made a doll for his daughter Lucette! "Seamstress and ragman. Well matched there. Are they well matched in age and looks?"

"Don't know 'bout that." Duval swung his hammer down on the hot iron. "She looks a little younger. Not much though. And he's got an interesting face. A fine face really. Wouldn't you agree?" Without waiting for LeBeau to reply, Duval continued, "She is, well, a little plain. Round face, brown hair done up in two big braids wound round her head. Nice grey eyes though."

The *Anglaise* niece to the last detail! LeBeau exulted. "Still in St Maurice?"

"Fraid not" Duval said as he shaped the horseshoe. "They left after the market."

LeBeau cursed the cast shoe that had robbed him of the chance to denounce the ragman and the woman with him. "Perhaps I'll see him later then. He's on his way to Le Havre, like me. Will probably stay at that inn – what's its name? – near Lillebonne. Or is it near Tancarville?"

"He's never said anything about an inn." Duval brought down his hammer for a crashing blow that made LeBeau jump. "Usually stays at the abandoned farm just beyond Lillebonne."

Duval having told him all he needed to know, LeBeau turned to his horse. "Should give the mare a quick rub down," he said

"Brush is over there." Duval pointed absentmindedly, his concentration once again on the task of shaping metal into a horseshoe.

To the sound of the blacksmith's hammer blows, LeBeau cared for the horse and imagined his friends' surprise when he told them he had captured two traitors to the Republic.

Late that afternoon, Verinder drove the cart inside an abandoned barn. "I know it looks dreadful." He tossed the reins to Elizabeth and jumped down from the cart's seat. Favoring his right leg a bit more than usual, he walked towards Angelique's head.

"This cold weather..." Elizabeth hesitated and then finished, "it makes the bones ache."

"It does." Verinder took Angelique's bridle and led her deeper into the empty building.

Elizabeth descended from the hard seat of the cart, stretched her back, and stepped out to Verinder's right.

"Don't move!"

Verinder's warning caused Elizabeth to freeze in mid-stride.

"Look ahead of you. About eight feet. Don't walk forward; just look."

As Elizabeth's eyes adjusted to the lack of light within the barn, she saw a patch of floor that seemed darker than the rest.

"The floor has collapsed." Verinder limped to her side. "A cellar, or understorey, was there once. Remember coming uphill to reach this building?"

"Past two other buildings that seemed to be in much better shape than this one." Elizabeth stared at the large hole in the floor and shuddered. That's why he chose this barn as our night's lodging. It's out of the way and it has...

"Let's unharness Angelique before we lose all of the light," Verinder said quietly.

When he had led Angelique to a corner of the barn, they unharnessed the horse in silence.

"I'll fetch some water for Angelique and for us," Verinder said. "You can start unloading."

"*Je t'accompagnerai,*" Elizabeth disagreed calmly. "I saw an old bucket near the door. I'll carry it, and you carry the two in the cart. In two or three trips, we can put enough water in the trough," she pointed to a stone one against the wall, "to see us all through 'til morning."

Verinder nodded and grabbed the two buckets.

When they trudged down to the small stream that lay a hundred yards beyond the barn, Elizabeth noticed how Verinder's eyes kept scanning the horizon. She forced herself to breathe deeply and evenly and to say nothing.

After they had poured the last buckets of water into the trough, Verinder said, "Help me with the door."

Together they manhandled the sagging, broken door, squealing and protesting, into a closed position. Although the light was now almost gone, Verinder could see Elizabeth's eyes looming huge in her pale face.

"We'll start our fire first and then eat something. Afterwards we can talk."

"*Ne t'inquiètes pas.*" Elizabeth walked over to the cart and waited. "What do you want me to carry?"

After hoisting himself into the cart, Verinder pushed what they would need towards the rear. "I'll bring the firewood. You take this." He handed Elizabeth her market basket and the bundle of clothes they used as bedding.

After Verinder gingerly lowered himself to the ground, he centered his weight on his left leg and picked up a large armful of wood. "We're heading over there." He pointed to a stone fireplace on the far side of the collapsed floor. "Just follow me. And stay close to the walls."

Verinder limped towards the left, inwardly cursing the bitter cold that was causing his leg to ache so badly. "This building is much like the one at the Martin's farm. With the same original use in mind, more than likely. People at one end, animals at the other."

"Only here, there was some sort of storage cellar below, dug into rising ground," Elizabeth said.

"That's right. And the corner we're heading for is the least drafty in the building." When they reached the fireplace, Verinder knelt to lay some kindling for the fire. He bit back a groan as his leg protested the new stress put upon it.

Soon a fire was burning brightly, and their belongings were laid out neatly by the hearth. Then while Verinder tended Angelique, Elizabeth prepared their supper.

After the meal, Verinder lay on his side before the fire, his head propped up by his forearm and resting on his hand. Elizabeth sat on a box. "Whatever it is," she said, "I would rather it was out in the open. Wondering whether my guesses are correct or the situation is worse than I imagine is what, is what..." Her voice faded.

"Fears of the unknown are always the worst," Verinder confirmed. "I told my..." This time it was he who left his sentence unfinished.

"Company under your command, perhaps? In the war in the former American colonies?" Elizabeth guessed.

Verinder nodded.

"Just like a man who used to visit my father. Lieutenant Smithson. William Smithson. He served with Howe." She paused. When Verinder said nothing, Elizabeth continued, "He said the officers – the good ones – had a sixth sense about danger. Could almost smell its presence."

"He's right. The ones without it didn't last long on the battlefield." Verinder's blue eyes were troubled as they gazed at her. "And today I reminded you of Smithson."

"Yes," Elizabeth said. "We've drawn a lot of attention in the past two days." Elizabeth sighed. "And attention is the last thing we need."

Elizabeth gave a desultory poke at the fire. "Today at the St Maurice market, that sixth sense kicked in. You decided we needed to stay some place, far away from prying eyes. Some place where my foolish tongue would not bring us more trouble." Elizabeth's voice broke on a sob, and she buried her face in her hands.

Immediately Verinder was kneeling beside her, pulling her hands from her face. "Look at me, Élisabeth," he ordered. "Listen to me."

When Elizabeth opened her eyes and saw Verinder on his knees, she cried, "I shall, but – oh, your poor leg; I have..."

Realizing that his kneeling had now made Elizabeth feel worse than before, Verinder suggested, "Let's turn that box of yours on its side and move it a bit farther back from the hearth."

As soon as they had done so, Verinder said, "Mademoiselle, pray be seated on this most elegant sofa while I beguile you with sweet words."

"You are so..." Elizabeth choked, halfway between tears and laughter.

"So, so what, Mademoiselle?"

"You are so..." The next word stuck in her throat. Elizabeth amended quickly, "Impossible!"

"Yes, you are right. I am impossible. To bring a lady to such a place is unforgivable." Verinder watched her face intently, hoping to see the return of the glint in her eyes that told him she was prepared to meet whatever came.

"No!" Elizabeth retorted, grey eyes blazing. "I have been the unforgivable one. Whining and fearful and...."

"And ready to eat stale bread in the rain, melt Madame Ridoubet's iron heart, and even play the shrewish wife on occasion."

"Oh, you are..."

"*Impossible.* We have already agreed upon that." Seeing Elizabeth about to reply, Verinder interrupted, "Peace now, woman; let me have my say." Suddenly the laughter left her eyes, but the overwhelming fear did not return to them. He nodded and then offered, "But perhaps you would like to have it for me."

Sensing that Verinder wanted her to voice her suspicions, Elizabeth began, "That sixth sense of yours made you decide to stay here. You made that decision this morning when you bought the firewood and feed for Angelique, from Etienne Duval."

"You saw them in the back of the cart?" Verinder paused. "Don't answer that question. You would have to be blind not to see them. All right. Next?"

"You've stayed in one of these buildings before, but not this one."

Verinder nodded.

"But this one is farthest from the road. And, since the back wall is still standing, the fire can't be seen from the road. And then there's the door." Elizabeth knew it would warn them if anyone tried to enter.

And a trap, Verinder added to himself. "Right again."

"You expect..."

"No, I expect nothing. I expect that tomorrow, early tomorrow, we shall be in Le Havre. Where we shall be safely housed. And with any luck on a ship sailing for England in a day or two."

"*Vraiment?*" Her eyes pleaded with him to be honest with her.

"*Vraiment,*" he answered with all the solemnity of an oath.

Elizabeth's sigh of relief seemed so heartfelt that Verinder longed to comfort her with more than words. "Bed for us both, I think," he said. "And as you sleep, just tell yourself that we shall reach Le Havre tomorrow."

"Le Havre!" Elizabeth whispered. Safety, she told herself, lay at the port.

Yet it was not the door but Angelique's whinny that warned them perhaps a half hour later. At once Verinder raised himself on an elbow.

"What," Elizabeth began before his hand across her lips stifled her question.

His ears could pick out the faint sounds of a rider approaching stealthily. In his mind's eye, Verinder saw a man inspecting the two other buildings, finding nothing, and heading towards the ruin where he and Elizabeth were.

No one rides in the darkness and bypasses a decent shelter near the road unless he is looking for something. For someone. For me, Verinder told himself grimly.

Knowing he had only seconds to explain, Verinder whispered urgently. "When the door creaks, jump up. Act surprised and frightened. Stand in front of the fire. Don't look at the floor. Follow my lead." He hoped Elizabeth understood his string of instructions. Then cursing himself for not reviewing with her earlier the possibility of their being discovered, Verinder gave Elizabeth's hand a reassuring squeeze and repositioned himself on their make-shift bed.

Immediately the broken door shrieked as it ground its way across the floor.

Verinder jumped up, the blankets falling about him in a heap. He shouted, "*Qui est là?*"

Elizabeth scrambled to stand beside him, careful to position herself at his side in front of the banked fire.

Henri LeBeau entered the dark ruin. He held one pistol and peered into the gloom. "Ragman," he barked. "*Sortez! Je suis que vous être là.*" He walked forward, waving the pistol back and forth. His eyes turned towards the barn's only light, his gaze fastening upon the two people standing in front of it.

Before Verinder could speak, LeBeau laughed in triumph. "Your friends in Caudebec and St Maurice were right. All of them spoke of the Ragman's wife Élisabeth." He made the name sound like a curse. "But I knew the Ragman has no wife." He pointed his pistol at Verinder. "Yet she is with you."

Verinder had heard enough to identify LeBeau's voice. Pretend not to understand, Verinder told himself. Keep his eyes focused on us. "*Mais oui, mà femme est ici, LeBeau.* Where else would she be?"

"Wife!? Pah! You said nothing about a wife to Dubois or anyone else in Rouen." He waved his pistol wildly in Elizabeth's direction. "She's not your wife. She's Mansard's niece, the *Anglaise*."

"You're mistaken, LeBeau." Verinder glanced at the box he and Elizabeth had sat on less than an hour earlier. "She is as French as you or I."

"*Anglaise*!" Elizabeth invested the word with scorn. "*Moi! Quelle farce!* Too bad my fellow servants in the chateau of the Comte d'Arnay can't hear you."

Verinder edged a half step closer to the box and hoped that LeBeau noticed his movement.

"Richard wants to surprise your friend Dubois," Elizabeth said, using the name Le Beau had mentioned. "Surprise him when we are next in Rouen." Her eyes flicked to the box Verinder sidled towards.

"*Une surprise, n'est-ce pas?*" LeBeau's eyes darted back and forth between Elizabeth and Verinder. "The surprise is mine." LeBeau caught another of Verinder's glances at the box. "Delivered when I drag you both to the Committee in Le Havre. Citizen Rouvault will be very interested in what I have to say. Remember him?"

"Of course, we remember Citizen Rouvault. We met him in Caudebec. You'll look very foolish taking us to see him. Best go back to Rouen, LeBeau," Verinder said dismissively, his words calculated to make LeBeau angry.

"This," LeBeau, shook his pistol at Verinder and took another step forward, "gives me the right to give the orders here." He looked at Elizabeth and demanded, "Walk towards me very slowly. You, Ragman," his eyes darted back to Verinder who had edged even closer to the box. "Stay where you are. We're all going to Le Havre together. See to the two of you first. Then my sister. Got a little surprise for her as well. A trip back to Rouen. Yours," LeBeau aimed the pistol first at Verinder and then at Elizabeth, "will be short and sharp." He gave an evil grin and then snarled at Elizabeth. "*Approchez moi lentement.*"

Elizabeth took a hesitant step forward. Then summoning a sob, she covered her face with her hands and dropped to the floor.

The moment she did so, Verinder leapt towards the box.

The roar of a pistol shot brought Elizabeth's head up in time to see Verinder crumple, blood pouring from the left side of his head. Without looking at Le Beau Elizabeth wailed, "You've killed him!" She scrambled towards the box and Verinder.

LeBeau saw Elizabeth's stumbling dive, fumbled for his other pistol, and ran forward. "Stay where you are or I'll..." Suddenly the floor gave way beneath his foot as his headlong dash carried his other foot forward where it found nothing under it. Releasing the pistol and grabbing wildly at the darkness around him, LeBeau screamed and plunged into the cavernous depths of the barn.

Her breath coming in labored pants, Elizabeth dragged herself to Verinder's side. The left side of his head was covered in blood. She began to cry. "Oh God, what will I do? He's dead, and he doesn't even know I..."

Then Verinder groaned. "He hasn't killed me. Though I probably look as if he had." Verinder's head felt as if it were exploding. Even worse his right knee, jammed against a corner of the box, seemed to be on fire, his fall reawakening the pain of his old wound.

"*Tu vis!*" Elizabeth sobbed now with joy. "I thought he had... But you're alive. Are you...how is..."

Verinder groaned again and struggled to sit up. "Must look to see if, if he's..." He pushed his back against the box and leaned into it. The name of the man who would have denounced them hung between them.

"Let me clean your wound first." As Elizabeth stated to rise, Verinder grabbed her arm.

"No," he insisted. "Not yet."

"But..." Elizabeth began.

"Scalp wounds bleed a lot. Surely your uncle," Verinder tried to smile and almost succeeded, "told you as much."

"Yes, but I'm not..."

"Help me up," Verinder interrupted her once again.

"You should be..." Elizabeth protested when Verinder began to heave himself to his feet. She could feel him sway unsteadily as they stood together, his arm heavy across her shoulders.

Verinder closed his eyes against the pain that shot up through his leg when he tried to put his weight on it and against the waves of nausea the pain brought with it. When he opened them, he saw Elizabeth staring anxiously at him.

"Somewhere outside is a horse," Verinder stated matter-of-factly. "And the cellar must be checked." He paused before continuing, "We need to know what's happened."

The thud that followed LeBeau's fall echoed in Elizabeth's ears. "Yes, yes, I..." She felt sick as she envisioned the man who moments before had been hurling threats at them.

"I'll need help. You'll hear me call from below." He stifled a moan as another wave of pain shot up his leg. "When you do, carry a brand from the fire over there." He pointed to the place where the flooring had given way. "Hold it so the light shines down." He took a tentative step towards the door. "I don't think anyone's near enough to have heard the shot. But I don't want to show a light outside."

Elizabeth nodded her understanding to Verinder's retreating back. "Are you sure you don't want me to come..." A vision of what lay beneath them caused her to pause and repeat, "To come?"

"*Il est plus important que tu restes ici,*" restated Verinder as he limped slowly to the door.

After Verinder disappeared outside, Elizabeth stoked the fire and put a kettle of water over it. Quickly she wiped up the blood on the floor with the first garment that came to hand. Then she prepared a torch by tying three sticks together with a strip torn from the blood-stained cloth and wrapping the rest of it securely at the top of the bundle.

"*Élisabeth.*" Verinder's voice resounded hollowly beneath her feet.

"*Je viens,*" Elizabeth replied. After touching the torch she had prepared to the fire, she carried it cautiously forward.

"*Attention*!" Verinder's warning was a reminder of the danger the rotting flooring presented.

"I shall," Elizabeth called back. Falling to her knees, she inched forward. She used her free hand to sweep the area in front of her. When her hand felt the edge of the hole in the barn floor, she lay prone on the ground. Then she stretched out her right arm so that the light from the improvised torch shone directly over the gap.

"Good work." Verinder's voice sounded miles away. "I see..." What he saw was obvious so he said no more. "Don't move the light."

Her arm aching from its awkward position, Elizabeth tried not to think about what Verinder was doing.

Beneath her, Verinder picked his way carefully over bits of collapsed rubble to the place where Henri LeBeau lay. The angle of the neck told him the man was dead. Yet he forced himself to touch LeBeau and feel for a pulse. When no fluttering heartbeat met his fingers, Verinder limped away from the body.

The sounds of tiny feet – mice? rats? – scrabbling in the darkness beyond the circle of light emitted by Elizabeth's torch made his stomach churn.

"You can move the light now." Verinder's voice reminded Elizabeth of how tired her arm was. "I'll be up with the horse in a few minutes."

Later as Verinder sat on a box and tried not to wince, Elizabeth finished dressing the bullet graze on the side of his head.

"*Tu as raison*," he agreed. "I've been fortunate. Fortunate that he was a poor shot. Fortunate that his bullet's path was not a quarter of an inch to the right. And fortunate that your uncle taught you well and thought to supply you with all that." Verinder nodded towards the small jars of salve and ointment and rolls of clean bandaging material that lay at Elizabeth's side.

"Uncle Léon insisted that I take all this." Elizabeth looked at the medical supplies her uncle had placed in the bottom of her market basket. "But I never thought we'd use any of it."

Elizabeth eyed her handiwork critically. She had cleaned the wound with hot water, applied some of her uncle's special ointment to it, and finally bandaged it. "*Ça va*."

"I'm sure it will." Verinder moved his head to look at her.

The intensity of his scrutiny held Elizabeth for a long, silent moment. Then she rose to her feet, her movement breaking the hold Verinder's eyes had on hers. "I'll get rid of this." She motioned with the basin of bloodstained water in her hands and walked away.

When she returned, Verinder was staring down at a piece of paper, a well-worn saddlebag open beside him.

"That bag," said Elizabeth. She sat down next to Verinder, her words drawing his attention from the page. "It's his, isn't it?"

"*Oui, c'est ça*," admitted Verinder. "I want to know why he was going to Le Havre and what made him look for us."

Elizabeth's eyes widened. "You don't think that he was, that he had…" She stared at the door. "That there might be others?"

"No," Verinder said at once. "And that is a most definite no." He held out the paper. "Read this."

Elizabeth shrank from Verinder's outstretched hand, as reluctant to touch the paper that had been among LeBeau's possessions as she was to use his name.

"Read it." Verinder put the paper into Elizabeth's hand. "You'll feel better if you do."

After a quick glance at his face, Elizabeth turned her eyes to the page in her hand.

Moments later, Elizabeth remarked with some surprise, "It's from his sister!"

"In Le Havre, from what it says about fishing and what he said to us."

"But though the news is sad..."

"The death of her husband," interrupted Verinder.

"There is much more about the man her husband and son worked for. About Armand Bertaux." Elizabeth scanned the letter again. "And about her son Guy. He's the one writing the letter for her." Then finding the place, she continued, "Yes, and Bertaux has given him an increase in wages."

"And given quite a lot of attention to the widow."

"Yes, I thought so, too, but wondered if I were reading too much between the lines."

"I think her brother was very good at reading between the lines," remarked Verinder.

"But when he said that he had a surprise for her, his smile did not make it seem a pleasant surprise." Elizabeth's brow wrinkled as she struggled to remember.

"And he mentioned a trip back to Rouen."

"*Ah, oui! Mais pourquoi?*" Elizabeth wondered aloud. "Why would she want to go to Rouen when her home, her son's job, and..."

"And Bertaux are all in Le Havre," finished Verinder.

"But she wouldn't, would she?" considered Elizabeth. "Want to return to Rouen, that is."

"No, I don't think she would," agreed Verinder.

"And now because he's, because..."

"She can remain in Le Havre," Verinder stated simply.

The two stared into the fire. Then Verinder said, "Madame Tellier's brother. He was the man I warned you and your uncle about."

"In Rouen, five days ago," Elizabeth sighed.

"Le Havre tomorrow."

"*Oui, je me souviens,*" Elizabeth replied. "But how did he find us? And why was he even looking for us?" Before Verinder could answer, she amended, "Me – I should say. I'm the one he was looking for, not you."

The guilt in Elizabeth's voice made Verinder ache to pull her close and comfort her. Resisting that temptation, he said, "You're right, but, thank God, he did not find you in Rouen at the home of your uncle."

"If he'd come, Uncle Léon would have..." Elizabeth began slowly.

"Your uncle would have given his life to try to save yours."

Elizabeth stared at Verinder. My life and Uncle Léon's. I owe both to him. "We still don't know how he found us."

"People in both Caudebec and St Maurice talked about us. He told us as much himself. But he knew the ragman he'd met in Rouen was not married." Verinder paused. As Elizabeth lifted her eyes to regard him gravely, Verinder continued, "Then I think Étienne Duval told him where we might be found. How he wormed the information out of Duval we shall never know. But I stupidly told Étienne where we intended to stay, and Étienne loves to talk."

"He does," Elizabeth agreed. "But why do you think it was Duval who told him?"

"Because I examined his horse," Verinder stated.

"*Son cheval, mais,*" Elizabeth frowned.

"Most horses can't talk. But this one can."

"And she said?"

"She said, 'I'm tired and I've been ridden hard.' So I looked at her legs and hooves to make sure she wasn't hurt. And saw one horseshoe different than the others. One newer than the others. One that looks very much like those made by a certain blacksmith in St Maurice d' Etelan."

"Duval." Elizabeth pictured the blacksmith as she'd last seen him, his laughing eyes and easy banter making him the perfect source of information. "It all fits, doesn't it?"

"It does. And now we get rid of anything that will make it fit for anyone else."

"Anyone else?" Elizabeth repeated. "Do you think..."

"No one else has followed us here or anywhere else. If Madame Tellier's brother had a partner, the shot would have brought him here." Verinder stood wearily. "He was alone, and I'm certain he confided in no one."

"So, if we can reach Le Havre without drawing any attention to ourselves, we should be safe." The rising inflection at the end of her sentence turned the statement into a question.

"*Oui, tu as raison.* But our clothes at the moment will not keep that unwanted attention at bay."

Elizabeth looked at Verinder and then down at herself. Everything they wore was splattered with blood.

"You have another dress with you, I believe."

"Yes."

"Our clothes will go into the cellar. Along with all of this." His foot moved the saddle and the other things he'd taken from LeBeau's horse. "And I'll turn the horse loose in the morning. Someone will consider himself lucky to find it."

Seeing some of the colour fade from Elizabeth's face and her shoulders sag, Verinder willed his own fatigue into the back of his mind. He said with as much cheer as he could, "I'll fetch some other clothes from the cart. You can prepare for bed. We've much to do tomorrow." Without waiting for a reply, Verinder limped off on his errand.

As Elizabeth removed her stained dress and let it fall to the floor, she shivered. She crawled into the bed they'd made earlier. Staring at the fire, she thought about the man who had done so much for her, the man she now owed her life to.

A change of clothes for them both in his arms, Verinder dragged himself back to the fireside. As he bent to put down his bundle, a grimace passed over his face. Elizabeth's "Let me..." prompted him to say, "Madame Verinder, some privacy *s'il vous plait.*"

"*Pardonnez-moi,*" Elizabeth apologized. "I wasn't thinking." She rolled to her other side, her back now to the hearth and Verinder.

Oh, but I think you were, Beth, reflected Verinder while he removed his bloodied shirt. But of what were you thinking so earnestly? He stifled another groan as he picked up Elizabeth's cast off garments and his own.

A soft whoosh followed by a low thud told Elizabeth that Verinder had flung the telltale evidence through the gap in the floor. She imagined it lying atop the dead man and shuddered.

"Don't think about it," Verinder ordered gently after he cautiously eased himself beneath the covers. "You have behaved bravely tonight. Better than many recruits who face enemy muskets for the first time. And before you tell me that those words are flattery, let me assure you they are not. You kept your head when his shot found its target and followed a plan that was never explained to you. When no one is there to give orders, undisciplined troops usually surrender or run. Few show the initiative you did."

Elizabeth stammered, "I only did what anyone would have done in the circumstances."

"You only saved our lives," Verinder stated simply.

When Elizabeth's unnatural stillness told him that heroism was as alien to her as it was to most of the men he knew with medals and battlefield commendations, Verinder changed the subject. "We'll be in Le Havre tomorrow. And, with any luck, you'll be back in the arms of your family soon."

The concern in his voice, the events of the past day, thoughts of her brother, and the realization of whose arms she wanted to be in caused another sigh to escape.

"*Élisabeth, tout ira bien.*" Verinder reached out to touch her shoulder. Feeling her shiver, he asked, "Are you cold?"

"*Non, c'est á dire, oui,*" Elizabeth replied in confusion.

"*Moi aussi.*" He turned on his side, hoping she would follow his train of thought. A moment later he felt her warmth against his back.

I am not the only one in need of comfort, Elizabeth understood with some amazement as she slid her arm beneath his and pressed herself closer to the safety of his presence.

"*Bonne nuit, Élisabeth.* Try to sleep."

"I will."

Yet the dead man lying beneath them was like a silent watcher in the barn. Thoughts of him kept sleep at bay.

## CHAPTER 6

# FRIDAY, JANUARY 25, 1793

"Wait here." Just after noon Verinder stopped the cart outside a waterfront wine shop in Le Havre and handed the reins to Elizabeth. "I'll not be long." He pulled down the cap that hid the bandage circling his head. Then grabbing the bundle under the seat, Verinder lowered himself cautiously to the ground and limped into *La Mer Tranquille.*

Once inside, Verinder sought Antoine Hivert. And found him sitting in his usual dark corner with another man. Hivert's ruddy face and thick sweater told of days spent at sea. But nothing made him look any different than the dozens of other sailors Verinder had seen along the waterfront. Nothing, except perhaps how the man with him kept ducking his head and leaning forward as he talked to Hivert, marked him as the captain of *L' Oiseau Vite.* And a smuggler.

Verinder put his bundle on the counter and ordered a measure of *vin ordinaire.* As he took his first sip, the man with Hivert mumbled something and stood. After a perfunctory handshake, he slunk off, passing Verinder without a glance.

A moment later Hivert also headed for the door, and Verinder turned slightly to face him.

"Ragman, you're back!" exclaimed Hivert in apparent surprise though no one entered or left *La Mer Tranquille* without his notice. "Find those things I wanted?"

"*Certainement.*" Verinder motioned to the bundle on the counter. "Want to see them now?"

"*Oui.*" Hivert turned back to the corner table. "But don't think I'll pay more than they're worth!"

"Have I ever tried to cheat you, Hivert?" asked Verinder.

"I don't know, have you?" retorted the smuggler.

Verinder opened the bundle and shook out a sprigged muslin bodice and matching skirt. "*C'est beau,*" Hivert commented before he could stop himself. "Where did you find them?"

"Paris."

"Anything else of interest in your cart?"

"*Certainement.*" Verinder drank the rest of his wine in one swallow. "It's right outside."

After the two men emerged into the chilly early afternoon light, Hivert saw Elizabeth seated on the cart and rounded on Verinder. "And who is this, Ragman?"

"My wife Élisabeth."

"Your wife, eh, Verinder?" Hivert stared at Elizabeth, his face hard and unsmiling. "Let me see what else you have," he demanded roughly. Verinder went to the rear of the cart and began to sift through what was piled there.

"If you're looking for the shirt I mended yesterday, it is here." Elizabeth reached behind her to a neat stack of clothing. She handed the shirt on top to Hivert.

After another sharp look at Elizabeth's face, Hivert turned his attention to the shirt. "Another Paris find, Ragman?" he asked.

"No," Verinder replied at once, realizing Hivert was not asking about the shirt. "This came from a doctor's *maison* in Rouen. I heard there was illness and death in the family and went to look for bargains. And found this," he touched the shirt, "and several other things."

Hivert locked his eyes on Verinder. "Not a piece of aristo finery then? A lot of that seems to be finding its way to Le Havre these days."

"Nothing like that here," Verinder said evenly while holding Hivert's gaze. "Though the cloth is foreign."

"*Ah, oui.*" Hivert nodded. "It is good cloth. Mostly likely English."

"Perhaps." Verinder shrugged. "Looks as good as any made here in France."

"Yes, it does," noted Hivert. "But with a dress for my wife, a shirt for me and …" He paused. "I always seem to be bringing things home after my trips in *L' Oiseau Vite.* Our clothes presses are nearly full. I don't know..." Hivert stared once more at Elizabeth.

"Two items or one," Elizabeth said quickly, understanding that the man staring at her was the ship captain Verinder had told her about. A captain who wasn't sure he wanted two passengers aboard his ship. "It hardly matters. Folded together, they will take up scarcely any room at all."

"It is as you say, Citizeness," decided Hivert finally. "I shall take them both." He dug into the clothes pile at the rear of the cart. "Huh," he said when he found what he was looking for. He held up a small pair of trousers. "Should fit the ship's boy I told you about, Ragman."

Fit Elizabeth. Verinder nodded his understanding.

"Now I have some other business to take care of, Ragman. And not much time. *L' Oiseau Vite* sails tonight," added Hivert, handing the trousers to Verinder.

"Then why not let us deliver all this to your house?" Verinder offered at once as he bundled together everything Hivert wanted.

"Come later this afternoon. I'll pay you then." Hivert stepped away from the cart and lifted a hand in farewell.

"And in the meantime, we'll look for a place to open a shop."

"A shop? *Vraiment?*" Hivert turned to stare at Verinder. "No more trips to Paris with the cart?"

"I'm a married man now," Verinder motioned in Elizabeth's direction.

"As you say." Hivert smiled for the first time. "And a married man belongs in his own place, his own house, *n'est-ce pas?*"

"He does," agreed Verinder. "But I need to sell the cart and horse first. Any ideas about who might give me a good price for them?"

"Leave them at Canivet's place. You passed it on your way here." Hivert pointed toward the city. "He's a scrap dealer. Got a small yard in the back where he keeps his own nag. Tell him I sent you, and stable the horse there for a few days. Then you'll have time to ask around and get the best deal."

"*Merci.*" And Hivert will sell the cart and horse later, Verinder thought. That's good. He's earned the money. "We'll go to Canivet's now."

"*Bien!*" Hivert added before he walked away, "And don't forget to bring all of this," he put his hand on the shirts and the muslin bodice and skirt, "to my house this afternoon."

"We won't," promised Verinder.

"Pay me when you pick up the horse. Empty stall's in back," Canivet said without interest, picking up a box and disappearing down a narrow aisle between shelves overflowing with discards of every description.

Minutes later, the cart resting in a corner of the shed behind the scrap dealer's shop, Verinder and Elizabeth unharnessed the mare.

"Take only what you need." Verinder said, his words sending Elizabeth to the back of the cart. She quickly found her few possessions and placed them together before reaching for her workbasket as well as the basket holding what remained of their food.

After Verinder saw to the mare, he gathered the things Hivert wanted. Then he took the trousers Hivert had found earlier and folded them together with a boy's tattered shirt and jacket. After putting everything into the middle of a blanket, he tied the blanket corners together. "Are you ready?" he asked as he slung the blanket over his shoulder.

"Wait, I want to find..." Elizabeth rummaged in the box full of Verinder's battered cooking utensils. "This!" Her hands held the small, chipped Sèvres bowl.

Verinder's left eyebrow shot up in silent inquiry.

"*Un souvenir de Franc.*" Elizabeth hid the bowl in the sleeve of a dress, knotted her bundled clothes together, and then put the two baskets near her feet.

"I'll take this one." Verinder picked up Elizabeth's workbasket.

"I can take the rest." Elizabeth slid her left arm through the handle of the market basket while her right hand grasped her clothes bundle.

"We should go."

"To…?"

"Look for a place for our shop. There are some likely places close to where Hivert lives." Verinder forced a smile and pushed himself to move towards the door of the shed. "Not far."

Elizabeth hesitated and then joined Verinder at the door. He felt her shiver beside him.

"The walk will warm us both. And by this evening, the ragman and his wife will be…" Verinder pointed towards the harbor and then looked down at Elizabeth. "Not long now."

By midafternoon, after buying some food and a boy's cap, Verinder and Elizabeth walked steadily through the St François district of Le Havre. The street was crowded with sailors, some speaking oddly accented English.

Just as Verinder whispered, *"Américain,"* a child's voice squealed, "*Guy! Maman,* it's Guy!"

A ten-year old girl ran past them towards a boy of perhaps twelve years coming from the opposite direction, a middle-aged man who appeared to be a fisherman at his side.

"Delphine, don't make such a fuss, *ma fille.*" A woman wrapped in a black shawl hurried to catch up with the girl. "*Souviens-toi de ton papa.* Your brother's only been gone two days."

Then as Elizabeth and Verinder continued walking down the street, the excited child threw herself into the arms of the grinning boy as the two adults with them looked on.

"Madame Tellier," Elizabeth heard the man say as she and Verinder moved closer, "your son has a job on my boat for as long as he wants it. He worked as hard as any man on the crew. His father would have been proud."

As she passed the four, Elizabeth noted the warm look the fisherman gave the woman. Her mouth lifted in a smile.

"*Une romance, crois-tu?*" questioned Verinder softly.

*"Possiblement,"* whispered Elizabeth.

"Does the name Tellier…?"

"*La lettre!*"

Neither commented further on the small drama they had witnessed, and for some time, they walked in silence, each rapt in thought.

After several turnings, Verinder stopped before a house that looked exactly like those on either side of it.

*"Ici."* The single word broke into Elizabeth's reverie.

Two brief raps brought Hivert to the door.

Seeing no horse with them, Hivert hurried them inside and shut the door. "Found Canivet all right, did you?"

"Yes," answered Verinder. "He said we could pay when we returned for the horse and cart."

"He would!" Hivert laughed as he started up the stairs opposite the door. "Don't worry I won't let him overcharge me. That is, you."

Elizabeth and Verinder followed him. Because Verinder was at the rear, neither of the others saw him bite his lower lip to prevent an inadvertent cry of pain as he struggled to force his protesting leg to move.

"My wife and children are out," Hivert said when they reached the landing where a ladder led to a trap door in the ceiling. "Marie knows you are staying here until we sail. But the children do not." He looked up at the trap door and then back at Verinder. "You can stay in the loft 'til we leave tonight. The children will be asleep then."

"*Merci.* And take these before we go up." Verinder handed Hivert the bundle of clothes he'd set aside for him. "Hivert, I..."

"No other thanks than these, Verinder." Hivert put the bundle under his arm. "*Mon frère...* I promised... a debt of honour," Hivert fumbled while staring at his feet. "My wife and the children will be home soon."

Hearing those words, Elizabeth put her foot on the bottom rung of the ladder and began to climb.

"It will push up easily." Hivert pointed to the door. "And in the loft, there's a pallet and some blankets. And a chamber pot," he added matter-of-factly. "The only window is covered with cloth. Don't touch it."

"We won't," Verinder assured him.

"*Bien,*" Hivert said. "Quiet and darkness. That's best. Try to sleep. The hours will pass quickly."

Moments later, after the trap door closed behind them, their eyes adjusted to the gloom of the loft. Both saw that, in addition to the items Hivert had told them about, a basin, ewer of water, and two cups had been left in a corner for their comfort.

"Change first. Then a meal while the light holds." Verinder whispered, "No talking. And as little movement as possible."

Soon the sounds of footsteps on the stairs and high-pitched children's voices could be heard. Elizabeth slipped out of her clothes and put on the boyish garments Verinder had laid aside for her. Then bread and cheese were consumed with painstaking slowness.

As the winter afternoon shadows fell, Elizabeth carefully lowered herself onto the pallet. Verinder, grateful for the necessity of physical stillness, wrapped himself in the blanket he had carried his bundle in.

How long will the crossing take? Verinder wondered. Two days with luck. Three days or more if the weather turns ugly. Despite what happened with LeBeau, we've been fortunate so far. If my leg buckles under me… No, I won't let that happen. Thank God, Hivert is trustworthy. He'll see us safe to England.

Meanwhile, memories of Elizabeth's only other sea voyage filled her with queasy dread. Then when she shut her eyes, the face of Jacques Rovault swam before her. What if he sees us walking to Hivert's ship? Of course, he won't, she told herself. At that time of night, he'll be home. And soon, so will I. But thoughts of home brought the faces of two other men to mind, her brother's almost purple with anger, and their neighbor's calculating and appraising. Elizabeth tensed, her shoulders hunched and tight as she rolled quietly on her side.

Verinder sensed Elizabeth's anxiety, and, gritting his teeth against the pain in his leg, inched closer to the pallet.

"Try to rest," Verinder breathed almost inaudibly, placing a hand on her shoulder. "You're safe with me."

The barest nod told him she'd heard and understood. Then Elizabeth covered his hand with her own, and little by little the tension eased from her shoulders. Soothed by his touch, she drifted into sleep.

Verinder, however, did not. Although he allowed his eyes to close, his ears were alert for danger. Consequently, hours later he heard the first rustle of footsteps on the ladder and shook Elizabeth awake, his hand over her mouth to stifle any surprised outcry, before Hivert raised the trap door.

"It's time," Hivert stated. "*C'est l'heure de partir.*"

## CHAPTER 7

# MONDAY, JANUARY 28, 1793

"'Fraid?"

"No!"

"Why yer lookin' over yer shoulder then?" Jack Harper nudged Jim Compton with the keg he shouldered, one beefy hand easily balancing it against the head of scraggly brown hair curling about his ears.

When Jim said nothing, Harper snorted. "Watchin' be you? Like you done in tha' stupid reg'ment you keeps on 'bout."

"That's right, Jack. I'm watchin'. If the revenue men come, I want a chance t' get out o' here with my skin in one piece."

Behind them was a boat, a dark shape off England's south coast. In front of them was a line of men, all carrying kegs of French brandy to the pack animals and wagons waiting a short distance from the shore.

Harper's eyes scanned the beach for their unnamed employer. "He knows 'is business. Most like those revenue men be snug in some place far from where we be. Most like they be downin' some of this here." Harper shifted his keg to a more comfortable position.

"You can trust him if you want to, Jack. But me--I'd just as soon keep my eyes open."

"Trust them bloody orficers, didn't you? N' look where it's got you. Same place's me."

"Tol' you b'fore, Jack, not all o' them were –"

Harper interrupted him with a laugh. "Fools? Well, I say them what served wi' 'em and them what gave the orders was both –"

"Stopper yer natterin', Jack Harper," hissed the man in front of them. "You heard 'im. No talkin' 'e said."

"T'was only," Harper began truculently.

"T'was only nothin'," finished Compton in a whisper. "We know what t' do, don't we, Jack?"

Harper grunted his agreement. The men deposited their kegs in a wagon near the pack train and headed back to the shoreline. Back to the cargo of French brandy being off-loaded from *L' Oiseau Vite's* cutter in the early hours' darkness, the wiry Compton stepping out sharply, the taller Harper striding behind.

"Orders! Someone's always givin' 'em to the likes of we." Harper looked for the man who had told him to keep quiet. Satisfied the man was not in front of Compton, Harper growled, "Who's 'e think 'e be? Some orficer may like, like 'im you always be braggin' 'bout."

Compton ignored Harper's taunts, his attention fixed on three people walking away from the last boat to come to shore. The first turned back to the boat crew and then pointed to the ship anchored off the coast. Near him, a taller man with a pronounced limp supported a smaller figure. Skirts! Compton noted with surprise. He watched the tall man and the woman as they plodded up the beach.

Émigrés! Compton considered the man he worked for. He won't be happy about them.

As Compton and Harper approached, the tall man seated the woman on a bleached driftwood stump.

"Orders n' orficers!" Harper muttered again. "Both as needful to the likes of we as--"

"Jack," whispered Compton over his shoulder, "I need this job, n' you do, too. You know what we were tol'."

"That little rat," Harper spat at the ground, "be nowhere near us now."

In reply, Compton jerked his head towards the two people they were now passing. As he did, the tall man with the limp turned towards them.

Compton's jaw dropped, and he stared in amazed recognition. "Sir!"

"Who you be sirring, Jim? Tha's only some mangy French Mon-sewer runnin' away from 'is own kind." Harper grabbed at Compton's arm. "Lez's go."

Compton shook off Harper's hand. "Capt'n Verinder?"

"You be tellin' me this here Mon-sewer..." Harper jabbed a finger in Verinder's direction. "This be yer precious Cap'n Verind'r? 'im?"

Harper's voice drew the attention of others on the shingle. Keg carriers stopped to gape. Hivert motioned the crew of the cutter to stay where they were and moved towards the gathering crowd. Farther up the beach a man in well-made boots headed in the same direction.

From her seat on the stump, Elizabeth raised her head to look at Harper, but the effort made the world spin once more. Weak from hours of unrelenting sea-sickness, she closed her eyes and put her head in her hands. Verinder – his ragged clothes, battered cap, grimy face, and ill-barbered hair making Harper's disbelief understandable – said nothing.

"This be tha' Cap'n you said saved those friends of yourn?" Harper laughed and shook his head. "Draggin' wounded -- theirs 'n ours -- off the battlefield! Frenchies n' a couple o' stupid privates, warn't that right? Workin' wi' the Frenchies more like, your precious Cap'n Bloody Verind'r!"

As Verinder stepped forward to face Harper, Hivert reached his side. "My brother was one of those 'Frenchies,'" he said before Verinder could speak. Hivert moved closer, forcing Harper to stumble back. "Verinder saved his life, and the lives of those two 'stupid privates.'"

The well-booted man walked up unnoticed behind Harper and Compton. "Wondered who your passengers were, Hivert," he stated evenly while recalling what he'd read recently about Verinder. "Always pay your debts. Aye, that's my motto, right boys?"

Their employer's voice startled Harper and Compton. Worried frowns appeared on their faces as he laid a heavy hand on each man's shoulder.

"Debts, we both agreed long ago," Hivert said, looking at his English counterpart, "are important."

"Aye, we did. And a profitable agreement it's been for us both."

Hivert nodded and looked back at *L' Oiseau Vite's* cutter, now empty of cargo and waiting to take him back to his ship.

"Yes, time to go," his partner said. "For all of us." He looked around at the curious keg carriers still standing nearby, and immediately they began to move off. Reading the newspaper has its uses, he thought, watching them go. They call me the man who knows things about people. The man from whom there are no secrets. Time to prove it, he observed to himself. "Including Colonel Verinder or should I say Lord Rossbury?" he added in a voice that caused the keg carriers to look back in fear.

Lor' Rossb'ry! Harper gulped in dismay. 'e's a lord! Trouble fer sure. Gawd help me.

Lord Rossbury! And Colonel! Compton was stunned. Shoulda guessed Capt'n Verinder'd be promoted.

Lord Rossbury! Hivert gasped. An aristo! *Mon dieu!* If the Jacobins in Le Havre...

Lord Rossbury! Elizabeth's brain screamed the title at her. She thought of how he'd emptied the bucket and wiped her face after each bout of retching. He can't be!

Damnation! fumed Verinder. Wanted to tell Beth in my own time, in my own way. Now this smuggler has ruined everything. Anger made his tired eyes blaze.

"And you'll be needing transportation. Especially as your companion seems to be ill." The free trader needed to clear the beach. The sooner, the better, he told himself. "And although the back of a wagon is not the most luxurious conveyance, it will take you faster than shank's mare to…?"

"Chichester." The anger drained from Rossbury as quickly as it had come. Hivert's partner couldn't have known that Beth – no, Miss Laurence, we are back in England now, Rossbury reminded himself – was unaware of my title.

"Chichester it is." The master smuggler turned and said sharply, "Harper, go find Huckaby and tell him to get ready for the Chichester run right away."

"Yas, sur," Harper gabbled, thankful he wasn't being sacked.

"Give Compton the Chichester run," Rossbury suggested. "I believe he knows the area well. And he can help me assist Miss Laurence to the wagon."

The sound of his name made Compton's eyes widen as he stared at the man he still thought of as Captain Verinder.

"Compton it is." The man in charge looked at his newest employee's glowing face and thought, No doubt Verinder's men would have followed him to the gates of Hell itself if he had asked. "Tell Huckaby to see to it, Harper."

"Yas, sur." Harper hurried away from the all-seeing eyes of his employer.

Rossbury turned to the French sea captain and offered his hand.

The gesture surprised Hivert's English partner. In his experience, those with titles did not offer to shake hands with men like Hivert. This Rossbury's a man of honor, the smuggler thought. So he'll say nothing about tonight since he owes his life – and hers, the smuggler shot a look at Elizabeth – to Hivert. He nodded, satisfied that everything was turning out to his advantage.

"A word of advice to you both." Rossbury's look swept over the two free traders. "No doubt you," Rossbury stared at the self-assured Englishman, "have made some sort of accommodation with one or more of the local revenue officers. But England and France will soon be at war. And that means a naval blockade of France or, at the very least, patrols of the Channel and the Bay of Biscay."

He paused to allow the two men to digest this information. "A zealous Royal Navy captain will not hesitate to fire a warning shot across your bow, Hivert, and order you to heave to. He'll follow that with a full broadside. Your ship would make a tidy prize for him and his crew."

The serious faces of his listeners told Rossbury that his warning had taken root. Yet he guessed the two men would not suspend their very lucrative business. They're probably already considering how to avoid the patrols. He left them talking together in low voices.

Rossbury limped back to Compton who stood as if on parade. "I am counting on you to help me escort Miss Laurence safely to the wagon."

"Yes, Capt'n Ver-, I mean Colonel, that is, Lord--"

"Sir will suffice, Private Compton."

"Yes, sir!"

Rossbury bent over Elizabeth. "Do you feel able to stand, Miss Laurence?"

Elizabeth felt wretchedly seasick still. Even worse, it seemed a huge gulf had opened between her and the man she had weathered so many dangerous situations with. "I am perfectly able to walk unaided, Lord Rossbury." She stood on wobbly legs.

Rossbury heard the distance that his title had forced into Elizabeth's voice. How can I explain? he wondered. She'll think me a liar. His anger over the free trader's careless words reignited.

Compton said, "It's not far, Miss. We'll have you there in a blink. N' I'll find somethin' t' keep you warm in th' wagon."

"Uncle Léon!" Elizabeth suddenly remembered.

The appeal in her eyes melted Rossbury's anger. He cursed the pain and fatigue that had swept the matter from his mind. "I shall ask Hivert," he told her.

Limping back to where the two smugglers stood deep in conversation, Rossbury called out, "Hivert, a request."

The partners looked up. Rossbury said, "Miss Laurence's uncle is Docteur Léon Mansard of the Rue St Vivian in Rouen." He put the bundle in his hand under his arm and dug deep in a pocket. "Please see that he receives this." He handed Hivert a creased paper. "It says the goods he entrusted to me have been delivered."

Miss Laurence, heh? thought Hivert's partner. Perhaps a relation of a Gideon Laurence? His own interest was in Laurence's neighbor Sir Augustus Tremaine. The baronet was one of a small group of men who had put up some of the capital for the ships being built to expand his business. All demanded anonymity. However, he had gathered information about each one. Information he'd use if any should prove difficult to deal with. And he'd heard something about Laurence's sister... He frowned in concentration. Soon as this lot's safe, he told himself with a look at the men carrying the last of the kegs up the shingle, I'll find out.

"Tell Miss Laurence her uncle's worries will soon be over." Hivert put the letter inside one of his own pockets.

"And tell your brother," replied Rossbury, "his life is doubly dear. The debt he truly never owed, you have redeemed with two lives."

Moved by Rossbury's tribute to his brother, Hivert called out, "*Avec plasir!*"

While Rossbury spoke to Hivert, Elizabeth remembered her one precious possession. "My bundle!"

"This it, Miss?" Compton picked up a knotted blanket near the driftwood stump.

"Yes." Elizabeth sighed gratefully. "And be careful. It contains something very dear to me."

"I'll be careful. Never fear, Miss."

A moment later Rossbury returned and took Elizabeth's left arm. "Where is this wagon, Private Compton?"

"Not far, Cap-, uh, sir. I was tellin' Miss Laurence here we'll have her there in a wink."

Elizabeth, ill and tired as she was, was aware of the limping man at her side. Gritted teeth, she felt certain, lay behind the thin line of his lips. "Slowly, Compton."

"Pardon me, Miss." Compton shortened his steps. "Slow it is. We'll be there soon. Wagons are just over there." He pointed to a spot about two hundred yards away. "N' after that, it's Chichester."

On the outskirts of Chichester, hints of dawn were lighting the sky. Rossbury stood beside the empty wagon driven by the former army private. "Remember there's a job in the stables at Rossbury House waiting for you."

"Come up t' London soon as I settle wi' one or two here," replied Compton, a grin splitting his thin face. "Matter of a couple of shillings owed n' a few good-byes to say. But come I will, sir, an' soon."

"Good." Rossbury looked at the ever-lightening sky. "And now you'd better be on your way with that wagon."

"Right you are, sir," agreed Compton. "Be glad t' see th' back o' this wagon, I will. Just let me get what I was promised, n' I'm on my way."

"Good!" Rossbury stepped away from his place near the wagon. "The Sergeant will be expecting you."

"Tell Sergeant Craddock, sir, I'm hoping t' share a loaf with him. One a bit tastier n' what we had at Yorktown!" Compton flicked the reins over the backs of the team of horses harnessed to the wagon. "N' thanks again, sir. You won't regret givin' me this chance, I promise you."

The wagon gone, Rossbury turned his attention to Elizabeth. The bumping and swaying of the wagon had worsened her seasickness. "A few minutes' walk will find us at the bakery. And walking may help you feel a bit better."

"I think you're right, Lord Rossbury." Elizabeth tried to smile, but her mouth didn't want to make the effort. "The wagon… I don't want to think about the wagon."

"Don't. Think about going there." Rossbury pointed in the direction of a cathedral spire visible in the pale dawn light. That damn title, Rossbury thought as he limped north. It's like a wall between us.

Rossbury's leg throbbed, every step an agony. His head ached, the blow from his fall on Thursday blurring his vision. Don't think about it. Say something. Anything.

"As you've already seen, Compton was in my company during the war with the American colonies." Rossbury clenched his fists, digging his nails into his palms as his leg protested anew against the demands being made upon it.

"And so was Sergeant Craddock. After Craddock was mustered out, he and his wife came to Chichester. Their daughter and her husband needed help with a bakery they'd opened."

"They're the Shaws." Elizabeth dragged the name from her memory. "The people you told Private Compton about."

"That's right." Rossbury forced the words out, the pain in his leg having increased to the point where thought was nearly impossible. "Sergeant Craddock's in the bakery." He gritted his teeth and said with an effort, "With his daughter and son-in-law." Another wave of pain made his eyes close for a moment, and he stumbled over a stone but did not fall.

Elizabeth heard his sharp intake of breath and lifted her heavy head. Rossbury's colorless face beaded with sweat frightened her. "You're ill!"

But Rossbury heard only Elizabeth's voice, not her words. "Almost there, Miss Laurence. Almost there."

Elizabeth realized that help was in a place only Rossbury knew how to find. We must get there soon. Before, before... Elizabeth stayed close to Rossbury and dragged along at his side.

"Turn here. Must go in the back. They live over the shop." Rossbury forced himself to continue walking and talking. His entire leg felt as if it were on fire.

Finally, Rossbury stopped. He knocked on a black door at the back of a row of shops. "Mrs. Craddock. Takes care of her grandchildren. The others will be in the bakery now." He pushed the words from his mouth.

But when the door opened, it was not Mrs. Craddock who stood before him. Instead a young girl of perhaps twelve years peered at them. "Saturday's the only day we give away bread."

She thinks we're vagrants, Elizabeth thought, not knowing what to say.

Rossbury leaned against the half-timbered building to try to reduce the pressure on his leg. "Please tell Mrs. Craddock you have a message from Verinder."

As the girl began to shut the door, Mrs. Craddock's voice called out. "Hannah, who is it?"

"A beggar. Says someone called Verinder gave him a message for you."

The name brought her grandmother clattering down the stairs. Though Mrs. Craddock's angular frame was a poor advertisement for the family's bakery, her heart was softer than her son-in-law's bread rolls. With one glance at Rossbury and the bedraggled figure drooping next to him, Mrs. Craddock ordered, "Hannah, go to the shop and get your grandfather. Lord Rossbury's arrived."

Her mouth agape, Hannah stared at Rossbury. Then she turned and ran to the door in the hallway, her apron ties flying behind her.

Rossbury dragged himself through the door Mrs. Craddock had opened wide. "Mrs. Craddock, allow me to introduce Miss Elizabeth Laurence."

Before Mrs. Craddock could reply, her husband bustled through the door connecting shop to house. Hannah was right behind him. "I'll see to Lor' Rossb'ry if the lady'd care to…"

"Miss Laurence, she is, Craddock," interrupted his wife. "And I think there be enough hot water left from the washin' to fill an extra tub for 'er. That is, if Miss Laurence'd like some nice hot water for a…" Thinking Elizabeth might find the word <u>bath</u> unseemly, Mrs. Craddock covered the gap in her sentence with a smile. "Then a posset and bed for you, my dear. Does that sound all right?"

Elizabeth managed a smile. "Oh, yes, Mrs. Craddock. It sounds wonderful. And thank you."

"No need to thank me. Any friend of his lordship's is a friend to the Craddock family." Mrs. Craddock saw Elizabeth's concerned look at Rossbury. "Craddock'll see to his lordship. You just come this way." She led Elizabeth towards a door at the back of the hall. "And Hannah?"

"Yes, Gran?"

"You fetch the linens I left upstairs and bring them to me."

Hannah immediately started up the stairs.

"Upstairs for us, too," Sergeant Craddock decided at once.

But as soon as Rossbury shifted his weight to his right leg to negotiate the first riser, pain so intense that it almost took away his breath stabbed through his leg. "Major Gresham. London. Important news," Rossbury gasped. Then he collapsed into the blackness of oblivion.

## CHAPTER 8

# WEDNESDAY, JANUARY 30, 1793

"Finished!" Sergeant Craddock pulled away the cloth around Rossbury's neck. He gave Rossbury's chin a final pat with his towel and then placed it over his arm. "I be no barber so's it's not th' job your Mallory'll do after he comes. But least I can say you look more like yourself now, sir." Craddock moved a basin of soapy water and a razor to the top of a small chest of drawers by the door of the small upstairs bedchamber.

"Thanks to you, Sergeant," Rossbury replied. Now if only my leg would take my weight for more than a few minutes! Another day of inactivity lay ahead. The Craddocks' room with its slant of weak winter light across the bed, meager deal furnishings, and picture-less white walls was beginning to feel like a prison cell.

Craddock turned and saw the frown creasing his former commanding officer's face. "Don't you fret none, sir. You'll be up an' about and back in London soon. Note I sent should bring th' carriage from Rossbury House here 'fore week's end. Meantime, Mrs. Craddock be doin' fine in th' girls' room. And the boys be wi' Ann and Will so's that nice Miss Laurence can have their room."

"So you've said, Sergeant." Rossbury leaned into the pillows propped behind him. "You've not changed a bit. The officers always said we should have made you quartermaster. No matter what we were lacking, you always found something we could use to replace it. And now here you are, sleeping in a closet and caring for two unanticipated guests. A puling invalid and a lady you don't even know."

"You be no invalid, sir. Just a bit knocked about. Did too much yesterday, you did. Thought you'd never be done wi' all tha' writin'," responded Craddock.

"My report was too important to put off another day." Rossbury looked at the neat pile of papers on the room's only table. "As soon as Major Gresham's courier arrives, my report and letters will be on their way to London, my duty to king and country done."

"Well, havin' you here be like serving king an' country meself, I reckon. An' Miss Laurence..." Craddock scratched his bald pate. "She be a lady, whatever she be wearin'. An' very good with the children. Even taken over darning and mending baskets. Insisted on havin' 'em th' first day." He lowered his voice and finished in a confiding tone, "Our Ann's never been one for sewin'. She'd rather handle a rolling pin than a needle."

Perhaps that's why I've seen nothing of Miss Laurence since our arrival, Rossbury considered. Making herself useful while I... His fist clenched in frustration. He thought of all the tasks awaiting him. There's so much to do, and I'm stuck here because this leg won't...

"Damn!" Rossbury muttered,

"Not quite the reception I was anticipating after haring down here from London."

Rossbury and Sergeant Craddock turned toward the voice. A gentleman whose slightly damp, wispy brown hair, cherubic face, and twinkling eyes gave him the look of a mischievous angel, stood in the doorway.

"Major Fitzhugh Gresham, reporting as ordered, Colonel." Gresham moved into the room, his smile unwavering as he took in the scabbed-over graze on Rossbury's left temple. A pistol ball? he wondered.

"Gresham!" exclaimed Rossbury. "I expected a subaltern, not you. And then not until tomorrow."

"The Lieutenant your Sergeant used as courier seemed to think giving up his leave and splashing through midwinter mud was some kind of lark. I believe a wager was involved, though I did not inquire too closely about that. And since Craddock's note said 'urgent,' I decided to come myself. And here I am." Gresham flung out an arm that encompassed the room.

"Where be my manners?" Craddock pulled the room's only chair over to the bedside. Then he motioned for Major Gresham to be seated. "An' I've not even bid you welcome to th' house."

"No need to apologize, Sergeant. When I stated my business at your front door, I was given a most courteous 'Good morning' and escorted upstairs by your…" Gresham paused, frowning for a moment before saying, "your daughter, daughter-in-law?"

"Nay," Craddock laughed. "Our Ann's in the shop wi' her Will. That be Miss Laurence, a lady Lor' Rossb'ry saved from that killin' machine those Frenchies got."

"Really Colonel," Gresham teased, his cherub's eyes brighter than before. "These rescues of yours are becoming a bit commonplace. I shouldn't think your dress uniform had enough empty cloth on it to accommodate any more decorations, but the General may disagree."

Craddock slung the towel over his shoulder and picked up the basin of shaving water. "I best be gettin' back to the bakery. If either of you need anythin', give a shout to one of the children. They'll come an' fetch me."

"Miss Laurence," began Rossbury after Craddock had left, "is not to be mentioned in any of your reports. Either written or oral."

"Chance encounter or…?" Gresham asked.

"A conversation overheard in Rouen. Miss Laurence's aunt had died, and her uncle, a doctor, was unable to accompany her to Le Havre."

There's much more to that story than Rossbury's telling, Gresham thought. His head wound's recent. That's means after Rouen. Ergo, Miss Laurence was with him when it happened. Whatever it was. As these thoughts passed through his mind, Gresham's left hand rearranged his wispy locks into an even more disordered state. "Is Miss Laurence pertinent to your report?"

"No." Not to my report, Rossbury added silently.

"Then there's no reason for me to mention her either. And," said Gresham, "I won't even ask how you reached England's fair shores. I have a feeling I would rather not know."

"Gresham, the astuteness of that comment is a credit to your remarkable intelligence." Rossbury recalled Antoine Hivert and *L' Oiseau Vite.* "But know this, the route is now closed."

As is the subject, Gresham realized. "Is that what prompted you to cut this trip short? Danger to your contact? Or perhaps the inevitability of war? For none of us expected to see you for another week or more."

"Neither." The grimness of that single word captured Gresham's full attention. "It was a page from the London *Times.*"

Rossbury visualized the garrulous Normandy wife who had proved such a good source of information because of her husband's trade. "A regular customer had replaced a broken window with newspaper used as packing for contraband brought over by her husband's employer."

Edward Verinder's obituary! Gresham realized at once. Rossbury saw it. In France. "I cannot tell you how sorry I am."

"Thank you, Gresham." Rossbury tried flexing the muscle of his right leg and grimaced.

Major Gresham ignored the grimace and returned to the subject of Edward Verinder's death. "Only hours after you left London, a letter from Earl's Wood came to headquarters in London. It related that your brother was gravely ill and asked that you go home at once. Within minutes, a rider was dispatched to the coast. But when he arrived, your ship had already sailed."

"My own arrival had coincided with the turning of the tide and a fair wind for France," recalled Rossbury.

"That explains why the courier missed your sailing."

For a few minutes, neither man spoke, Rossbury remembering an elder brother's love and support, Gresham realizing sadly that his friend would resign his commission to take up his new position at Earl's Wood.

Rossbury broke the silence. "And now another courier waits."

"He does."

"Good. My time in France yielded some new information. Information the General will be interested to read in this dispatch," reported Rossbury.

He reached for the papers on the bedside table and handed them to Gresham. "As you can see, there are a few letters as well."

"I'll see they're delivered, of course." Gresham scanned the top page of Rossbury's report. "This," he added, "does look interesting. The courier can wait another quarter of an hour - can he not? – while you share a few of the main points?"

"He can," Rossbury replied before beginning. "Let me start with what I saw and heard outside an encampment near Paris."

The heavy tread of hastening footsteps alerted Geoffrey Hamilton-Smythe, Baron Bardstow, to the presence of his brother in the Baron's London townhouse before the door to the study opened.

"He's back!" shouted Tyler Hamilton-Smythe disgustedly as he burst into the room. "That murdering swine is back!"

Accustomed to his younger brother's outrageous statements, Baron Bardstow did not raise his head. Instead he continued replying to the latest letter from his eldest son James, a promising lad of eleven who was at Eton.

"His servants are acting like the second coming's been announced," added young Hamilton-Smythe darkly. The chatter of Patience Downes, a maid at Rossbury House, fluttered through his memory. How easy it had been to gain her confidence and to learn about the doings in his hated brother-in-law's London home. Shivering a little, for the day was a cold one, Tyler turned his back to the warmth of the coal fire burning on the grate. His handsome face was flushed with anger, his bright gold locks disordered by his agitated hands, his hazel eyes hard with hatred,

Baron Bardstow wrote his signature at the bottom of the page and put his pen down. "And who is it, Tyler, that has so irritated you this time?"

"Our dear brother-in-law, who else?" Hamilton-Smythe's tone made the name sound like an imprecation. "Colonel Richard Sinclair Verinder." And then when the Baron said nothing, he added, "Or shall I say the Earl of Rossbury as he now styles himself."

"Since Edward Verinder died a bachelor, surely you are not suggesting that the title does not now belong to his brother Richard? Or are you, Tyler?" Bardstow pushed his chair away from his writing table and stretched his legs towards the heat of the fireplace.

Eight years Tyler's senior, the Baron, with his domed forehead, large nose, and brown eyes spaced a bit too closely together, could not be described as good-looking even by the most generous of his friends. But acquaintances and enemies alike admired his honesty and sound management of Stowe Manor, the Essex estate left to him in dire financial straits by his father. However, his brother Tyler was not among their number. To Tyler, Bardstow was a 'dry stick' who didn't know how to make the best use of the barony. Meanwhile, Tyler chafed under the restrictions that were his lot in life as a second son.

"He's brought a woman back with him, Geoff. From France!" Tyler threw the statement down like a challenge. He hoped this information would make his brother his ally against the man Tyler regarded as an enemy. When the Baron merely looked questioningly at Tyler, the younger man was forced to continue.

"Don't you see, Geoff? She's probably some kept woman he's been seeing wherever he's been hiding out these past several years. He's not dared to show his face in London for more than a few days at a time in ages. He knows what everyone's saying about him!" Tyler's explanation ended on a triumphant note.

"And what is everyone saying, Tyler?" asked Bardstow.

"Surely you know, Geoff," remarked Tyler with some surprise. "That devil murdered our sister -"

"No!" Bardstow jumped from his chair and took a step toward his brother. "No, Tyler, I know nothing of the sort. I know that your friend," his voice shook with fury as he repeated, "your friend, Tyler, her lover, the less than Honourable Patrick Kincade, pushed our sister hard during one of their innumerable quarrels. So hard she fell down the stairs and broke her neck. And that is what everyone except you, Tyler, is saying."

"But who drove Sarah to take a lover, Geoff?" countered Tyler stubbornly. "If Rossbury," he emphasized, grudgingly giving man he hated his new title, "had been any sort of man, Sarah would never have been driven into Kincade's arms."

"Have you forgotten, Tyler, that Rossbury, Captain Verinder as he then was, was gravely ill at the time and had just been transported home? With wounds received while rallying his troops to prevent a disaster in his section of the line during Cornwallis's failed attempt to break out of the Yorktown stranglehold. Wounds so severe that he was fighting for his life for weeks. But what did Sarah do? Did she stay with her husband? No, she abandoned Simon to the care of a nursery governess and herself to the pleasure of London with that damnable rascal you introduced her to!"

"Only you and Rossbury would have expected Sarah to stay in that dreary mausoleum in the wilds of Shropshire with only Edward Verinder and a five-year old son for company," Tyler shot back. "Sarah needed light and laughter, color and company, and music and gaiety around her. She was, she was…" Tyler groped for a word to make his brother recognize that their sister should not have been judged by the same rules that governed others.

"Let's leave the nomenclature applied to our sister out of this discussion, Tyler." Bardstow fought to keep his voice under control. "I do not want to sully her memory by recalling, much less recounting, some of the words that have been coupled with her name."

"Nurse, Geoffrey, nurse!" retorted Tyler. "That was the word, your precious Rossbury wanted to tie to her. Sarah – a nurse! Geoff, you know that suggestion was entirely unreasonable!"

"Unreasonable? Unreasonable, Tyler, to expect his wife to remain with him during a long and difficult convalescence?" ground out Bardstow, fighting the urge to shout.

"Sarah was never any good in the sickroom, you know that, Geoff. She hadn't the patience for anything--"

"Unpleasant. How right you are, Tyler." To contain his anger, Bardstow began to straighten the objects on his writing table.

"No, that's not what I meant at all, and you know it!" Tyler glared at the back of his brother's head. "Why shouldn't she have gone to London? The great military hero hardly knew who was in the house for the first month or more anyway! And changing dressings for a fevered convalescent is a job for some lackey, not a lady like Sarah."

The Baron moved his ink stand a fraction of an inch, lovingly touched a miniature of his two youngest children Georgiana and John, and turned slowly to face his brother. "Are you suggesting, Tyler," he asked with deliberation, "that my wife Eleanor, whilst she cared for our mother during her recent illness, our mother whom you never bothered to visit during her recovery, is less than a lady?"

"But Sarah -" explained Tyler.

"Are you, Tyler?" The Baron's words cut across the younger man's with biting ferocity. "I think Eleanor deserves an answer to my question."

"No, of course not," admitted Tyler grudgingly. "But I am willing to wager that she didn't take on Mother's care alone."

"You're right, Tyler," replied the Baron. "She had a good deal of help. Exactly as Sarah would have at Earl's Wood Park. But for the first two days, when Doctor Carlyle said it was impossible to know whether Mother would pull through, Eleanor scarcely left her bedside." His voice shook with remembered emotion he could not conceal. "And, by God, Tyler, she has never been more of a lady than she was then!" The Baron dashed a hand across his face to wipe away the moisture that the incident and his pride in his wife brought to his eyes.

"But Sarah was young, Geoff. No one can expect a young, vibrant woman like Sarah to hide herself in a sickroom for months! And besides," Tyler hurried on before his brother could stop him, "Rossbury could have come up to London for the Season. If he had--"

"The man was learning to walk again. Very painfully, I might add. And you want him to spend his nights dancing?"

Tyler Hamilton-Smythe faced the fireplace and kicked pettishly at the grate. Geoff will never see the truth. He's not even listening. He doesn't care about Sarah. Or me.

"No matter what you think of Rossbury, Tyler," continued the Baron," he's a hero to all those who have served with him. His appointment to the General Staff..."

"Didn't help me, did it, Geoff?" interrupted Tyler. He glared at his brother. "He can't wait to see the back of anyone who doesn't idolize him the way his little clique of toadying junior officers does. I should have known before I was even commissioned that his interference would ruin my chances in the army."

"His interference, as you call it, saved you from a court-martial, Tyler. And as far as your chances for advancement were concerned, your intemperate behaviour was the cause of their ruin," countered the Baron.

"The devil it was!" shouted Tyler. "He went to Colonel Hardcastle behind my back. Lieutenant Napier told me. And what chance did I have to explain the incident afterwards, I ask you?" Tyler gave his brother no time to answer before stating emphatically, "None! And now, that hypocrite's brought some woman back with him from God knows where!" He waved his hands wildly as if to underscore the point. "Who can tell how long he's known her. He probably had her hidden away somewhere while Sarah was alive!"

The nameless woman Tyler keeps mentioning, who is she? Bardstow wondered. Probably an English widow. Someone Rossbury's escorted home from wherever he's been. Doing God knows what. But without details, Bardstow found himself unable to defend Rossbury from Tyler's accusation though he was certain it was baseless. "Rossbury -"

Tyler cut across his brother's remark. "Rossbury's not fit to inherit the title. Or to guide the upbringing of our nephew Simon. Have you seen that 'thing' he's engaged as Simon's tutor? The man's hideous. Yet Rossbury seems to think he's a suitable companion for his son." Suddenly the solution to all Tyler's problems was clear. If England somehow did not contain the person of

Richard Sinclair Verinder, the Earl of Rossbury, then guardianship of the young Viscount Verinder and the Rossbury fortune might very well fall into the hands of Simon's uncles. Or perhaps into the hands of one of his uncles. "We should call him out. Demand satisfaction for the dishonour done to our sister Sarah."

Bardstow cast a quick glance at the door, still securely closed, and prayed that no servant waited in the hall to see to the fire or to bring him a message. "Your jest is in exceedingly poor taste, Tyler." He paused and stated, "You are jesting, of course."

"I am not! Don't you see, Geoff? A duel or..." Tyler shrugged his shoulders. "There are two of us, and once Rossbury's out of the way, Simon –"

Tyler's plans for his nephew remained unknown as the Baron hissed, "Are you mad? Have you taken complete leave of your senses?"

"I am saner than our monarch has appeared to be on occasion." Tyler's eyes glittered with excitement. "Don't you see, Geoff? This is the answer to everything!"

"What I see," replied the Baron, restraining himself with effort, "is that you are doing your best to destroy our entire family! After the details of Sarah's death were blazoned across the front of every London newspaper and burned into the memories of every decent family in the country, securing a place for James at Eton was difficult enough. If word of your despicable scheme were bruited about, finding any sort of preferment for John, who'll not want to live in his older brother's pocket all his life," and here he cast Tyler a look which made the younger man take an involuntary step backward, "and finding a husband for Georgiana will be impossible."

"But –"

"No, Tyler. No more buts. No more excuses. Eleanor and I haven't worked to restore the family name and put Stowe Manor on a secure footing once again to permit you to plunge us all into another base scandal. I have allowed you to live here at Hamilton Place because you are my brother. But, damn your eyes, I will not allow you to destroy my children's futures."

"I'd never –"

"Never what, Tyler? Demean a man who – considering how Sarah hurt him – has been more generous to us all than anyone else in his place would have been?"

"He's despicable, Geoff! Why are you the only one who doesn't see it?" shouted Tyler, stung by his brother's denunciation.

"Why are you the only one who does?" retorted the Baron

Tyler was incoherent with fury. What he saw as continual treachery by his brother-in-law Rossbury had made his dependence on his own brother necessary. All his sources of income were gone, his inheritance spent long ago. His mother lived at Stowe Manor and was unavailable for loans. His sister Sarah, generous with her own allowance was dead. And his military career had been ruined over a few paltry documents copied and sold to pay a gaming debt. Wanting to tell his brother that he was moving out but powerless to do so, he turned quickly on his heel, strode to the door, and slammed it behind him.

I shall make Geoffrey see the truth, Tyler fumed to himself in the passageway. And I shall make Rossbury pay for Sarah's death. One way or another.

Major Fitzhugh Gresham pulled the bedroom door shut behind him, Rossbury's report and three letters in his hand. He looked at the papers and shook his head. Just these and nothing more. He's told me nothing of himself. As usual. But perhaps, Gresham thought, I may be able to winkle something from Miss Laurence. If I can find her.

Then halfway down the stairs, faint strains of music caught his ear.

"Since first I saw your face, I resolved
To honour and renowne thee.
If now I be disdained, I wish
My heart had never known thee."

A clear mezzo-soprano carried the sweet melody, and drew Gresham towards the door of the Shaws' first floor parlor. He smiled, his head nodding in satisfaction as he pushed the door inward with the final note.

Ensconced in the window seat, Elizabeth restitched a torn seam on a child's shirt. Two thick plaits wound over the top of her head like a coronal. She wore a faded blue gown, and a heavy knitted shawl covered her shoulders. She looked up as Gresham entered, the dark smudges beneath her gray eyes revealing a recent lack of sleep.

"Major Gresham, I presume you are seeking your coat and hat?" Her hands occupied, Elizabeth motioned to the left with her head.

Looking where Elizabeth had indicated, Gresham spied his hat on the floor and his greatcoat spread out over an oak settle standing before the room's fireplace. The heat coming from it had dried the garments that had been dripping wet earlier.

Elizabeth said, "I think you'll find they are both quite dry. And now that the rain has stopped momentarily, they are likely to remain so. At least for the rest of the morning."

"Miss Laurence," said the Major, "I fear you have been chased from your comfortable seat by the fire by my troublesome coat."

"Oh no," Elizabeth protested with the hint of a laugh. "Your coat has not chased me anywhere. This," she patted the worn tapestry cushion in the window seat, "is a pleasant place to spend a rainy morning." Her glance fell upon the nearby basket of items in need of mending. "And since Mrs. Shaw and her mother Mrs. Craddock have been more than kind to me," Elizabeth finished stitching the seam she worked on and took another item from the mending basket, "the least I can do to repay their hospitality is to use my one talent to help them."

"From what I heard as I came downstairs, your skill with a needle is not your only gift, Miss Laurence," offered Gresham.

"Oh, the ayre by Thomas Ford?" Elizabeth asked. She lifted her right shoulder. "Mine is a small talent, fit only for the drawing room although..." Elizabeth's mind wandered to the inn at Caudebec and her impulsive singing of *La Marseillaise.*

Elizabeth's unfinished sentence hung in the air. Although what? Gresham wondered. Then hoping to tempt Elizabeth to say something, anything, about Rossbury's journey from Rouen to Le Havre, he asked, "Although perhaps not during your recent travels in France?"

Elizabeth lowered her head, apparently intent on placing her next stitch perfectly. "No, not then. And probably not in my next position either. Most likely as a companion, I think. At least for a time. And that will rather be like being a soldier." Elizabeth laid her mending aside and stood. "For, I believe, obedience to orders is necessary to both." Elizabeth forced a smile to her lips and motioned towards the papers in Gresham's hand.

"Orders, Miss Laurence," replied the Major, realizing, with chagrin, that he'd been outmaneuvered. "They are the essence of a soldier's life. And mine are to return to my quarters at the Dolphin and Anchor here in Chichester and give my enthusiastic courier Rossbury's report and send him off at once." He gathered up his greatcoat from its place on the settle and drew his arms through the sleeves as Elizabeth walked to the door.

Moments later, Gresham was walking down the street, his usual cherubic smile replaced by a frown. She told me as much as Rossbury did, he thought in frustration. *And that is precisely nothing!*

"This is a most interesting piece of correspondence, Laurence."

Gideon Laurence stood in the doorway to his study, surprise written large on his face. Elizabeth's brother had been told that Sir Augustus Tremaine had called. But he did not expect to find the owner of neighboring Throck Manor standing near the window of his study at Hopeden Hall and holding a letter. A letter Gideon was certain had been placed safely inside a drawer of his desk.

Tremaine set the letter casually on the top on the desk and walked to the fireplace. Sir Augustus turned his back to the blaze. "What reply do you plan to make?"

Gideon strolled to his desk and picked up the letter. "What do you mean by 'What reply'?" Gideon said at last. "The letter is addressed to Elizabeth, and-"

"Miss Laurence is not here." Tremaine paused for an instant before finishing with deliberation, "And you, my friend, are."

"Yes, but..." Gideon began uncertainly. He stared at the tall, rapier thin man standing before him, his arm resting on the mantle. Tremaine's expression was impossible to read. Heavy lids veiled his hard, slate eyes and gave his face with its high cheekbones a reptilian look. Tremaine's ash blond hair, tied back with a black ribbon, was so pale that its silvering was unnoticeable. And the well-tailored dark clothes the baronet habitually wore gave him an elegance Gideon knew he could never achieve.

Gideon dropped his eyes to the letter, wondering if he had missed something important. He reread the contents quickly. Catherine Calvert, sister of his maternal grandmother, had died. With her children and husband long gone, the old harpy had left Elizabeth everything. Rosemont, her unentailed estate in

Gloucestershire. And £5000 in Bank of England investments. And not a penny for him.

Tremaine said nothing while Gideon scanned the letter's contents. Such a fussy man, he thought, viewing at his neighbor's stocky frame, old-fashioned gray wig, and patterned waistcoat with a critical eye.

When Gideon looked up, Tremaine appeared to be studying the fingernails on his left hand. "The letter-"

Tremaine interrupted impatiently, "Names you, Gideon Laurence, as both trustee and secondary heir."

"It does. But..."

"And you have not heard from your sister in..." Tremaine's rising inflection invited a response.

"Years. There were quite a few letters at first, but then nothing." Both men knew none of the letters had been answered.

"Then for all you know, she may be..."

"Married to some Frenchman, living God-knows-where, or..." Suddenly Gideon understood what Tremaine had in mind.

"Or..." Tremaine prompted.

"Or dead." And if she is, she deserves to be, Gideon told himself. He remembered how Elizabeth had thwarted his wishes years earlier and let his anger grow. "And this, this..." Gideon searched the letter for the solicitor's name.

"William Clewett," filled in Tremaine smoothly.

"Cannot expect me to search all of Europe for a willful termagant who is probably in some French churchyard!"

"Surely not. A man like yourself – with an estate that must be managed, a son who needs your nurturing hand, and two daughters who will be soon be of marriageable age – can hardly be asked to accept such a hopeless commission. And with war between England and France imminent..." Tremaine allowed his sentence to trail off.

"A war that will make crossing the Channel doubly dangerous, if not impossible."

"I fear you are correct. And as émigrés and aristos have been fleeing France for the past three years or more, all our countrymen have fled, too."

"That's true. And if my sister had left France, she would have come to Hopeden immediately."

"Where else could she go?"

"So she must be..."

Tremaine was wise enough to say nothing. When Gideon tried to gauge his neighbor's opinion, Sir Augustus was once again contemplating his beautifully manicured nails.

"Rosemont includes two farms." Its income added to Hopeden's would make all manner of things possible, Gideon thought. "I am the trustee."

"And," observed Tremaine, "£5000 would make an exceptionally fine dowry for Emma or Marianne."

"It would." Gideon rubbed his chin and stared at the letter he still held.

Only the crackling of the fire broke the long silence that followed. When Gideon tore his eyes from William Clewett's neat script, he found Tremaine's gaze fixed upon him.

"You are wondering perhaps why your decision in this matter seems to me a good one?"

When Gideon did not reply, Tremaine thought, Good. Maybe he is, at long last, learning to hold his tongue. "Of course, my main desire is to serve my neighbor and friend. In the absence – or, at least, the failure to appear – of the primary heir, it seems perfectly acceptable that you, the secondary heir, should secure what is yours."

Gideon nodded and remained silent, waiting for Tremaine to continue.

"However," Tremaine added, "should the primary heir return to England..."

This caveat was not one Gideon had anticipated, and he was betrayed into saying, "But, I thought you said..."

"I may have implied that such an event was unlikely, but it is not impossible."

"And if Eliz-" Gideon paused and then amended, "If such an event did occur?" He swallowed hard, the possibility of a charge of fraud or theft seeming more real than the £5000.

"Then I should be happy to oblige you by immediately renewing my previous offer of marriage. An offer I feel sure would meet with your approval and hers. As my wife, your sister could gainsay none of my decisions about the handling of her legal or financial affairs. The law is very clear on that point."

"But she..." Gideon decided not to speak his thoughts aloud. Why Tremaine would still want to marry his sister Elizabeth, a scold who had pointedly refused him, seemed a mystery. Tremaine did not accept refusals of any sort meekly. Gideon's own experience had taught him this truth well.

"Of course, the likelihood of a return to England is remote, as you know." Tremaine pretended that he had not heard Gideon's thoughtless phrase. "Yet if by some chance she does, you'll find that her time abroad has made your sister more tractable. Of this I am sure."

Spoken with chilling assurance, the last five words called up a vision of two very different women in Gideon's memory. The first was Edith Tremaine. Sir Augustus had wed the Northumbrian woman only months after Elizabeth's departure. Her constant bruises were always said to be the result of falls or accidents. Her fear of her husband was politely ignored. Her death, a drowning ruled 'death by misadventure' since suicide was a horror not to be contemplated by the gentry, came as a relief to all in the neighborhood. The second was a madam. Only the rouge on her cheeks rivaled the redness of the woman's hair. She owned a house Tremaine and Gideon had visited together the previous year. Her question – "Is ye like yer friend here? Like to play rough, do ye?" – earned her a sharp rebuke from Tremaine. But Gideon almost immediately pushed his memories of both women aside. Elizabeth's refusal to bend to his will still rankled in his memory. Women, he reasoned, are meant to be obedient to men.

"And," Tremaine said, "I am also sure that you can find some worthy uses for £5000."

The thought of the money erased any other qualms Gideon might have had. Besides, he reassured himself, Elizabeth will not return. "Indeed, I can."

"Then I had best leave you. You'll want to write to Mr. Clewett today."

Moments later Sir Augustus Tremaine drove away from Hopeden Hall. He handled the reins automatically and permitted himself a tight smile as he recalled the naked greed in Gideon Laurence's face as he realized the value of the property that could soon be his. The fool never once considered that knowledge of the inheritance fraud could be used against him. Knowledge, Tremaine thought, is more useful than money – if used correctly. He had no doubt that one day soon, it would be very useful. To him.

Then Tremaine saw another face. Elizabeth's as he had last seen her in '88. She's by no means a beauty, but I want her. Want to see fear in her eyes. He considered the wife and the doxies he had bedded in the last five years. None of them had purged his blood of his craving for Elizabeth Laurence, of his craving to tame her. And, he promised himself, should Elizabeth ever return to England, tame her I shall!

# CHAPTER 9
# FRIDAY, FEBRUARY 8, 1793

"Arriving Tuesday? Accompanied by Mrs. Craddock?" Martha Pearson looked at Beatrice Rowley, Dowager Marchioness Farnsworth, in the dressing table mirror. Then she put down the comb in her hand and picked up a hair pad. "Isn't Craddock..." She paused as she placed the pad at the top of her mistress' head and eased some hair over it.

"He is." Lady Beatrice sat at her dressing table while Martha Pearson arranged her hair. Lady Beatrice gazed critically at her mirrored reflection and then caught the eyes of her maid, a woman who had served her ever since she was fifteen. Both recalled the questions Craddock's note had excited among Rossbury's servants and hers.

"Humph! Wrote a bit more than he should have, didn't he?"

"He did." Lady Beatrice frowned.

As Martha waited for Lady Beatrice to continue, she glanced around the beautifully appointed boudoir where the Marchioness received her closest friends. From the delicate Meissen shepherd and shepherdess on the mantle to the brushes and combs on the dressing table, from the pale pink cushions plumped on the day bed to the comfits in the Waterford dish on the piecrust table near it, Lady Beatrice's boudoir had been Martha's domain ever since the Fifth Marquis Farnsworth had died and his widow had moved to her townhouse situated on a fashionable but quiet London square. And now there's to be... "A companion," Martha said, without realizing she'd spoken her thought aloud.

"Yes, a companion. My letter has most likely reached Miss Laurence by now. And how we are to explain her?"

"You'll come up with something. You always do, Lady Bea." Martha resumed her work on Lady Beatrice's hair, teasing a few errant strands into place.

"Stop fussing," ordered Lady Beatrice. "You've done your best."

Martha laid the comb on the vanity and stood expectantly behind her mistress.

"We've got better things to do than primp and preen." Lady Beatrice reseated herself so that she faced Martha rather than the dressing table mirror. "And I can't talk to you while you're looming over me." She pointed to one of the room's comfortable chairs.

"Betty'll be up shortly," Martha muttered as she took a seat.

"We both know Dolly. We've plenty of time to talk before Betty announces her arrival." Lady Beatrice glanced at a small, decorated porcelain-cased clock standing near the Meissen figurines. Punctuality about morning calls was not one of the Duchess of Lewisham's virtues. "She won't arrive for half an hour at least."

"And when she does, you're going to tell her about Miss Laurence."

"That's right. My companion, Miss Laurence. Whom I've never met." The dowager Marchioness sighed in frustration as she considered the task her godson had given her.

"Why you need a companion is beyond me. Seems like all London's traipsed through the drawing room at one time or another."

"Be that as it may, Martha, I need a companion." Seeing Martha ready to protest, Lady Beatrice said, "That's what Richard wants everyone to believe. I'll tell you what he told me last night. But it's not much. And he attached a warning to what little there is. None of this is to leave the room."

Martha nodded.

Lady Beatrice hesitated, not sure where to begin. "As we know from Craddock's note, my godson's been in France."

And sensing Martha's question before it was asked, Lady Beatrice added, "No, Richard did not tell me why he was there." She paused, both mistress and maid remembering that war had been declared the previous Saturday.

"And somehow while he was there, he saw Edward's obituary notice in the *Times*."

Martha gasped, her hand coming up to cover her mouth as she shook her head in dismay.

"Seeing the notice and knowing war was imminent made him decide to end his 'visit.' His word, Martha, not mine." Lady Beatrice scowled. Visit, my foot. Who does he think he's bamming?

"Apparently," Lady Beatrice continued, "this occurred while he was in Rouen. There by some fortuitous coincidence – which he did not explain – he learned Miss Laurence needed to be escorted back to England." Lady Beatrice hesitated momentarily and then added, "He also omitted to mention whether anyone else was in their party. But his warning about keeping what he said last night to myself leads me to believe they were a party of two."

"Two?" repeated Martha. "From Rouen to…"

"Rossbury omitted that detail as well, but I suspect it must have been Le Havre. God only knows how or with whom they traveled from Le Havre to wherever it was they came ashore.

Obviously somewhere near Chichester, since Richard traveled from there to London last week."

"More omitted details, Lady Bea?"

"Very astute of you, Martha." The Marchioness gave her maid a tight smile. "Rossbury can be rather stingy with words, as well you know."

Both women recalled the months that followed Lady Sarah Verinder's death. It was a time of ugly talk from others and even fewer words than usual from the newly bereaved husband. "He'll not be hurt by another scandal, will he, Lady Bea?" asked Martha anxiously.

"Not if I can prevent it," declared the dowager Marchioness. "No thanks to Craddock!"

"Craddock's note just said that Miss Laurence returned from France to England with Lord Rossbury, didn't it?" asked Martha.

"It did," confirmed Lady Beatrice. And seeing immediately what her maid was hinting at, she nodded. "So they simply returned on the same ship. From Le Havre."

Martha recalled what the Farnsworth House butler had told the assembled staff only that morning. "And Dunhill has warned everyone here not to spread tittle-tattle about Lord Rossbury."

"And Harris over at Rossbury House has done the same. So perhaps no damage has been done."

"Let's hope so." Martha narrowed her eyes in concentration. "Miss Laurence has been in France then. For some years?"

"She has," confirmed Lady Beatrice. "Rossbury described her as a gentlewoman in need of employment. She's been living in Rouen with an uncle – a doctor– and an aunt, who was the sister of one of Miss Laurence's parents."

"Was, Lady Bea?"

"Not much gets by you, Martha Pearson," complimented her mistress. "The aunt died shortly before Rossbury's arrival."

"That explains why her uncle couldn't travel with Miss Laurence. But it doesn't explain why Miss Laurence needs a position unless her aunt was the only member of the family yet living."

"Her relations are Hampshire gentry," related Lady Farnsworth, "but Rossbury omitted…"

"To tell you why Miss Laurence isn't returning to them." Both women were silent, the only sound the ticking of the clock on the mantle. "Bit of a mystery, isn't she?"

"Just like Richard's time in France. And I'll wager that's where he's being disappearing to for months now."

"Perhaps this Miss Laurence will know something about that," asserted Martha.

"Miss Laurence won't be sharing whatever she knows with us, Martha. If Richard had thought she would..."

"He'd never have asked you to take her on as a companion." Martha sighed in frustration. "Can't be as closed mouthed as his lordship, can she?"

"I doubt it, but…" Lady Beatrice trailed off.

The visit with Rossbury the preceding evening had been frustrating in the extreme. Rossbury limped so painfully that she had felt guilty about his rising and escorting her to a chair near the fire when she entered the drawing room. And then there was that fresh scar on his left temple. When she had asked Rossbury about the injury, he said, 'It's nothing.'

"Did he say anything about why he wrote to ask you to employ Miss Laurence as a companion?" asked Martha.

"Nothing at all. All I know is that Miss Laurence will be here on Tuesday. And my Valenciennes lace will be mended at last."

"I told you, Lady Bea, I'd repair it just as soon as…"

"Don't apologize, Martha. If your eyesight is only half as bad as mine, I don't know how you can thread a needle. I know I couldn't. And I hate losing the pleasure of books and correspondence. There's no skirting around it – we're both old. And mending lace takes younger eyes than either of us has."

Seeing Martha about to disagree, Lady Beatrice hurried on. "And one of the few things Richard told me about Miss Laurence is that she is an expert needle woman."

"Well, the weeks of Lent are the doldrums of the social year. And with Ash Wednesday coming next week, a new face might be just what's needed 'til the season starts."

"Oh, this new face is guaranteed to enliven my days, Martha." Lady Beatrice's eyes twinkled as she recalled the one other detail about Miss Laurence her godson had shared.

"You've got that look in your eyes, Lady Bea, that tells me enliven isn't quite the word I'd have used," said Martha suspiciously. "What else did Lord Rossbury tell you about Miss Laurence?"

"That when Miss Laurence arrives, she will be free of the encumbrance of cases, trunks, valises, portmanteaux, and boxes."

"Miss Laurence will have no baggage!" Martha exclaimed. "None at all?"

"One small bag, and nothing else. And that alone should make for some interesting days, Martha, wouldn't you agree?"

"Between filling in the omissions in Lord Rossbury's story and in Miss Laurence's wardrobe, I'd say the next few weeks look to be a lot more than interesting!"

"Rossbury even asked me, as if I couldn't figure it out for myself, to advance Miss Laurence most of her wages. He had no doubt that she will want to pay for her own purchases."

While the two considered this statement, both nodded. Independence was a trait they admired.

"But," realized Martha, "a wardrobe costs more than any companion earns in a year, Lady Bea."

"Rossbury asked me to insure Miss Laurence has whatever she needs and to forward the excess bills to him!"

"But you won't, will you, Lady Bea?"

"Of course not!" asserted the Marchioness. "And if I'm right about Miss Laurence, she'll not be so easily flummoxed. Whether in Rouen or London, anyone who has done what she apparently has on this journey with Rossbury isn't likely to make errors about the cost of anything."

"Lord Rossbury's no fool either, Lady Bea," reflected Martha sagely.

Again both women considered the situation. Puzzling and intriguing, it promised to add spice to the normally bleak days of February and March.

"Now, Martha, your job is to present Miss Laurence to the rest of the staff as my companion. Someone engaged to relieve the tedium of this dull time of the year. Recently arrived from Le Havre after an extended stay with relations in France, she has been recommended to me as needing a position."

At that moment, a knock sounded on the door. Martha rose and moved towards the dressing table.

Upon hearing Lady Farnsworth's "Enter," Betty, the upstairs maid, opened the door and saw Martha Pearson putting the finishing touch on the Marchioness's hair. "The Duchess of Lewisham has arrived," Betty announced.

Her head down to minimize the buffeting of the chill wind, Elizabeth hastened down North Street. Her destination was the Cathedral Church of the Holy Trinity. A place that promised a quiet not to be found in a house with four active children next to a busy bakery.

As Elizabeth hurried past the Council Chamber and Bishop Edward Story's Market Cross, the words of the brief letter she'd received from the Dowager Marchioness of Farnsworth scrolled through her head. A letter stating that she was being engaged as a companion and expected at Farnsworth Place on Tuesday.

Hunched against the cold, Elizabeth passed the Dolphin and Anchor and turned right through Canon Gate into Canon Lane, past the houses of the Vicars' Close towards St. Richard's Walk.

Once on the stone flagged path used by the godly Bishop of Chichester from 1246 to 1253, she allowed her steps to slow, thinking not of the saint, but of another man with the same name.

Lord Rossbury is behind this. He knew from what I said on *L' Oiseau Vite* that I was seeking a position as a companion. Only he could have made inquiries in London. And only he would have found an employer willing to bring me to London in a private post chaise with Mrs. Craddock as my traveling companion.

"And I will probably never see him again," whispered Elizabeth. "And if I do, I must address him as Lord Rossbury. Not…"

Shaking these thoughts from her mind, Elizabeth stepped from the walled walkway into the cloister and quickened her pace once more. Soon the cathedral door closed behind her, and the nave with its Norman arches lay before her.

For the second time in less than three weeks, Elizabeth thought as she sat where nave and choir met, I am sitting in a great cathedral and trying to look into the future before I begin a journey. Then the cathedral's organ broke the stillness. A practice session for the organist, Elizabeth decided. The music was soothing, and she listened for a moment. If only my thoughts were as harmonious as the organ!

Images of Hopeden Hall and neighboring Throck Manor flitted across her mind. Had Sir Augustus taken a wife at last? Perhaps someone in London will know, she thought. Or perhaps I could risk a letter?

Elizabeth pictured her letter being placed on the entryway table in Hopeden Hall. Then another scene flashed across her memory – Sir Augustus Tremaine idly picking up her brother's mail and turning letters over in his long fingers. Elizabeth shivered, huddling deeper within the cloak she had borrowed from Ann Shaw as memories of Tremaine's touch pressed close

I will make my own way, she promised herself. And the first step will come at Farnsworth Place in London.

Meanwhile, the organist, having completed his practice of pieces suitable for preludes and postludes, began to experiment with common meter hymn melodies. Soon the familiar rhythm of eight, six, eight, six – the beats regular and sure – wrapped itself around Elizabeth and cemented the peace she had found in her decisions about the future.

Then the unseen organist transitioned into another common meter hymn, and words surfaced in her mind. When the hidden fingers began to repeat the music, Elizabeth sang softly unaware of how well her voice carried.

"Oh, for a closer walk with God…."

On the organ bench, John Marsh heard William Cowper's words sung by a barely audible mezzo voice. If I decrease the Swell somewhat, he thought, voice and organ should blend well.

Instead of switching to another common meter tune, Marsh continued to play the one he had already played twice. After the voice moved through the words of the second and third stanzas, Marsh improvised a counter melody in the tenor on verse four and another in the soprano on verse five. On the sixth verse, above the melody that he now played in the alto line, a descant soared gracefully.

"So shall my walk be close to God,
Calm and serene my frame…"

"Calm and serene," repeated Elizabeth quietly as the echoes of the music dissolved. "And ready now for whatever comes." She rose from her seat and saw a plainly dressed man of two score years hurrying towards her from the direction of the choir. Her face flushed crimson as she prepared to accept his wrath over being disturbed.

"Don't apologize. You didn't bother me one wit," said the man at once. "Nor anyone else," he added, looking around. "We seem to have the cathedral to ourselves this afternoon. Cowper's lines and a fine old tune." He smiled broadly. "A fitting pleasure in this place." His hands spread, and his glance encompassed the whole of the nave, "Don't you agree?"

"Indeed, I do," said Elizabeth. "Being the organist here must be a very satisfying profession."

"Would that it were mine!" Noting Elizabeth's look of confusion, he clarified, "Allow me to introduce myself. I am John Marsh. I deputize for the cathedral's organist. But being but a talented amateur, like you, Mrs…?"

"Miss Laurence," Elizabeth supplied. "And talented amateurs, Mr. Marsh, do not play Couperin, Schütz, Handel, and Stanley." She matched composers with pieces of music she barely recalled she had heard.

"Your familiarity with liturgical music goes beyond that of the *Olney Hymns* of Newton and Cowper, I see, Miss Laurence." He looked at Elizabeth with surprise. Good diction, wonderful knowledge of music, but her clothes. They're fit only for the ragbag. "I am surprised I have not seen you at any of our subscription concerts here in Chichester."

"I'm only visiting the city for a few days. But I enjoyed your playing this afternoon." Elizabeth held out her right hand. "Now, I have overstayed my time, and my friends are expecting me so I must bid you 'Good day,' Mr. Marsh."

Moments later while John Marsh adjusted some music at the organ, he shook his head in wonderment. He saw himself bowing over the hand of a woman clothed in a well-worn dress made of inexpensive fabric and watching her glide down a side aisle.

Poor women do not visit friends in other cities. Or walk with elegant steps, or extend their hands upon saying farewell, or read Cowper, or recognize Stanley, or end a conversation with... Words escaped him. Bless me, he thought, I've been dismissed! Simple as that. By…? A lady? Marsh shook his head. Miss Laurence is a mystery. One you will never solve, John Marsh. Yet he knew he would never hear Cowper's "Closer Walk with Thee" without recollecting a beautiful blending of voice and organ in Chichester Cathedral.

"Joseph's brothers were cruel!" stated young William Shaw firmly that evening. "I'd never treat Tom the way they treated Joseph!" He put his arm around his younger brother's shoulder as they sat near the parlour fire.

"I know you wouldn't. William." Elizabeth closed the Craddock family Bible.

"Finith `tory, Miz Lizbeth." Ruth snuggled close to Elizabeth's left side. "I want Jothup to get out of the big hole."

"I'll finish reading the story tomorrow," promised Elizabeth. "Now I want to see how your sister's progressing with her lace."

"But it'th dark in that hole and Jothup's `fraid," insisted Ruth.

"You know how the story ends, Ruthie." Her brother Tom was eager to show Miss Elizabeth how much he knew. "Grandad read it to us last year. Joseph's brothers sell…"

"No! No!" Ruth yelled. "Want Miz Lizbeth to read_`tory. Now!"

"Miss Elizabeth will never read us any more stories, and she'll be glad to leave on Tuesday if you keep shouting at her like that," scolded William. "You're acting like a baby."

Elizabeth and Hannah, sitting on Ruth's right, exchanged a smile. "Chain three," Elizabeth whispered to Hannah.

"I'm not a baby, Miz Lizbeth," murmured Ruth.

"Prove it, Ruthie," demanded Hannah without taking her eyes from the fine line of lace beginning to appear at the edge of the collar she held.

"Thorry, Miz Lizbeth." Ruth's head hung contritely. "I thorry I yelled. You finith `tory tomorrow." She yawned and sidled closer to Elizabeth.

Elizabeth, noting that Hannah was crocheting the lace border slowly but correctly, bent to pick up the only item left in the mending basket. As she did so, the door to the parlour opened, and Sergeant Craddock and his wife entered. The sergeant held a yellowing newspaper in his hand.

"This be th' newspaper I was tellin' you 'bout." Craddock raised a 1792 edition of the London *Times* in his hands. "The part about Lord Rossbury's brother is right here." He pointed to an article on the back page.

Elizabeth dropped the mending back into the basket and took the newspaper Craddock offered her. The words, *Edward Verinder, Earl of Rossbury*, leapt off the page.

"Young Will, Tom, you come over here with me and leave Miss Laurence to read in peace." Sergeant Craddock motioned towards his usual chair in the chimney corner. "I've a new story for you, one 'bout Private James Compton."

Mrs. Craddock squeezed next to her eldest granddaughter. "What's this then, Hannah?" She looked at the rows of stitches on the collar in the girl's left hand.

With Ruth asleep, her head resting on Elizabeth's lap, Elizabeth was free to give her entire attention to the newspaper article. She read it twice and then added the newspaper's information about the Verinder family to the Sergeant's stories about Lord Rossbury. The precious details merged into a portrait. Still, Elizabeth thought, there is much I don't know. She looked again at the obituary's list of heirs. Simon, now Viscount

Verinder. He's Lord Rossbury's son. And his mother must be dead or she'd be mentioned as well. So why does no one speak about her? Elizabeth glanced at Sergeant Craddock.

"And so," finished Sergeant Craddock some minutes later, "Jim Compton who once almost unseated Captain Verinder, as Lord Rossbury were then, when that musket of his went off right under the nose of the Captain's horse now be on his way to work with horses at Rossbury House in London!"

"Can't believe I'm going to London, too," put in his wife. "I'll be able to see Mary and Seth an' our new grandson!" Mrs. Craddock shook her head in wonderment. "Never been in a private post chaise before."

"I shall be glad of your company." Elizabeth turned to Mrs. Craddock with a smile. "You can help me keep my courage up on the way to Farnsworth Place."

"Nay!" exclaimed the Sergeant. "Can't be tha' you're a bit worrit 'bout companionin' one Marchioness." His voice reflected his incredulity. "Anyone who can handle this lot," here his loving glance enfolded his four grandchildren, "can entertain a widow lady any day."

During this conversation, Will and Ann Shaw quietly opened the parlour door. Tired after a long day in the bakery, they were content to stand in the doorway for a moment and observe their family. Both noted Ruth asleep on Elizabeth's lap and then simultaneously turned to one another and smiled. Will put an arm about his wife's waist, and Ann drew close to his side. With the ease of the long-married, each read the other's thought: Here's a woman who was born to have children of her own.

"Bed for you," announced William Shaw to his children when his wife's father had finished speaking.

Sergeant Craddock said, "I'll take young Will an' Tom up." Then leading the boys to the door, he confided, "Tell you 'bout 'nother daft thing our Private Compton did 'fore bed."

While her husband bent to gather the sleeping Ruth in his arms, Ann Shaw stated, "Hannah, you can finish that row I see you're workin' on and then it's bed for you as well."

Roused from slumber by her father's lifting, Ruth mumbled, "Finith 'tory 'morrow, Miz Lizbeth." Following her husband out, Ann Shaw shut the door behind them.

When only Mrs. Craddock and Elizabeth remained in the parlour with her, Hannah held out the collar with its minute edging of lace. "Am I doing this right?"

"I believe you are. In fact, it looks very good," complimented Elizabeth while examining the collar. "What do you think, Mrs. Craddock?"

In lieu of a reply, the trio bent over Hannah's work.

# CHAPTER 10

# MONDAY, FEBRUARY 18, 1793

"Beatrice!"

Hearing the familiar voice of Dolly Dalrymple, both Elizabeth and Lady Farnsworth turned. Behind them, the Lewisham carriage pulled up in front of Eastons, the two titled ladies' favorite Bond Street linen drapers.

The carriage stopped, and a footman opened the crested door. "Something to say, Bea." Lady Dorothy patted the seat next to her.

"Shall I wait for you inside, Lady Farnsworth?" Elizabeth said.

"We'll join you shortly, won't we Dolly?" Lady Beatrice looked at her friend who nodded.

Leaving the two to their conversation, Elizabeth entered the bow-fronted shop.

Moments later, Tyler Hamilton-Smythe slipped from the hack he'd hired as soon as the Marchioness' carriage had pulled into Carlington Square that morning. He'd been watching Farnsworth Place ever since Patience Downes had told him about two newcomers to Carlington Square. Rossbury's new stable man, James Compton, was of no interest to him. Stupid cow, he thought as he slunk into Eastons, thinks I'll be jealous. As if any former private's a rival!

The other newcomer was a different story. Miss Elizabeth Laurence. Tyler scanned the crowded shop and found her among the ladies near the linen draper's long counter. Though he'd seen Elizabeth earlier when a footman had handed her into the Farnsworth carriage, he still found it hard to believe this was the woman Patience had told him about. He stared at Elizabeth's ugly bonnet and shabby clothes and saw that he was not the only one to notice that Lady Farnsworth's new companion looked like someone's poor relation.

Yet Patience had gone on and on about her arrival in a private post chaise from Chichester. Chichester, where Rossbury's own carriage had been sent at the end of January. And that meant Miss Laurence was the woman Rossbury brought to England with him. His kept woman.

As Tyler watched, Elizabeth approached the far end of the counter. Then she picked up a card of lace left there by a busy shop assistant. He grinned as a way to hurt his hated former brother-in-law surfaced.

Without further thought, Tyler shouted, "Stop, thief!"

These two words immediately silenced everyone in the shop. They turned towards the well-dressed, handsome young man who had raised the alarm. His pointing finger shifted their eyes to Elizabeth.

With the card of lace still in her hand, Elizabeth looked up and was shocked to find Tyler's accusing finger transferring everyone's scrutiny to herself. Then a woman behind the counter echoed, "Stop, thief!"

Those closest to Elizabeth recoiled in horror. One customer screamed. The senior assistant bustled forward. Tyler slid towards the door. His head down to shield his face, he collided with someone coming in and rushed off without a word.

Pausing to look at the back of the man who had bumped into him, Rossbury heard Elizabeth say, "I see no thieves here."

Thieves? Has someone accused... Rossbury scanned the shop, saw the horrified looks on customers' faces, the semicircle of space around Elizabeth, and realized what had happened. As he watched, Elizabeth laid the card of lace in her hands back on the counter.

Looking at the hostile crowd, Elizabeth concluded, "I see only ladies wishing to make purchases."

Rossbury silently applauded Elizabeth's calm denial but knew he had only a moment to help her salvage the situation. "Miss Laurence," he said in matter-of-fact but carrying tone, "my godmother and Lady Lewisham require your presence outside."

Lord Rossbury! He can't be... Elizabeth's eyes shifted from those who believed her a thief to the man who had somehow appeared to rescue her. Again!

The ladies in the shop also turned their attention to this newest player in the little drama unfolding in Eastons.

Rossbury, having come from another early morning session with the General, was resplendent in his uniform, the red tunic with its gleaming buttons and colonel's insignia gaining immediate respect.

As Rossbury took a step forward, the crowd parted. One woman whispered, "That's the Earl of Rossbury," another murmuring, "His godmother's the Dowager Marchioness of Farnsworth."

"Is it convenient for you to join them?" asked Rossbury.

"It is, Lord Rossbury," Elizabeth replied, relieved that her voice did not shake.

When Rossbury reached her side, he smiled, gave a slight but perfect bow, and offered his left arm as if they were a couple preparing to take a turn about a ballroom. Elizabeth immediately placed her trembling right hand upon his arm. Rossbury deliberately but gently covered her right hand with his before escorting her to the door.

Removing his hand from Elizabeth's only to open the door, Rossbury heard the hushed whispers behind them and sensed the fixed stares at their backs. And when the door closed behind them, he knew the observation continued, the large windows at the front of the shop affording an unobstructed view of the next scene in the drama.

Elizabeth was also aware of the watchers behind Eastons' windows. But she unhesitatingly took her cue from Rossbury, just as she had done so often in France, and strolled with him toward the Lewisham carriage.

Once at its side, Rossbury's glance at the footman caused the man to dart forward to open the door. The two ladies inside turned to question the interruption and saw Rossbury and Elizabeth standing side by side within the space framed by the door. Both women's eyes were riveted at once upon Rossbury's hand laid protectively over that of Elizabeth.

Rossbury observed, "The day is a chill one. Perhaps something warm – taken at Rossbury House? – might be in order after the exertions of the morning."

Lady Lewisham scented a story and diplomatically said nothing. Lady Farnsworth, completely mystified by Rossbury's appearance with Elizabeth on his arm, refrained from saying that they had not yet had the opportunity to exert themselves on this raw February morning and that her carriage was not due back in Bond Street for another hour. Instead she inquired, "Is Lady Dorothy included in this impromptu invitation, Richard?"

"Of course," replied Rossbury smoothly. "That is, if Lady Lewisham will honour me by accepting."

"Delighted to accept, Rossbury."

"I told Weaver to wait here with my carriage when I saw yours leaving Bond Street, Godmother," Rossbury noted in rather oblique fashion.

"Be happy to have Bea accompany me." Lady Lewisham looked at her friend to see if this arrangement was acceptable.

Nodding her approval, Lady Beatrice said, "We shall meet you then at Rossbury House."

Observing Eastons from a shop doorway down the street, Tyler Hamilton-Smythe cursed under his breath. *Why did Rossbury come to Eastons today? And how did he prevent an arrest?* he wondered. He fumed over his bad luck. He watched Rossbury hand Elizabeth into his carriage and swore, *I'll make him pay for what he did to Sarah. I'll find a way. If it's the last thing I do!*

Inside Rossbury's carriage, Elizabeth settled herself on the banquette facing forward, Rossbury on the one opposite. "Thank you, Lord Rossbury, for once again providing help in a time of need."

"From what I observed, you didn't really need anyone's help." Rossbury noted the dark smudges under Elizabeth's eyes but said nothing.

"I doubt that I would have been permitted to walk out of Eastons without your intervention."

"Do not give me too much credit, Miss Laurence. My happening to spot the Farnsworth carriage pulling away from Eastons was mere coincidence," Rossbury said with less than total honesty. He'd spent the early part of the morning with the General, the two reviewing his latest report. Then Rossbury had ordered Weaver to drive slowly down Bond Street, his godmother's preferred place to shop.

"Just as it was coincidence that led to your hearing of the danger I may have encountered in Rouen?" Elizabeth asked. "Some react to such coincidences by remaining spectators. I thank God that you, Lord Rossbury, are not one of them."

"A title or a uniform smooths the way," Rossbury said dismissively.

"They do," agreed Elizabeth. "But other men with such advantages abuse privilege rather than use it to help others. And, in France you had neither of those advantages." Enough, she told herself. Watching Rossbury's face had shown her once again that gratitude made him uncomfortable. "All in all, I am in your debt."

"Perhaps you could repay me by telling me all you remember about the unpleasantness at Eastons. Beginning with your entrance into the shop," requested Rossbury while trying to recall why the back of the man who jostled him in the doorway seemed familiar.

"Gladly." Elizabeth closed her eyes and pictured the shop. She described everything she could remember – the other customers, the bolts of cloth on display, her plan to buy material for a dress, her examination of the card of lace, and her accuser's surprising charge.

Rossbury interrupted. "Would you recognize him again?" Elizabeth's description, added to the familiarity of a retreating back, had caused a memory to awaken. But the face in his recollection refused to come into focus.

"Yes, I would." Brow furrowed, Elizabeth hesitated and then added, "At least, I would in the next few days. If you think it is important, I can write down what I recall."

"That could be useful. Do you remember anything else? Perhaps someone standing close to the man who shouted?" Rossbury asked.

"No, there is nothing more to tell. I don't think he had an accomplice. It was probably some sort of prank." Elizabeth looked down at her frayed dress with a self-deprecatory smile. "The result of a dare, perhaps."

"If you are correct, it was a vile one."

Into the moment of silence that followed this comment, as both considered the consequences had the situation become ugly, Elizabeth exclaimed, "How glad I am that Lady Farnsworth was not with me!"

"If she had been," grinned Rossbury suddenly, "neither you nor anyone else would have had the opportunity to say anything." The scene began to play in his mind, white-faced assistants fearing the loss of Lady Farnsworth's patronage, some in tears, the Marchioness' imperious demands that the accuser be apprehended. "My godmother does not suffer fools gladly."

"When Lady Farnsworth wrote to me, she never said she was your godmother," protested Elizabeth.

"If she had, you would have turned down the offer. Am I right?"

Since the answer was obvious, Elizabeth instead said, "And Lady Farnsworth is hardly in need of a companion!"

"I disagree," insisted Rossbury.

"But visitors come to the door, and the carriage is in use almost every day. Something I am sure you already know. She only needs help with lace mending, letter writing, reading... "

"Things you do well," Rossbury interjected.

"You knew Lady Farnsworth's eyesight was troubling her and made her believe she was doing you a favor by hiring me!"

"I confess it, Miss Laurence. I am guilty," Rossbury admitted. Not wanting Elizabeth to think about the matter further, he changed the subject. "And as I must soon travel to Earl's Wood Park in Shropshire for some time, you might oblige me by reminding my godmother that I expect letters. Weekly."

"Of course, Lord Rossbury." Then Elizabeth's eyes widened as, through the carriage window, she saw Farnsworth Place coming into view.

"But this is..." Unable to keep the disappointment from her voice, Elizabeth did not complete the sentence.

"Carlington Square," noted Rossbury, not understanding why Elizabeth was upset.

Then the carriage, instead of continuing left to Lady Farnsworth's residence, turned right. "But," Elizabeth said in confusion, looking back at Farnsworth Place on the south side of the square, "Carlington Square is where..."

"...my London home is located," supplied Rossbury as the carriage turned left and then halted.

The footman opened the carriage door and lowered the steps. Rossbury exited and then offered his hand to Elizabeth. The door in the centre of the Georgian townhouse swung inward as they mounted the five steps leading to it. Upon the threshold, Elizabeth looked over her shoulder at Farnsworth Place directly across the tree-lined square from where she stood. Everyone thought I knew who lived here so no one ever said anything! she realized.

"Welcome to Rossbury House, Miss Laurence."

In the entrance hall, its cantilevered staircase leading first to a landing lit by a large window in the style of Palladio and then to the first floor, Harris, the butler, hovered anxiously. As soon as the door had closed behind Rossbury and Elizabeth, he thrust the silver salver in his hands forward. Rossbury removed a single sheet of folded paper. "Must see you. Urgent. Confidential. Bardstow."

Harris explained, "The gentleman awaits your pleasure in the book room, milord."

"Pardon me, Miss Laurence," Rossbury apologized. "An unexpected matter requires my attention. Perhaps you'd like to go upstairs to remove the grime of this morning's outing?"

"Yes, thank you," Elizabeth replied at once, knowing Rossbury needed time to speak with whoever was in the book room.

"Ask Mrs. Green to see to Miss Laurence's needs, Harris. And then light the fire in the morning room and tell Mrs. Ballantyne to prepare some refreshments. Lady Lewisham and Lady Farnsworth should be arriving at any moment. Conduct them to the morning room and tell them that I have been detained and shall be with them shortly."

"Very good, milord."

"You will excuse me, Miss Laurence." After a perfunctory nod of his head, Rossbury strode across the hall.

His leg must be much better, Elizabeth thought as she watched Rossbury disappear. His limp is scarcely noticeable. A voice at her elbow interrupted her thoughts about Rossbury's health. "Miss Laurence," said the middle-aged woman who stood there, "I'm Mrs. Green. Would you like to accompany me upstairs?"

Inside the book room, which was a combination small library and study, the pacing of Geoffrey Hamilton-Smythe, Baron Bardstow halted as soon as he heard the click of the door's opening. Turning to the man he had come to see, he waited until Rossbury pulled the door shut behind him before speaking.

"It is good of you to see me, Rossbury," Bardstow observed as Rossbury stepped toward him. "Please accept my condolences on the death of your brother."

"Thank you for your sentiments and for the letter you and Lady Bardstow sent." Rossbury noted Bardstow's agitation. "Would you care to take a seat?"

"No." Bardstow's refusal sounded blunt even to his own ears. "Forgive me, Rossbury. What I must say is so painful that I don't feel I have the right to sit in your house." He paused and gulped some air. "Believe me, I hardly know how to begin to..."

Rossbury waited while his visitor fought for enough composure to control his voice.

With a shake of his head, the baron hurtled headlong into his story. "About a fortnight ago, Tyler stormed into my study at the house here in London and poured out a tirade of abuse..." He bit his lip and looked at the floor. "On you, Rossbury."

Bardstow resumed his pacing. "He'd heard you'd returned to town. He said you'd brought a woman with you."

Rossbury's face hardened at this news, his mouth a mere line, his eyes cold as snow melt. Bardstow's words had jostled the memory of the familiar back seen at Eastons.

Bardstow plunged forward with his confession. "I realized that she was probably some widow you were escorting home. But Tyler insisted that she was someone you had known before Sarah's..." He gasped for air as if he had been running. "And that she was, she was..." Bardstow floundered desperately, unable to repeat his brother's terrible allegation.

"Miss Laurence required a safe passage back to England. The imminent war with France has made that country an inhospitable place for anyone of English birth." With difficulty Rossbury reined in his anger. What he feared after he learned that Craddock had forwarded an unauthorized message to Rossbury House had come to pass.

"Good God, Rossbury! You have been in France! When Tyler said...I thought he was... You could have been..." Bardstow stuttered incoherently and stared at Rossbury, now appearing dangerously aloof.

"Tyler's source of information was..."

"Servants." Bardstow ran a hand distractedly over his high forehead. "No one who knows you will believe anything Tyler says. You know the set he idles away the days with at that damned club of his." His previous apologetic tone disappeared under an angry outburst. "Bunch of know nothings and do nothings. Just like Tyler unfortunately. All hell-bent on finding the fastest way to Newgate or perdition!"

The baron's brown eyes closed for a moment as his anger dissipated. Then Bardstow continued his painful revelations and his pacing. "I will, of course, scotch any ugly rumors I hear though I am not likely to hear much news from town as I return to Essex tomorrow."

After yet another hesitation, Bardstow added, "Which brings me to the real point of my asking to see you today."

Rossbury's face was expressionless as he waited for Bardstow to continue.

"I considered writing to you, but using a letter to tell you what, to tell you what…" Bardstow swallowed, steeling himself to finish what he had come to say. "It seemed dishonourable."

"No one could think you so," stated Rossbury. "Your care for Stowe Manor and its people, if nothing else, is an irrefutable proof of your integrity."

"Thank you, Rossbury." The Baron smiled bleakly. "Your praise, however, makes telling you what I must even more unpalatable."

Seeing his visitor struggle again to master his voice, Rossbury observed calmly, "This has something to do with Sarah, doesn't it?"

The Baron's chin, which had sunk to his chest, was raised, and a determined look entered his eyes. "Yes," he admitted grimly. "Yes, it has. Tyler blames you for Sarah's death. Doesn't matter that his beliefs are based on nothing. He worshiped Sarah and finds it impossible to blame Kincaid for what happened because, because…"

"Doing so would be the same as blaming himself," finished Rossbury.

"Exactly!" Bardstow was relieved that Rossbury understood this point. "Just as he will never blame himself for his dismissal from the army."

"Another sin he lays at my door."

"Now that he has chosen to believe that Miss Laurence is…" Bardstow decided to leave the rest of that statement unsaid and hurried on, "Tyler has concluded that you are unworthy both to possess a title and to raise your son."

The allusion to Simon stopped Rossbury's breath for a moment. Chilled by fear, he was unable to speak.

As if reading his listener's mind, Bardstow explained, "Simon would never be a target for Tyler's anger. But you might. That's why I felt I had to see you before I left town. Tyler proposed that the two of us call you out. I put paid to that idiocy. And while I do not believe Tyler is brave enough to resort to physical violence on his own, if something happened, if Tyler..."

"Nothing has happened yet," Rossbury lied. Telling Bardstow of the morning incident in Eastons will heap more coals on a head already burning with shame. "And thanks to your warning, I should be able to blunt anything Tyler might try to do, whatever it might be."

Bardstow reached for his greatcoat and hat lying upon a nearby chair. "And now I've a favor to ask."

Rossbury's lifted eyebrow, a gesture familiar to Bardstow from their close association in the past, caused him to smile briefly. "I should like to leave through the mews. I have reason to believe Tyler's keeping a watch on Rossbury House at times. He wasn't when I arrived, but now..." He shrugged uncertainly and stared at the floor.

Rossbury digested this additional information in silence.

Bardstow continued bitterly, "I'd not blame you for wanting nothing more to do with my family, Rossbury."

"As you are uncle to my son, that's not possible," Rossbury said at once.

Rossbury's words brought Bardstow's eyes to his face. "Thank you."

During this exchange, Rossbury considered how to spirit Bardstow out of the house. A possibly watchful Tyler Hamilton-Smythe was not the only problem. The chance of servants' gossip must be avoided also. Rossbury looked around the book room and nodded when he saw no tray with a glass or decanter.

When Rossbury opened the door, he found Harris waiting in the hall. A slight movement of his hand brought the butler to his side.

"My guest" – Rossbury emphasized the vague description of his visitor and saw immediate understanding in Harris's face – "would like to leave through the mews. I'd like you to show him out yourself."

Harris nodded. "Very good, milord."

Meanwhile, Elizabeth and Mrs. Green ascended the stairs to the second floor. During the climb up the two flights, the housekeeper had spoken only once. "You're Lady Farnsworth's new companion, aren't you, Miss Laurence?" To Elizabeth's simple assent, the housekeeper had added nothing.

The morning had been so full of unexpected occurrences that Elizabeth welcomed the quiet. And the chance to admire the house, from the fine barley sugar turnings supporting the well-polished banister to the series of portraits and landscapes on the walls.

Once the second floor had been gained, the two women turned from the staircase into a hallway and passed an open door. Elizabeth glanced inside and stopped. Within was the loveliest bedroom she had ever seen. A maid was dusting the top of a low chest of drawers. It stood to one side of a canopied bed, its posts gleaming, the canopy itself a rosy crown that seemed suspended above the bed and connected to the posts by mere swags of fabric.

"Perhaps you would like to enter this room for a few minutes, Miss Laurence?" Mrs. Green motioned Elizabeth to step forward. "You may continue with the dusting, Downes," the housekeeper instructed the startled maid who had looked up at the sound of voices.

The room itself was filled with light and a sense of warmth even on this bleak winter day. Directly opposite the door, a bank of south facing windows overlooked Carlington Square. To the right of the open door was the magnificent bed that had first captured Elizabeth's attention. To the left was the fireplace, fronted by an intimate grouping of two comfortable chairs upholstered in striped satin, a small marquetry-topped table between them.

Elizabeth gazed in silence at the lovely proportions and understated elegance of the room and its furnishings. At the same time, Patience Downes was surreptitiously inspecting Lady Farnsworth's new companion. Those clothes, Patience observed, don't look fit to be seen on Molly, the scullery maid.

"What a beautiful retreat!" exclaimed Elizabeth softly.

Mrs. Green nodded. Retreat is exactly the right word for this room, she thought. "The ninth earl, Lord Rossbury's father, designed this room himself. It was a birthday gift for Lady Rossbury. Originally it was two smaller rooms. The adjoining wall was pulled down, and this chamber was the result. Unfortunately, before she ever saw it, Lady Mary died unexpectedly at Earl's Wood Park – that's the family's Shropshire estate – and the room hasn't been used since."

Elizabeth, who had wandered toward a painting, a landscape she guessed to be by Poussin, turned and remarked, "What a pity!"

"There's some who haven't liked the arrangement. Lord Rossbury's dressing room was through there." Mrs. Green pointed to a door at the far side of the bed. "But the room itself is both bedchamber and lady's boudoir."

Both Mrs. Green's words and her slight sniff caught Elizabeth's attention. "But everything is here." Her hand gestured towards the dressing table with its large cheval glass and the chairs in front of the fireplace.

"Some would have it that a lady's boudoir should be a separate room, Miss Laurence." Mrs. Green thought of Lady Sarah Verinder, late wife of the present Lord Rossbury. His brother, the Earl, had offered the use of Rossbury House for the young couple's honeymoon. But the bride, upon hearing of the arrangement of the principal bed chamber, had asked her father for the use of his London townhouse, with its more conventional arrangement, for the first and last days of the wedding trip.

"But surely," insisted Elizabeth, "anyone who saw the room..." She turned in a slow circle. "It's beautiful."

Mrs. Green neither agreed nor disagreed. Instead she noted, "The hot water that's been brought up for you is probably the right temperature by now."

Reluctantly Elizabeth returned to the hall. Soon she found herself in a pleasant guest chamber, a bowl of slightly steaming water before her, a fresh towel at its side.

"The commode is through that door." Mrs. Green touched on the delicate matter in a practical tone.

"Thank you, Mrs. Green. I can think of nothing I could want that is not provided here," Elizabeth observed courteously.

A pretty speech. Very proper too, thought Mrs. Green. "When you are ready, you may simply return to the ground floor. Harris will be waiting in the hall to conduct you to the morning room." Then with a nod and a smile, Mrs. Green left.

The Rossbury House morning room was a cheerful place to receive visitors. Its lemon walls, three large windows opening onto the square, gleaming white enameled wood around the fireplace with its pair of tapestry fire screens before it and identical mahogany drop-leaf card tables on each side of it made an ideal setting for the rest of the furnishings. In one corner was a lady's escritoire, in another a cherry wood nest of tables. At a right angle to the fireplace was a comfortable camel backed sofa designed by Hepplewhite. Facing the sofa, a pair of matching upholstered chairs, a satinwood marquetry tea table between them.

When Rossbury entered, he saw his godmother seated on one of the chairs and Lady Lewisham occupying a spot on the sofa.

"Forgive me for not being here to greet you. An unanticipated business matter required my attention." He saw that their outer garments had been collected and the fireplace was emitting a pleasing warmth. "I trust Harris has made you comfortable?"

"Harris never puts a foot wrong as well you know, Richard." Lady Beatrice peered up at her godson. "What I want to know is what happened in Eastons that made you cancel a morning's shopping."

Rossbury seated himself on the vacant chair at his godmother's left and leaned forward. "Someone accused Miss Laurence of trying to steal a card of lace." He did not say that he believed the accuser to be Tyler Hamilton-Smythe. This revelation could wait until later.

"A shop assistant then seconded the accusation. Miss Laurence was extricating herself from this unpleasantness when I entered. I simply informed her that the two of you awaited her outside and offered to escort her to your carriage." Rossbury looked at Lady Lewisham. "Fortunately for me, you were there."

"You thought you'd find Bea inside Eastons, didn't you, Rossbury? But when you found only Miss Laurence and remembered seeing my carriage on the street…" Lady Lewisham's head shook in approval. "Always said you were intelligent."

"It was those awful clothes, of course." Lady Beatrice frowned. "And the whole purpose of going to Eastons was to make a start on a new wardrobe!"

"I have some ideas about that. I'll share them once Miss Laurence joins us."

Rossbury's neutral tone gained him a sharp look from Lady Beatrice. "They'd best be good ones, Richard. Miss Laurence needs no more scenes. Two accusations of theft in as many days is more than sufficient excitement for anyone." Her listeners' expressions and Rossbury's "What on earth?" sped the rest of Lady Beatrice's tale.

"Yesterday when we returned from St Etheldreda's, Betty accused Miss Laurence of breaking and then removing a small Sèvres bowl."

"*Un souvenir de France.*" Rossbury saw the warm apples Elizabeth put in the bowl for the meal in the Martin's barn and then Elizabeth's hands cupped around it in Canivet's small stable in Le Havre.

"That's exactly what Miss Laurence said when Betty told me she'd found the bowl in Miss Laurence's room!" Lady Beatrice looked expectantly at Rossbury, who said nothing.

Frustrated, she turned to Lady Dorothy and explained, "The bowl, Dolly, was not mine although the pattern is the same as the Sèvres in my set. This piece is a memento that Miss Laurence brought back from France. And after Miss Laurence stated that a thief would scarcely place a stolen object in plain sight on a bureau, Betty had the grace to apologize."

"Knows how to keep her head, this Miss Laurence of yours, Beatrice. I like that. No swoons, no tears, no hysterics, no angry words." Lady Dorothy's head nodded with each item ticked off on her list. "I'd say she deserves a bit of help. This business at Eastons this morning, for example. It's bound to be spoken of. The crowd of ladies who were there are not about to keep a delicious little incident like that to themselves."

Rossbury agreed grimly. "It will be all over town by tomorrow."

"Tomorrow!" Lady Beatrice exclaimed derisively. "You have been away too long, Richard. The scene will be replayed over teacups this very afternoon!" And the accusation won't be the only part of the scene replayed, she thought, recalling Rossbury's hand covering that of Miss Laurence.

"But," insisted Lady Lewisham, "you and I, Beatrice, can squash it. Our morning calls on Wednesday. We both sing Miss Laurence's praises. A woman of impeccable integrity and all that. Never met anyone who could talk both of us down or turn a conversation we're determined to keep going. Remember that afternoon at Agatha Moreland's?"

The pair of titled conspirators exchanged grins.

"Besides Miss Laurence will accompany you to my party on the 28th," observed Lady Dorothy thoughtfully. "Cards and a little music perhaps."

"You never mentioned planning an evening party this month, Dolly," said Lady Beatrice.

"Well, I'm planning one now!" Lady Dorothy loved entertaining, and already her mind was sorting through what refreshments to offer. "You must admit that an invitation to one of my evenings carries a certain cachet with it. Slighting someone I've invited will be difficult even for the worst of our society tabbies."

Then the door to the morning room opened, and Elizabeth entered. Harris and a parlor maid followed, both carrying trays.

Rossbury rose to his feet. Lady Lewisham patted the sofa cushion at her side. "Miss Laurence, please sit by me."

Harris asked, "Where do you wish me to set the tea things, milord?"

"Godmother, would you like to pour?"

"If you don't mind having the tea in the saucers and over that beautiful uniform tunic of yours, I should be happy to. But if you want the tea in the cups, I suggest you let Miss Laurence pour," Lady Beatrice exaggerated.

Soon the business of arranging tables and the items on the tea trays was complete. Then Elizabeth began the ritual of asking each person how he preferred his tea. The two dowagers exchanged an approving glance. They held their delicate Meissen teacups while Rossbury rose to accept a cup of tea from Elizabeth's hands.

Next the tiered dessert plate was handed 'round, and the slices of Mrs. Ballantyne's seed cake were pronounced delicious. Only then did Lady Beatrice broach the subject on everyone's mind. "Rossbury told us what occurred in Easton's this morning. No doubt I shall be receiving an apology from Mr. Easton himself for the part his clerks played in this unpleasant little drama. Still returning to Eastons just now seems less than wise. Yet we must do something about your wardrobe."

"All I need is cloth, something better than this." Elizabeth glanced at the skirt of her dress and looked up with a shrug and a smile.

Rossbury set the cup in his hand on its saucer. "While I know you, Miss Laurence, are an excellent seamstress, I believe you would be better served by a modiste." Seeing Elizabeth about to protest, he continued, "The one I have in mind, Emìlie Villiers, is a recent French émigré. Her own small establishment has nothing in common with Eastons."

"Where is Mlle Villiers' shop, Richard?" Lady Beatrice removed the napkin in her lap and placed it on the table near her elbow.

"Out of your ordinary shopping orbit, I'm afraid. Mlle Villiers' customers are mostly merchants' wives and daughters." Rossbury handed his cup to Elizabeth to be refilled. "My proposal – if it suits you, Godmother – is to escort you all – Lady Dorothy also, if she would like to come – to Mademoiselle Villiers' after we finish our tea."

"That suits me admirably, Richard. Though I assume you'll not be staying with us as we look through pattern books and materials."

Rossbury could not suppress his grin. "As it happens, I've another appointment to keep. One to see some preliminary designs for Edward's stained glass memorial window."

Cheeky devil, thought Lady Beatrice. Knows I'm ready to cross-examine this French modiste and doesn't care what I find out. "Excellent! We can stay as long as we like." She ignored Rossbury and looked directly across at Elizabeth. "Men are never to be taken to a modiste's, Miss Laurence. They fume and fuss and tell you that you have been an age when barely five minutes have passed."

"I shall remember that, Lady Beatrice," said Elizabeth. "Though it seems that I'm the only one causing any fuss."

"Bit of fuss'll do me good," stated Lady Dorothy firmly. "Going to a modiste none of my acquaintances has ever heard of. Sure to be more interesting than morning calls during this time of year." She looked at Elizabeth as she finished her sentence. "Besides I want to be certain this new wardrobe of yours includes something suitable for my evening party on the 28th."

"But Lady Lewisham," protested Elizabeth, "I couldn't possibly accept an invitation to an evening party."

"Who's going to find me a chair out of the draft, separate me from long winded matrons and poor whist partners, fetch my wrap if I'm cold, find me something more fit to drink than that insipid punch Dolly always insists on serving, fuss over me, and report it all to Martha if you don't, Miss Laurence?" Lady Beatrice recited in a slightly waspish tone.

"Certainly not I, Godmother. Both Simon and I are leaving for Earl's Wood Park on Wednesday. I've much to do there." Rossbury finished his second cup of tea.

"A pity, Rossbury. The young Viscount Verinder would have been a welcome addition to my guest list. His new position, you know. Well, there's bound to be speculation. Especially by doting mamas," commented Lady Dorothy.

"That's another rumor we can scotch, Dolly." Lady Beatrice turned her head left to look at her godson. "A Shropshire girl – local gentry, if memory serves – has already captured his heart. Correct me if I am wrong, Richard."

"Your memory serves you well. Her name is Lucy Clare. She's the one drawing him to Earl's Wood this time." His smile was a bit rueful as he continued, "I have promised Simon that we shall both speak to Mr. Clare as soon as possible. And Simon has promised me that he will attend Cambridge and complete his studies before he makes any other plans for his life or Lucy's."

"Very sensible," approved Lady Dorothy, her head nodding twice.

Rossbury and Lady Beatrice exchanged glances. "Almost too sensible," added Rossbury. "Although if the war with France is a long one, as I fear it will be, then I shall pray that Simon continues to be sensible and does not seek a commission."

"Such a wish made by his father in uniform seems a bit odd." Lady Dorothy leaned forward, her curiosity piqued.

"Today is the last day I shall be wearing it," observed Rossbury. He rose and walked to the fireplace. "My resignation is official." He did not tell them of the reluctance with which it had been accepted. "After the General's dinner this evening, Mallory will, no doubt, inter it with its fellows."

"And a uniform of sorts is exactly what Miss Laurence needs," Lady Beatrice concluded. "And sitting here talking won't put any clothes into that empty armoire in her room."

"I concur." Rossbury reached for the bell pull and tugged on it once. "You certainly don't want Miss Laurence to arrive at your party looking like a..." He paused and repeated, "Like a..."

"Ragman's companion," Elizabeth said demurely as she placed her cup and saucer back on the tea table.

"Might raise a few eyebrows. Could even be interesting," noted Lady Dorothy.

"Interesting, yes, Dolly," Lady Beatrice inserted, "but we have raised enough eyebrows for one day, don't you agree, Richard?"

Before Rossbury could reply, Harris reentered the morning room in response to the bell. "The ladies will be needing their cloaks, Harris."

"If you are leaving us at Mademoiselle Villiers', why don't we travel in my carriage?" offered Lady Dorothy. "It will accommodate four easily."

"Agreed," said Rossbury at once, realizing that the Lewisham carriage would be of no interest to Tyler. "Harris, please ask Lady Lewisham's coachman to bring her carriage around."

After Harris left to relay the order, Lady Dorothy wondered aloud as she rose from the sofa, "Going to a new modiste is a bit like placing a wager – exciting but risky. I hope we are not disappointed, Bea." Preceding the others, she walked towards the door.

Rossbury reached for the door handle. "I don't think you will be, Lady Dorothy. In fact, my wager is that you will be very pleasantly surprised."

"Daughter, come quickly!" Pere Villiers' voice was excited. "A carriage with a coat of arms on the door has stopped in front of the shop!"

Emìlie Villiers darted through a narrow door into the front of *Maison d' Villiers.* Her father, a stoop-shouldered man with dark eyes that missed little, then retreated behind it.

Mlle Villiers smoothed her pale brown hair arranged simply in a low knot on her neck and shook out the full skirt of a becoming but modest moss green gown. She stared at the door, wondering if these aristocratic customers would be anything like her family's former employer.

Years earlier, the Duc du Lantier had kept the entire Villiers family busy, Pere Villiers and his son Jean Jacques tailoring suits and constantly adjusting seams and waistbands for the Duc and his three sons, Madame Villiers and her daughter Emìlie creating the latest fashions for his wife and their two daughters.

Then in the early spring of 1789, the du Lantiers traveled to their villa in Italy for a three-month stay. Among the servants left behind at the Lantier chateau were the Villiers. But the Bastille fell in July, and the du Lantiers did not return. And long before the autumn months, the result of the Duc's youngest son brutal attack upon Emìlie on the eve of the Lantiers' departure made the Villiers fear the fanatical local revolutionaries.

The family had fled to London. There the family's luck changed when M. Villiers became lost, his questions in French mere gibberish to those passing by. Then a gentleman had stopped to help. Seen M. Villiers to the family's single room apartment, heard their story, and lent them the money to start *Maison d' Villiers.*

A loan we have already repaid. By doing a bit of everything, Emìlie thought. Basic tailoring, millinery, and even home furnishings, like table drapery and matching cushions.

Emìlie glanced around the shop. A gleaming wooden counter separated shelves stocked with bolts of material and cards of various trimmings and pattern books from the parlor-like front of the shop. Since *Maison d' Villiers* occupied a northeast corner of the street, light entered the shop from the two south-facing windows on either side of the door as well as a west-facing window. In each corner near the front of the shop was a small table draped with a floor length cloth of lemon-colored muslin. The three chairs at each table were cushioned in matching material.

It looks well, Emìlie thought. Then the door opened, and a smile of recognition lit her face, "*Bon jour*, Colonel Verinder." Emìlie stepped forward to greet the man who had lent her the means to begin her business.

Rossbury removed his hat and made the introductions, the modiste replying politely to all three women and not showing her surprise at Elizabeth's frayed sleeves and hem.

"As you can see, Miss Laurence requires a new dress," stated Lady Beatrice without further ado. "More than one new dress."

When Elizabeth opened her mouth to object, Lady Beatrice laid a hand on her arm. "I'll not have you going 'round looking like – what was the phrase you used this morning?"

"I believe it was 'ragman's companion,'" Rossbury answered, with a glance at Elizabeth.

"Yes, so it was," Lady Beatrice said. "And it won't do, as, I'm certain, Mlle Villiers would agree."

"I'm certain she would, Godmother. And so I shall leave you in her capable hands."

Moments later, Rossbury was gone, and Lady Beatrice picked up the thread of conversation he had started. "I don't know how much my godson knows about dressmaking, Mlle Villiers, but I'll wager those capable hands he mentioned are experienced in putting together a wardrobe," she said with a look at Elizabeth who, she knew, was concerned about cost, "that won't strain limited resources."

The modiste understood at once what was wanted. "Fabrics already on my shelves. Designs," Mlle Viller's picked up the latest copy of *La Belle Assemble* and set it on a nearby table, "from a pattern book such as this one." She looked at Elizabeth as she spoke as saw the signs of worry disappearing from her face.

"That sounds perfect." Elizabeth's smile was immediately reflected in Mlle Villier's face.

Lady Beatrice nodded her approval. "However, Mlle Villiers, I am also considering ordering a new gown myself. Something for an evening party on the $28^{th}$."

"Can't have you showing me up at my own party, Bea." Lady Dorothy looked at some bright blue material peeking out from the other side of the counter. "That means I'll have to order something, too."

Emìlie Villiers was struck dumb for a moment. A companion's wardrobe. Evening dresses for two titled ladies. All seen by others. And perhaps admired, she thought as she invited them to be seated at the table. "I can modify any design in this book or even sketch an original design for you."

As they seated themselves, Lady Dorothy said, "I'd like to see an original design, wouldn't you, Bea?"

"Three, Mlle Villiers," added Lady Beatrice, motioning towards Elizabeth. "Let's make the $28^{th}$ something special."

Emìlie's heart beat faster. "*Certainement*!"

"However," concluded Rossbury late that evening in Lady Beatrice's boudoir as he finished relating what he had learned from Bardstow, "I believe that I am Tyler's real target."

Seeing Rossbury grimace as he shifted his weight and leaned more heavily against the fireplace, Lady Beatrice wordlessly cursed the General. Dratted man and his dratted reports. Kept Richard an hour after the others had left.

"Do you think Tyler will follow you and Simon to Shropshire?" Lady Beatrice asked.

"No. From what Bardstow said, Tyler's finances will keep him close to Bardstow's townhouse here in London."

"If that young ne'er-do-well thinks he can besmirch reputations with impunity, he'd best think again." Lady Farnsworth clenched her fists in a most unladylike fashion. "No one of any consequence will believe the miserable whelp, Richard."

"Bardstow said as much this morning." Rossbury picked up the Meissen shepherdess and twirled it in his fingers without seeing it.

"He's right, you know, Richard. In fact, no one will give any more credence to Tyler's ravings than to those libelous newspaper accounts a decade ago."

Rossbury did not ask to which accounts she referred. The headlines remained etched in his memory.

"Have I your permission to lay a few of the details before Dolly?" asked Lady Beatrice as she rose stiffly from her chair.

"Yes, of course." Rossbury limped over to where his godmother stood. He saw that her anger was spent. Her shoulders sagged in spite of her attempt to maintain an upright carriage. "I'm counting on the two of you to scotch any rumors that reach the drawing rooms in your sphere."

"And our sphere includes everyone who counts for anything, Richard." Lady Beatrice stifled a yawn. "Don't worry about rumors. Dolly and I will put paid to them."

"I know you will." Rossbury saw that Lady Beatrice could barely keep her head up. "And now, Godmother, it's time I took my leave and allowed you to go to your bed."

"You're the one who looks in need of a good night's sleep, not I, Richard!" Lady Beatrice straightened with an effort.

"I shall concede that point, Godmother, without argument." Rossbury moved toward the door and opened it. "I'd hoped to be here earlier, but the General...."

"And Bardstow before him. There's always someone." Lady Beatrice complained as she walked into the hallway.

Rossbury followed her into the hall. "Thank God, Barstow came to me. He could have said nothing."

"Yes, he could have." Lady Beatrice turned to Rossbury and said a trifle waspishly. "Be thankful he didn't take a page from your book."

"But…"

"But me no buts, Richard. It's the truth, and you know it. Keep too much to yourself!" Lady Beatrice glared at Rossbury with a fierce, protective look.

"It's to…"

"And don't tell me you're trying to spare me from fretting, Richard," Lady Beatrice cut across Rossbury's attempt to speak as the two neared the stairs. "Being left in the dark…that's enough to make anyone fret!"

"Don't fr-," Rossbury began, then stopped. "You'll fret no matter what I say."

"Not if you give me no reason to!" She lifted her cheek for the kiss she knew was coming.

"I'll do my best, Godmother." Kissing her affectionately, Rossbury added, "Good night, and thank you."

"I don't want your thanks, Richard. I'm tired and want my bed." Lady Beatrice put her hands to Rossbury's chest and pretended to push him towards the first step. "Off with you!"

"I'm…"

"Don't! Don't!" Elizabeth's desperate cries rang out from her room and stopped the words in Rossbury's mouth. The fear in her voice startled Lady Beatrice.

Rossbury whispered, "Beth." Then he dashed awkwardly down the hallway. Lady Beatrice followed.

Outside his godmother's best guest room, Rossbury heard a thump followed by a muffled sob. Without hesitation, he opened the door. The interior of the room was so dark that, at first, he could see nothing. "Beth?"

Muffled sobs were the only reply. Tangled in the last remnants of her nightmare as well as the sheets and coverlets from the bed, Elizabeth huddled on the floor.

His eyes straining against the darkness, Rossbury groped his way forward. When his outstretched hands met the tangle of bed linens half dragged from the four-poster bed, he bent to find Elizabeth.

Wresting a blanket from the pile, Rossbury lifted Elizabeth into a sitting position. "Another nightmare, wasn't it?" He put the blanket around her shoulders.

Rossbury backed towards a chair he had touched when he crossed the room. He sat, his arms still cradling Elizabeth.

Elizabeth leaned into him and grabbed the front of his dress uniform tunic with her trembling left hand.

"Beth," Rossbury whispered, "he cannot hurt either of us. He's dead." Closing his eyes, Rossbury rested his cheek against Elizabeth's hair loosely bound for the night in a long plait. "And that's what makes it so awful."

Outside, Lady Beatrice listened. Heard her godson call her companion Beth. Again. Heard him say, "He's dead." She adjusted the door. Left it open – just a crack for modesty's sake. Then she turned to see Martha and Mrs. Featherstone hovering at the far end of the hall.

"Only an unpleasant dream. Miss Laurence is fine and resting peacefully now as all of us should be doing." Lady Beatrice pulled the door a fraction of an inch towards her. Then she strode back towards her own room.

As Martha detached herself from the cook who turned towards the servants' stairs at the far end of the hall, Lady Beatrice ordered in a tone designed to carry, "Martha, please tell Dunhill to lock up if he hasn't already."

Without a word, Martha descended the stairs.

She'll be up in a minute to see me to my bed, thought Lady Beatrice. And expect me to tell her everything. While Richard will leave the way he did when he was a boy. Lady Beatrice entered her room and heaved a tired sigh. That means Martha must go back downstairs in half an hour to lock the French window in the morning room.

For a few minutes, Rossbury simply held Elizabeth in his arms, saying nothing. Then as the frightened galloping of her heart steadied, he said, "Your nightmare. You've had it before."

Elizabeth shook her head and burrowed deeper into the front of Rossbury's tunic. "It's…" she began haltingly before shaking her head again.

"I'm a good listener, Beth. Trust me." Rossbury waited for Elizabeth to begin. When she didn't, he remembered the fear in her voice as she shouted his name and linked it to her cry in the deserted barn near Tancarville. "It's LeBeau, isn't it?"

Elizabeth relaxed her grip on Rossbury's coat and closed her eyes. He doesn't know, she thought. Doesn't know it's… Elizabeth would not name the man from Rouen even in her thoughts. Him and…

"I'm running," Elizabeth whispered at last. "From something. From someone. Then I see his face grinning, his mouth opening and closing. I can't understand what he's saying. There's only his face. Angry. And threatening. Like he was in the barn." Elizabeth swallowed, the nightmare scrolling forward in her memory. "His face comes closer. I try to back away from it, but I can't."

When Elizabeth paused again, Rossbury's arms tightened about her. Poor Beth, he thought. Even in sleep, she tries to run from a dead man.

"Then just as his face is about to touch mine, I realize he is behind me." Elizabeth bit her lip. But the man she felt behind her was not LeBeau. It was Sir Augustus Tremaine, the man she had run from five years earlier. And it was his cool calculating eyes she felt behind her.

Elizabeth began to shake again. One in front, the other behind. In her nightmare, she was hemmed in, trapped.

"There is nowhere to run. And then hands are grabbing for me. And he is falling. And, and I know that if he touches me..."

Elizabeth's voice broke on a sob. "If he touches me, I will fall, too."

Elizabeth pressed her hand to her mouth and squeezed her eyes shut. "I try to back away, but I can't move. Then he screams. And suddenly I'm falling …" Did I shout his name aloud, Elizabeth wondered, as I do in the nightmare?

"And I scream – because I am falling..." Elizabeth's voice dropped to a mere breath. "With him." Elizabeth shivered. "And he's dead. Because of me."

Darkness pooled around them, each of them recalling the night in the ruined barn. And the man who had fallen to his death.

"In my first action in America," Rossbury said at last, "I was a raw untried lieutenant. It was only a skirmish, not a battle. We were marching when we were attacked, the rebels faceless enemies emptying their muskets into the column. By the time we formed a line, the rebels had begun to melt into the trees. We were ordered to pursue them, so we did. We charged a group of them. Probably some sort of rear guard. Overwhelmed them in seconds, and my sword nearly decapitated a lad who was about the age I was when I first joined the army. He had light brown hair and freckles across his cheeks, and his mouth was open in a scream he never had time to utter.

"That boy was the first person I killed. And when I looked at his blood on my sword, I was sick. Literally, physically sick. I had no time even to stumble behind a bush before I embarrassed myself in front of all my men. And I have never forgotten the contempt on a corporal's face afterwards or the agony in the boy's eyes."

"You?" Elizabeth asked while Rossbury's stillness hinted at the clarity of his nightmare faces.

"Yes, me," Rossbury admitted quietly. Sighing, he added, "Causing a death and remaining untouched..." He shifted his body slightly so that her weight was not upon his right leg which was beginning to throb. "And then there are the questions you ask in the middle of the night."

"How did you...?" Elizabeth blurted out. Then before she completed her question, she answered it. "You've asked them yourself."

"Who hasn't? Questions laced with fear because we do not know ourselves as well as we thought. Questions about pain, suffering, and death. Questions without answers. Questions that frighten us even to think about. They are a part of any brush with violence and death, and they raise doubts about what, at other times, seems so certain. Right and wrong, purpose, meaning, even God."

And now, thought Rossbury, is not the time to explore any of them. With reluctance, he rose and carried Elizabeth to the four-poster looming large in the shadows a few steps from his chair.

"I'd best say, Good night," Rossbury, stated simply, unwilling to refer to the cry that had brought him at such an improper hour to Elizabeth's room. Then he bent to gather the sheets and coverlets that trailed from the bed.

"Yes," Elizabeth agreed quietly, tired now but as reluctant as Rossbury to end their conversation. After Rossbury pulled the bed linen into some semblance of order, she added, "Thank you."

Elizabeth felt Rossbury's lips brush her forehead, listened as his footsteps reached the door, heard his promise, "We shall speak of this again" before the latch clicked. And although she believed the thoughts circling her head would keep her awake until morning, within minutes of Rossbury's departure, she slept, the nightmare a phantom of the past.

# CHAPTER 11
# TUESDAY, FEBRUARY 19, 1793

"Your affectionate sister, Elizabeth." Elizabeth put down her pen and read the letter she written to her brother Gideon while Lady Farnsworth napped. As she did, she realized that she must rewrite the letter. Again. She looked at the pieces of paper on the floor and sighed. "How am I to find out what I need to know, Gideon?"

"I wish I had the answer for you," replied Rossbury. He had entered the morning room of Farnsworth Place a moment earlier and soundlessly closed the door behind him. "Or knew what the questions are."

Elizabeth rose hurriedly from the writing table. "I hardly know myself, Lord Rossbury," she said, a little less than truthfully.

Rossbury crossed the room and glanced down at the paper he had seen Elizabeth's head bent over when he entered. "You are writing to your brother, I gather."

"I am."

"And having some difficulty." He motioned towards Elizabeth's previous attempts now lying at her feet.

"Yes." Elizabeth picked up the letter. "And this, too must be rewritten." She folded the letter in quarters, and dropped it to the floor.

"Perhaps not."

Rossbury's calm disagreement brought Elizabeth's eyes to his face. "I could wait a bit longer, but there are things that I need to know, things..." She trailed off, unwilling to say anything of her brother's neighbor at Throck Manor. "Perhaps," she continued, speaking her thought aloud, "I should simply tell Gideon that I have returned to England and accepted a position as companion to Lady Farnsworth."

"And," Rossbury added quietly, "that you have been offered a new position, one I hope you will accept."

"A new position? Who would offer me another position?"

"The position – Countess of Rossbury; the offer – mine."

Impossible, Elizabeth thought at first. He wants me to be... The word hung before her, tinged with amazement. His wife! Elizabeth was filled with joy so singingly sweet she ached with its sudden appearance.

Rossbury watched as Elizabeth's emotions chased one another across her face and smiled at her small, voiceless 'O.' Realizing that happiness had robbed her of the power of speech, he stepped towards her, his arms raised and welcoming.

Immediately Elizabeth walked into Rossbury's embrace, her left hand seeking his shoulder, her right half-circling his waist, her head nestled against his chest as his own arms held her close and his cheek rested against her hair. She whispered, "Richard." Her use of his name was all the answer Rossbury needed.

Much as he enjoyed holding Elizabeth in his arms, Rossbury knew he had much to discuss with his newly betrothed wife-to-be and little time to do it. Taking Elizabeth's hand, he led her to the Hepplewhite sofa angled before the fireplace. Once they were seated, his left arm gathered Elizabeth close to his side. She leaned into him and put her right hand into his, a response that touched his heart. Her next words confirmed the promise of her actions.

"But it's Lent."

"It is." Rossbury understood that this apparent non-sequitur was a complaint. Marriages could not be solemnized during Lent. "But the recentness of Edward's passing necessitates some postponement." Rossbury continued quickly before Elizabeth could apologize for forgetting his bereavement. "Never fear. Edward would not have begrudged me this. Nonetheless, we must wait until after Easter. That means sometime in April."

Easter Sunday was March 31, Elizabeth easily recalled. And suddenly her time in Chichester Cathedral only eleven days earlier sprang to her memory. "Wednesday, April 3."

When Rossbury looked puzzled, she added, "The feast day of St. Richard."

"Of Chichester." Rossbury thought about the city that had sheltered them on their return to England and its thirteenth century bishop. "We share a name, but unlike him, I am no saint."

"Living with a saint would be quite uncomfortable. I would rather live..." She hesitated, not wanting to seem too bold, then ducked her head and added shyly, "With Richard Verinder."

Rossbury raised her hand to his lips and then threaded his fingers through hers as his hand carried hers to his side. "I am glad to hear it. Yet now that my family's title – with its all its honours and responsibility – has been thrust upon me, you must also live with the Earl of Rossbury."

Raindrops pattered against the windows of the morning room. For a moment, neither spoke, content to savor a warmth that owed nothing to the fire burning in the grate.

At last, Rossbury pressed Elizabeth's hand and said, "You will find Earl's Wood full of people who need you, as I do." His voice caught on the phrase. "People of all types, from villagers, tenants, servants, and labourers to neighbors; people of all ages – from old retainers to families and children."

"Children!" Elizabeth murmured.

"One of Simon's first remarks," Rossbury noted lightly, "after I told him of my intentions this morning, touched upon that very subject. He appears to think that having a young sibling would be rather..." He paused as he tried to remember his son's wording. "'Jolly' was, I believe, his term."

"And do your son's thoughts reflect your own?"

"'Jolly' is not the word I would have chosen," Rossbury admitted. "Nevertheless, it will do nicely until we can think of a better one. Perhaps in a setting and a time more conducive to such reflection."

"Indeed? Have you a setting and a time in mind, Richard?"

"Indeed," Rossbury echoed, "I have. And I shall reveal all in due course. But I believe we should discuss the wedding itself before moving on to other more interesting arrangements." As Elizabeth leaned against him, Rossbury pulled his mind away from those 'arrangements' and focused on the list of details he had mentally organized before coming to Farnsworth Place that afternoon.

"You are right, of course, but..."

"<u>But</u> is a horrid word; let us agree upon that."

"Yes," Elizabeth answered. "And I have been distracting you with talk of..."

"Oh, it is not your talk which has provided the distraction, Beth."

"If you say so, Richard."

"I do say so. Now may we move on to the wedding plans?"

"Yes."

Much as Rossbury enjoyed their word play, the next day would see his departure for Earl's Wood Park, and he knew that he had much to do before the start of his journey.

"Edward's death makes a lavish ceremony out of the question. Yet everything still must be done properly."

When Elizabeth nodded but said nothing, Rossbury continued. "That means having the banns called…"

"At St Etheldreda's," Elizabeth interrupted suddenly, "by the Reverend Mr. Souther."

"Souther," Rossbury repeated. The Reverend Mr. David Michael Souther and he had enjoyed several discussions over the years during his irregular sojourns at Rossbury House. Rossbury respected the middle-aged clergyman who had come to his priestly vocation after an earlier stint in the military. "I'll speak to him today, that is, unless you would prefer your home parish."

Images of the Reverend Mr. Jeremiah Cuthbertson, the vicar at St Mark's in Little Throckton when Elizabeth left England in 1788, surfaced. And standing behind him in her mind's eye was Sir Augustus Tremaine, for the incumbency was in the baronet's gift.

"Hampshire is no longer home." Elizabeth thought, That's the truth, at least. "And St Etheldreda's," Elizabeth hesitated, then added, "is a place we both know."

"Then your brother must come to town in April. I shall write to him at once."

The title alone will be enough to secure Gideon's consent, Elizabeth thought. "Gideon may decide to bring his family with him. My nephew Peter will be at school, but his wife Felicity and his two daughters will welcome the chance to come to London." Elizabeth recalled her oldest niece Emma and smiled.

"A simple ceremony, held after morning prayer, with your brother's family, and, of course, Godmother, and Simon in attendance." As Rossbury visualized Elizabeth and himself standing before the altar at St Etheldreda's, one person appeared to be missing. Grantleigh, he thought immediately. He was about to mouth his best friend's name when he recalled Grantleigh's continuing grief over the death of his wife Louise. I'll write first, he thought, saying instead, "And perhaps Simon's tutor John Naismith. He arrived at Rossbury House last night with Simon. You'll meet him tonight at dinner."

"And I'll meet Simon," added Elizabeth.

"And Simon," Rossbury affirmed, "though the two of you won't have much time to get to know each other." He hesitated a moment before continuing, "Simon, as well as Naismith, will be accompanying me to Earls' Wood. We leave tomorrow morning, I'm afraid. Urgent estate business for me, and a visit to Piers Clare for Simon."

"About Miss Lucy," Elizabeth said, recalling what Rossbury had related the day before.

"Since he and Lucy are barely seventeen, Simon will ask Clare only for a 'formal understanding,' as he calls it, rather than an engagement."

"Very proper," noted Elizabeth. "Unlike Simon's father."

"Oh? Are you saying, Miss Laurence," Rossbury queried, "that it is propriety I lack? Are you suggesting that I imitate my son, unsay my offer of a quarter of an hour ago, and apply first to your brother?"

"No!"

"I thought not, Miss Manners." Rossbury struggled to appear stern. "Instead I shall pen an elegant epistle to Mr. Gideon Laurence, Esquire of..."

"Of Hopeden Hall, Little Throckton."

"In Hampshire," Rossbury finished. "And most earnestly request the honour of his sister's hand in marriage on the 3rd of April at St Etheldreda's."

"Very proper," noted Elizabeth for the second time.

"Unlike some of my actions yesterday."

"You were..." Elizabeth began to disagree. Then she recalled his hand covering hers as they had exited Eastons together. And the time spent alone last night. And, she glanced around the morning room, once again they were unchaperoned.

"However, society's notions of propriety have not guided my actions today, Beth."

"No one could ever make me believe they had." Elizabeth's heart swelled with love.

"However, I admit my original intention was to wait until April to speak to you and to suggest a summer or even an autumn date. But certain events of yesterday cast a different light upon the matter."

Elizabeth blushed and edged closer to Rossbury.

"Consequently," Rossbury finished, "the reasons for delay seemed trifling while those for immediate reaction became pressing."

Because this comment did not call for a reply, each spent the next few moments lost in contemplations neither cared to reveal to the other.

Finally, Elizabeth asked, "One of those pressing reasons was your departure for Shropshire tomorrow, wasn't it?"

"Yes."

"I…" Elizabeth paused and completed her thought softly, "I shall miss you."

"You do see the necessity of the journey, don't you, Beth?" Rossbury took both her hands in his and turned her towards him.

"Of course, I do, Richard," Elizabeth answered. "Yet…"

"A betrothal followed by an immediate separation looks suspiciously like the erstwhile groom has had second thoughts about the whole business!" Rossbury rose to his feet and slammed one fist into the other. "Blast!"

Rossbury paced to the French window that opened onto the square. Its leafless trees and sodden aspect now echoed his mood perfectly. His leg was aching again, the activity of the past days and the cold, damp of a London February taking their toll. I thought of everything except how others might view my absence.

Elizabeth joined him at the window. She bit her lip, considering how to lighten Rossbury's mood. "Perhaps Lady Farnsworth will occupy my time so completely that I shan't have a moment to miss you, much less to consider whether you and Simon have decided to roam the countryside, incognito, in a cart to determine what your neighbors think of the new Earl and the young Viscount."

Retaking her hand, Rossbury brushed the backs of her fingers with his lips in silent thanks. "Then perhaps I should warn Lady Beatrice to guard her wardrobe if she is unable to occupy your time well."

"Oh, do you think setting up a market stall is too impractical?" she retorted. "I thought Lady Farnsworth and I could form a more effective partnership than a certain ragman and..."

"Wretch!" Rossbury pulled Elizabeth into his arms. "I must insure that you have too much to do in the coming weeks even to suggest such escapades to Lady Beatrice, who – heaven forbid– might encourage them."

"Indeed? You would pile more labors on the back of a poor over burdened woman, would you?" Elizabeth pulled away from him, placed her hands on her hips, and attempted to look angry.

"Of course!" Rossbury countered. "First," he said, using his fingers to tally his points, "there is the matter of letters. Yesterday you gave me an assurance regarding correspondence and I intend to hold you to it."

"Happily."

"Next," Rossbury listed as a second finger was lifted, "is the matter of purchases you may now want to make." And seeing the word no forming on her lips, he rushed on. "No objections from you. This morning I spoke to a director at my bank and set aside £500 in your name."

Her eyes grew wide at both his forethought and generosity. "Were you so certain of my response?"

"As certain as I am of my love for you."

To this simple confirmation, Elizabeth could only murmur, "Richard!"

After he was able to refocus his thoughts, Rossbury raised a third finger, "Finally, there's the matter of a wedding trip. I thought that the first evening..." The intimacy his words suggested made him pause.

"That beautiful room with the Poisson!"

How Elizabeth knew about the bedchamber, Rossbury did not know, and his voice was husky as he replied, "Yours if you want it, Beth."

"Mine?"

Elizabeth's question puzzled Rossbury until he realized what it implied. "Ours."

The glow in her eyes told him that the closeness they had shared in France was not something simply born of fear but of a deeper need that would be consummated with their nuptials.

"Ours," Rossbury repeated firmly. "However, after the first evening, we can go..."

"Home."

Home, he knew, meant not her brother's house but Earl's Wood Park, the house Elizabeth would turn into their home.

"Are you sure?"

"There is but one thing of which I am more sure."

Rossbury had not thought she could surprise him and was touched to discover he was wrong. "And if, Beth, I should require corroboration?"

"I should be most happy to provide it, Richard."

Then back within the arms waiting to encircle her, Elizabeth gave and received proofs of love that both found more than satisfactory.

A quarter of an hour later Martha stood outside the door of Lady Farnsworth's boudoir and saw Rossbury and Elizabeth in the hallway.

"Lady Beatrice is asking for you, Miss Laurence." Martha was relieved that a trip down and up the stairs was unnecessary. With a nod at Elizabeth's "Thank you, Mrs. Pearson," Martha continued down the hall.

As Elizabeth opened the door to the boudoir, Lady Beatrice asked, "Did you finish the letter to your brother?"

"I shall be writing to Gideon Laurence," answered Rossbury as he entered the room behind Elizabeth.

Lady Beatrice barely prevented herself from exclaiming, 'Already!' Instead she waved Elizabeth into a chair and waited for her godson's next words.

"I have asked Miss Laurence for her hand in marriage and she has done me the honour of accepting." After moving the dressing table bench next to Elizabeth's chair, Rossbury sat down and reached for Elizabeth's right hand.

They will tell me none of what I really want to know, thought Lady Beatrice. Not even if I sit with this foolish look on my face for the next hour. Lady Beatrice recalled the words she had overheard the previous night: 'He can't hurt either of us. He's dead.' Something happened in France, and it's forged a bond between them. And neither of them will tell me a thing about it.

"The only surprise here is your timing, Richard," Lady Beatrice remarked at last. "I was anticipating some sort of announcement by summer."

Elizabeth turned towards Rossbury in surprise. But Rossbury simply gazed at his godmother with diplomatic blandness and said nothing. Maddening! Lady Beatrice thought before asking, "Have you set a date?"

"April the 3rd," noted Elizabeth at once.

The date surprised Lady Beatrice in a way the announcement had not. Had her godson chosen to be married on the anniversary of his baptism? She remembered standing at St Giles' font beside her best friend – Lady Constance Verinder, Countess of Rossbury – nearly thirty-eight years earlier. Constance had blessed the coincidence that allowed the christening of her second son Richard Sinclair Verinder to occur on the feast day of St Richard of Chichester. St Richard! Lady Beatrice repeated to herself. Of course, Miss Laurence chose the date. Look at her. She leans towards Richard like a flower turning towards the sun.

"Congratulations, Richard. I am very happy for you both."

"Thank you, Godmother."

"However, introducing Miss Laurence into my household for a week and then sending her back home to prepare for a wedding seems unfair," Lady Beatrice teased

"We shall be married at St Etheldreda's after morning prayer," Rossbury said.

"Does that mean that Miss Laurence and I will have all of the work of planning everything while you and Simon are amusing yourselves at Earl's Wood?"

"I'm afraid it does. But the ceremony will be a simple one, and I shall do as much as I can by letter from Earl's Wood."

"And are you still intending to be gone a month, Richard?"

"Yes. I doubt that what must be done at Earl's Wood can be done in less time. But I should be back just after the banns are read for the first time."

Lady Beatrice turned towards Elizabeth. "That will give you time to gather a wardrobe that will set my godson back a guinea or two."

"Richard has already set aside £500 for the purpose. He has spoken to..." Elizabeth looked at Rossbury who supplied, "Mr. Elliott of Tellson's Bank."

Lady Beatrice nodded. Elliott, known for his discretion, was her banker, too. I wonder, she thought, what ideas whirled through his brain when Rossbury gave him that order!

"So when I return to Mlle Villiers, it will be to prepare a..." Trousseau! The word seemed so unreal Elizabeth was unable to say it.

"Trousseau," finished Lady Beatrice helpfully. "You can also increase your order tomorrow when we go to look at her designs."

"But, I've already ordered three, and..."

"My dear Elizabeth, you'll triple that order, at the very least, if I have anything to say about it!"

And seeing Rossbury's nod of approval and Elizabeth's look of dazed happiness, Lady Beatrice said, "That's settled then." She rose from her chair, Rossbury immediately doing the same, Elizabeth standing as well. "And unless you have more surprises for me, I shall do what I should have done a half hour ago – check on the arrangements for dinner this evening."

"This godson of mine, Elizabeth," continued Lady Beatrice as she walked towards the door, "seems too accustomed to giving orders. Yesterday it was about dinner here this evening. Ordering invitations for two more as Simon and his tutor John Naismith are now at Rossbury House. Today it's wedding plans. Tomorrow..." Lady Beatrice put her hand on Elizabeth's arm and drew the younger woman to her side. "Who knows what demands he'll make."

Although Rossbury knew his godmother was teasing, he put on a penitent face that did not deceive her in the least, bowing low as she and Elizabeth passed through the door into the hallway.

"You really are impossible at times, Richard." Lady Beatrice shook her head and sniffed her apparent disapproval. "I cannot think why I put up with you."

"Nor can I, but I am glad that you do." Stepping between the ladies, Rossbury took his godmother's left arm and Elizabeth's right and escorted them towards the stairs.

"Then make me glad that I do, Richard," riposted Lady Beatrice. "by giving us time to make our preparations for this evening by going home and making yours!"

Because he wanted to compose a letter to Gideon Laurence before he dressed for dinner, Rossbury allowed himself to be hurried away. "Your wish is my command, Godmother. Until this evening then."

After a quick but warm grasp of both Elizabeth's hands in his, he hastened down the stairs.

Elizabeth gazed wistfully at his retreating back. But her sigh became a chuckle when Lady Beatrice hurled her departing demand down the stairs.

"And make certain that all three of you are dressed properly and arrive on time!"

That evening the three gentlemen from Rossbury House arrived punctually. Each was suitably attired, all looking as if they were ready to be presented at court. One delectable dish after another came from Mrs. Featherstone's kitchen to the dining room. Conversation at the table flowed so freely that the gentlemen limited themselves to one glass of port before joining the ladies in the drawing room.

"If you'd like, I will accompany you," offered John Naismith after hearing Lady Beatrice's request for a song and Elizabeth's assent.

Simon Verinder found himself astonished once again on a day that seemed to be full of surprising events. Never before had Naismith volunteered to accompany anyone.

Simon recalled the early morning conversation with his father at Rossbury House as he watched Elizabeth and his tutor walk to Lady Farnsworth's spinet. Father's announcement was so unexpected that I didn't know what to say and so I made that inane comment about a possible sibling. And then I started thinking about how I could prevent the marriage. I was sure Miss Laurence was a fortune-hunter who only wanted a title and a large bank account. A golden ringleted, befrilled, simpering hoyden only a few years older than I.

Now as Elizabeth and Naismith looked through the music lying atop the spinet, Simon noted again the simply dressed brown hair and shabby gown so at odds with the mental picture he had conjured up that morning. Instead of the coy smiles and false modesty of his imagination, he had found a forthrightness and serenity that made conversation easy. And then, as Lady Farnsworth and Elizabeth were leaving the dining room, he had intercepted the glance of pure adoration Elizabeth had cast at his father. I felt like an interloper. Thank God, I didn't tell Father what I thought this morning.

Fool! Simon called himself for the third or fourth time that evening. You ought to have had a bit more faith in Father.

Then as John Naismith began playing an introduction to "Caro Mio Ben" by Giordani, Simon recalled Elizabeth's initial reaction to his tutor. She gave him the same warm smile she gave me when we were introduced. She saw beyond his scars to the man behind them.

For splinters from a caisson's explosion had scored the right side of Naismith's face into a mass of livid, shining red brands. His disfiguring scars had cost him the woman he loved, caused him to resign his commission, and turned him into a hermit in his elder brother's home. Only the request of a former fellow officer, that he serve as his son's tutor, had drawn Naismith out of his self-imposed seclusion.

And tonight, this woman who will soon be my stepmother has drawn Naismith out of another kind of seclusion, thought Simon.

The Italian words of the song erased all other thoughts for the next few minutes.

*...Caro mio ben*
*Credimi almen*
*Senze di te, languise il cor.*

However, Simon noted that before the last line retarded, the eyes of both singer and accompanist met and that Naismith's head nods served to mark the tempo.

"Lovely!" Lady Farnsworth's simple compliment after the music ended brought Naismith to his feet. As the three listeners applauded, Naismith extended his hand to Elizabeth. The curve of her lips as she placed her hand in his hid none of the repugnance or pity often seen behind the forced smiles on the faces of other ladies meeting him for the first time.

After the two musicians bowed together, Lady Beatrice asked, "Perhaps you will give us another?"

"What say you, Miss Laurence?" asked Naismith while turning to face Elizabeth.

To his question, Elizabeth replied easily, "Of course."

As Elizabeth and Naismith conferred upon what piece to perform next, everyone present had his own version of the same thought in mind: that the future for the newly betrothed couple would be a happy one. Elizabeth and Naismith's choice of "Fairest Isle" by Purcell as their second selection served to confirm that conclusion.

# CHAPTER 12
# SATURDAY, FEBRUARY 23, 1793

"I'm ruined! Ruined!"

Disheveled and wigless, Gideon Laurence slumped disconsolately over his desk as Sir Augustus Tremaine entered his study.

"Surely, it's not as bad as that, Laurence," said the baronet. "Your note said to come at once, that the matter was urgent, not a catastrophe."

"But it is! Because she's come back! Come back and ruined me!" Gideon pushed the paper he'd been staring at to the edge of his desk. "Read it yourself."

Sir Augustus picked up the letter, looking first at the signature. Rossbury, he noted. Without seeing the other words on the page, he concentrated on the name. The memory of a recent obituary clicked into place.

"Elizabeth is back from France – God knows how she managed it – and staying in London. At the home of this, this," Gideon groped for the name, "this Rossbury's godmother!"

Tremaine found the name – the Dowager Marchioness of Farnsworth! He read on quickly, motioning at the same time for Gideon to continue.

"And he wants to marry her," Gideon moaned. "Says I must come to London. For the wedding! There will be a request for her dowry! His solicitor will want to speak to mine! And if I say nothing about, about…" Gideon gulped convulsively. The terms of Catherine Calvert's will loomed before him. "If I say nothing about it," he finally said in despair, "that damned solicitor of hers, that…" The name fled as thoughts of charges of perjury, theft, and prison pummeled his conscience.

"William Clewett." Tremaine filled in the name while scanning the rest of Rossbury's letter.

"He will read the betrothal notice or someone he knows will read it and, and…" The door of the prison his brain had conjured up clanged shut. "I'm ruined." Gideon put his head in his hands. Title to the bank of England stock had already been transferred and used for collateral for several small loans. Clewett, like all solicitors, had filed Gideon's letter – of that he was sure. Proofs of his unethical and illegal actions were everywhere, actions an earl was unlikely to excuse or forgive.

"There will be no betrothal announcement in the *Times* until Rossbury returns from Earl's Wood Park in Shropshire to Rossbury House in London." Tremaine had read Rossbury's letter thoroughly. He saw the trap Gideon feared had an unlocked door

Tremaine's assurance brought Gideon's head up. "Yes, Rossbury asks me to write him there, but--"

Sir Augustus interrupted. "A busy man like yourself has other obligations more pressing than this letter." Rossbury's brother died last year, he recalled. Rossbury will have much to occupy him on his estate and in his local solicitor's office. If no letter arrives from Hopeden Hall immediately, its absence won't be noted for some time. By the time Rossbury does notice, it will be too late. He smiled. When he looked again at Gideon, his neighbor was staring at him.

"But the wedding date is--" Gideon began.

"April 3rd. Over five weeks away." Tremaine saw Gideon's look of confusion. Dolt, he thought. A man should never forget the power he exercised over women. Particularly the women in his own family. Sir Augustus dropped the letter onto the desk and strolled to the fireplace. His eyes narrowed. Having power over a woman like Elizabeth Laurence would be... Not now, he told himself, tearing his mind from the thought of subjugating the woman who had dared to reject him. He turned his back to the fire and waited for Laurence's next but.

"But he expects me to give–"

"Give your consent?"

"No." Gideon's brain finally started working. "He said nothing about that. Though I am Elizabeth's brother."

"Her closest male relative – acting in lieu of a father."

"That's right, I am," noted Gideon slowly. "But what reason could I give for refusing an earl's offer?"

"That is your trump card," observed Sir Augustus with slight impatience. "And you may never have to use it. For now, go to London. See the sister you have not seen in years. What could be more ordinary than that? And because you are concerned about Elizabeth's happiness, inquire about the suitability of the man who has offered for her hand."

Gideon, still at sea, burst out, "But he is suitable so what good–"

"And," Sir Augustus cut across Gideon's words as if the other man had not spoken, "then escort Miss Laurence to her home. Here. Because, naturally, you want your sister to be wed at St Mark's at Little Throckton. A request – perhaps, a demand – she cannot deny you."

"But how will that help? Mr. Cuthbertson will be only too happy to officiate at the marriage of an earl!" exclaimed Gideon in exasperation.

"He'd be happier, I think, to officiate at the marriage of a baronet." Cuthbertson, Sir Augustus knew, would do whatever he was told.

"But Elizabeth doesn't..." Gideon stopped abruptly. He didn't want to remind Sir Augustus that Elizabeth had rejected him years ago and would, no doubt, do so again – particularly after having had an offer from an earl.

"Miss Laurence will be guided by her brother who has her best interests at heart," Sir Augustus inserted smoothly. "And we will convince her that her best interests lie in a marriage closer to home."

Suddenly Gideon understood Tremaine's plan. The conversation they'd had at the end of January replayed itself. And since marriage to Tremaine erased the threat of prosecution for fraud, Gideon was only too happy to help himself by helping Tremaine to what he wanted: Elizabeth.

"I shall go to London on Monday." Gideon stood up and began to gather up various papers strewn over his desk. Rossbury's letter in hand, he looked up to see Tremaine, his fingers outstretched, standing directly before him. Without a word, he gave Tremaine the letter.

"Monday will do nicely." Sir Augustus walked to the hearth and tossed the paper onto the flames. When he turned back towards Gideon, he found the other man still fussing over his desk. Cold, stone dark eyes raked Gideon's stocky figure. "You will tell no one here, Laurence, about the receipt or the contents of that letter."

"Of course not," protested Gideon, thankful that his earlier fear had made Tremaine his sole confidante.

"While you are in town, perhaps you can take care of a few small commissions for me." Laurence, Tremaine considered, could hand deliver some letters. And as Gideon was always strapped for cash, the letters would be an excuse to give him the funds he'd need. "You'll be saving me a trip so, of course, I'll contribute to your traveling expenses."

"Only too glad to help a friend." Gideon's chest swelled with importance. Sir Augustus had never trusted him with any of his business in the past. And Tremaine's assistance with expenses was a godsend. "A friend who will soon be a relative."

"Indeed." Being kin to Gideon Laurence was the only drawback to the whole business Sir Augustus saw. Yet there were also more than sufficient compensations. Elizabeth and Rosemont, he gloated. For Catherine Calvert had willed Rosemont to Elizabeth, and Elizabeth would soon be his wife. And a wife's property becomes her husband's, Tremaine thought, the corners of his lips lifting briefly. "Indeed, I shall."

Gideon saw what passed for a smile on Sir Augustus' face and felt it spelled approval. His chest swelled a bit more. Tremaine, he convinced himself, would make an excellent husband. Any qualms, raised by certain phrases sometimes linked to Tremaine's name, were shoved aside.

"And as a friend and future relative, perhaps I may be permitted to give a bit of advice about..." Sir Augustus waved his tapered fingers in Gideon's direction. "About how to make the most of your appearance."

Gideon stood a bit straighter. Looking down at his clothes for the first time that day, he realized that he had been too upset to dress properly. Embarrassment flooded over him. "Your advice would be very welcome."

"Your decision to stop wearing a wig suits you." Tremaine knew Gideon had merely forgotten to put one on, but throwing a sop to his neighbor's pride cost him nothing.

Gideon preened a little. A footman had brought the post to him while he was still in bed. Rossbury's letter had sent him into a maelstrom of anxiety. Dressing was a blur. Once safely in his study, he had scribbled an urgent message to Sir Augustus and then remained there, staring at Rossbury's words, until Tremaine's arrival. However, after he ran a hand over his hair and recognized its uncombed state, his bubble of pride burst. "Do you really think so?"

"Dress it simply, perhaps tie it back in a queue." Sir Augustus gazed appraisingly at Gideon. He must appear, Tremaine considered, a well-to-do country gentleman. "Use a sober coloured ribbon that matches your coat." Then as if adding an afterthought, Sir Augustus appended, "And tell your man to pack your most modest waistcoats."

"I will." Gideon almost gushed in his eagerness to show his appreciation. "Thank you."

"And since you are going to London on business of mine, one of my traveling carriages will take you there." The second-best coach should do nicely, Sir Augustus told himself. "But don't take your man with you. You can stay at my townhouse on Hanover Crescent. Inchcomb will see to all your needs."

Gideon's eyes widened at the prospect. He had been to the baronet's small but fashionable London home only once. "That is very generous, Sir Augustus."

That Gideon Laurence thought generosity ever played a role in his plans brought another twitch to Sir Augustus' lips. Inchcomb, the townhouse's permanent man of all work, would be Tremaine's assurance that Gideon did not lapse into bad habits as well as his eyes and ears.

"Once in London, a call at Farnsworth House to congratulate your sister must be your first order of business."

Gideon listened carefully. The disaster he feared was becoming a pleasurable stay in Tremaine's townhouse and a chance to control the sister who had thwarted his wishes.

"And after I offer my congratulations, I'll tell her how eager Felicity and I are to plan her wedding. Here at her own parish church. A wedding all of her family and friends want to attend."

"Exactly."

Eager to show Sir Augustus that he understood his part, Gideon continued, "Then I'll bring her back to the Hall and..." Suddenly a vision of Felicity and Elizabeth together in the same room crystallized. It was not an encounter that boded well for any of them. "And then..." Gideon stumbled, unable to see what would happen next.

"Leave all the rest to me."

Sir Augustus' statement brought Gideon's eyes back to his neighbor. But the baronet, studying the beautifully manicured fingernails of his left hand, appeared oblivious to Gideon's scrutiny.

Elizabeth will never return to Hopeden Hall, Sir Augustus calculated. His coach would bring her to an out-of-the way inn where an overnight stay would decrease her options to one. Imagining the lessons he would teach the only woman who had ever refused him made Sir Augustus burn in anticipation.

Some instinct warned Gideon not to question Sir Augustus further. It's only right that Elizabeth marry the man I've selected for her, he told himself. "If I am to travel to London on Monday, I must order my affairs here and set my man to packing my trunk."

"Of course, you must," replied Sir Augustus smoothly. He had plans of his own to make as well as letters to write. That these plans would take him west to Gloucestershire rather than north to London was something Gideon need not be told.

Both men headed for the door. Once in the corridor, Sir Augustus announced, "And thank you, Laurence, for your willingness to complete those commissions for me while you are in London. I shall deliver the necessary papers tomorrow after morning worship at St Mark's if that suits."

"I am always pleased to oblige a neighbor," replied Gideon as the two men walked towards the entrance hall.

"I am especially grateful for your offer to go up in my traveling carriage so that Townsend and Sons can refurbish the interior." As Tremaine reviewed his plan, it seemed flawless. His coachmen, he knew, would follow his orders.

While one servant scurried off to have Sir Augustus' horse and conveyance brought around and another to fetch his hat and outdoor coat, the two men shook hands in the entrance hall. Yet as Sir Augustus murmured polite words of farewell, he was estimating how many days would pass before he and Elizabeth's brother called upon the Reverend Mr. Jeremiah Cuthbertson to arrange a hasty and very private wedding.

It's beautiful!" Elizabeth smiled at her reflected image. She was trying on the first of the dresses Mlle Villiers was making for her – a gown suitable for social calls in a delicate shade of lavender, only its hems left to be finished

"Now let me help you into this," offered Mlle Villiers. She eased Elizabeth's arms into the jacket she had designed to complement the dress.

The front of the fitted jacket had a military look about it, Lord Rossbury's tunic having provided the idea. However, the collar and cuffs were soft and feminine.

"*Merci.*" Elizabeth admired the way the braid sewn on the jacket front accentuated the ingenuity of its cut. "*Merci beaucoup!*"

"*Je vous en prie, mademoiselle,*" replied the French seamstress. "*C'est un plaisir travailler pour celle qui admire mon travail.*" Miss Laurence, realized Mlle Villiers, has a good head behind that plain face. She knows this jacket was not designed and sewn in the last two days. "As companion to a Marchioness, you would have gone everywhere, your clothes seen and noted, a good advertisement for a struggling modiste. As wife to an earl, you will move in the same circles. But as a countess, your clothes will excite a little closer scrutiny, some admiration, and – I hope – a desire to visit the shop you patronize."

"If this ensemble is followed by more of the same quality," Elizabeth turned before the mirror to scan the set of the jacket's sleeves, "by summer you should be besieged with customers."

"I pray you are right," replied Mlle Villiers. "The quality of my designs – this I can control. The vagaries of fashionable ladies are far less certain." Mlle Villiers visualized the women upstairs in her workroom. "A business like mine needs customers."

"I will be one of them. For years to come, I hope."

"Then perhaps you would like to meet those in my workroom?" Mlle Villiers asked suddenly. "Seeing the lady they sew for will make their work *prendre vie*."

With Elizabeth's agreement, they were soon climbing the stairs to the floor above which served as a workroom during the day and living quarters for the Villiers family at night.

As they entered the south-facing room, the hum of voices stilled. Seated at various tables were four women. The oldest among them, Elizabeth guessed, was Madame Villiers. In one corner, a man bent over a length of rose-coloured material, a pair of long scissors in his hand. After he straightened and, with his forefinger, pushed his spectacles higher on his nose, he gazed approvingly at Elizabeth's dress. "*Très bien, ma fille.*"

Then a black-haired boy darted from where he had been playing with scraps of cloth near Madame Villiers. "*Maman! Maman!*" he shouted excitedly.

Emìlie Villiers ruffled the dark curls of her three-year-old son. "Alain, remember to use a small voice in the workroom."

"Yes, Maman." The child's brown eyes were bright and unabashed as he stared at Elizabeth. "She's in your dress."

Elizabeth leaned forward to look directly at the boy. "Yes, I am, Alain. And it's a beautiful dress, don't you agree?"

As Alain sought confirmation of what Elizabeth had said in his mother's face, a girl engaged in setting a sleeve whispered to her worktable companion, "Looks a treat on 'er, don't it?"

"It does, Mary." Mlle Villiers' sharp ears had caught the whispered comment. "You have all done your work well. And because you have, Miss Laurence has ordered a complete wardrobe." Mlle Villiers paused for a moment. "Actually, a trousseau."

Oh's of amazement greeted her announcement. Emìlie Villiers smiled at Elizabeth and then added, "Miss Laurence will soon be the wife of the Earl of Rossbury."

A reed slim woman barely past adolescence nudged the seamstress to her left. The side seam she had been stitching was momentarily forgotten in her lap. "Betty," she hissed, "does that mean these dresses we's makin' 'ere are for a countess?"

Betty, a large-boned Londoner whose stubby fingers had a deft touch for fine stitchery, replied, "What it means, Kate, is that there'll be plenty of work for the likes of us for weeks to come."

Awestruck by the romantic aspects of Elizabeth's situation and her own good fortune, Mary blurted out, "When's the 'appy day, Miss?"

Her impudence elicited a frown from Madame Villiers; but before anyone could reprimand the young sleeve-setter, Elizabeth replied, "April the 3rd after Morning Prayer at St Etheldreda's near Carlington Square."

"So we have only five weeks to prepare the trousseau of *Madame la Comtesse,*" Madame Villiers warned sternly. Four heads immediately bent over appointed tasks.

Once they had returned to the fitting room downstairs, the seamstress unhooked the tiny buttons at the back of the lavender dress. Moments later Elizabeth was once again wearing the faded garments she had worn as the ragman's wife.

"The women in your workroom seem happy," noted Elizabeth, picking up her cloak.

"They have employment. It is more than can be said of many." Mlle Villiers thought of her hours of work for the du Lantier family and the complaints and slaps that followed if so much as a single stitch was crooked. "And now they are part of our little family here at *Masion d' Villiers*. And when they are happy…" Her shoulders moving slightly in an elegant Gallic shrug, she continued, "…their work reflects it."

"I am glad. They are, after all, the ones who shall be converting my rather tattered appearance" – Elizabeth spread her arms in a self-deprecatory gesture – "to lady-like elegance, are they not?"

"However, you dress, no one could ever mistake you for anyone other than a lady, Mlle Laurence." The modiste opened the fitting room door.

"But one who needs a wardrobe." Elizabeth did not want to return to Eastons. "And a linen drapers."

"Such a shop is only two doors from my own," related Mlle Villiers without thinking. "But you may not find its goods suitable to your needs. The women who run it – Mlles Faith and Charity Plover – their customers are not – that is, they are…" She stopped abruptly.

"They are women who have the same needs as I do." Elizabeth moved quickly towards the street door. "Mlle Villiers, please tell Lady Farnsworth's coachman to go to the linen drapers when he arrives."

A few minutes later Elizabeth entered the Plovers' shop. Gleaming wooden counters and brass fixtures attracted her attention. Behind the counter a few drop-fronted drawers were open to display the merchandise housed within the large phalanx of storage drawers.

At one end of the counter stood a gray-haired woman. Her ringleted hair and frilly bodice did not suit someone of either her years or short stature. Her face like an unshaped lump of dough with two currant dark eyes was animated as she spoke to two customers.

"May I help you?" Miss Faith Plover summed up the new customer with one sweep of her tawny eyes. Tall and rail thin, she was the antithesis of her younger sister Charity, the woman who twinkled at the customers at the opposite end of the counter. Faith's ramrod straight posture, business-like attire, and severe hairstyle contrasted sharply with her sister's bows and curls.

"Yes, you may." Elizabeth placed a list she had written on the counter so that the woman on the other side could read it. "I need every item here."

Faith Plover's eyebrows raised a fraction of an inch as she scanned the paper.

"It's a trousseau, isn't it?" Miss Charity Plover, co-proprietor with her elder sister of the linen draper's shop, joined Faith in scrutinizing the list.

Elizabeth's slight blush answered the question even before she murmured, "Yes, it is."

"You'll find, Miss…?"

"Laurence," supplied Elizabeth.

"Miss Laurence," continued Charity Plover, "you will find we have stocked all the articles you require."

Charity's slightly wistful tone was, Faith Plover knew, the prelude to another attempt to sell the costly items purchased during Faith's sole absence from the shop in thirty-two years. "Charity," began Faith Plover, glancing again at Elizabeth's dress, "I think we should…"

"Excuse us for a moment, Miss Laurence." Charity bustled towards the bank of storage drawers. "Sister, could you assist me please?"

Inwardly fuming, Faith Plover followed Charity and bent low to help her sister lift the entire drawer at the bottom corner. The two then carried it forward and placed it on the counter.

In it were beribboned chemises, stockings that felt like gossamer, and delicate undergarments. As Elizabeth touched the exquisitely soft items, a little frisson of pure pleasure went through her. Wearing finery that no one could see but… The unbidden thought and her own boldness even to imagine it brought another blush to her cheeks. Charity Plover smiled approvingly.

"I am certain that…" began Miss Faith Plover.

"I shall take everything in the drawer." Elizabeth had observed that the items were small and knew those that did not fit would do so after minor alterations she could do herself.

The whole drawer! Faith shouted inwardly. A woman dressed as she is cannot afford a single item in it.

As Faith's lips framed the word "But," Charity remarked, "Of course, Miss Laurence. I knew these items would please you."

"However, I am unable to wait for you to wrap all these lovely things for me." Elizabeth knew the Farnsworth carriage would come at any moment. Lady Beatrice insisted upon punctuality, and her coachman would arrive on time. "Perhaps they could be delivered tomorrow?"

Hearing the hiss of indrawn breath that was a prelude to Faith's objection, Charity quickly answered, "Certainly, Miss Laurence. We shall need your direction, of course."

"Farnsworth Place, Carlington Square."

Before Faith Plover could echo Elizabeth's last four words, the door of the linen drapery swung inward. A liveried footman entered.

"Miss Laurence?" Matthews called a bit uncertainly, drawing the attention of everyone in the shop – including Charity Plover's original two customers who had remained near the windows to exchange news and gossip before going their separate ways. As

Elizabeth turned towards the voice, James Matthews recognized the woman he had been sent to find.

"Carriage's waitin', Miss Laurence." Then Matthews grinned cheekily. "An' I've been 'structed to report tha' a letter 'as arrived an' is waitin' on the morning room mantle – with your name an' Lor' Rossb'ry's seal on it."

His words sent Elizabeth hurrying towards the door.

"I look forward to your delivery tomorrow." Then, as Matthews opened the door, Elizabeth turned and smiled brilliantly. "And if you have any other items as lovely as those you showed me, please save them for me."

And on this promise of a return visit, the door closed behind Elizabeth and left four women's mouths shaped in identically perfect O's.

# CHAPTER 13
# WEDNESDAY, FEBRUARY 27, 1793

"There must be something," Tyler Hamilton-Smythe muttered to himself as he circled Carlington Square. "Something that'll convince Geoff that Rossbury's no saint."

He slowed his steps, recalling what he learned about Elizabeth Laurence. She's Rossbury's mistress. I know it. So's that Frenchie dressmaker. And her son's probably Rossbury's by-blow.

And tomorrow Patience will tell me all about the Laurence woman's engagements, he told himself with satisfaction as he passed Rossbury House. Useful little cow. Chatters constantly about all the 'doings' over at Farnsworth Place. He looked at the house across the square. Just then the front door opened, and he stopped to watch.

Gideon Laurence jammed his hat onto his head as he descended the steps of Lady Beatrice's townhouse. The smile he had forced onto his lips disappeared. He strode down the pavement without even thinking about where he was going.

Tyler Hamilton-Smythe observed the departing visitor with curiosity. His clothes said he was not a member of London society or the Farnsworth family. And a solicitor would be carrying papers. Who is he? Tyler wondered. Determined to find out, Tyler began walking in the same direction.

Unaware that he was being followed, Gideon fumed over Elizabeth's refusal to return home and be wed at St Mark's. If Rossbury's solicitor begins looking into Elizabeth's affairs... No, Gideon told himself, when he begins...

"Damn Elizabeth," he swore softly. Stopping abruptly, he looked back at Farnsworth Place. "And damn this Rossbury!"

As Gideon turned, Tyler cannoned into him.

"Excuse me," Gideon mumbled, recognizing the collision was his fault. "No insult intended, I assure you. I was... I was only... That is..." To tell a complete stranger that he wished the Earl of Rossbury in Hades was impossible.

However, Tyler scented an ally. "You said, 'And damn this Rossbury,' did you not?"

"I, I may have. What of it?" Gideon glared at Tyler.

"I damn him, too. He as good as murdered my sister, his late wife."

"Murdered!" gasped Gideon. "His wife, you say? But my sister..." Gideon's eyes narrowed. Getting Elizabeth to return home suddenly seemed possible again.

Her brother! Tyler gloated, blessing his good fortune. And no friend of Rossbury! "Let me introduce myself," Tyler said at once. "The Honourable Tyler Hamilton-Smythe, at your service." Tyler inclined his head slightly in Gideon's direction and waited for a reply.

"Gideon Laurence," supplied Elizabeth's brother. "Of Hopeden Hall, Hampshire."

Then affecting surprise and dismay, Tyler blurted out, "That deluded Miss Laurence Rossbury wishes to wed is your sister!"

"She is." Gideon looked back at Farnsworth Place for a moment. "A most contrary sister who ignores the advice of her brother." He returned his gaze to Tyler. The younger man was well-dressed, dark pantaloons and shiny Hessians visible below his fashionable, many caped greatcoat. "You say, Rossbury is, or was your brother-in-law?"

"Unfortunately, yes, though blackguard would be a better word for him. And now it seems that he's…" Tyler dropped his eyes, as if unwilling to say more. "There are rumors. Rumors about Rossbury and Miss Laurence. Has she told you how they met?" Tyler looked up, his anxiety real. Let him say 'No,' he pleaded silently.

"She has not. As I questioned her, we were interrupted by…" Remembering Lady Farnsworth's regal self-assurance as she overrode all his objections made Gideon angry all over again.

"The Dowager Marchioness of Farnsworth," Tyler filled in quickly. "Rossbury's godmother. She'd do or say anything to help him."

"That's her, interfering old gorgon!"

"Between the murder and these ugly rumors currently circulating about France, and about Rossbury's arranging for Miss Laurence's wardrobe to be made by his French mistress, the mother of his bastard son, well…" Tyler stopped when he saw Gideon's mouth gape and his face turn an ugly shade of red. Then he glanced up and down the street.

"This is no place to share such information," Gideon agreed. "But these rumors about my sister…" He hesitated, not wanting to appear too eager. "They are disturbing." He began to walk away from Carlington Square, Tyler keeping pace with him.

"Hamilton Place, my London home, is not far from here," Tyler stated as soon as the square was behind them. And Geoff's gone back to Stowe Manor so we'll have the house to ourselves, he thought. "We can speak freely there."

"And you'll share everything you know about Rossbury?"

"Everything."

A short time later, the two men stepped out of a hackney onto a quiet London street lined with townhouses. Hamilton Place was far less imposing than the houses on Carlington Square, but the shiny brass work of the knocker and the well-scrubbed steps told Gideon that this was the home of a man with capable servants, a man of some status. He nodded in satisfaction.

"Welcome to Hamilton Place, Mr. Laurence." Tyler ushered Gideon into the entry hall. Watley, one of the two servants in the house, took their coats without comment.

"A substantial tea, Watley, in the study." Tyler motioned his guest to the stairs at the rear of the hall. "Something warm, I think. And as soon as possible."

Watley watched Tyler and his guest mount the stairs. Mr. Laurence looks to be a different sort of gentleman from most of them the master's brother brings here, he thought. Then he turned to the door that hid the stairs leading down to the servants' hall and kitchen in the half-basement. As he opened it, he heard Tyler repeat, "As soon as possible, Watley."

"If you have not returned in an hour, I shall send Matthews to fetch you. London's streets are no place for you to be alone after dusk," Lady Beatrice replied to Elizabeth's observation that a brisk walk to St Etheldreda's and back might clear her aching head.

The two women stood in the entry hall of Farnsworth Place. Around them was a bustle of activity. Footmen carried in several parcels carefully wrapped by Mlle Villiers and one package from the Plovers' shop.

"An hour, no more," Elizabeth promised.

Elizabeth was still upset by Gideon's visit. She had expected her brother to write, not appear on the doorstep of Farnsworth Place. Throughout their time together, Gideon had harped on her duty to return to Hopeden. Fortunately, Elizabeth recalled,

Lady Beatrice joined us and told Gideon that we had another engagement

That appointment had been at *Maison d' Villiers.* There Mlle Villiers had eased Elizabeth into a gown designed for Lady Dalrymple's evening party. It was a vision in rose silk, the fitted bodice revealing the curve of neck and shoulders, the full skirt looped up over an under skirt in a complementary shade of pink. But the airlessness of the fitting room had simply added to the claustrophobic feeling tightening around Elizabeth ever since Gideon had entered the Farnsworth morning room.

"If she tried on all of these," Martha muttered under her breath, "it's no wonder her head aches." After she had handed two bulky packages to Betty, she observed, "Wardrobe like this needs taking care of."

Lady Beatrice had said the same to Elizabeth during the carriage ride back to Carlington Square.

Now feeling two pairs of eyes upon her, Elizabeth relented. "You are right, of course."

Lady Beatrice seized the opportunity to convince Elizabeth of the soundness of her change of heart. "A word, Elizabeth, before you go?"

"As many as you wish, Lady Beatrice."

Dunhill stepped to the door of the morning room and opened it.

Once inside, Lady Beatrice moved toward the warmth of the fireplace and then turned to face Elizabeth.

"If I must have a lady's maid," began Elizabeth immediately, "I should like to employ a young girl I can train."

"A most sensible idea," agreed Lady Beatrice.

"I also think promoting someone currently at Rossbury House would be good for morale."

"It would; there is no doubt of that. Servants are generally pleased to see one of their own receive preferment." Lady Beatrice smiled and asked, "Have you someone in mind?"

"Yes." The memory of the beautiful bedchamber that she and Rossbury would share was briefly linked to the name of girl dusting it when Mrs. Green had allowed her to inspect the room. "It's Downes as I recall. She is, I believe, at present only an upstairs maid, but..." The connection Elizabeth had formed between the startled young face and the lovely room could not be explained.

"I shall arrange an interview for the morning," stated Lady Beatrice. "If she is capable, she can begin her duties by helping you prepare for Dolly's party tomorrow evening." Lady Beatrice started towards the door.

"Thank you, Lady Beatrice." Elizabeth walked to the door and opened it.

"For what, my dear? Admiring your good sense?" Lady Beatrice passed through the doorway and reentered the hall. "Now you are eager for that brisk walk so be off with you."

Dunhill was alone in the hall. Elizabeth's cloak was draped over his arm, her gloves in his hand. As he gave Elizabeth the gloves, Lady Beatrice admonished, "One hour, no more."

"I assure you I shall be gone no longer." Elizabeth drew on her gloves. "I have a letter to complete."

Yes, your letter to that absent godson of mine needs its daily installment, remembered Lady Beatrice as Dunhill slipped Elizabeth's cloak over her shoulders. "You shall have plenty of time for your correspondence this evening. I am expecting no one." With Elizabeth attired warmly and ready to go, Dunhill opened the door that faced Carlington Square. "No one except you, Elizabeth, in one hour."

Impulsively Elizabeth turned and kissed Lady Beatrice's cheek before she hurried through the door and down the steps.

Noting his mistress' startled but pleased reaction to the familiarity, Dunhill stored the moment in his memory as one to be shared later in the servants' hall.

The bareness of the trees in Carlington Square and the feebleness of the weak winter sun did not prevent Elizabeth from finding the miniature park beautiful. She emptied her mind of everything except her enjoyment of the crisp air and the shadows cast by the tree branches. Taking long walks had been one of the pleasures of her years in Hampshire.

Elizabeth imagined the coming of spring in Shropshire and being shown its glories by someone who had grown up among them, someone who would, by then, be her husband. Then across that vision of Rossbury and herself rambling in a rural landscape came a vision from the past – one she had tried to forget. Sir Augustus Tremaine's intruding on her excursions and insisting upon escorting her home. Touching her and… She shivered.

Elizabeth's memories brought her to the door of St Etheldreda's. Nothing will make me go back, she told herself. Nothing.

The door separating narthex from nave thunked. Martyn Ballard looked up from the pile of music he was digging through on the organ bench. Here again, he thought, curious about the unseen listener who sometimes came during his afternoon practices and left before he finished.

Then finding the Stanley voluntary he wanted in the music stacked on the bench, Ballard placed it on the organ's music rail.

After his right hand pushed back the sandy colored hair that tended to fall over the left side of his face, he tucked both hands under his armpits to warm them. Whether in the nave or the organ loft, the chill of the stone church penetrated the bones of anyone who sat there for more than thirty minutes in winter. Having studied the music for a moment, he rubbed his hands together, flexed his fingers, and began to play.

From the last pew, Elizabeth let both the music and the beauty of the nave with its timber trussed ceiling drive out the anxieties caused by her brother's appearance.

Then the voluntary that had filled St Etheldreda's with its joyous rhythms finished with running eighth notes in the bass and a magnificent final chord. "Don't leave," Martyn Ballard called out, "before I introduce myself. I'm coming right down."

As soon as Elizabeth walked into the aisle, the door to the nave opened. Within its frame was the organist – perhaps ten years Elizabeth's junior – with unruly hair, eyes the color of sherry, a crooked nose, and a wide, generous mouth curved in a smile of welcome.

At the same time, Martyn Ballard saw a petite woman of some thirty odd years wearing a beautifully tailored afternoon dress of pale lavender and a matching jacket, a cloak folded over her arm.

"It's as cold here as it is in the loft." Ballard rubbed his hands together to try to warm them before offering Elizabeth one in greeting. "I'm Martyn Ballard, the organist here at St Etheldreda's."

Elizabeth put her gloved but cold right hand briefly into Ballard's. "And I am Elizabeth Laurence."

Ballard observed, "You must be as bone-chilled as I am."

"And so you are wondering what draws me here on such a cold day? The sublime nature of the place or the music?"

"Pardon me, Miss Laurence. And let me assure you it wasn't vanity that prompted me to meet you but curiosity. Mr. Souther has warned me that mine..." The youthful organist stumbled over his apologies. "Well, that doesn't matter. What does is that St Etheldreda's is a house of prayer and I have disturbed yours."

"No," Elizabeth insisted, "it is I who disturbed you. Practice requires concentration and solitude. And I have allowed you neither."

"Miss Laurence, I must contradict you," Ballard replied immediately. "I have a lesson to give in half an hour. That is the only disruption."

Although Ballard's words were obviously sincere, Elizabeth admitted ruefully, "Yet it seems disrupting church organists seems to be something of a habit of mine lately."

"Who else?" Ballard's curiosity betrayed him into blurting out before the memory of the Reverend Mr. Souther's warning could stop his tongue.

"Mr. Marsh who, like you, was good enough to insist that some unsolicited accompaniment was no disruption."

"Although I cannot speak for Mr. Marsh, I can assure you that your presence here has not been a distraction. And please, don't let anything I've said stop you from returning whenever you like."

"I won't," promised Elizabeth. "Thank you, Mr. Ballard."

The interior of the church darkened suddenly. The sun, which had been stroking the top of a west-facing stained glass window of the Conversion of St Paul disappeared behind a neighboring structure.

Turning to face the door, the organist observed, "I must be going."

"I also," replied Elizabeth.

Pausing in the narthex, Ballard inquired, "Do you require an escort?"

Outside, the light was fading rapidly, Elizabeth's features a blur in the gloom of the church's interior.

"Your offer is kind, Mr. Ballard, but unnecessary. Farnsworth Place is only a few steps away. But thank you for your concern."

Then with a polite 'good evening,' Elizabeth settled her cloak over her shoulders and left.

Ballard hurried up the stairs into the loft. No wonder she looks familiar, he told himself as he gathered some music. She's Lady Farnsworth's companion, the one Mr. Souther says will be wed here.

He picked up his engagement diary from its place atop another pile of music and scanned its pages. On April 3rd to Lord Rossbury! And she has heard Marsh. Most likely in Chichester Cathedral, Ballard considered while he pictured his more accomplished fellow organist. The two had met twice and carried on a sporadic correspondence.

Music gathered under his left arm, Ballard headed back towards the stairs. "'Unsolicited accompaniment,' Miss Laurence said." As he spoke the thought aloud, the meaning of the ambiguous phrase struck him. He halted at the top of the stairs. A bold idea surfaced in his mind. Why not? All he can do is refuse.

Having decided to write John Marsh that every evening, Martyn Ballard sped down the stairs. He had a music lesson to give first.

# CHAPTER 14
# FRIDAY, MARCH 1, 1793

Her arm jostled by another customer, the three volumes in Elizabeth's arms thudded to the floor of Stanfield's Bookshop.

"Pardon me," the young man said at once. Then he bent to pick up the books lying at Elizabeth's feet.

The afternoon sun angled through Mr. Stanfield's large windows and gilded the auburn hair of Elizabeth's book rescuer with gold. "These are unusual for a..." Realizing that he had nearly committed a *faux pas,* he halted. His embarrassment was evident in the abashed look on his angular face with its startlingly green eyes.

"For a lady?"

"Most women of my rather limited acquaintance would have selected *Romance of the Forest.*" Seeing Elizabeth smile, he added, "Not for you the castles, chains, and cloaks of Mrs. Radcliffe then?"

"I'm afraid not. Though I do like Mrs. Burney." Elizabeth walked toward the front of the bookshop as she spoke, the young man keeping pace with her.

"Mrs. Burney cannot be compared to ..." He glanced at two of the books he held. "Fielding and Sterne."

When they reached the front counter, Phillip Stanfield looked up, a book in his hands, a smile wreathing his face. His uncombed hair like a white halo atop his head, his perpetually stoop-shouldered posture, and the small square-lensed reading glasses perched near the tip of his nose made him appear like a friendly gnome.

"Mr. Farquhar," he beamed, "I have here your Adam Smith. Is there anything else I can assist you with?"

"There is, Mr. Stanfield."

The elderly bookseller's pale blue eyes regarded him patiently.

"The name of this lady."

"Bless me, you've not been introduced?" Mr. Stanfield's eyes twinkled. "Let me do the honours then," he said as Elizabeth and Farquhar turned towards each other. "Miss Laurence, allow me to introduce the Honourable Nigel Farquhar." After a fractional pause, he added, "Mr. Farquhar, Miss Elizabeth Laurence."

The two nodded politely in acknowledgement, Farquhar struggling to recall why Elizabeth's name sounded familiar.

Stanfield took Elizabeth's books from Farquhar and read the titles with interest. "Earl's Wood," he noted, "has a fine volume of *Tristram Shandy*. The late Earl was rather fond of Sterne."

"Was he?" Elizabeth took the Sterne and set it to one side. "And what other authors might I expect to find in his library, Mr. Stanfield?"

"A better question might be what authors might you not expect to find."

As Stanfield spoke about Edward's Verinder's collection and the volumes that had flowed from the bookshop to Earl's Wood over the last twenty years, Farquhar remembered where he'd heard Elizabeth's name.

Only two days earlier, Sir Godfrey Carruthers, second cousin to his uncle, Lord Somerville, had visited the Marquis. An inveterate gossip, Carruthers had shared what he'd heard about the 11th Earl of Rossbury. In reply, his uncle had snorted derisively.

"Scurrilous nonsense. Don't know where you hear such tales, Godfrey. If you're wise, you'll not repeat them. I have known the Verinder family all my life. And I tell you the only mistake Richard Verinder ever made was marrying that Hamilton-Smythe beauty. Wasn't her brother Tyler who told you this taradiddle, was it? I can see from your face it was. I shall remind you, Godfrey, that Rossbury is still a colonel on the general staff. His being in France and returning with this Miss Laurence will turn out to have all the makings of a heroic tale, if we ever know the truth. In the meantime, consider Godfrey, that time in the not too distant past when your son was branded as a libertine by those who love tittle-tattle?"

His recollection faded when Stanfield said, "So the other two volumes will be fine additions to the Earl's Wood library, Miss Laurence, for I never could interest Edward Verinder in novels by Mr. Fielding or verse by any of our modern poets."

"I believe it is not unusual for someone to be fond of literature but care little for verse," replied Elizabeth.

"Tell that to young Mr. Farquhar here!" Mr. Stanfield chuckled. "He would debate that point with you. In fact, I am surprised he has not interested you in a volume by Mr. William Blake."

"William Blake?" Elizabeth repeated. "Should I add another book to those on the counter, Mr. Farquhar?"

"Yes, you should, Miss Laurence. *Songs of Innocence* is," Farquhar began excitedly before holding up his right hand as if to stop himself. "No, I shall say nothing more. You shall judge for yourself."

As Gideon Laurence huffed towards Stanfield's Bookshop, his anger grew. Three times in the past two days he'd gone to Farnsworth Place to talk to Elizabeth. And three times he'd been turned away. In the morning, Elizabeth was interviewing a lady's maid. Later, she was resting and needed to be fresh for an evening engagement!

Then this afternoon, she's not at home. She's gone out! To a linen drapers owned by an imbecile, he told himself, remembering the flutings of Miss Charity Plover. At least, the older one recalled that Elizabeth intended to visit a bookshop. And gave me its direction.

Gideon pulled open Stanfield's door and glowered at Elizabeth's back as she chatted to Nigel Farquhar.

Mr. Stanfield saw Gideon enter. "May I be of some assistance, sir?" His question caused both Elizabeth and Farquhar to half turn towards the door.

Gideon ignored the bookseller and glared at Elizabeth. "Information which is most disturbing has come to my attention." He ground the words out from between his clenched teeth. "It is imperative that I speak to you immediately."

Elizabeth, embarrassed by her brother's behaviour, stepped to his side and forced a smile onto her lips. "Gideon, I should like to introduce the Honourable Nigel Farquhar and Mr. Stanfield. Mr. Farquhar, Mr. Stanfield – my brother, Mr. Gideon Laurence."

Gideon remarked curtly, "Farquhar, Stanfield, pleased, I'm sure. Now Elizabeth, we must go." Turning on his heel, he headed towards the door, certain that Elizabeth would follow him.

"Your books, Miss Laurence?" Mr. Stanfield motioned towards the stack on the desk behind him. "I'll have them delivered to Farnsworth Place later today."

"And I shall speak to my uncle, Miss Laurence, and arrange a time." Farquhar had proposed a visit to William Blake's engraving shop followed by refreshments in his uncle's London residence. Farquhar believed that his uncle, a rheumatic who was often in pain, would enjoy Miss Laurence's company.

"Thank you." Elizabeth smiled once again. "Thank you both."

Because Gideon had already left before Elizabeth reached the door, Farquhar hastened forward and opened it for her. "Thank you, Miss Laurence," he emphasized with a slight bow.

A light touch on his arm, another smile, and a swish of skirts, and Elizabeth was gone.

Farquhar strode back to where Mr. Stanfield stood, his anger at Gideon Laurence's rudeness plainly visible on his scowling face.

"The less said about that, the better, Mr. Nigel." Mr. Stanfield bustled about his desk. "Ah yes!" He picked up a paper and pushed at his glasses with one ink-stained finger. "Your uncle's list. I believe I have these in stock." He laid the list back on the desk. "Some new books and soon a visitor who loves them as much as he does. That will brighten the Marquis's day, won't it, Mr. Nigel?" Stanfield asked, his pale blue eyes twinkling under silver eyebrows. Anger dissipated, Farquhar grinned and nodded in agreement.

As soon as the morning room door at Farnsworth Place closed behind Gideon and Elizabeth, Gideon erupted. "The man you propose to marry is a murderer!"

Elizabeth paled, for Gideon's last word caused LeBeau's scream and the thud as his body broke itself in the undercroft of the barn outside Tancarville to echo in her mind. How did Gideon find out? Elizabeth asked herself before realizing almost in the same instant that he couldn't have.

"A murderer, Elizabeth!" Gideon repeated before Elizabeth could speak.

"Impossible!" What has Gideon been told? she wondered. Knowing he would tell her if he were angry enough, she asked tartly, "Who gulled you into believing this pack of lies, Gideon?"

"Who, Sister? The Honourable Tyler Hamilton-Smythe, his brother-in-law. Rossbury did tell you that he'd been married before, didn't he?"

"His son, Viscount Simon Verinder, was a guest at Lady Farnsworth's table on the 19th of last month."

"Nevertheless," Gideon hissed, "I'd wager that no one at the table told you Rossbury practically murdered his wife, Simon's mother."

"Practically, Gideon? Is Lord Rossbury accused of murdering Lady Verinder or not?" Elizabeth's eyes blazed with challenge.

In spite of himself, Gideon flinched. "He expected Lady Verinder to play nursemaid to him at Earl's Wood Park," he blustered. His brain groped for words. A phrase Tyler had used drifted into his memory. "To dance attendance on him at that great mausoleum of a house in Shropshire."

Her back stiff with tension, Elizabeth looked skeptical and willed Gideon to continue.

"Rossbury was involved in that stupid war with the American colonies where, no doubt, he acted the gallant soldier, dallied with the ladies, and enjoyed a bit of freedom from the confines of marriage." Gideon placed his hands behind his back and began pacing the carpet in front of the cold grate. "Yet during his absence, he expected Lady Sarah to sit idly alone at home and await his return."

Elizabeth remained silent and motionless, her lips pinched together, not wanting a word or movement to stop Gideon from telling her all he knew. Or thinks he knows, she considered.

"By war's end, he was laid up with a trifling leg injury. Demanded that Lady Sarah closet herself twenty-four hours a day in the sick room with him. Even wanted everyone to treat him as sort of war hero. Humph! If he had acted more like one when he was in those damned colonies, perhaps the war would have been won rather than lost! Well, imagine what sort of husband he'd make, Elizabeth."

Gideon darted a look at his sister. Elizabeth's look of horror convinced him she saw the situation as he did. Gideon resumed his pacing.

"Of course, Lady Sarah refused to meet such unreasonable demands. She fled to London to escape Rossbury's tyranny – fully believing that Rossbury would join her in town." Gideon paused, anticipating an interrupting question from Elizabeth. But when none came and another glance showed him that she now stood statue still, wide-eyed and aghast, her hand held to her mouth in a gesture of dismay, he continued.

"But Rossbury preferred to play invalid. Complaining that the scratch he'd received while playing soldier did not allow him to leave his bed. Naturally the unhappy Lady Verinder, without a husband to guide and protect her, fell into some unfortunate company and, and..." Gideon fumbled for the phrase Tyler Hamilton-Smythe had used earlier. "Then a tragic accident caused her premature death." Tyler had not elaborated upon this accident so Gideon merely reiterated, "A tragic accident that would never have occurred if Rossbury had cared for Lady Sarah as he should have." His pacing halted, Gideon glared at Elizabeth as if daring her to contradict him.

Stunned by the portrait Gideon had presented, Elizabeth remained speechless.

Convinced that his sister was properly appalled by his tale of marital failure, Gideon barely prevented himself from smiling. "Afterwards, to avoid the scandal, Rossbury went to France where he resumed his dalliance with..."

Too late Gideon realized that he should have left this part of Tyler Hamilton-Smythe's story unsaid.

"With me, Gideon?"

Elizabeth's low voice and matter-of-fact tone caused the fury within Gideon to boil over. He spat out, "Do you deny the two of you returned from France together? How Claire Mansard could have allowed that..." He moved his hands in a gesture of abhorrence, his mouth working as if something distasteful were in it. "I told you no good would come of your stay in her house!"

"Aunt Claire is dead, Gideon." Without realizing it, Elizabeth had backed away from Gideon as he spilled out his malicious account of Rossbury's first marriage. Now feeling the satinwood writing table behind her, Elizabeth gripped it with both hands.

"Dead?" he repeated. "But you never said..."

"You never asked. Not about Aunt Claire or Uncle Léon." Tears sprang to Elizabeth's eyes as memories of her beloved aunt returned. "Aunt Claire died on the day before King Louis XVI was executed in Paris." She paused. Letting Gideon absorb the implications of the two events.

"Feeling against foreigners – particularly those from England because of our support of the monarchy – was high. Uncle Léon had Aunt Claire's funeral to plan. But perhaps, Gideon," Elizabeth speculated calmly, "you would have preferred him to plan two funerals. Aunt Claire's and mine."

Elizabeth's level gaze disconcerted Gideon. Her question was too close to the truth. "No, no," Gideon assured her. "Of course not. Undoubtedly you had to come home." Determined to regain the offensive, he bombarded Elizabeth with a series of questions. "But why not with some other Englishwoman? Another woman would have made a more appropriate traveling companion than Rossbury. And what was Rossbury's business in France anyway? Unless his business was my sister and the rumors about the two of you are true!"

"There were no other English women in France, Gideon. And none of the women I knew wanted to travel to a country France would soon be at war with. And after Uncle Léon met Lord Rossbury..." As Elizabeth said these words, a picture flashed across her mind. Léon Mansard and Rossbury shaking hands when she returned from gathering clothes upstairs and her sense that some secret had been shared. Uncle Léon knows who Richard is. Richard told him!

"Mansard met Rossbury?" repeated Gideon Laurence incredulously.

"In his own house," confirmed Elizabeth. "Where Uncle Léon accepted Lord Rossbury's offer to escort me home. Especially as Lord Rossbury knew a ship captain willing and able to take an extra passenger aboard his vessel to England."

Gideon opened his mouth to speak, but no words came.

Elizabeth watched Gideon's features as he understood that she and Rossbury had not returned to England alone. She was thankful that her brother had forgotten Léon Mansard lived in Rouen, some distance from the coast.

"As for Colonel Lord Rossbury's business in France" – Elizabeth's underscoring of the military title caused Gideon's eyes to goggle and his jaw to drop – "I can only suggest that you speak to Major Fitzhugh Gresham. He met us at Sergeant and Mrs. Craddock's home in Chichester. Or perhaps to the man the Major referred to as the General on whose staff Lord Rossbury served."

Elizabeth's catalog of military officers dumbfounded Gideon. Tyler had said nothing of Rossbury's continuing military service, and Gideon had believed that Rossbury's stint in the army had ended with his return from the war with the former American colonies.

"And you will recall, Gideon, that my own residence in France began years after the American colonial war had ended." Elizabeth released her grip on the hard surface of the desk and walked toward the Hepplewhite sofa. She sank gratefully onto its cushions.

Elizabeth's last statement puzzled Gideon. He screwed up his face in an effort to recall exactly when Elizabeth had left for France. "1789, no, 1788. Yes, 1788, that's right, isn't it?"

"Impossible then, is it not, Gideon," observed Elizabeth, her stomach clenching at the nature of the rumor apparently circulating, "to have resumed a 'dalliance' supposedly begun with Lord Rossbury before the war with the American colonies?"

"Well, perhaps that was an exaggeration," blustered Gideon.

"Exaggeration is hardly the word to describe a lie, Gideon."

"Humph! Well, if I see young Hamilton-Smythe again, I shall inform him that the lady in question is not my sister. But there is still Rossbury's treatment of Lady Sarah Verinder, his late wife."

Gideon started to pace again, thought better of it, and took a seat on a chair opposite the sofa on which Elizabeth sat. "Rossbury's behaviour was..." Gideon groped for words. "Well, it was definitely outside the bounds of what most would expect from a husband."

"It was, indeed."

Surprised by Elizabeth's apparent agreement, Gideon could only mumble, "Yes, quite. Outside the boundaries of ordinary expectations. Glad that you see that, Elizabeth."

"It was certainly outside the bounds of what you would expect as a husband."

"Thank you, Elizabeth." Gideon smiled.

Elizabeth rose from the sofa, forcing Gideon to stand as well. Turning her back on her brother, she walked towards the window. However, she saw nothing of the square outside. "During the second December of your marriage, you expected Felicity to remain at Hopeden with you when you were ill. Even though she'd been looking forward for months to spending Christmas with her brother Robert and his wife."

"Of course, I did." Gideon nodded approvingly. "For a wife's place is with her...." His eyes widened as he saw where Elizabeth's apparent non-sequitur had led.

"Husband. Yes, it is." Elizabeth faced her brother and observed calmly, "Perhaps especially after he has been wounded in the service of his country in a foreign land and endured a long sea crossing."

Gideon felt as if he'd been slapped across the face. He'd been duped. And Elizabeth was the one who'd torn the arguments that had sounded so solid only two days earlier into tatters. In a blind rage, he lashed out at her.

"Living in France and now in this," Gideon's arms circled wildly nearly knocking a vase of dried flowers off a nearby table, "fine house has made you think you are too great a lady to be married in your own parish church."

The accusation stung. Silently Elizabeth considered yielding to part of Gideon's wishes.

But Gideon gave her no time to reply. "You always were selfish, caring for no one in the family but yourself. And now, Elizabeth, you appear poised to ally yourself to another such as you. The scandalous stories are all over London," Gideon exaggerated freely. "And once you have wed this Rossbury, they will taint everyone in the family, too! Blighting Peter's chances to make a name for himself and Emma and Marianne's opportunities to marry well." Gideon rushed toward Elizabeth, his fist shaken before her face. "I won't have it!" he shouted. "I am your brother! You need my consent!"

Gideon's threat, now out in the open, caused the prickings of conscience that his earlier appeal had awakened in Elizabeth to evaporate. Back stiff with resolve but knees trembling, Elizabeth countered in a voice scarcely louder than a whisper, "Then you shall have to refuse it. And be prepared to state your reasons for doing so before witnesses and the Reverend Mr. David Souther in St Etheldreda's on April 3rd."

Elizabeth's answer enraged Gideon. His face grew redder, the veins at the side of his neck bulging with frustration. But before he could shout his ultimatum, the door to the morning room opened to admit Lady Farnsworth.

Sailing into the room, Lady Beatrice smiled brightly first at Gideon and then at Elizabeth. "Elizabeth, you should have asked Betty to tell me you had a visitor." Not waiting for a reply, Lady Beatrice turned immediately to Gideon. "Your sister is most remiss." The Dowager Marchioness looked about the room. "She has not requested that the fire be lit nor has she called for refreshments."

Concerned about Elizabeth's pallor, Lady Beatrice then crossed the room and gave Elizabeth's arm a gentle squeeze. "We must rectify that or Mr. Laurence will find my hospitality lacking." However, she did not reach for the bell chord to call for a servant.

Instead, raising her hand to her chin and gazing at the unlit grate to avoid staring at Gideon's startled face, Lady Beatrice appeared to be considering. "Hmm? Let me think. We have been so busy, you understand, Mr. Laurence. Dressmaker's appointments and fittings. All the business of gathering a trousseau. Well, you, of course, are not interested in any of that, are you?" She threw another bright smile towards Gideon who stood with his mouth agape, his face now a nearly normal shade.

Then Lady Beatrice exclaimed, "Tomorrow night! You must come to dinner tomorrow night. Lady Dalrymple will be here and some other people," she added vaguely, "whom you will enjoy meeting. Do say that you shall not disappoint us?"

"I shall be happy to accept your invitation, Lady Farnsworth," Gideon replied with a slight nod that seemed to indicate that such invitations were his due.

"Good!" Lady Beatrice interjected before the man whom she knew only slightly but was beginning to despise could speak further. Quite deliberately turning her back on Gideon for a moment, she spoke gently to Elizabeth. "My dear, another letter has arrived for you. You'll find it next to your Sèvres bowl."

If only that small piece of china could speak! Lady Beatrice knew it could tell her a story she would never hear from either her godson or his affianced bride whose face had been transformed the moment the word letter had been mentioned.

"That godson of mine must have written a letter at every posting inn between London and Shropshire," Lady Beatrice remarked more for Gideon's benefit than Elizabeth's. Giving Gideon no opportunity to object, she added, "Mr. Laurence and I shall excuse you if you would like to read it now, Elizabeth."

"Thank you, Lady Beatrice." Elizabeth hurried towards the door, which the Marchioness with some disgust noted Gideon Laurence made no move to open. "Gideon, we'll see each other tomorrow evening."

"I shall come early," announced Gideon, determined to assert his authority, "for I want another word with you in private."

Come as early as you like, decided Lady Beatrice immediately, but you shall have no private conversation with your sister!

Not three minutes later, Gideon Laurence found himself on the street outside Farnsworth Place. No fire, no tea tray. Nothing! Just a lot of talk about return visits, he fumed.

Gideon settled his hat on his head and began to walk away. "I've been turfed out!" he exclaimed aloud. Embarrassed by his reaction, he stared guiltily about him. No one else was in sight. Then the memory of his first meeting with Tyler Hamilton-Smythe struck him. Hamilton-Smythe's to blame for this mess, he told himself. Him and his cock and bull stories about Lady Sarah Verinder! A sudden urge to confront Tyler overwhelmed Gideon. Striding off angrily in the direction of the townhouse he believed Tyler owned, Gideon began to rehearse what he would say.

A sharp rapping of the knocker brought Watley to the door of Baron Bardstow's London residence.

"Tell Hamilton-Smythe that I must see him at once!" Gideon pushed his way into the entry hall, removed his hat, and thrust it into the hands of the startled Watley.

"Let me see if Mr. Hamilton-Smythe is at home," stammered Watley, leaving Gideon to struggle with his greatcoat alone.

Moments later, Tyler pounded down the stairs. One look at his visitor's face told him that Laurence's news was not what Tyler had hoped to hear.

"Watley," Tyler ordered, "some refreshments for my guest." With Gideon ready to erupt, Tyler wanted Watley safely out of the way. "Immediately, Watley!" Smiling, Tyler turned back to Gideon.

Watley scuttled towards the door that led to the half-basement where the kitchen, scullery, and pantry were located. But when the door had closed behind him, he did not continue down the stairs. Instead Watley waited, ear pressed to the doorjamb while hardly daring to breathe.

"You're a liar, young man!" Gideon shouted as soon as Watley had left the entrance hall. "And your sister Lady Sarah, well…" Gideon snorted derisively.

The mention of his sister's name wiped the smile from Tyler's face. Presented with Hamilton-Smythe's stony look, Gideon hastily revised his sentence.

"Well, she's not what you…"

"Who told you about my sister?" Leaping to Lady Sarah's defense, Tyler counterattacked before Gideon could finish. "No doubt Rossbury or that opinionated, self-righteous godmother of his, Lady Farnsworth, filled your poor deluded sister's ears with lies. Of course, she has believed them. And now, despite what you told me Wednesday about her obstinacy and desire to oppose you in every way, so do you!"

Faced with Tyler's certainty and a viewpoint he desperately wanted to believe, Elizabeth's arguments faded. Gideon's anger at being opposed had made half of what she had said a mere roaring in his ears. He shook his head as if to clear it.

"Come upstairs, Laurence," Tyler invited. "Tell me what's happened to upset you. To tell you the truth, I was expecting you yesterday," Tyler lied, for he knew, from a brief meeting with Patience, that Elizabeth had not seen her brother. First because she'd spent the morning with Patience who'd been full of the news of her elevation to lady's maid, and the late afternoon with preparations for Lady Dalrymple's party.

The memory of being sent away from Farnsworth Place on Thursday scalded Gideon still. "Elizabeth," he snarled, "was too busy to see me yesterday."

"That's what she told you?" Tyler's voice oozed consolation and understanding

"No," Gideon declared like someone relating a great injustice, "that's what some lackey told me, 'The ladies are resting.'"

"Hatching schemes more likely."

With those words, Gideon's eyes riveted on Tyler's face.

"We can hatch a few schemes of our own, can we not, Laurence? Perhaps we can convince your sister that London is a dangerous place. A small but frightening accident might make her happy to return to the safety of Hopeden Hall."

An accident! Gideon was startled. But before he could speak, Tyler invited soothingly, "Let's go up to my study. And put you in a comfortable chair in front of the fire. Then you can tell me what's happened over something to eat."

Moving noiselessly from his post by the door, Watley hastened towards the kitchen. What he had heard disturbed him. But now, he knew that he and his wife, who between them cared for Bardstow Place while the Baron was at Stowe Manor, must quickly prepare a warm meal before the clanging of the study bell announced Tyler's displeasure over his delay.

## CHAPTER 15

# MONDAY, MARCH 4, 1793

"They are all lovely, Mr. Danforth!" exclaimed Elizabeth. Three pairs of earrings sparkled against a square of dark velvet laid upon the counter of Robert Danforth's shop.

Rossbury's letter of Friday had directed Elizabeth to visit the London jeweler, to select a pair of earrings for herself, and to charge them to Rossbury's account.

"You'd not go wrong with any of them, Miss Laurence." Danforth's large hands and solid frame seemed more suited for a rugged rural life than one shaping intricate trinkets.

Then another customer entered the shop. Robert Danforth recognized Mrs. Cholmondeley-Musgrove whose purchases from Danforth's were quite regular.

"If you will excuse me, Miss Laurence."

"Of course," replied Elizabeth as she studied a pair of small enameled pendants.

As Danforth went to assist Mrs. Cholmondeley-Musgrove, his assistant Kenneth Weatherholt took his place.

"A cravat pin for my husband's birthday," the rather large woman at the other end of the counter announced.

"Perhaps these?" Weatherholt put a pair of delicate filigree-work earrings into Elizabeth's hands.

"Perhaps," replied Elizabeth. However, her attention had strayed to the other customer's comments about the cravat pins she was looking at.

Finally, after Mr. Danforth had opened the street door of the shop and seen Mrs. Cholmondeley-Musgrove through it, he returned to where Elizabeth was standing. "Have you made a selection, Miss Laurence?"

"No." Elizabeth looked up from the earrings displayed on the velvet square. "However, I would like to see your cravat pins."

"Of course," Danforth noted smoothly without so much as a blink. Weatherholt went to retrieve the tray and placed it in front of Elizabeth.

She immediately lifted a slim cravat pin, its head a fingertip of black jasper circled by diamonds so small she marveled at the skill required to fashion them into an elegant piece of jewelry.

"This is perfect!" Elizabeth envisioned the pin nestled in the folds of Rossbury's cravat.

Then the street door of the shop opened again, and Gideon Laurence strode in. A glance through the front window had told him that Elizabeth was inside exactly as he heard on Saturday evening she would be.

Thoughts of that evening still rankled. All through dinner, Gideon had exercised a supreme effort to control his temper and to present a loving face to his sister and an amiable one to Lady Farnsworth's guests. Particularly that old harridan Lady Dalrymple, Gideon recalled. Never gave me a chance to speak privately with Elizabeth. But her questions about Rossbury's letter were useful. Let me know that Elizabeth would be here picking out a pair of earrings this afternoon. Alone.

Gideon Laurence plastered a smile on his face as he walked towards the counter.

"May I be of assistance?" inquired Kenneth Weatherholt.

"It is the assistance of my sister, Miss Laurence, that I require." Gideon sidled next to Elizabeth and touched her arm awkwardly. "But my need of your advice, Elizabeth, will wait until you are done here."

Gideon's appearance and congenial tone surprised Elizabeth. Saturday evening at Farnsworth Place cannot have been easy for him, she considered. Perhaps he has accepted the situation. Elizabeth smiled warmly. "I shall not keep you long, Gideon."

On the other side of the counter, Robert Danforth and Kenneth Weatherholt listened in silence to this exchange. Now turning to them after a swift glance at Gideon, Elizabeth said, "Gideon, this is Mr. Robert Danforth and his assistant Mr. Weatherholt. Mr. Danforth, Mr. Weatherholt – my brother Mr. Gideon Laurence. Of Hopeden Hall in Hampshire," Elizabeth added quickly as she knew her brother believed his residence gave consequence to his name.

Gideon nodded. The two jewelers bowed slightly. The expected acknowledgements of names and murmurs of 'Your servant' were repeated.

Introductions to shopkeepers! What will she think of next? Gideon wondered. But he forced his lips to curve. "Let me see the earrings you have selected."

"They can wait until Lord Rossbury returns. Instead I have bought this." Elizabeth lifted the cravat pain and held it up towards Gideon. "Isn't it elegant?"

The small thing in his sister's hand was not to Gideon's taste. After a quick scan of the other pins on the counter, Gideon's eyes were drawn to an ornate piece, a large jewel at its head.

From their position on the other side of the counter, both Danforth and Weatherholt observed Gideon's attraction but said nothing.

While privately calling Elizabeth foolish for discarding an opportunity to acquire something valuable for herself, Gideon lied smoothly, "Indeed, it is. Most elegant, Elizabeth. An excellent choice."

Danforth noted dryly, "That your opinion and Miss Laurence's are the same is a credit to the craftsman who designed this piece – Mr. Weatherholt."

"You designed this?" Elizabeth looked at Danforth's assistant with appreciation.

With a modest inclination of his head, the young jeweler confirmed, "I did, Miss Laurence."

"Your skill and pride in your craft are both evident here."

"They are, Miss Laurence," agreed Robert Danforth. "And I am glad that both are put to work at Danforth's." The jeweler placed a hand upon Weatherholt's shoulder. "My daughter Henrietta and Kenneth Weatherholt here will be wed this Michaelmas. Danforth's will someday be in his good hands." He beamed upon his prospective son-in-law.

Danforth's comments about the future of the business intrigued Elizabeth. She quickly drew Weatherholt out with questions about his betrothed and his own jewelry making techniques.

Meanwhile, Gideon's fingers itched to take his watch from his pocket, an impulse he resisted. However, he could not prevent himself from turning to peer out of the jewelry shop's front window or shuffling his feet or harrumphing often.

Elizabeth recognized the signs of her brother's boredom and ended the interesting conversation. "I have kept you both from your business for too long and denied my patient brother the interview he has asked for."

"It has been our pleasure to make your acquaintance, Miss Laurence," Mr. Danforth replied. "We shall be happy to serve you at any time and hope to do so often in the years to come." He handed Elizabeth a small wrapped box containing the cravat pin and bowed slightly.

"Let me carry that for you." Relieved that Elizabeth was finally leaving the jewelry shop, Gideon was prepared to be courteous.

"Thank you, Gideon." Elizabeth smiled and turned towards her brother. "I am glad you found me here today."

Gideon Laurence merely glued his own smile more tightly to his lips. He took the small package from his sister's hands and offered his arm as Mr. Weatherholt stood ready to open the street door.

Once outside, Elizabeth frowned. "I had planned to go to *Maison d'Villiers* next. Lady Farnsworth's carriage is due to arrive there in an hour to take me back to Carlington Square."

"A boy can be sent to Farnsworth Place with a note saying the carriage is not needed," Gideon said at once. "We can do that as soon as we reach my house on Hanover Crescent. Over some tea, you can read Felicity's latest letter. She is worried about Peter. We thought perhaps Lord Rossbury..." Gideon hesitated for a moment as a hackney drawn by a dejected looking horse trundled down the street. "Well, you can read the letter yourself and then give me the benefit of your advice."

"I'll be happy to, Gideon. You know I'd do anything I can to help Peter." Elizabeth decided not to say anything about Gideon's reference to a town house. He must have brought it while I was in Rouen, she concluded.

"A hackney will bring us to Hanover Crescent in a trice. In fact, we are in luck, for here comes one now." The hackney Gideon had seen earlier slowed to a stop beside him, the driver all but invisible under an enormous cloak and wide brimmed hat pulled low over his forehead.

Inside the coach, cracked upholstery, an unswept floor, a slightly sour smell, and a general air of dilapidation greeted Elizabeth. She gingerly took a seat, Gideon clambering in after her and settling himself opposite her.

As the hackney rolled along, Gideon said nothing, his silence convincing Elizabeth the problem with Peter was serious. Meanwhile, the hackney turned often and then neared the river. This can't be right, Elizabeth thought. "Gideon," she began, "we appear to be–"

Suddenly, the coach lurched forward, its abrupt motion throwing Elizabeth against Gideon and then onto the floor.

"Runaway!" screamed the driver as the hackney shot down the street. "Runaway!"

A man with a handbarrow and a mother with one child by the hand and another balanced on her hip leaped out of the way to avoid being run down. They stared at the hackney careening down the street, its driver using his whip to lash his frightened animal into more speed.

Meanwhile, the extreme swaying of the vehicle kept Elizabeth on the floor. She disentangled her feet from her skirts, while Gideon hung onto the door frame, his eyes wide with terror. Then as she tried to lever herself back onto the seat, the hackney hurtled around a corner. Its two-wheeled navigation of the right turn toppled Elizabeth off her feet and against the door. It gave way behind her. At the same time, Gideon was thrown from the cushions. With a startled 'oow', he fell atop her.

Elizabeth scrambled for something to hang onto. Then the door handle loosened at her back. Suddenly she was suspended precariously over the street. Her feet were wedged under Gideon's body while both hands clasped the door handle, the only object preventing her from plunging headlong onto the cobbles below.

"Gideon, help me!" Elizabeth's arms felt as if they were being pulled from their sockets, her shoulders and wrists on fire with pain. Beneath her back, the ground blurred while the hackney plummeted down the street.

Then Elizabeth sensed her legs being edged towards the open door as her brother lumbered to his feet inside the hackney. "Stop! Gideon, you're pushing me out!" Elizabeth attempted to gain some leverage for her legs, but Gideon's movements were slowly causing her feet to lose their hold. Gasping as the hackney careered over a hole, Elizabeth struggled to maintain the perilous foothold that kept her from falling.

"Gideon, grab my legs or the door!" Elizabeth shouted desperately.

"Can't, can't get my balance!"

Then Elizabeth saw the dray. "Stop! Stop!" she screamed.

Pulled by two huge draft horses, its ponderous weight crept slowly across the intersection of streets directly in front of the wildly swaying hackney. A collision seemed unavoidable. Elizabeth knew falling from the hackney was preferable to being rammed into the heavy dray. Her eyes glued to the other vehicle as the distance between it and the hackney shortened, Elizabeth steeled herself to release her grip.

At the same time, Daniel Smallwood, the dray driver, looked over his left shoulder. He saw the hackney driver, whip in hand, urging his terrified beast on while shouting, "Runaway!" Then Smallwood spotted Elizabeth hanging outside the hackney, her fingers clinging to the open hackney door, her feet somehow remaining inside.

As the dray inched its way across the street, a quick heave from his seat took Smallwood to the ground. He ran towards the wild-eyed animal, lathered with exertion and fear, between the shafts of the hackney.

The hackney driver immediately slowed his horse with a tremendous pull on the lines, the coach veering right simultaneously. "Jump," Smallwood yelled as he pounded forward. "I be here. Jump!"

Her feet slipping more with each turn of the hackney's wheels, Elizabeth saw Smallwood leap from his seat and felt the hackney slow and then swerve right. In the next heartbeat, her brain screamed at her, If you stay where you are, you'll be slammed into the back of the dray and then dragged under the hackney. Jump!

Lips clamped together and eyes shut tight, Elizabeth released her grip on the door handle and pushed her feet as hard as she could against the coach's interior. At the same time, Smallwood dived forward, his momentum propelling him towards Elizabeth. Barely missing the swinging door, the two tumbled to the ground together. Elizabeth pulled her legs towards her as the pair rolled on the muddy road.

"Oof!" Smallwood felt the breath forced from his lungs as Elizabeth's head landed in the middle of his chest, his arms clamped about her rib cage.

Then the tumbling and bumping stopped. Elizabeth opened her eyes cautiously. The winter sky loomed above. The hackney was nowhere in sight. A pair of brawny arms pinioned her; a stranger's chest cushioned her back. Aches and pains immediately invaded every part of her body. Tentatively she flexed her legs. Thank God, she prayed in gratitude, nothing seems to be broken.

Smallwood, feeling her movement, asked, "Miss, 'e all right?"

"Yes, I believe I am." Elizabeth lifted a hand to her throbbing head and immediately winced. "Thanks to you."

"Roll a bit to your right, Miss." Smallwood moved in that direction himself. And as Elizabeth did the same, he remarked, "That's right, Miss. Then I can," he withdrew his arms and clambered to his feet, "help you up."

Gideon Laurence, panting as if he had been running, rounded the corner of the dray standing motionless in the intersection of the streets. "What are you doing to my sister, you oaf?" Gideon shook his fist as he hustled towards Elizabeth and Smallwood. "Elizabeth, are you quite…? You look…"

With a glance at her clothes, torn and mud covered, Elizabeth noted wryly, "I am fine, Gideon, thanks to this gentleman…" The man whose diving catch, Elizabeth was sure, had saved her from serious injury was a broad-faced giant whose shaggy brown locks were peppered with grey. His stillness and calm manner cloaked him with a natural dignity.

"Dan'l, Miss." The drayman's hand rose to his head in search of his cap. Spying it in a nearby puddle of murky water, he bent to retrieve it. "Dan'l Smallwood, Miss Elizabeth."

"Mr. Smallwood…" began Elizabeth.

"What on earth happened, Elizabeth?" demanded Gideon before she could introduce him to Smallwood.

"I assume, Gideon, something startled the horse and the driver could not control it. You must have heard him shouting, 'Runaway!'" Elizabeth rubbed her left wrist. "It was an accident. And, thanks to Mr. Smallwood, it was not …" Elizabeth shivered.

"Well, it's over now," Gideon said gruffly, "and you're…" He glanced at Elizabeth and then turned to look up and down the street. "Never heard of a runaway in Little Throckton."

"Beg pardon, sir." Daniel Smallwood stood motionless, gazing intently at Gideon. "That weren't no runaway. Tha' driver – well, he were whippin' tha' poor beast, makin' 'er go fast as she could. An' when I tried to catch hold of 'er, he just swerved purposeful like. An' then--"

"Are you mad?" Gideon rounded on Smallwood with a threatening growl. "Didn't you hear him shout, 'Runaway' as a warning to other vehicles? You should have moved your damned dray out of the way. We almost collided with you. It's no thanks to you my sister wasn't killed!"

"Gideon!" Elizabeth stepped between the two men. "Mr. Smallwood saved my life. His dray forced the hackney to slow."

"That'd be right, Miss Elizabeth," insisted Smallwood. "When tha' other driver seen th' dray, he pulled back hard on his lines. Don't know what he were tryin' to do earlier. Seems he must o' heard you screamin' f'r him t' stop. Heard you myself, if you'll pardon me sayin' so." Smallwood held his cap in his hands as he spoke while looking back and forth between Elizabeth and Gideon.

"Well, then the man must be a lunatic!" huffed Gideon. "We are both fortunate to have escaped with our lives." He saw Elizabeth and Smallwood staring at him and explained, "When that swine slowed down on the other side of the dray, I jumped out." His fingers brushed imaginary dust from the sleeves of his coat. "Naturally after I saw you fall, Elizabeth..." Gideon's eyes appeared troubled, his voice concerned as he stepped forward to take Elizabeth's hands. "Well, my only thought was to come to your aid. I even managed to save your package." He fumbled the small wrapped square from his coat pocket and gave it to Elizabeth.

"Tha' were a bit o' luck," Smallwood noted as Elizabeth cradled the package from Danforth's in her hands. "Hackney's long gone now, I 'magine, sir."

In Daniel Smallwood's quiet statement, Gideon glimpsed a hint of accusation and suspicion. The drayman's motionless stance, still hands, and steady gaze unnerved him.

"Of course, he is," Gideon snapped. "Raced off as soon as I leapt from his blasted hackney." Unable to meet Smallwood's eyes, Gideon turned his attention to Elizabeth. "This would never have happened in Little Throckton, Elizabeth. You must admit, my dear, that Hampshire is a far less dangerous place than London. I want you to be safe. That's why I want you to come home."

Elizabeth's hand touched her pounding temples for a moment. "Right now, Gideon, we need to find a way back to Carlington Square."

Daniel Smallwood remarked, "No hackneys 'bout here, Miss Elizabeth. Don't know where you comed from, but this were a funny way to get to Carlington Square if that be where you were goin'. Pr'aps your driver didn't unnerstand your directions." He looked at Gideon for an answer.

Gideon recalled with a start that he had given no directions. Giving Elizabeth no time to recollect that fact, he demanded, "How far to the nearest hackney stand?"

"Mile or more."

Elizabeth fought a desire to weep. Normally a mile's walk would be a pleasure. But now the distance seemed interminable.

"But if you'd not mind ridin' with me on the bench..."

"You will take us to Carlington Square?" Elizabeth seized on Smallwood's offer.

Smallwood had intended to drive to the nearest hackney stand, but the relief in Elizabeth's eyes made him say, "Yes, Miss, that I will."

Before Gideon could even voice an objection, the drayman lifted Elizabeth onto the high seat and handed her a large piece of sacking to use as a lap robe. "Tha'll help keep off the cold, Miss Laurence. It's dry but not too clean, I'm afraid."

"Neither are my clothes, Mr. Smallwood," observed Elizabeth. "Thank you for your thoughtfulness."

Then Smallwood heaved himself onto the box, his single fluid movement the result of his years of guiding the bulky wagon. Gideon was forced to follow.

Driving required little of Smallwood's concentration. He knew his horses, his vehicle, and London's streets well. He let his mind drift to the scene he had witnessed earlier. He saw Elizabeth hanging from the hackney and wondered why her brother had done nothing to help her.

Then Elizabeth asked a question about his work. One question followed another; and Smallwood began to share details about his life

"I be good wit' beasts an' there's no end o' work totin' things from one place t' 'nother – 'specially for us as has a strong back an' no fear f'r any sort o' weather. 'Sides my horses be good company, better 'n some folk." A slow grin made his eyes dance with mischief, and his look invited Elizabeth to share the joke with him.

"I am sure they are," replied Elizabeth. She paused to allow Gideon to comment, but he appeared lost in thought. "Nevertheless, I hope your life also includes human companionship."

"Oh, aye, it does, Miss Elizabeth." Without intending to do so, Smallwood related the whole story of his courtship and marriage to Hannah Kendall. "Couldn't believe someone like her – vicar's daughter wi' all her books and learnin' an' pretty ways – would be interested in th' likes of me. But she were. Vicar didn't even object." Smallwood shook his head in amazement at this miracle. "Said Hannah'd never marry cause o' this little – well, 'tis only a splash o' color on the side of her face – 'tis nothing, Miss Laurence."

Elizabeth recalled one of Doctor Mansard's patients, a spinster with a wine-colored birthmark across her left cheek. Some had been afraid of her; and no matter the season whenever Elizabeth saw her, a thick wool scarf was wrapped about the woman's face. "You are right, Mr. Smallwood. Such things are trifles."

"Trifles," repeated the drayman. "Tha' sounds like one o' Hannah's words. She's taught our Will and Nan their letters n' numbers n' proper ways. Both o' 'em talk like summat out of a book." His pride in his children was evident. "Will's got a job as a clerk. Only thing on his hands is a bit of ink. Mr. Maxwell – that's the man he works for – well, he says our Will's got a head for business."

The dray had entered the London of fashionable shops and elegant town houses. Well-dressed pedestrians and footmen on the backs of gleaming equipages stared as Smallwood effortlessly navigated his team around a corner.

"And our Nan, she's workin' in a big house. Upstairs maid, she is now. But she's determined to get on, an' find a place where she can use her head."

Smallwood paused, waiting for Elizabeth to comment. When she didn't, he stole a quick glance at her face. Her eyes were closed, a bruise on her forehead beginning to purple and swell.

"I'm the one who should o' used my head, Miss Laurence. Doan know what's come over me. Talkin' away at you when you needed a bit o' peace n' quiet," Smallwood apologized.

"Damn right." Gideon grabbed the opportunity to repay the insult of Smallwood's assumption that his story would have any interest for him. "My sister is obviously unwell, and your chattering has been enough to make anyone's head ache!"

"I should o' thought, Miss Elizabeth…" began Smallwood.

Elizabeth stopped his apology by laying her hand on his arm. "If I'd not been interested in your family, Mr. Smallwood, I would not have asked you to tell me about them." Elizabeth watched the hurt melt from the drayman's face. "Someday I hope to be blessed with children as fine as both of yours."

"Tha' were kindly said, Miss Elizabeth."

"It was truly and kindly meant, Mr. Smallwood."

"Carlington Square at last!" Gideon had seen the square ahead and almost shouted its name.

"Is tha' 'er?" Smallwood asked Elizabeth while motioning with his hand towards Rossbury House.

"No." A sudden thought brought a smile to Elizabeth's lips. "But it soon shall be, Mr. Smallwood. I live in the house opposite."

Immediately the drayman directed the team to the left and then eased the dray to a halt in front of Farnsworth Place.

"Wait here, Elizabeth, while I fetch one of Lady Farnsworth's footmen to assist you up the steps." Gideon scrambled unceremoniously down from his seat on the dray.

"I can--" began Daniel Smallwood.

"This is for your trouble, Smallwood." The coin Gideon tossed flew by the astonished dray driver and fell onto the cobbles before Gideon headed around the vehicle and towards the front door.

"Mr. Smallwood, would you be so kind as to help me down." Elizabeth moved aside the sacking covering her legs while Smallwood made his descent from the dray's high seat. Then she slid to her left and put out her arms. Smallwood said nothing but lifted Elizabeth easily and set her lightly on her feet next to him.

"You must excuse Gideon, Mr. Smallwood. I believe he means well." Elizabeth stooped awkwardly to pick up the coin Gideon had thrown and placed it on the seat of the dray. "Perhaps Mrs. Smallwood would like some new ribbon for her best hat."

As Daniel Smallwood nodded his understanding and acceptance, Elizabeth put out her hand. "Good-bye, Mr. Smallwood. I thank God that He appointed you my guardian angel today."

Taking her hand in his, the drayman responded, "T'were my pleasure, Miss Laurence."

Suddenly there was a flurry of activity at the front door. Two footmen hurried down the steps, one reaching for the small box from Danforth's Elizabeth clung to. Gideon offered his arm amidst declarations that 'such things never happen in Little Throckton.' Elizabeth climbed stiffly up the steps. A bevy of aproned maids presided over by a black coated Harris fluttered and fluted their dismay in the entrance hall. The little procession disappeared into the house. The door closed.

After Daniel Smallwood again took his seat and moved the lines slightly, the dray rumbled forward. Guardian angel! he recalled with a slow smile. Won't I have a story t' tell my Hannah t'night.

"Father, I am leaving for Gylston Priory now."

Rossbury turned from his work in the Earl's Wood library to glance at his son. Ledgers, correspondence, and papers littered the top of his desk.

"Are you certain that you won't join me?" Simon inquired.

"I dined with the Clares only last evening, Simon." Rossbury rose from his chair behind the desk and flexed shoulders stiff from bending over paperwork for hours. "Naismith and I will do very well together here. Mrs. Garrison will believe we consider her cooking inadequate if all of us dine at our neighbors' homes every day."

"Do you think I should decline the Clares' invitation?"

"No, Simon. Go and enjoy yourself. And if the Clares are free on Wednesday, invite them to join us here."

Simon's face brightened with anticipation. "Lucy here!"

"Be sure to include Mr. and Mrs. Clare, as well as Anthony and Anne, in your invitation, Simon," Rossbury reminded his son with a smile. "And perhaps you can convince Naismith to make our numbers even."

"I'll speak to him tomorrow. But now I must be on my way."

"Yes, you must. Being tardy to any engagement is not the habit of a gentleman."

After Simon had left the library and closed the door behind him, Rossbury returned to his desk. But instead of reviewing the latest accounts, he considered his son Simon and Lucy Clare. The two glowed in one another's company.

"Elizabeth," Rossbury said aloud. "How I wish I could see your face across the table tonight." Simon, he thought, you do not know how fortunate you are!

Pushing the papers on his desk aside, he reached for a piece of stationary and his pen.

*Beth dearest,* he wrote. *The afternoon sun streams through the library window here at Earl's Wood Park, but the house seems dark. It needs you, and I need you, too...*

A thunderous knocking on the front door of Hamilton Place brought Mrs. Watley scurrying up the servants' stairs. Outside, his hand raised to pound on the door again was Gideon Laurence.

Once in the entrance hall, Gideon demanded, "Where's your master?"

Before Mrs. Watley could reply, Tyler Hamilton-Smythe answered from halfway down the stairs. "I shall see to my guest, Mrs. Watley." He descended the remaining steps and cast a searching look about the hall. "Watley should answer the door. Where is he?"

Mrs. Watley, having taken Gideon's greatcoat, gloves, and hat, noted a flash of motion on the first-floor landing. "In the pantry, I expect."

"Tell him, Mrs. Watley, that I expect him to bring a tray of refreshments to the study in a quarter of an hour."

On the landing above, Watley heard his wife's lie and scuttled into the dining room, its door not quite shut.

Soon voices drifted up the stairs.

"Your reckless driving nearly killed my sister!"

"How is she?"

"Badly bruised, but she refused to let Lady Farnsworth send for the doctor. And I've a few bruises of my own. You drove like a bedlamite."

"The purpose was to frighten her, was it not?"

"But you didn't need to loosen the hackney door latch to do that!"

"A piece of sheer inspiration, Laurence. And it worked, didn't it? She was frightened."

The two men reached the landing and walked towards the study.

"Oh, she was frightened all right."

"Enough to return with you to Hampshire?"

"That I do not know."

"Well, if she is still bent on remaining in London, perhaps another accident can be arranged."

Tyler Hamilton-Smythe's chuckle made Watley's skin crawl. The voices receded down the hallway.

"Not inside of another filthy hackney!"

"No, Laurence, no. I have quite another idea altogether. I'll explain it to you later. But first tell me all your afternoon's adventures."

Watley heard the study door close and counted to ten slowly. Easing the dining room door open, he saw that the hallway was empty. Cautiously and quietly, he made his way down the main stairs.

He's up to no good. I know it. And whatever it is means trouble for Lord Bardstow, Watley thought unhappily. If he only knew… The servant shook his head. Maybe if I…

Watley mulled over the idea taking shape in his mind as he hurried down the stairs to the kitchen. Don't want to be a sneak, but don't want Lord Bardstow to be hurt again. A letter. It's the only way. He opened the kitchen door and saw his wife putting a cake plate on a tray. Mary will help me find the words.

Her back propped against several pillows, Elizabeth, clad in a soft white night dress, sat in her four-poster bed. Across her knees was a portable writing desk. She glanced at her bedside bureau. There the cravat pin box sat beside the Sèvres bowl.

What to tell Richard? Elizabeth thought. Certainly not everything I told Lady Beatrice and Lady Dorothy.

The Dowager Duchess of Lewisham had been at Farnsworth House when Elizabeth arrived, disheveled and mud-covered. So keeping the story of the hackney accident to herself was impossible.

But, Elizabeth remembered, some good came of it. When I related what Mr. Smallwood said about his daughter Nan, Lady

Dorothy said, "Winifred Braithwaite" and threw an almost triumphant look at Lady Beatrice.

The memory caused her to smile because the discussion that followed soon became a monologue.

"A vicar's granddaughter, you say? And she can read and write. Definitely an improvement on that lazy creature Winifred Braithwaite's saddled with now, wouldn't you say, Beatrice? Of course, Winifred's is a quiet house. Not much to interest a young girl. The entailment's been hard on her. And that cousin who inherited! No help at all. But it sounds as if this Miss Smallwood and Winifred would suit excellently."

The Smallwoods. Richard would enjoy hearing about them Elizabeth thought. And Mr. Danforth and Mr. Weatherholt. No need to write about the hackney accident at all, she thought. She uncapped the ink bottle and dipped her pen.

Twenty minutes later, portraits in words of the three men Elizabeth had met that day filled a page. Then she added, *Despite these encounters, the days since your departure for Earl's' Wood Park seem like an eternity. That I should need you as much as I do seems impossible – but my need is an ache that fills every waking minute.*

## CHAPTER 16

# THURSDAY, MARCH 7, 1793

To stand up with Richard at his wedding in London! Andrew St John Beresford, Viscount Grantleigh, stared at his friend's letter with its startling request without seeing it. Meanwhile, the rest of the day's post lay forgotten and unopened on the desk in his study at Brookfields in Gloucestershire.

Grantleigh's sea green eyes grew dark with memories. His wife Louise was less than three years in her grave as was the stillborn son she had died giving birth to. Since then, weddings had become something to avoid.

But Richard wants me there with him, Grantleigh told himself. I cannot let him down.

Grantleigh picked up the letter to search for the name of the bride. Elizabeth Laurence, he read. A frown creased his handsome face. The name was familiar, and he'd heard it recently. But where? Suddenly the memory surfaced. But that Elizabeth Laurence is dead, he recalled. Quickly he reread the letter from Earl's Wood Park. Details sprang up from the pages – Gideon Laurence, Hopeden Hall, Hampshire, France.

Moments later Grantleigh entered the morning room at Brookfields. His mother Cecily Beresford, the Dowager

Viscountess Grantleigh, sat in a comfortable wing chair, her feet on an upholstered stool. Her white hair was elegantly but simply dressed; and her cheeks, though crossed with their share of wrinkles, retained the lovely damask rose colour that had made her one of the most beautiful women in London forty years earlier. Her hands were busy with a piece of tapestry.

Grantleigh, the oldest of her two surviving children and the only son, dropped a kiss on her cheek. "Mother, I need to sift through your memories of Catherine Calvert."

"Catherine?" The dowager Viscountess looked up at her son in surprise, her tapestry forgotten in her right hand. Strange, she thought, when only this morning...

Grantleigh seated himself on a small sofa opposite her chair. "Yes, Mrs. Calvert," he repeated.

"My friendship with Catherine Calvert predates your birth, Andrew," Lady Cecily noted without a trace of sarcasm. "What exactly do you want to know?"

"I am not certain. What do you recall about her connections with Rosemont." Grantleigh paused and then added, "And her will."

"Her will? But why..." Lady Cecily began.

"Perhaps you should start from the beginning."

"The beginning..." Lady Cecily sifted through her many memories of her late friend. "Catherine was a Morestone. And Rosemont has belonged to the Morestones for over a hundred years."

The image of the Elizabethan manor house with its linenfold paneling, barrel-roofed long gallery, and mullioned windows arose in the minds of both mother and son. Two farms were part of the estate, a home farm long in the care of the Bell family and a smaller holding now tenanted by a younger Bell son.

"And there's no entail," Grantleigh recalled.

"Nevertheless, Catherine's brother Matthew wanted Rosemont to stay in Morestone hands. When it was apparent that he would die childless, he willed Rosemont to his younger sister Catherine. Never guessing that both Catherine's children would predecease her."

"And afterwards she came to live at Rosemont."

"Yes, she did," Lady Cecily continued briskly, remembering that her son wanted to know about Catherine Calvert's will. "And that's when she thought about how to continue the Rosemont-Morestone legacy. Her thoughts soon fell on Elizabeth Laurence, the granddaughter of her older sister, Elizabeth Cavenaugh. You met Miss Laurence, on more than one occasion, at one of Catherine's parties. Of course, that was years ago.

"Miss Laurence was the only one who showed any interest in the Morestone family, the only one who loved Rosemont and its gardens as Catherine did. So Catherine decided to leave Rosemont to her. I witnessed her will, and afterwards was sworn to secrecy. Catherine wanted to give her grandniece a lovely surprise."

Lady Cecily sighed deeply. "Thank God, the news that Elizabeth Laurence died in France did not arrive until after Catherine's death."

Grantleigh asked, "Do you know how William Clewett learned of Miss Laurence's death?"

"According to Mrs. Higgs," Lady Cecily named Rosemont's housekeeper, "Mr. Clewett received the news of her death in a letter from Miss Laurence's brother Gideon. Mr. Clewett had written to Miss Laurence. Her brother's reply stated that Miss Laurence had died during a visit to relations in France. And it is her brother, of course, who now inherits Rosemont."

"And Mrs. Higgs learned all this ...?"

"From Mr. Clewett. Laurence's reply stated that he would visit Rosemont sometime this spring. Clewett wants Mrs. Higgs to be prepared to meet the new owner. And now she is worried that Laurence will dismiss her and the others at Rosemont and replace them with his own servants."

"Mrs. Higgs, I believe, has nothing to fear from…from the new owner."

"I hope you are right, Andrew. And so does Mrs. Higgs, for she told me only this morning that a friend of Mr. Laurence has already visited Rosemont thinking he was in residence."

"Mrs. Higgs was here this morning?" asked Grantleigh.

"No, not here, Andrew. I encountered her in Ashcoombe. Your father's grave needed tending." Lady Cecily said no more on the subject.

Grantleigh rose and walked towards the morning room's window where he rested his forehead against the cool glass. Two reminders in the space of an afternoon. First Richard's letter. Now Mother's visit to St Timothy's churchyard. Where another grave needed tending. Then he turned from the window and asked, "And this friend of Laurence. Who was he?"

"Sir Augustus Tremaine. He came on Tuesday of last week. Said he was touring the county and Laurence was expecting him. According to Mrs. Higgs, Sir Augustus seemed quite put out to learn Mr. Laurence was not at Rosemont. Whatever had happened, she thought the least she could do was to prepare a meal for Mr. Laurence's friend. Afterwards, Sir Augustus asked if she would take him 'round the house. She did, of course, thinking that Sir Augustus could tell Laurence how well Rosemont is being cared for. An hour later, Sir Augustus left, apologizing for being confused about the date of Laurence's arrival."

"A person could mistake a date," noted Grantleigh. "It is a common error."

"Mrs. Higgs thought the same at first. But when she saw the Bell family, they all described the grand traveling coach with two postilions coming up the Northcote road on that Tuesday. And returning down the Northcote road that afternoon." Lady Cecily hesitated only a fraction of a moment before adding, "No one touring the county would take the Northcote Road." Lady Cecily frowned as she pondered again what Mrs. Higgs had told her. "Besides..."

"Besides," Grantleigh finished her thought, "late February is an odd time to be touring Gloucestershire."

"So Mrs. Higgs thought. And now she wonders if she should write to Gideon Laurence and tell him about Sir Augustus. The poor woman's afraid that Laurence will blame her no matter what she does. That's why she spoke to me this morning. To ask my advice. I told her it was probably best to do nothing unless this Sir Augustus returns. But now, Andrew, your interest in Catherine Calvert's will makes me suspect I made a mistake."

"Read this, and decide for yourself." Grantleigh gave his mother Rossbury's letter.

"Richard Verinder is marrying Elizabeth Laurence. Elizabeth Laurence!" Lady Cecily repeated aloud when she had finished reading and set the letter on a table by her chair. "Why did her brother say that Miss Laurence was dead?"

"Richard writes that he and Miss Laurence returned from France at the end of January. I'm guessing that Gideon Laurence wrote to Clewett before he learned of his sister's return." Grantleigh's face was grim.

"But Laurence has had time to write Mr. Clewett and tell him Miss Laurence is alive."

"But he hasn't. Richard would have said that his future Countess had recently inherited a property near Brookfields if he knew."

"So this Gideon Laurence," Lady Cecily pronounced his names as if they were the worst words she knew, "is trying to rob his sister of Catherine's bequest. To rob her of Rosemont."

"Yes." Grantleigh tried to imagine how Rossbury would react to this news.

"What are you going to do, Andrew? Rossbury must be told."

"I'm going to Earl's Wood. Better that Richard hear something like this from me than from a letter. But the matter is not urgent, and Richard says the business that took him to Earl's Wood will not allow him to leave for London until the 21st. I'll travel north sometime early next week. There are a few matters here I must attend to first."

And that means something's happened at Chelbourne Court, Lady Cecily thought with irritation.

Grantleigh stood and walked to the fireplace. Leaning a shoulder against the mantle, he turned to face his mother. "It's Eustace this time." Grantleigh ran a distracted hand over his fair hair while thinking about what his former father-in-law Nicholas Carstairs had said about his son. "The business should be fairly simple to put right, and then I'll be free to help Richard."

"And that means you probably won't return to Brookfields before Richard's wedding on the 3rd of April," concluded Lady Cecily

"It does."

Lady Cecily picked up her tapestry once again. "Then after you leave for Earl's Wood, I shall plan a trip to London. Being there to see Richard wed Miss Laurence will be a pleasure. He writes that the ceremony will be a quiet affair, as it must be with Edward's passing so recent. Yet I do not think Richard will object to my presence, do you?"

"No, of course not," confirmed Grantleigh. "You and Simon can share a pew," he added good-naturedly. "No doubt there will be several available." Then as he envisioned the wedding – himself at Rossbury's right, Miss Laurence to his friend's left, the thought of who would be standing to the bride's left caused his brow to furrow.

The same thought had occurred to Lady Cecily. "The matter of who answers, 'Who giveth this woman?' could be rather problematic," she noted slowly, her tapestry once again forgotten in her lap.

Meanwhile in the library at Earl's Wood Park, Rossbury speculated briefly upon the same topic, for he had received no word from Gideon Laurence. Then he reread Elizabeth's latest letter. One sentence in the paragraphs of the 27th of February stuck in his mind. *How I wish that, rather than with my arms wrapped about a pillow in a lovely four poster bed, my night's rest were to be taken amidst a pile of worn blankets in the Martins' barn...*

This was the night of Elizabeth's nightmare, Rossbury easily recalled. A nightmare prompted by fear of a nameless pursuer. But neither of us knew about LeBeau that night. He frowned and read the entire letter again, but these additional readings gave him no clues to Elizabeth's fear

His vague unease led Rossbury to make two decisions. First, to reply to Elizabeth's letter tonight and post a reply tomorrow. Second, to complete his business at Earl's Wood by the end of the next week. By either the 16th or 17th of March, he promised himself, I'll be on the road south to London – and Elizabeth.

That afternoon when Jim Compton entered the Rossbury House mews stable, Damson, the mare who was currently its sole resident, whickered softly in greeting.

"Hullo, old girl." Compton gently scratched a place between the mare's ears as she nudged at him with her head. "You an' me has somethin' important t' do t'day." After he opened the stall door, the mare moved forward into the corridor that ran the length of the stable. "Aren't you a clever one?" said Compton as he turned towards the tack room. "Want t' help me, don't you?" The mare's answering snuffle and stomp made the former private smile.

Although the mews stable had always been well kept, it was now a showpiece, thanks to Compton. He spent hours currying and grooming the thirteen-year-old Damson, once part of a team that pulled a luggage wain between Shropshire and London and now just a stable mate to younger and stronger horses. He also kept the mews dogcart in good repair, its iron parts clear of rust, its axles greased.

This small vehicle Compton now hitched to Damson while clucking over the mare, patting her rump, and checking and re-checking the harness. "You n' me'll pick up that order for Mrs. Ballantyne. Though th' Capt'n's said naught 'bout a wedding breakfast, our Mrs. Ballantyne's worrit 'bout not havin' all in readiness 'case he changes his mind at th' last minute."

Compton led the mare, now securely harnessed to the cart, out of the stable yard into the cobbled area behind the house. "But 'fore we comes home, you n' me's got important business of our own t' take care of."

The mare's ears twitched, and her head bobbed up and down once.

"Clever lass," said Compton as he hoisted himself onto the seat and gathered the lines in his hands.

An hour later, the cart stood at the side of an intersection about a half-mile from Carlington Square. His hat pulled low over his forehead, his coat collar turned up, Compton examined Damson's legs slowly and methodically. Then with painstaking care, he made minute adjustments to the placement of the items loaded in the bed of the vehicle.

When a couple came into view, Compton began to inspect the cartwheel farthest from the street. Surreptitiously watching the couple by looking under the wagon, Compton clenched his teeth to bite back a curse as the young, well-dressed gentleman took the girl at his side into his arms and kissed her casually.

Then Compton watched, as did Tyler Hamilton-Smythe, while Patience Downes walked in the direction of Carlington Square. Compton knew she would return immediately to Farnsworth Place, for he had followed her the previous Thursday.

As soon as Compton had been introduced to Patience in the servants' hall at Rossbury House, he had been taken with her. Compton told himself that, as someone fifteen years her senior, he had no chance with Patience Downes. But his heart refused to heed the warnings of his head. When he learned Patience's free afternoon was Thursday, he asked for Thursday afternoon off as well. This was the day Patience carried a basket of delicacies to a sick aunt. Compton hoped to be allowed to carry the basket for her. But his request was refused. And behind Patience's refusal, Compton glimpsed a hint of fear. He then began to wonder whether Patience's visit to an ill relative was really something else, something she didn't want anyone to know about.

A fortnight earlier Compton had followed Patience to a large, noisy public house. He had returned to Rossbury House after learning Patience had met a young gentleman there in a private room.

Last Thursday he had waited outside the Hare and Hounds slightly before the time he guessed Patience would make her way back to Carlington Square. Following her and her young gentleman, he had witnessed their leave taking on the street corner where he and Damson currently waited and then trailed her to Farnsworth Place.

This afternoon he was determined to learn something about the gentleman's identity. Compton did not blame Patience for falling in love with someone else. Instead he saved his anger for the hazel eyed, golden haired stranger. Compton was sure that the man, who had the kind of good looks – and probably the charm to go with them, Compton reflected – likely to sweep a young girl off her feet, was up to no good. And given the time and place of Patience's meetings with the man, Compton was also sure something more than simple seduction was on the man's mind.

*Got t' help Patience,* Compton thought. *N' if I know th' man's name, p'rhaps I'll be able t' figure out what he wants wi' Patience.* He climbed slowly into the driver's seat of the dogcart and turned Damson in the direction Patience's gentleman friend was heading.

When the man entered a hackney, Compton knew he had been right to use Damson and the cart. He had guessed that the Hare and Hounds was nowhere near the gentleman's home.

Looking bored as if he were a common carrier making a delivery, Compton kept the hackney in sight while staying well behind it. After it stopped outside an elegant townhouse, Patience's friend descended and went inside.

Compton stared at the house, memorizing the address, as he and Damson passed it. He knew the mews stable at Rossbury House needed little attention after his efforts of the past weeks. *N' with Weaver in Shropshire, I'll have a free hour b'fore next Thursday.* "Time enough to come back here without you ol' girl," he told Damson as he turned the dogcart around. "Time enough for a little plan o' my own."

## CHAPTER 17

# SATURDAY, MARCH 9, 1793

"Your visit today gave Uncle Gerard a great deal of pleasure." Nigel Farquhar escorted Elizabeth from the London home of his uncle, the Marquis of Somerville, to Stanfield's Bookshop.

"The pleasure was mutual. And," Elizabeth added mischievously, "your warnings about his irascibility were quite unnecessary. He was every inch the gentleman."

"Miss Lawrence," asked Farquhar, "are you implying that I am less a gentleman than my uncle? Granted his inches are greater than my own, but..."

"But what Lord Somerville's nephew lacks in inches is more than made up in his kindness to his uncle."

"It is Uncle Gerard who has been kind to me," insisted Farquhar.

The two walked in silence for a few moments, the pale March sun warming their backs.

"And you, too have been more than kind," Farquhar said, remembering his uncle's animation during Elizabeth's entire visit. "Never once did Uncle Gerard refer to the fire at Hillgrove and the inconveniences of being in London while the repairs are made. How can I thank you?"

"By helping me choose some books for my sister-in-law," Elizabeth replied at once. "While he is in London, my brother Gideon wants to send some new books to his wife and..." Elizabeth trailed off, remembering how Gideon had come to Farnsworth Place on Tuesday to ask how she was feeling after Monday's frightening hackney incident and to ask her to choose a time to meet him at Stanfields. Gideon had seemed so anxious to have Elizabeth's help and good opinion that she had immediately named a time on Thursday afternoon.

"And you are thinking that your tastes and your sister-in law's might not be the same," Farquhar concluded.

Then seeing that they had reached Stanfield's Bookshop, Farquhar opened the street door to allow Elizabeth to enter before him. Elizabeth glanced about the bookshop and saw that Gideon had not yet arrived and that Mr. Stanfield was occupied with another customer.

"Yes. And I also thought that your sisters might be fond of books."

"They are. And I believe that two volumes my younger sister recently asked me to send her might interest Mrs. Laurence." Farquhar motioned towards an aisle near the centre of the shop.

Taking a deep breath, Jim Compton rapped on the tradesman's entrance of the elegant town house where the hackney had stopped two days earlier. Uneasily he shifted the bulky package under his left arm, a brown papered and neatly corded parcel containing old newspapers. With his right hand, he straightened his cap.

Suddenly the door swung inward. Mary Watley, drying her hands on her apron, stood in the opening. The presence of a deliveryman with a package surprised her. "Are you sure you're at the right house?" she asked without waiting for Compton to state his business. "We've ordered nothing."

Compton pulled the cap from his head and stated abjectly, "I know you haven't, Mrs. Fact is, I'm lost. Haven't been in London long, n' Mr. Smithson'll sack me if I don't make this delivery n' get back t' th' shop soon. His directions just flew out of my head, I'm afraid." Compton let his shoulders slump. "Hopin' you could help me out. Give me some directions maybe?" He hung his head, his eyes downcast as if too ashamed and disheartened to look his listener in the face.

"Hmm." He looks harmless enough, Mrs. Watley thought to herself. "Where's the package supposed to go?"

Sprinkling a generous number of "thank you's" throughout his description, Compton stumbled through a request for directions to an address he knew to be a quarter mile and five turnings distant. "If you could tell me how t' get there, maybe draw me a picture like, few lines on a scrap of paper so's I don't lose my way again, I'd be that grateful, Mrs."

"Who is it, Mary?" Watley, working inside the butler's pantry, had heard the knocking on the areaway door and then the sound of two voices.

"A lost delivery man. He's new to London. Needs a bit of directions. Think you can help him, Alfred? I need to get back to those pies."

A moment later Watley stood in the narrow passageway leading between the pantry and a storeroom to the servants' hall and kitchen. "You go back to your baking, Mary," Watley told his wife who quickly headed towards the kitchen. "And you," he jerked his head in Compton's direction, "come on in and be sure to use the boot scraper or Mrs. Watley'll give you a tongue-lashing you'll never forget. And," he called over his shoulder, "close the door behind you."

With a "Thank you, Mr. Watley," Compton followed Watley into the servants' hall and laid his package on its scrubbed deal table. He felt almost suffocated by the warmth coming from the kitchen and his own nervousness. "Hope me bein' in here doesn't land you in trouble with your master, Mr. Watley, sir."

His back to Compton, the butler opened a drawer in a dresser ranged along one wall of the hall and looked for a scrap of paper. "Baron Bardstow's very reasonable about our visitors. However, he's not here at present but in residence at his estate Stowe Manor in Essex."

"Well, everythin' here looks fit for his inspection." Could I have mistaken the house? Compton asked himself. "Judging by the look of this room, two o' you work as hard as a staff o' four or five." Perhaps, Compton thought, Bardstow left for Essex this very morning n' a bit of flattery will winkle out th' information.

Watley smiled at the praise. "When Lord Bardstow's family is here," noted Watley proudly as he put a small piece of paper on the table, seated himself, and waved Compton into a chair, "we are fully staffed. But with only his Lordship's younger brother, the Honourable Tyler Hamilton-Smythe, at home, Mrs. Watley and I can manage quite easily."

From the kitchen, Mrs. Watley's loud sniff and "Humph!" were clearly audible. Compton decided it was better not to remark on Mrs. Watley's addition to their conversation especially after he recalled where and when he had heard the names Bardstow and Hamilton-Smythe before. Too excited to risk speaking, he remained silent.

Watley, approving of his wife's sentiments but disapproving of their expression with a stranger present, simply ignored her. "Where is your delivery to be made?"

With the information he wanted safely locked in his memory, Jim Compton repeated the address he'd given to Mrs. Watley and then watched as Watley drew a small map to a house Compton would never visit.

Nigel Farquhar, making his way back to his uncle's London home, absentmindedly put a hand into his coat pocket. There his fingers found a folded piece of paper. As soon as he touched it, he remembered the note from his uncle to Mr. Stanfield. A note he'd forgotten to give to the bookshop owner.

"Blast!" exclaimed Farquhar softly. He turned abruptly and headed back towards Stanfield's shop.

Meanwhile, Gideon Laurence's right hand also dug into his coat pocket and removed a large white handkerchief. His brow and upper lip were beaded with sweat. His left hand toyed with his watch chain, his eyes constantly straying to the street beyond the bookshop's front windows. Gideon mopped his forehead while Philip Stanfield carefully wrapped brown paper about the three books he had purchased for his wife Felicity.

"You seem a bit anxious and somewhat flushed, Gideon." With concern Elizabeth asked, "Are you feeling unwell?"

"I am finding it a bit warm in here, Elizabeth. That's all," Gideon remarked sharply. His left hand flicked open his watch-case. Four minutes to the half hour, he told himself. Slipping his watch back into its pocket, he stretched his mouth into a smile. "I shall be fine as soon as we go outdoors, my dear. Don't fuss."

"There!" stated Stanfield, the neatly packed trio of books extended in his hands. "They are a bit heavy. Are you certain you want to carry them with you? They can easily be delivered."

"I prefer to take them with me," stated Gideon.

"As you wish." Stanfield handed the bundle to Gideon. "I am certain that Mrs. Laurence will enjoy these. And if you find that you require any other volumes, I hope you will allow me to serve you again."

After grasping the package with his left hand, Gideon offered his right arm to Elizabeth. "Ah yes, I will. That is, you may." Gideon looked at the door, moved his left hand towards his watch pocket, realized his hands were full, and said, "Thank you for your help," as the bookshop owner hastened towards the door. "Shall we go, Elizabeth?" The question was a matter of form since Gideon was already heading towards the door, his pace compelling Elizabeth to walk quickly to keep step with him.

But Gideon was forced to halt abruptly when, just as Mr. Stanfield opened his street door, another customer entered the shop.

"Mrs. Cholmondeley-Musgrove!" greeted Stanfield. "I shall be with you in a moment."

"Thank you, Mr. Stanfield," replied the stout matron with a nod in the direction of Gideon and Elizabeth before she strode towards the counter.

Once outside Stanfield's shop, Gideon halted again a few paces beyond the door. "Just a moment," he ordered, a hint of irritation in his voice as if it were Elizabeth and not he who had set the pace.

"Of course, Gideon." Elizabeth watched in surprise as her brother fastened the buttons of his coat and drew up its collar.

"It's a bit chilly for March," Gideon observed with a shiver. "Don't you agree, Elizabeth?" He passed the bundle of books from hand to hand and cast a surreptitious glance down the street.

Instead noting her brother's shiver and restlessness, Elizabeth asked, "Wouldn't those volumes be better delivered than carried?" Once back inside the bookshop, she hoped to persuade Gideon to let her send for the Farnsworth coach.

"These?" Gideon hoisted the package now in his left hand and once more offered his right arm to Elizabeth. "The weight is nothing at all." Then he added brightly, "Let's find this French dressmaker of yours. Perhaps I can find something there for Felicity." Grasping Elizabeth's arm tightly, he hustled forward.

Two men from opposite ends of the street observed these activities. One was Tyler Hamilton-Smythe. From his now familiar perch atop a borrowed hackney, he watched the front door and saw Gideon and Elizabeth Laurence emerge. He smiled to himself as Gideon played the scene as they'd planned.

"Sarah," Tyler promised silently, "she'll never replace you." He cracked his whip. Between the shafts of the hackney, the startled horse bolted forward.

The other observer was Nigel Farquhar. Nearing the bookstore, he was surprised but pleased to see Elizabeth and her brother Gideon exiting its door and then standing outside for a few moments. As he was about to call out a greeting, the pair began to walk away from him. Farquhar quickened his pace to catch up.

Burning up and freezing at the same time, Gideon felt his heart was pounding so loudly that Elizabeth must hear it. He kept a smile glued to his lips while only vaguely listening to what Elizabeth was saying. His mind was fixed on the hackney speeding towards them.

"...and although you could not purchase one from Mademoiselle Villiers, I'm sure Felicity would like a fine shawl of some soft..."

The hackney but a half block distant, Gideon gulped and interrupted. "These books are deuced heavy, Elizabeth. I think I'll have them delivered after all."

Gideon gave Elizabeth no time to respond. Instead he gripped Elizabeth's left arm firmly and pivoted abruptly on his left leg while simultaneously thrusting out his right leg.

Immediately Elizabeth felt herself being propelled to her left, Gideon's right leg hooking around her left ankle and causing her to stumble back towards Stanfields. She tried to steady herself on her brother's arm. But his vise-like grip relaxed, and she continued to stumble unevenly, unable to stop while Gideon corkscrewed to the side while trying to keep his own balance.

Then the bundle of three books was driven into her back as it flew from Gideon's hand. The corners of the bindings hit her ribs and caused her to cry out in pain. The blow sent her diving towards the cobbles. Elizabeth sought to break her fall with her arms, but her wrists and elbows collapsed beneath her. At the same time, the books, torn from the brown paper wrapped about them, fell over her shoulders, one landing sharply on her left hand. The impact of her forehead and cheek bone hitting the cobbles of the street left her dazed, breathless, and unable to move. Sounds – hoof beats, coach wheels, voices calling her name – seemed distant. Her cry of "Help!" came out as a whisper as she shut her eyes to lessen the pain in her head.

"Miss Laurence!" shouted Nigel Farquhar as Elizabeth stumbled towards the street. Accelerating his pace to a run, he commanded, "Laurence, grab her arm!" But to Farquhar's amazement, Elizabeth's brother sent the parcel he carried into his sister's back as Elizabeth fell onto the cobbles. Then movement farther down the street caught Farquhar's eye. Barreling down upon Elizabeth was a speeding hackney. The driver, rather than pulling back on the lines, cracked his whip over his animal's back and urged it forward. Meanwhile, Gideon Laurence was pressed motionless against the side of the building, apparently so paralyzed with fright that he could do nothing to save his sister. Farquhar sprinted forward, his concentration divided between the hackney and Elizabeth's position on the street.

The sound of wheels was loud in Elizabeth's ears and her entire body ached. Then she heard, "Miss Laurence, raise your left arm! Your left arm! Now!" Somehow Elizabeth knew that this shouted order was important and lifted the correct limb. The effort caused her to groan. Her arm felt as if it were being jerked from its socket when it was grabbed and wrested sharply to the side. The rest of her body followed and bumped painfully over the paving stones as Nigel Farquhar pulled her to the side of the street a hair's breath before the hackney passed over the spot where she had lain.

Sitting at his desk at Stowe Manor, Geoffrey Hamilton-Smythe, Baron Bardstow, stared at Watley's letter. Its contents disturbed him profoundly. Tyler was once again involved in something that could prove disastrous to the entire family.

Bardstow stood, his brown eyes troubled. A few steps brought him to the window. Outside a gardener carrying a spade over his shoulder whistled tunelessly as he crossed the lawn. Quiet and peace. What he always found at Stowe Manor. Bardstow thought of his wife Eleanor closeted with the housekeeper and his daughter Georgina probably reading her grandmother a story. He sighed heavily. And because of Tyler's latest schemes, I must leave all of this for London and...

His mind refused to consider what he might discover upon his return to Hamilton Place. He passed a hand over his forehead and began to pace agitatedly before the fireplace. As he did, he mentally reorganized the contents of Watley's letter.

Somehow Tyler has made the acquaintance of Gideon Laurence, brother of Elizabeth Laurence. This Laurence has been closeted with Tyler at Hamilton Place on several occasions.

On one visit Tyler mentioned "arranging an accident," and on the next visit Laurence charged Tyler with driving a hackney so recklessly that Miss Laurence had nearly been killed. And now another accident is being planned. An accident Watley thinks I may be able to prevent if I come to London.

"He's using Miss Laurence to hurt Rossbury. Threatening the life of a woman he has never even met to avenge himself on a man who has always looked out for his good!" As Bardstow spoke his conclusion aloud, his anger rose. "This time Tyler, you've gone too far!" Suddenly a picture of his mother's youngest brother in Canada slid across his memory. I will ask Mother for Uncle Josiah's direction today, he told himself.

Bardstow strode back to his desk and sat down abruptly. Pulling a piece of paper towards him, he tried to decide whom to write first. Rossbury must be told, he reflected wearily.

Bardstow puzzled over the connection between Elizabeth and Rossbury for some moments. Could it be, he wondered, that Rossbury intends to make Miss Laurence his Countess? Would Tyler seek to destroy Rossbury by harming someone he loved? He would, Bardstow thought sadly.

Bardstow struggled to find the words to tell Rossbury what had occurred, hoping all the while that Rossbury had already been informed and was dealing with the situation in London. Then he remembered Tyler's suggestion about calling Rossbury out. Tyler's trying to… Bardstow gasped. He abandoned his attempt to couch Tyler's schemes in polite language and rapidly covered the page with words that bluntly told Rossbury of the danger to himself and Miss Laurence. Hastily he addressed the letter to Richard Sinclair Verinder, the Earl of Rossbury, Earl's Wood Park, near Myndton, Shropshire.

Dear God, Bardstow prayed, if Rossbury is not already in London, let the letter reach him in time!

"Mr. Stanfield," called Farquhar urgently when he entered the bookstore with Elizabeth drooping on his arm. "Have you a chair where Miss Laurence may sit?"

Both the bookseller and Mrs. Cholmondeley-Musgrove, interrupted in their examination of a large illustrated volume on Stanfield's desk, gazed towards the doorway. There they saw an ashen-faced Gideon Laurence and Nigel Farquhar who was half-supporting Elizabeth, her clothes torn and dirty.

"What on earth happened?" gasped Stanfield.

Stanfield pulled out the chair behind his desk, and Elizabeth limped over to it. Gideon stammered, "An accident. It was an accident. She tripped. Fell into the street. All a terrible mistake. That is, a mishap," Gideon corrected wildly. "Driver couldn't have seen her. I'm sure he wasn't trying to, to… I tried to help her, but, but I, but I…" He broke off abruptly, aware that he was talking too much.

Although Gideon's account of the incident did not mirror either Elizabeth's or Farquhar's recollection, neither noticed. Elizabeth was yearning for Rossbury's arms and trying hard not to cry. Farquhar was considering the best way to convey Elizabeth back to Carlington Square quickly.

Gideon fluttered over his sister and babbled, "Nothing like this ever happens in Little Throckton. I did try to tell you, Elizabeth, that London's a dangerous place. We should both go home."

"I think," inserted Mrs. Cholmondeley-Musgrove, "Miss Laurence needs to be taken to a place a bit nearer than Little Throckton." She bent over Elizabeth's chair. "And that would be?"

"Farnsworth Place," Elizabeth whispered. The kindly face looming close to hers looked familiar. "Not a hackney," Elizabeth pleaded.

"Of course not," assured Mrs. Cholmondeley-Musgrove. "You shall travel in my carriage. It is just around the corner and large enough for all of us." She knew that both Gideon and Nigel Farquhar would want to see Elizabeth safely home. "Mr. Stanfield shall tell my coachman to bring it to the front of the shop." Her large honey-colored eyes, the only beautiful feature of a face far too angular to be called handsome by anyone's standards, never left Elizabeth, who struggled to identify the comforting woman at her side.

"A generous offer," commented Philip Stanfield. He immediately headed for the door.

"But my sister and I have never been introduced to you!" exclaimed Gideon. He was annoyed that a stranger was usurping the role he was supposed to play.

At the door, Stanfield stated unceremoniously, "Mrs. Cholmondeley-Musgrove is a fine lady and one of my oldest customers." Then he exited the shop.

"I am certain you will agree, Mr. Laurence," observed Mrs. Cholmondeley-Musgrove smoothly, "that, for today at least, the needs of your sister must take precedence over convention." Straightening, she directed the force of a smile full of understanding upon Gideon before bending over Elizabeth once again. "And besides in a sense, we have all met, I believe, at Mr. Danforth's?"

Elizabeth felt she was being willed to remember something, something more pleasant than the brush with death that had left her shaken and unnerved. Suddenly her eyes widened and she smiled at Mrs. Cholmondeley-Musgrove for the first time. "The cravat pin!"

"I returned to purchase a second pin only to be told that it had been selected by another customer."

Then Elizabeth remembered, "My appointment with Mademoiselle Villiers! And Lady Farnsworth's coach will be there!" She ignored the pain in her aching left shoulder and ankle as she stood and laid a compelling hand on Farquhar's arm. "We must send a messenger at once."

While Farquhar scrawled the necessary words on paper found upon Mr. Stanfield's desk, Mrs. Cholmondeley-Musgrove moved to Elizabeth's left side. "Here's Mr. Stanfield come to tell us that my carriage is outside, Miss Laurence."

"It is," acknowledged the bookshop owner. One hand held open the door he had just entered; the other cradled the three books, now tattered and dirty, he had salvaged from the street.

"You must tell your coachman to drive very carefully, Mrs. Cholmondeley-Musgrove." Gideon Laurence hastened to Elizabeth's right to escort her to the waiting carriage. "London is a most dangerous place," he informed Elizabeth as he took her arm, "and I shan't be easy in my mind 'til you are safe at Hopeden Hall." Then both he and Mrs. Cholmondeley-Musgrove assisted Elizabeth as she limped towards the carriage standing beyond the door.

Nigel Farquhar put the note he'd written into Mr. Stanfield's hand. "Can you find a lad to deliver this at once?" Upon seeing the shop owner's nod, Farquhar dug in a pocket, pulled out a coin, and gave it to Stanfield. "For the messenger."

Soon Farquhar was seated within a spacious carriage next to Gideon Laurence, their backs to the horses. Opposite them sat Mrs. Cholmondeley-Musgrove and Elizabeth, whose legs were covered by a large traveling rug. Elizabeth's eyes were shut. Gideon appeared to be lost in thought. Mrs. Cholmondeley-Musgrove laid a finger to her lips and smiled at Farquhar. And silence suited Farquhar perfectly as his mind replayed what he had seen in front of the bookshop and tried to make sense of it.

"This second hare-brained plan of yours worked no better than the first!" shouted Gideon later that afternoon in the study of Sir Augustus Tremaine's London town house. "Elizabeth appears no more likely to return to Hampshire with me than she was when I first arrived!"

"And whose fault is that?" demanded Tyler Hamilton-Smythe. "When her friend – Farquhar, you said? – came pounding down the pavement, you shouldn't have stood there, glued to the wall, quivering like a terrified rabbit. You should have–"

"I should have what?" Gideon stepped within inches of the younger man and glared up at him. "Tripped him perhaps? Grabbed his arm? Let you run over my sister with that blasted hackney?" Gideon punctuated each of these questions with a raised fist shaken right below Tyler's nose.

"No, of course not!" Tyler batted the fist away and turned sharply on his heel. "The intent, after all, was to frighten her, and I couldn't do that without bringing the hackney close, could I?"

"Too damned close!" Gideon hurled his frustration at Tyler. "While Farquhar dragged her out of the street, your left wheel ran over part of her dress!"

"You said yourself she was only bruised so there's no real harm done." Tyler sank into a comfortable armchair and crossed his legs. "We must simply make a better plan."

Maddened by Tyler's self-congratulatory smirk, Gideon echoed, "No harm done! A better plan!" He paused to gulp some air. The cell in Newgate he had nightmares about appeared all too real. "Lady Farnsworth informed me – informed me, mind you," repeated Gideon, "that Elizabeth would be keeping to her bed for the next four to five days. And three weeks from Wednesday next, she'll marry Rossbury. I'm running out of time."

Yes, you are, reflected Burke Inchcomb. Tremaine's man of all work in London hadn't needed to remain close to the study door to learn why Gideon Laurence had been upset when he returned to the Hanover Crescent townhouse. Shortly after

Hamilton-Smythe's arrival, their loud angry voices could be heard all over the house.

Sir Augustus will be furious when he learns what a mess this fool Laurence has made of everything, Inchcomb thought, remembering Tremaine's secret orders enclosed in the envelope Gideon had delivered in February. But, he considered with a calculating smile as he padded down the stairs to the ground floor, Sir Augustus will reward the person who tells him about it. Particularly if he can use Laurence's blunders to force those two idiots up there to help him get what he wants.

And when has Sir Augustus not gotten what he wants? Inchcomb chuckled softly to himself as he made his plans. First, to learn more about Tyler Hamilton-Smythe without arousing anyone's suspicions. Next, to send a letter to Throck Manor.

And before Miss Laurence is out of her bed, Inchcomb made a silent wager with himself, Sir Augustus will be here with a plan for how to put her into his!

Lady Beatrice lay wakeful and restless in her bed at Farnsworth Place. The house was quiet. Her godson's intended bride was safe in her room. Doctor Patterson had said Elizabeth was "badly bruised but otherwise fit."

Two accidents in a week. The phrase circled inside Lady's Beatrice's mind. Part of her wanted to credit the events to coincidence or misfortune. Part of her said she was simply an old lady who was making a mare's nest out of nothing.

Yet, yet – another corner of her mind said – something is amiss. But the dowager could not lay her finger on what it was. She moved to her side in a vain attempt to get comfortable, the scene in her entrance hall replaying itself in her memory.

Nigel Farquhar had seemed worried but preoccupied. Gideon Laurence had gabbled and made no sense. Mrs. Cholmondeley-Musgrove had declined to come in. Her footman had presented her card, her compliments, and her request to return on Monday to ask after Elizabeth.

A pity she didn't see what happened, thought Lady Beatrice, moving her pillow to the right. Still I shall be at home to her on Monday. Any woman who has the sense not to thrust herself into a distressing situation is someone to be cultivated. Perhaps she heard something at the bookshop.

Suddenly Lady Beatrice's eyes flew open as another memory surfaced – Rossbury's relating the details of the ugly accusation at Eastons. But not telling me everything he knew. Three incidents then, not two

Rossbury must be informed at once, she told herself. If my suspicions are groundless, he will discount them as such. If he knows anything that reveals otherwise, he'll be here by the end of the week. Elizabeth – on Doctor Patterson's orders – will be in bed for most of that time. Lady Beatrice nodded her head in the darkness and began to compose exactly what she would say in the letter she'd send to Earl's Wood Park the very next day.

# CHAPTER 18
# TUESDAY, MARCH 12, 1793

"Yes, Betty." Lady Beatrice looked at the upstairs maid standing in the doorway of her boudoir, the letter she was writing to her son forgotten.

"There's a man downstairs, milady. A carter. With a large trunk. He says it's for Miss Laurence." Betty Kemp bobbed her head in Elizabeth's direction. "He won't say who sent him. And he says he can't leave 'til he delivers the trunk into Miss Laurence's hands."

At the sound of her name, Elizabeth finished a stitch and laid the piece of lace she was mending in her lap. When she started to rise from Lady Beatrice's day bed, the Marchioness made a peremptory gesture to halt her.

"There's no need for you to go downstairs, my dear," Lady Beatrice stated firmly. "Doctor Patterson ordered you to rest, and I have already given way to your insistence that you were well enough to leave your room. I won't have you overtaxing yourself."

The dowager turned once more towards the upstairs maid. "This man has been told that Miss Laurence is receiving no visitors?"

"He has, milady. Mr. Dunhill told him. More than once. But he says he has orders. And his orders are to 'deliver the trunk and a message to Miss Laurence personally.'" As Betty recited the words the man downstairs kept repeating, she looked nervously first at Lady Beatrice and then Elizabeth.

"Then he shall do so," decided Elizabeth, rising a bit stiffly from the day bed and walking immediately towards the door before Lady Beatrice could stop her. "Perhaps Gideon has ordered what I left behind at Hopeden to be delivered here," she considered hopefully as she and Lady Beatrice preceded Betty to the stairs.

When Elizabeth turned at the newel post at the bottom of the staircase, she saw a wiry man of middle years who appeared much like the hundreds of other carters in London. But what caught her eye was what was at his feet.

"My trunk!" Elizabeth exclaimed. Without thinking of her bruises, Elizabeth dropped to her knees. She ran her hands over the familiar length, now corded securely. "How did it get here?" she asked aloud, seeing it in the attic of Doctor Mansard's house in Rouen where she had last left it.

"Be you Miss Laurence?" The nameless carter grinned.

"I am," answered Elizabeth, still kneeling by the trunk on the floor.

"I been 'structed t' put this trunk inter yer keepin' n' t' give you th', th'..." The man struggled to recall the words he had been ordered to memorize. When the phrase popped into his mind, he finished in a rush, "Th' complermints o' Capt'n Bird n' his partner."

Elizabeth stood slowly, her left leg complaining about the extra bending after Saturday's fall. Captain Bird? She mulled over the name over. Then like a dark room lit by a taper, the meaning of the words became clear. Clever man, Elizabeth thought.

Cautious, too! "Can you deliver a note to Captain Bird and his partner?"

"Not t' th' capt'n hisself, Miss. But t' them as knows him." Not knowing either man suits me, thought the carter with an involuntary shake of his head. "It'll get t' 'em all right."

"Use the desk in the morning room," suggested Lady Beatrice. "I'll stay here with," she paused invitingly.

The carter sensed an interrogation was forthcoming and said, "Abel Black," his cheeky grin telling the dowager that the name was not his own.

"I shall keep Black here company while you write your note of thanks." Lady Beatrice ordered two footmen supervised by Dunhill to carry the trunk to Elizabeth's room and uncord it there.

"That trunk," Lady Beatrice mused aloud when the servants had gone, "seems to have traveled a goodly distance."

"Tha' it may of, ma'am. But I knows aught 'bout it. Me," the so-called Black jabbed his chest with a dirty finger, "I takes it on my cart here to Carlington Square like I been told t'. T' Rossb'ry House first. The foreman, he says, Miss Laurence won't be there, but th' people there'll know where she be." His smile broadened. He knew Lady Beatrice wanted to know where he had picked up the trunk, but he had been working at his trade long enough to know that the best way to keep his job was to follow orders, ask no questions, and speak about his work to no one. "When they tol' me she was right 'cross th' square, well I says t' myself, you're a lucky man, Abel Black. Miss Laurence bein' right 'ere. Saves me a bit of a trip n' my mare, too!"

"You are fortunate," noted Lady Beatrice dryly.

Elizabeth hurried back into the hall, a fat note in her hand. Inside her short note of thanks for 'Captain Bird' was another one for her uncle. It said, *All is well here. The delivery was made. The ragman and the doctor's sometime assistant will wed on April 3.* The message will keep Uncle Léon from worrying, Elizabeth thought.

"Thank you for waiting, Mr. Black. Please give this note to your master. And if you will wait a moment more, I'd like to give–"

"Don't need anythin' more, Miss Laurence." The carter edged towards the door. "Was tol' yer might give me somethink like this." He held up the note. "But foreman was tol' I weren't to–" He stopped abruptly, aware he had said more than he needed to. "I'll just be on my way then." After a bob of his head, the man jerked the street door open and hastened down the steps.

Lady Beatrice and Elizabeth watched him as he bounded onto the driver's seat of his cart, gathered up his lines, and urged the horse forward.

"Well, my dear," suggested Lady Beatrice as she closed her own front door, "let's see what's in that trunk."

Soon the trunk lay open in the middle of the floor of Elizabeth's room. Martha's hands busily unpacked each item with practiced care.

Forced to recline in the room's upholstered wing chair, her feet resting on the matching hassock, Elizabeth felt like an invalid.

"Unpacking's easy," Martha assured her. "Pressing and hanging's the real chore. And Patience will do that. So don't fret, Miss Elizabeth." Martha lifted a dark pink gown from the trunk and shook out its folds.

"That is one of my favorites," Elizabeth said.

"Pink is a good colour for you," observed Lady Beatrice as Martha laid the dress beside the others already on the bed.

"What's this then?" Martha stooped to grasp a piece of paper that had lain under the pink dress. She handed the folded note to Elizabeth.

Elizabeth swiftly read its few lines. She pictured Doctor Mansard penning it in haste as Captain Hivert or someone sent by him waited.

"It's from Uncle Léon. And in French, of course. He says – this is a rough translation – *I packed these after the funerals. I thought that what is old may bring pleasure to a new life. I am well, and Alain and Delphine will arrive soon. Thank the ragman for his message.*

After refolding the note, Elizabeth saw the questions in the others' faces and recognized that she should have changed funerals to funeral and ragman to Rossbury. "Alain is the second son of Uncle Léon's youngest brother. Delphine is his wife. They have not been married long. Alain has expressed a wish to study medicine. And after Aunt Claire died, Uncle Léon decided to ask if they would like to come to Rouen so Alain could study and work with him. Obviously, they have accepted."

"That will be good for all of them." Lady Beatrice waited for Elizabeth to explain the other references in León Mansard's guardedly worded note.

"And 'what is old' refers to these pieces of Aunt Claire's jewelry Uncle Léon packed in my truck." Elizabeth opened one of the small boxes that Martha had earlier found in the trunk and now lay in her lap. "Knowing that two of them, this brooch and these earrings," Elizabeth picked up the two items and smiled, "belonged to Grandmother Cavenaugh makes them doubly dear."

Elizabeth put those pieces down and touched another box. "And dear Uncle Léon put my own jewelry in my trunk, too. Much of it was mother's."

"You'll have something of hers to wear at your wedding then, if you like," suggested Martha.

"I will." Elizabeth looked up from the jewelry boxes to find both Lady Beatrice and Martha still gazing at her with undisguised curiosity. "Perhaps Uncle Léon included some of my books in the trunk," she said brightly. "He would put them at the bottom. Martha, can you feel them beneath the clothes?"

"Funerals. That's two at least, Lady Bea," reminded Martha as she brushed her mistress' hair that evening in Lady Beatrice's boudoir. "Who else died besides Claire Mansard? That's what I want to know."

Lady Beatrice stared into the mirror without seeing her reflection. Martha's questions echoed her own.

"And this ragman? Who is he?" Martha harrumphed. "Some friend of Captain Bird's?"

"I think," stated Lady Beatrice carefully, "that Elizabeth believes whatever it is she is not saying is really not hers to tell, but Richard's."

Martha stopped brushing and considered the idea. After her eyes met those of the dowager in the dressing table mirror, she nodded slowly.

"When my godson returns, we may learn more."

"Less, more like. A good one for keeping things private is our Dickon." Martha resumed her downward brush strokes.

"That's true," admitted Lady Beatrice. "I confess I am most vexed by Richard's refusal to be more open with me."

"That was always his way, Lady Bea."

"It appears to be Elizabeth's as well."

Martha put the brush down on the dressing table. "These accidents…" She halted, unsure of how to complete the sentence.

"Accidents, yes," repeated Lady Beatrice. But are they? she wondered again. And as her eyes again met Martha's in the looking glass, she saw her unspoken question reflected in her maid's troubled glance. Tomorrow, Lady Beatrice hoped, Rossbury will receive the letter I posted to him and answer it by coming to London at once.

"Shh!" reprimanded Tyler with a laugh. "Wake everyone, and there's trouble, I know." With one arm, he supported Gideon Laurence. They stumbled towards the door of Sir Augustus Tremaine's townhouse, its fanlight a beacon of gold.

The rest of the street was dark in the hour just past midnight. The hackney behind them stood quietly. Then the horse blew noisily and stamped once.

"Shh!" repeated Gideon to the animal. He hiccupped, tripped on a step, and fell to his knees. "No noish, no noish. We'll jush..."

When the door swung inward and spilled an oblong of brightness onto the steps, they looked up. Standing with one hand on the door was Inchcomb. His look was not welcoming.

"Sir Augustus will see you both in his study." Inchcomb strode past them to pay off the hackney. "Immediately."

"Thought this was your place?" whispered Tyler while Gideon rose and began to scuttle forward as fast as his drink-wobbled legs would move.

"Loan."

"And Sir Augustus?"

"Tremaine," puffed Gideon wishing the alcohol fog would lift from his brain and wondering how much Sir Augustus knew. Too much, he told himself and groaned aloud. "Neighbor. Should be my brother-in-law 'cept tha' Elish, Elizsha." He gave up the attempt to pronounce his sister's name. "Doesn't want him." He stood on the landing, winded by the effort of climbing the stairs so quickly. "Ungrateful, tha's wha' she ish."

A picture began to form in Tyler's mind. He unbuttoned his greatcoat and shrugged out of it. Then he tugged at cuffs and waistcoat, pulling both into a better semblance of order. "And Sir Augustus?" he whispered when he heard Inchcomb padding down the hall behind them. "Did he ask you..."

"Sent me here to bring her home." Gideon felt sick. A cell at Newgate loomed large. He leaned against a wall and rubbed his eyes with a hand that felt grimy.

Then Inchcomb passed them, opened the door to the study, and announced, "Gideon Laurence and the Honourable Tyler Hamilton-Smythe, Sir Augustus." The two men followed close behind him.

At his desk, Sir Augustus Tremaine folded a piece of paper, let a drop of wax fall on the fold, and applied his seal. "I need no reply to this."

Inchcomb took the note. "Understood, Sir Augustus."

"That will be all, Inchcomb."

"Very good, Sir Augustus." Inchcomb bowed and left the room, the door's click sounding unnaturally loud in the ears of the two men who faced the immaculately dressed, blank-faced figure now rising behind the desk.

Sir Augustus' hooded eyes, devoid of expression, revealed nothing. Without uttering a word, the baronet walked to the fireplace, turned, and stood before it.

Finally Gideon burst out, "Was all an accident! Tha's all. Only a mis, a mis…"

"Accidents," interrupted Sir Augustus. "With a hackney. And an extraordinarily reckless driver." His eyes caught and held those of Tyler Hamilton-Smythe for a moment until the younger man lowered his.

Gideon's jaw dropped. "How did…" he began to ask before deciding questioning Sir Augustus' sources was not the best idea. "Thought to frighten her out of London. Kept telling her tha's ssh, shafer in Hampshire."

The word <u>frighten</u> caused Sir Augustus' imagination to catch fire. "And has she agreed to come?"

"No," admitted Gideon.

If a fall from one hackney and a close brush with the wheels of another did not frighten her off, thought Sir Augustus, taming Elizabeth Laurence will be an even bigger challenge than I thought. And challenge, evoked by fear and reluctance, was what he wanted. Upon his return from Rosemont, he had stopped at the house of a madam who understood his needs. But the experience had palled. He wanted to face scorn and change it to fear, to intimidate. And though the latter was possible, most of the women he had used had been as spiritless as his late wife Edith. Yet controlling someone such as Elizabeth Laurence – a woman never bedded, unwilling and frightened by little... His body burned with anticipation.

"Before these accidents," Sir Augustus' voice was patient, that of a schoolmaster questioning a dull pupil, "did you try to reason with your sister?"

"Of course, I did," shot back Gideon, stung more by the condescension than he would have been by sarcasm. "Won't give up this Rossh, Rossh-b'ry. Won't hear a word sshp, 'poken against him." He glared at Tyler. "Won't return to Hopeden – not for any reason."

"And should you withhold your consent?"

"Shays she'll marry without it!" The memory of what Elizabeth had said drove Gideon from terror over Sir Augustus' reaction to fury over his sister's refusals. "You know what she's like after she's made a decision," Gideon wailed. "Nothing will persuade her to change it! Nothing!" He covered his face with his hands, scrubbing his temples as if to erase the drumbeat the night of revelry with Hamilton-Smythe had brought on.

"I doubt that, Laurence," rejoined Sir Augustus smoothly as he examined the perfectly manicured nails of his left hand. "A different tactic, a more amiable but less direct approach, I think, would be quite successful."

Gideon's hands dropped. He stared, goggle-eyed, disbelieving at the baronet. "Sus, sus-sessful," Gideon repeated clumsily.

"Indeed." Sir Augustus tugged at the bell pull hanging to the right of the fireplace. "But more of that tomorrow. Or," he continued with a smile that left his eyes unblinking and cool, "should I say later today."

The door clicked open. "Mr. Laurence is ready to retire now, Moss," Sir Augustus told the servant who had entered. "You will be sure to ask Moss for anything you require, won't you, Laurence?"

Surprised by the sudden end to the interview, Gideon opened his mouth to speak and then shut it again. He had expected – he did not know what he had expected, but not this. Not the implication that all would be well. He swallowed. "Thank you, Sir Augustus." He turned to follow the servant to his room.

After the door had closed once more, Sir Augustus gave his full attention to Tyler Hamilton-Smythe. "Shall we be comfortable?" Sir Augustus motioned to a pair of chairs near the fireplace. "Perhaps a little brandy would be welcome."

While Tyler seated himself, he watched Sir Augustus pour two measures from a decanter on a nearby table and framed a question about Tremaine's interest in Laurence's sister. He had observed the baronet's handling of Gideon Laurence and recognized that Sir Augustus would make an excellent ally – and an implacable enemy.

However, as Tyler took his first sip of Tremaine's excellent brandy, Sir Augustus asked, "The new Lord Rossbury is a relation of yours, is he not? By marriage? A bit of good fortune for you having an earl as a brother-in-law."

Tyler almost choked on the fiery liquid. He removed the glass from his lips, unaware that the fingers clenched around it and the scowl on his face were the signs Sir Augustus wanted to see. "Relation he is, to be sure. Good fortune the connection assuredly is not," spat Tyler. "Married my sister Sarah and good as killed her. And then put paid to any chances of advancement I might have had."

"Oh?" Though Inchcomb had told Sir Augustus a great deal about the Hamilton-Smythe family, the baronet looked at Tyler questioningly, his gaze inviting Tyler to explain his previous remark.

Spurred by Sir Augustus' apparent commiseration, Tyler poured out his torrent of grievances against Rossbury. Then he tossed back the remaining brandy in one gulp. "Now Rossbury wants to replace Sarah with Gideon Laurence's sister and –"

"Something you want to prevent," interrupted Sir Augustus smoothly.

"Yes, by God I do," ground out Tyler. "Rossbury doesn't deserve to be happy with her or anyone else."

"I concur," agreed Sir Augustus. "No one deserves to make himself free with what belongs to another man."

"Another man?" echoed Tyler. "You."

Sir Augustus said nothing.

Tyler laughed mirthlessly. "Rossbury – and everyone connected to him, save for my poor sister Sarah – has the devil's own luck. And Laurence and I have been damned unlucky in our attempts to…" He left his sentence dangling when he remembered that Tremaine wanted to marry the woman he had been about to call stupid. "Now we have all but run out of time," he continued. "The banns will be read for the first time this Sunday at St Etheldreda's, and Rossbury's due back in town in a week."

Sir Augustus masked his surprise. Inchcomb had reported neither of these facts. "For someone who claims to dislike Lord Rossbury so actively, you appear to know a great deal about his plans."

"One of Rossbury's female servants likes to talk. To me."

Sir Augustus nodded approvingly and waited for him to continue.

"And for once, luck was with me. Patience – Patience Downes, that's her name – was promoted from upper house maid at Rossbury House to lady's maid at Farnsworth Place. Lady's maid to Miss Elizabeth Laurence." Tyler smiled smugly.

Sir Augustus' eyes gleamed appreciatively. Young Hamilton-Smythe has a bit more sense than I thought, he told himself. "An unwitting spy in the house of your enemy."

"Stupid cow thinks I am Viscount Armbruster. Tells me everything." Tyler relaxed in the chair for the first time, his feet stretched out in front of him. "I know, for instance, that this Friday Lady Farnsworth has appointments with both her banker and then her solicitor in the forenoon and that on Saturday they are invited to some doings at Lady Dalrymple's."

Sir Augustus' brain began to form a plan. "Friday morning?" he asked. "You are certain?"

"I can check, can't I?" Tyler said. "On Thursday afternoon. Patience's free afternoon. That's when I meet her at the Hare and Hounds."

"An appointment you will keep." And, thought Sir Augustus, in a few days Elizabeth will not be in St Etheldreda's listening to the banns being read but in St Mark's at Little Throckton listening to the Reverend Mr. Cuthbertson pronouncing her my wife.

Less than a half hour later, Sir Augustus swirled the remains of the brandy in his glass and smiled. Hamilton-Smythe, who had been sent home in Tremaine's coach, would be back the next day.

Today, Sir Augustus noted with satisfaction. However, Gideon Laurence will not be here when he arrives. Gideon's a weak reed.

He must believe he is speaking the truth when he sees Elizabeth on Friday.

After Tyler's departure, the baronet had written a postscript to the note he had earlier given Inchcomb, and Moss had taken it to Inchcomb's room. Now Sir Augustus considered his plan anew, ticked off each point. No, he considered, there is nothing more to be done tonight. All that remains is to spring the trap. And catch Elizabeth in it. Before the end of the week, Tremaine promised himself, she shall begin to learn who her master is.

Sir Augustus raised his glass. "Lady Tremaine. May you prove to be a wonderfully stubborn pupil."

## CHAPTER 19

# WEDNESDAY, MARCH 13, 1793

At mid-afternoon, Andrew St John Beresford, Viscount Grantleigh, climbed down from his traveling carriage stopped near the steps to the entrance of Earl's Wood Park. He flexed the muscles of his back and looked up at the front of the beautiful Georgian house designed by Robert Adam.

"Drew!"

Grantleigh turned. From the stable block, Rossbury strode quickly forward.

"I heard a carriage pull up but thought it was a neighbor."

"It's good to see you, Richard." As Grantleigh and Rossbury shook hands, "Or do you prefer Rossbury?"

Rossbury's left eyebrow quirked upward in surprise, a characteristic response that put a wider grin on Grantleigh's face. "We have known each other too long to regress to formality now, Drew."

"Agreed."

The two men stood for a moment while assessing each other's appearance, Rossbury thinking the Viscount seemed a trifle thin, Grantleigh noting the new Earl looked lean and hard but content.

Rossbury gestured towards the steps, and the pair began to mount them. "Thank you again for your letter of condolence."

"Edward's death was a shock to both Mother and me. He was a good man. We shall miss him."

"As will I." Rossbury opened the front door and led the way to the library.

"Simon acquitted himself well at Edward's funeral. You can be proud of him," stated Grantleigh, "as I am certain others have already told you." After having sat for hours during the carriage journey, he declined Rossbury's offer of a chair.

"They have, and I am. Nonetheless, hearing you confirm the general opinion is gratifying." Rossbury took up a position familiar to Grantleigh – back to the unlit fireplace, one shoulder eased against it, weight centered on his left leg.

"Simon was rather anxious about you at the time." Grantleigh knew that Rossbury would understand that he too had been concerned. "He feared he might find himself an earl rather than a viscount when all was said and done."

"There was never much danger of that." Faces – Jacques Rouvault's aflame with fanaticism and Henri LeBeau's twisted with hatred – loomed before Rossbury; but his expression remained calm.

"Nevertheless, I – and I imagine Simon agrees – am glad to hear that you will be taking no more trips to France in the immediate future." Grantleigh concluded, "You and I have seen too little of one another of late."

"And is this visit an attempt to remedy that situation?"

"It is."

With a rueful shake of his head, Rossbury observed, "I feared as much. Your visit is unfortunately ill timed and gives us little time for conversation. First, the Clares are expecting me to join them this evening. In fact, I was preparing to leave when you arrived. But I anticipate no difficulty about your making a ninth at supper. The numbers will be uneven, but Mrs. Clare has declared it a family affair and is not a hostess who becomes ruffled at the appearance of an unanticipated guest. Simon and his tutor John Naismith are, in fact, already at Gylston Priory."

"I should say my timing is excellent, for having the opportunity to dine with your neighbors sounds delightful. Particularly as your letter indicated Piers Clare has consented to an understanding between his daughter Lucy and Simon. And the talk I wanted to have with you can wait until tomorrow."

"It cannot. Tomorrow I must leave for London." Rossbury thought of the contents of Lady Farnsworth's letter received at midday. Godmother does not frighten easily, he told himself. And the absence in Elizabeth's letter, containing her wishes for his birthday, of any mention of the events related by the dowager only increased his concern.

"Your letter indicated that you intended to travel south next week."

"That was my intention. However, I now find I must return to London at once." The urgency of Lady Beatrice's words, her underscoring of the word accident, her distrust of Gideon Laurence again scrolled across Rossbury's mind. Without his realizing it, his posture changed. Rossbury stood upright, a determined set to his jaw.

"Does this business concern Miss Laurence?"

"It does," rasped Rossbury, his voice suddenly hoarse with emotion, his blue eyes demanding answers.

"Then it may be that my reason for coming here has some bearing on the matter." Grantleigh plunged into the story. Relate essentials now, time for details later, he told himself. "Catherine Calvert, a neighbor of ours at Brookfields, died in January. She was a widow whose children had predeceased her and the owner of an unentailed property, Rosemont. Mrs. Calvert's will left

Rosemont and £5000 to Mrs. Calvert's grandniece – Elizabeth Laurence." Grantleigh paused to order the next set of facts in the story he had heard from Lady Cecily.

Rossbury, at Grantleigh's mention of Elizabeth's name, grew very still. He waited silently for Grantleigh to continue.

"Upon Mrs. Calvert' s death, her solicitor William Clewett, wrote to Miss Elizabeth Laurence at Hopeden Hall in Hampshire to inform her that she was the principal beneficiary in her great-aunt's will." For a second time, Grantleigh halted briefly. Thinking about what he must say next angered him.

Meanwhile, Rossbury's mind leapt forward, seeing motives for the accidents Lady Beatrice had written about.

"Then Clewett was informed by a letter written by Gideon Laurence, Miss Laurence's brother, that while visiting relatives in France Miss Laurence had died."

Grantleigh's last word turned Rossbury's face to stone. "And Gideon Laurence is the secondary legatee."

"He is," confirmed Grantleigh as Rossbury strode to a desk where a silver pen and inkstand rested and seated himself. "Furthermore, although I do not know how important the incident is, Rosemont has already had a visitor." He stopped in confusion, for Rossbury's attention appeared fixed on a letter.

Pulling a sheet of paper toward him, Rossbury rapidly penned an apology to Mrs. Clare for his absence that evening. "Continue."

"The visitor," Grantleigh related, "was Sir Augustus Tremaine, a friend of Laurence. He told Mrs. Higgs, the housekeeper, that he had been traveling through the countryside and that Laurence was expecting him at Rosemont. But Laurence was not in residence. Before he left, Tremaine said he must have mistaken the date."

"And the date of this visit was?" Rossbury continued writing.

Grantleigh cudgeled his brain. First the arrival of Rossbury's letter, then Lady Cecily's voice saying, 'Last Tuesday' surfaced. He made a mental calculation. "Tuesday, February 26th."

So, concluded Rossbury while signing and sealing the note to Mrs. Clare, Sir Augustus Tremaine could be the driver of the hackney.

"Yet," Rossbury began to speak his next thought aloud as he drew out a second sheet of paper which he headed 'Simon.' "Yet," Rossbury wondered, "for Tremaine to mistake the date of his friend's arrival at a newly inherited piece of property seems more than odd."

"Exactly what Mrs. Higgs thought." Grantleigh paced the room restlessly. "Especially after the Bells, who tenant Rosemont's farms, reported seeing a traveling coach arrive and depart on the Northcote Road on that Tuesday."

Rossbury stopped writing. Tremaine's visit was not a stop on a tour. And it coincided with Laurence's journey to London as if... As if, Rossbury concluded, Tremaine wanted to keep his visit a secret from his neighbor.

"There's more amiss here than Gideon Laurence's attempt to cheat Miss Laurence of an inheritance, isn't there, Richard?"

Rossbury found Lady Farnsworth's letter. "Read this."

Grantleigh took the offered paper and read it while continuing to prowl the room. The deeper into its contents he delved, the more concerned he became.

Meanwhile, Rossbury completed his note to Simon, a brief explanation of his urgent need to go to London that very day and instructions for handling two pieces of business. As soon as he had dusted the sheet with sand, a disturbing memory returned. Tyler Hamilton-Smythe, hat pulled low, hurrying from Eastons after making his accusation. Bardstow relating

Tyler's desire to provoke a duel. And Bardstow's mews exit from Rossbury House because he feared Tyler was keeping watch in the square.

A frightening possibility arose as his brain searched for answers. Tyler transferring his watch to Farnsworth Place after I left for Earl's Wood Court. Tyler seeing Gideon Laurence at Farnsworth's door. Tyler scraping an acquaintance with Laurence and enlisting him as the ally Bardstow refused to be.

Rossbury's eyes narrowed while his fists clenched. If either of you has harmed one hair of Elizabeth's head, he vowed silently. He saw his sword and pistols in his room at Rossbury House and nodded. He rose and tugged the nearest bell pull.

"Miss Laurence is in grave danger." Grantleigh folded Lady Farnsworth's letter and returned it to Rossbury's hand. One look at his friend's face told him he need not say more. What he saw there was deadly purpose. Rossbury appeared to be seeing an enemy at a distance, one he intended to destroy.

The door to the library opened; Trevor, the Earl's Wood butler, entered, on his features a servant's habitual polite inquiry.

"Trevor, see that these are delivered to Gylston Priory at once." Rossbury handed the notes he had just written to the butler. "Then send Philips to tell Brown to saddle a horse--"

"Two," Grantleigh interrupted quietly.

The friends exchanged a level look before Rossbury turned back to Trevor. "Two horses. Raven and…" He made an instant assessment of his late brother's stable, "Warrior. Brown should bring them around in half an hour."

Rossbury glanced to his left and saw Grantleigh's nod. "And ask Mrs. Garrison to send a cold collation – anything at all will do – to this room in a quarter of an hour."

"Very good, milord." Trevor, letters in hand, exited the room.

Before the door closed, Grantleigh moved toward Rossbury's desk.

"Feel free to use whatever you need as I know you also must write a note or two of explanation."

"I'll send them and my coach back to Brookfields with Garrett," stated Grantleigh, already scribbling a few words to Lady Cecily.

"Raven and Warrior should carry us as far as the hours of light left enable us to go." Rossbury sketched his plans aloud. "I intend to push them through part of tomorrow morning and then to stop at a posting inn for new mounts. If we continue to exchange horses often, we should be in Carlington Square by midday on Friday."

Rossbury did not say what he planned to do once they reached London. I must be sure Elizabeth is safe. Dear God, let me find her well at Farnsworth Place. He forced from his mind thoughts of what he would do if all were not well. Time enough to deal with that problem later. So first, reach London. Then, find those responsible for the accidents Godmother wrote about.

Thoughts of those events caused him to feel both the chill of fear, greater than any he had experienced when his own life was endangered, and the heat of revenge. And a desire to hurt those who would harm the woman he loved so intensely that the possibility of her loss was akin to a physical wound.

Rossbury's continuing silence caused Grantleigh to lift his head and look at his friend. Rossbury's grim face made him look like a duelist who intends to kill his opponent. "I could not let you go to London alone," Grantleigh said more lightly than he felt. "Standing beside you now will prepare me to stand beside you on the third of next month."

"Thank you, Drew." Rossbury walked purposefully to the door. "I shall gather a clean shirt and a few necessities and tell

Garrett to do the same for you. By the time, I return, our meal should be ready."

Grantleigh nodded and kept writing.

With a hand on the door, Rossbury glanced about the library, a room where he knew Elizabeth would enjoy spending time. I must be in time, he told himself. For Elizabeth. His lips compressed into a tight line. For us.

Micah Whitbread stirred restlessly as he stared into the darkness, his narrow face creased in a frown. Beside him, his wife Sally heaved a sigh and shifted her bulk. Man's gonna be the death o' me, she thought. Alwa's worrit 'bout somethin'.

"Yew know t'was right thing f'r you t' do, Micah," Sally Whitbread stated impatiently for the third time since the couple had gone to bed that night.

"I be no man's lick spittle," whined Micah as an image of a well-booted man whose name he did not know rose before him. "Least ways, not his," he amended, recalling the man whose visit had caused his present anxiety.

"Inchcomb 'e said 'is name woz," reminded Sally, a horse-faced woman with a rawboned body and meaty hands, each of which could easily grasp two tankards. Of the two, she had the better memory for name and faces. Once she had been told a customer's name, no matter how seldom he stopped at the King's Arms, she never forgot it or him. Her memory of names was an asset she had developed along with a hearty, rough good humour. Both made her popular with the travelers and regulars she pulled a draft of ale for.

"Cockscomb more like!" groused her husband. He chewed a thumbnail. "How'd yew think that..."

"Tremaine, Sir Augustus Tremaine," supplied Sally, wondering if her memory had played her false for once. The name meant nothing; the face that should have sprung to life in her mind was only a blank.

"How'd Tremaine find out 'bout this place, Sal? How'd 'e find out?"

Both Sally and Micah pondered the question – as they had done immediately after Inchcomb had delivered Sir Augustus' note to the King's Arms earlier that day. They knew some of the men who financed the smuggling of contraband – ship owners some of them, men able to bribe customs officers to look the other way – were gentlemen who willingly collected the profits but who would deny all knowledge of what sort of cargoes their ship captains were transporting. But such men were far removed from day-to-day business itself. Such men would not know that the cellars of the King's Arms, a very ordinary tavern where costly French products were never served, was a store house for rare vintages held back from the market until the profit margin was astronomical.

"Think 'e be the owner, Sal? That'd 'splain ever' think," Micah wondered aloud.

The pair considered this new question for a moment.

"We's spoken 'bout this afore, Micah. Yew knows what we 'greed."

Micah's voice dropped to a whisper. "That 'e's the owner, y' mean?" The slight stress on the word <u>he</u> was overlaid with awe. He was the nearly invisible, powerful head of their brotherhood, someone they thought they had seen once.

"If this here Tremaine's the owner, why'd 'e send this Inchcomb wit' a piece o' paper, Micah? Why'd 'e use a name?" Sally's eyes shut tight as she reasoned the matter out. "Nothin's ever put in writin'. Yew knows that. 'Sides, only person we's ever seen is tha' Huckaby."

"Tha's right, Sal," Micah's breath came out with a soft whoosh.

"Whosomever the owner be, 'e won't be happy, Micah. No one involved ever 'posed to show 'is face 'ere when customers are 'bout. Tha's a rule. Allwa's followed 'fore now. Yew did right to send word 'bout it."

"So's even if the owner's – "

Sally cut her husband's question short. "'e's not, Micah."

"But even if," Micah insisted.

"Even if," Sally allowed, "'e's no call to come 'ere. Wants to use the King's Arms for some dirty work of 'is own, yew mark me, Micah. Doesn't want to foul 'is own nest, I warrant. Why else would some gennelmun send us a message 'bout needing the best room on Friday, I asks yew?"

"Tha's right, Sal," agreed Micah.

"Course, I's right," snorted Sally Whitbread into the darkness. "N' you be right t' send word t' 'im, Micah."

"'ope so, Sal, 'ope so," Micah worried. "You know wha' we're tol'. Never –"

Sally interrupted again. "'cept when we're 'spicious 'bout somethin', Micah. N' yew knows well as me tha' this Inchcomb n' 'is note 'bout as 'spicious as a ten-penny piece!"

"Still, Sal, if 'e thinks we done wrong in sendin' word n' we lose our places 'ere." Micah's fears had grown ever since Inchcomb's visit earlier and were not easily quieted.

"Won't 'appen, Micah. Somethin's wrong 'ere, n' t'weren't yew sendin' word. 'e knows we never bothered 'im 'fore this n' don' jump at 'ares, Micah. We've served 'im well. Done all we been asked t' do n' more. N' asked no questions. Yew mark me, Micah. Us'll not be ones in muck. Might even give us somethin' extra, 'e might." Sally hoped her last supposition was true. Their first grandchild was due any day now, and a few extra shillings would not come amiss in their daughter and son-in-law's home. "Be nice to be able to help Maggie, wouldn't it, Micah?" Sally's voice softened just as it always did when speaking of their only child.

"T'would, Sal," sighed Micah. He reconsidered his wife's arguments. They seemed sound, and he wanted to believe that his decision had been the correct one. Had he not sent a message as he had been instructed to do if he suspected any trouble and then a problem had arisen, he knew that his and Sally's tenancy of the King's Arms would be terminated without notice. Yet if he had caused concern in the free traders' hierarchy for naught, the result would be the same. Stuck between the Scylla and Charybdis of these choices, he – with Sally's prompting – had plumped for the latter and then been torn with anxiety ever since.

"Yew did right, Micah," Sally reiterated, knowing that her husband was still second-guessing himself. "It'll all come out right in th' end. Don' yew worrit. 'e'll take care o' whatever this all be 'bout."

"'ope so, Sal."

"'Tis out o' our 'ands now, Micah. N' we got 'nuff on our plates t'morrow." Sally turned on her side, put her hams of hands on her husband's shoulders, and began kneading. She heard him expel a long breath. "Yew did right," she stated again. "Yew knows 't, Micah. N' so will 'e."

# CHAPTER 20
# THURSDAY, MARCH 14, 1793

"Now, Patience, you know I don't like tears," cajoled Tyler Hamilton-Smythe, one hand on the door of a private room at the Hare and Hounds.

"But you always..." insisted Patience Downes, tears threatening to spill over despite her best efforts.

"Not today, my love." Tyler transferred the basket Patience always brought with her from his hand to hers. "If you'll be a good girl, next Thursday we shall do something special."

Patience's face brightened. "Something special!"

"I can't tell you about it now. It's a surprise," lied Tyler. "You do remember that we won't be meeting here again?"

Though Patience nodded, her eyes betrayed her doubt.

"I'll send you word of where we can meet next week." Tyler lifted Patience's chin and stroked her cheek with one finger. "Trust me."

"I do, Geoffrey. I will." Patience stumbled over her misgivings as Tyler twined a curl around one finger. "But I do look forward to, to – "

"Next week, my love." Tyler lowered the door lever and edged Patience into the opening. "Next week a special surprise and a long walk afterwards. But now you really must go."

"Yes, Geoffrey."

"Until next week then." Tyler smiled brilliantly and shut the door in Patience's face.

Tyler turned his back to the door and leaned against it, his smile widening. Done, he said to himself. And next week there will be no message to Patience, no walk, no meetings anywhere. Viscount Geoffrey Armbruster will simply disappear. That will be Patience's surprise. And there'll be one for Rossbury, too. Tyler's countenance darkened. A surprise long overdue and well deserved.

So engrossed was he in his thoughts, Tyler did not see Sir Augustus Tremaine slipping into the room through a door almost invisible in the inn's dark oak paneling.

"She is gone, I trust, for good." The baronet studied the room, his distaste for it and for its previous occupant clear in both his expression and tone.

"She is." Unable to resist the impulse to show off before Sir Augustus, Tyler preened a bit. "You must have heard the little cow prate on about –"

"Lady Farnsworth's plans for tomorrow. Yes, I did. She was very clear on that part. Tiresomely so." Sir Augustus paced a few steps to a diamond paned window overlooking a courtyard.

"She does go on a bit," confirmed Tyler. "But I had to appear interested in–"

"That was understood," interrupted Sir Augustus once again. He whirled to face Tyler. "But Lady Farnsworth's errands make tomorrow morning the perfect time for a brotherly visit."

Outside, Patience stood uncertainly near the door of the public house, her eyes wet with unshed tears. The gray skies reflected her mood. Her mind scrolled through the events of the afternoon; and when it arrived at Tyler's announcement that the usual stroll towards Carlington Square must be omitted, her tears began to fall. Patience fumbled in her basket for a handkerchief. It was not there. Gulping in terror, she frantically tore through the basket. The handkerchief, borrowed without permission, was gone.

"I'll be turned out for sure," Patience whispered to herself, whimpering a little. "Without a character!"

Her frightened eyes scanned the pavement, but no trampled handkerchief was seen. Then she saw herself taking the dainty lace-edged morsel of cloth from the basket when the promised walk was canceled.

Dropped it. That's what I did, Patience thought. He'll be angry with me for coming back. But if Miss Laurence misses it and says I'm a thief...

Patience hurried back into the Hare and Hounds, torn between fear and hope. Fear that the man she loved would scold her. Hope that the precious handkerchief had not been taken by some serving girl or potboy.

Once outside the door of the private room, Patience hesitated. Two low voices could be heard within. Quaking with fright, Patience put her hand on the door lever and lowered it slowly.

As the door inched open, snatches of conversation drifted out. "...experience as driver..." was followed by familiar laughter. Geoffrey's still there! Patience sighed with relief. Then there were words from a voice in a lower register.

Patience cautiously pushed the door inward. "... to the King's Arms... Surrey road..." The other voice faded. Patience gnawed on her lower lip. They won't like being interrupted, but if I don't put the handkerchief back... She felt desperate. "... traveling coach ...early afternoon ...plans coincide..." filtered from the room as she tried to decide what to do.

Finally, Patience took a deep breath, grasped the door handle firmly, pushed the door forward, and entered the room as if she had just arrived.

"Geoffrey," Patience began before quailing beneath the icy stare of Sir Augustus Tremaine. Patience shriveled under the baronet's disdain, which somehow made her feel dirty.

Patience hoped the man she had loved for the past eight weeks would speak, would rescue her with soothing words or even an introduction. But one look at her lover's face told Patience that returning to the room was an unforgivable sin.

Her mouth opened and closed without a sound coming from it. She felt paralyzed, unable for moment to remember why she had come. Her glance darted about the room, wanting to look at anything but those two accusing pairs of eyes.

"Get rid of her," hissed Sir Augustus Tremaine venomously just as Patience spotted Elizabeth's handkerchief a few feet in front of her.

"Patience, you must–" Tyler Hamilton-Smythe walked forward.

"Miss Laurence's handkerchief!" blurted out Patience. She snatched up the precious scrap of cloth and immediately began backing away from the two men in the room. "Missed it. Knew it must be here," she gabbled, retreating towards the door. "Had to come back. Pardon me if I, if I..." Patience swallowed hard, unable to think of anything else to say. Then she turned and fled through the door.

Once on the street again, Patience hurried in the direction of Carlington Square. When a glance over her shoulder showed her that the Hare and Hounds was no longer in sight, her pace slowed to a walk.

Never see him again. Never see him again. The unsaid words beat against her like a funeral knell. Never see him again. With one sleeve, Patience dashed away the tears trickling down her cheeks.

And underlining her tears was fear. The memory of the cold stare of the tall gentleman sent a shiver through her. Questions about who he was and how long and how often he had been there tumbled over one another. Patience shook her head, frightened by what she did not understand.

If only I could tell somebody! Patience moaned softly. But confiding in anyone meant risking her position at Farnsworth Place, perhaps being turned out. Daft I've been! Daft! There's no one to…

Jim! Jim Compton! The stableman's name leapt into her mind, and she recalled his offer to carry her basket, his kindly questions, and the smile he directed at her when he related a particularly amusing incident from his soldiering years to the Rossbury House servants.

But how can I tell him about…? Especially after I turned him away. No, Patience thought sadly, I can't tell Jim. Or anyone else.

Should've known! Should've known! Patience chastised herself while again wiping away tears with her sleeve.

Recognizing that she had reached the corner where her Thursday afternoon's walk usually ended, Patience stopped. After taking a deep breath, she scrubbed at her eyes with the heels of both palms to erase the traces of tears. Say nothing, Patience told herself. Forget this ever happened. The face of the rapier thin man, elegant in black and white, rose before her. She prayed she'd never see him again.

And next Thursday, Patience vowed, I will take a basket to Aunt Franny. Maybe cook'll give me a sweetmeat for the children. And if I'm lucky, maybe Jim'll ask to carry the basket again.

These decisions made, Patience set out briskly for Carlington Square as rain began to fall.

"Shall I go after her to…?" Tyler asked once the door of the Hare and Hounds' private parlour had closed behind Patience for the second time.

"No." Sir Augustus spoke in a peremptory fashion. "Her worry now will be to restore the handkerchief to its proper place."

He paced the few steps to the fireplace, its grate bright with coals, and put his back to its warmth.

"But we were discussing the coach when she–" Tyler protested.

"Yes, we were." Sir Augustus again cut across Tyler's words. "And little Patience Downes will, therefore, be unsurprised when the message you promised to send her does not arrive." He examined the nails of his left hand as he continued his explanation. "And to whom can your Patience confide her own deception about how she has been spending her Thursday afternoons? Employers will not tolerate any sort of clandestine relationships in their servants. A slip of the tongue would lead to an immediate order to pack her bag." Sir Augustus returned his gaze to his companion. "Patience Downes will hold hers."

"Yes, yes, you are right, of course." Tyler was relieved Sir Augustus had not faulted the way he had dealt with Patience. His palms felt wet, and he suddenly found himself wanting a drink. He licked his lips. An evening at the club, Tyler thought, will soon put me right.

"So, our plans are destined for success." Tyler grinned. What will Rossbury do when he learns of my role in his fiancée's abduction. Suggest pistols? Blades? Which would be more satisfying to drive into Rossbury's body? Tyler half-turned towards the door. "Will meeting you in Hanover Crescent at eleven o'clock tomorrow morning suit?"

"Yes, for all must be ready by eleven." Sir August had been watching Tyler from under hooded lids. "But I believe we should return to Hanover Crescent. Now. Together."

Surprised by this change in their previously discussed plans, Tyler faced the baronet, his mouth slightly agape.

"While I speak to Gideon Laurence about tomorrow's invitation, you and Inchcomb can rehearse your parts in the morning's drama." Before Tyler could claim that a rehearsal was unnecessary, Sir Augustus continued, "If you are like most of us," he moved his hands in a fluid, expansive gesture, "you have either had few dealings with those in the medical profession or been unobservant of their ways." His eyes bored into Tyler. "Tomorrow you must play the part of Doctor Adams to perfection. Everything," he exaggerated, "depends upon it."

Tyler unconsciously straightened his bearing, smugly reveling in his importance.

"Though your time on our stage will be very short, it is vital. Thus, as our best actors do, you too must memorize your role." Sir Augustus paused. "It would be a pity if your revenge were delayed. Again."

Tyler's mouth tightened. "Inchcomb will assist me, you say?"

"He will. He has everything you will require. The bag. The dose you must administer. And as you must look the part, he also has the clothes you must wear. I'd like you to try them on this afternoon." Sir Augustus shrugged. "It would not do to have your coat sleeves cover your hands or bare your shirt sleeves."

"No, it would not," agreed Tyler with a wolfish grin.

"And perhaps a slight alteration of your appearance as Miss Laurence will expect to see an older man. A few gray hairs. Spectacles and…" The baronet recalled Tyler's inability to look at him when questioned about previous encounters with Elizabeth. Sir Augustus suspected there was something Tyler did not want to relate. Sir Augustus let his gaze travel over Tyler's face. "You'll find Inchcomb will know what to do. His knowledge of the actor's paint box is quite remarkable."

"I shall play Doctor Adams so thoroughly I'll be half-believing I've a medical degree myself," assured Tyler.

"Excellent. And then tonight perhaps you will be so good as to dine with me. I'll require help," the baronet lied, "convincing Gideon Laurence that his best hope of winning his sister's cooperation is to treat her kindly. I plan to suggest some amusements in town that he and Miss Laurence might enjoy together in Rossbury's absence. As you have resided in London for a number of years..."

"Of course. I shall be happy to accept," replied Tyler, his chest expanding a bit. "If you need my help."

"I do," Sir Augustus assured him. "And as we have already agreed, we will tell Laurence nothing of Doctor Adams and our journey to the King's Arms. The less he knows, the better," Sir Augustus concluded as if sharing a secret with a close friend. "If Laurence had done his part earlier, Miss Laurence would already be in Little Throckton." The falsehood rolled easily from his lips.

"He panicked both times. Never seemed to realize it was a neck or nothing venture. Whereas I– "

"Whereas you," interrupted Sir Augustus, "are the man I need at my side tonight to help me keep Laurence in blissful ignorance. I fear," said the baronet in his most confiding tone, "that if Laurence knows our plan, a careless word or something in his manner would betray our intentions to his sister." His voice underscored the word <u>our</u>. "An ignorant man cannot reveal what he does not know. And with your help this evening, Gideon Laurence will remain ignorant."

Tyler nodded. "Only too happy to oblige."

And while you are speaking to Gideon Laurence at my table, thought Sir Augustus, I can be assured that you, Tyler my fair-haired idiot, are not revealing my plans to your wastrel friends at that hellions' haunt you frequent.

The baronet then mentally listed his plans for the rest of Tyler's day. A long session with Inchcomb. An even longer dinner. Then a suggestion that, due to the lateness of the hour, Tyler stay the night at Hanover Crescent. Where I can be assured that he does or says nothing to jeopardize tomorrow's venture.

Stepping away from the fireplace, Sir Augustus looked distastefully about the room. "Now the sooner we return to Hanover

Crescent, the better. I wish to be at home when Laurence arrives. Besides, you, Doctor Adams," Sir Augustus added, "need some tuition in the medical arts."

Sir Augustus opened the door and, with a gesture, indicated that Tyler should precede him through it.

"To Doctor Adams. May all of his doses work as intended," laughed Tyler softly as he exited the familiar parlour for the last time.

To Elizabeth Laurence, thought Sir Augustus Tremaine as he closed the door behind them. May this be the last day I cannot claim her as mine.

Hours later and miles north, Elizabeth was also the centre of Rossbury's thoughts as he urged his tired mount south along the road that led to London. Though heavy rain had been falling for hours and his legs were plastered with mud, he was only aware of the persistent throbbing of the old wound in his right leg. Punishing hours in the saddle had undone the good of the past month of recuperation. He rode stiffly, the pain from his leg seeming to penetrate every inch of his body. Meanwhile, chilling possibilities made him push his horse and himself onward.

"The horses are spent, Richard," remarked Grantleigh after his mount had stumbled twice in as many minutes. And so are you, he observed silently while noting Rossbury's rigid posture and compressed lips.

The faint lights Grantleigh had seen before he spoke became brighter. "Continuing tonight and risking a broken leg or worse – whether ours or one of the horses…" Grantleigh left the conclusion unstated.

Aroused from his thoughts of nightmarish possibilities, Rossbury fixed his attention on the road ahead. It was barely visible. Rain had turned its surface into a treacherous mire, and sodden skies had hastened the evening darkness, his drooping horse's head a grey blur in the quickly disappearing light.

"You are right, Drew. Going any farther tonight would be folly," admitted Rossbury, his voice flat with disappointment.

A folly you would commit had you been alone, thought Grantleigh.

Rossbury peered through the water dripping steadily off the brim of his hat. More lights blinked in the distance. A hostelry, not a mere cottage then, considered Rossbury. "The number of lights ahead indicates an inn."

"The Bull and Bush." Grantleigh recalled what they had been told the last time they had changed horses.

"A fire, a warm meal, and a dry bed for us and some decent stabling for these two," Rossbury listed as he gave the exhausted animal he rode a pat on the neck.

"Fresh mounts for the first leg tomorrow with any luck," added Grantleigh. He knew that night would be a mirror image of the previous one. Rossbury would eat what was set before him without even knowing what was on his plate, pace restlessly in front of the fire, and spend black hours on whatever bed was available staring sleeplessly at the ceiling while awaiting their pre-dawn departure.

"If not, we must press these two old soldiers into service for a few more miles until we reach a posting house." Rossbury absently patted his mount's neck again, his mind already on the road ahead.

Hearing the impatience in Rossbury's voice, Grantleigh reminded, "Nevertheless, barring an accident, mid-day tomorrow should find us in Carlington Square."

Rossbury glanced up at the leaden sky above them, now a dark ceiling from which rain descended in sheets. Even if the deluge stopped by morning, the roads would remain what they had been all day, ribbons of churned mud, mud which slowed their pace and made urging their horses to greater speed risky. A risk the danger to Elizabeth compelled him to take.

"Mid-day tomorrow in Carlington Square," Rossbury repeated grimly. It was a promise to both Elizabeth and himself.

"I have nearly finished, Lady Beatrice," Elizabeth noted from her place at the writing table as she heard the morning room door open and the rustle of skirts.

Moments later she signed her name to the letter she'd written. "I can address it tomorrow." She stood and turned towards Rossbury's godmother.

"To the Reverend Mr. Dean and his sister. The cousins you wish to come to London to see you wed?" Lady Beatrice asked.

"Yes," Elizabeth confirmed with a smile. "Rossbury has written that I may send them the funds for the journey."

"Has all this writing made your arm tired, my dear?" Lady Beatrice's concern forced the question from her.

"Only a bit," said Elizabeth honestly. "The bruises are already fading, and I have nothing more difficult to do tonight than to hold up Mr. Blake's little volume."

Lady Beatrice nodded her head in approval. "I expect you to pursue similar activities tomorrow morning." She disliked the idea of leaving Elizabeth alone but told herself that no harm could come to her godson's fiancée during the time it would take her solicitor to add a codicil to her will. "I do not want to find you and Betty cleaning the attics upon my return!" Lady Beatrice's exaggerated warning was half-teasing, half-scolding.

"My morning will be devoted to the business of writing more letters. First to Richard, and then to Lord Somerville," Elizabeth related.

"Ah yes, Lord Somerville's invitation for Tuesday. Delivered by his nephew, I believe."

"That's right. Just a quiet, early afternoon social. Only the four of us. But Mr. Farquhar says the company and conversation will brighten his uncle's whole week, for Lord Somerville is lonely."

"As is Winifred Braitwaite." Lady Beatrice thought about a widowed friend living on a small annuity.

"Mrs. Braitwaite?" Elizabeth echoed, her voice sounding puzzled. "Isn't she the woman Nan Smallwood's now companion to?"

"Yes, she is, thanks to Lady Dorothy. And that has made me think that perhaps I might play companion-maker, too."

"For?

"Lord Somerville, of course."

"Lord Somerville?" Elizabeth repeated in confusion. "I don't understand."

"I know you don't, my dear. Let me explain." Lady Beatrice's face softened, her eyes seeing a crowded ballroom where the future marquis and an eighteen-year-old girl danced, both with eyes only for the other. "Eons ago, when Dolly and I were young, Winifred Napier, as she then was, and Gerard Farquhar were..." She sighed. No need to say more, Lady Beatrice thought with a look at Elizabeth curved lips and gleaming eyes.

"His father, the third Marquis, wanted a titled bride for his son, and six months later hers had betrothed Winifred to a local squire." Lady Beatrice gave an eloquent shrug. "And now that Lady Somerville and Mr. Braithwaite are both long gone, I thought perhaps..." She trailed off, lost for a moment in memories.

"Then you plan to play matchmaker on Tuesday?"

"Not on Tuesday," admitted the Dowager Marchioness. "On Tuesday, you and I will behave so well that Gerard Farquhar will be eager to issue other invitations."

"In other words, we are to be perfect guests."

"We are." Lady Beatrice said emphatically, showing that she had no more to say on that subject. "And as the topic of guests has been raised, may I remind you of your obligations on this score?"

Elizabeth could think of none and cast a quizzical look at Lady Beatrice.

"The wedding breakfast, my dear," reminded the Marchioness.

"But there will only be..." Elizabeth began to count those who would be present. "A dozen?"

"The guests are few, I grant you, and that is as it should be so soon after Edward's death, but inviting those few to Rossbury House for a modest wedding breakfast is perfectly acceptable. Besides," Lady Beatrice used her final argument, "Rossbury's servants will expect you to do something."

"Yes," agreed Elizabeth, "they will. First, a menu and then a talk with Mrs. Ballantyne next week."

Elizabeth returned to her chair at the writing table, Lady Beatrice moving another small chair in position beside her. Elizabeth pulled out a fresh sheet of paper, picked up the pen, and wrote, "Menu. Wedding Breakfast. 3 April 1793." Then the two bent their heads and minds to the task of deciding what dishes the twelve guests might enjoy.

About the same time, in the entrance hall of Baron Bardstow's London residence, Watley took his master's dripping greatcoat and hat as a footman and the Baron's valet carried his trunk into the house. The arrival of the carriage from Stowe Manor, Watley immediately realized, was an answer to the letter he had written ten days earlier.

Baron Bardstow frowned at the water puddling around his feet and removed his gloves. "Good evening, Watley. I apologize for giving you no notice of my return to town. Some unexpected business," he finished vaguely while watching the two servants trundle his box up the stairs.

Watley's face remained impassive even as the reason for the Baron's slight deception registered. His lordship's told no one about my letter – 'cept p'rhaps Lady Bardstow. Keep family business within the family. Best way. Least said, soonest mended.

"As you can see," added the Baron, "I have brought Phipps, Larkin, and Carr with me. And we are all famished and more than a bit wet."

"Mrs. Watley'll manage, m'lord," replied Watley. Always does, he thought with a certain amount of pride.

"I know she will. Mrs. Watley is a treasure, and I shall be down later to tell her so myself," Bardstow observed while listening hopefully for footfalls on the stairs.

"Shall I have dinner set forward, m'lord?" inquired Watley.

Bardstow replied with a query of his own. "Is my brother at home?" His gaze unconsciously lifted to the landing where he expected Tyler to appear.

"Mr. Hamilton-Smythe is out, but he is expected to return for dinner," supplied Watley.

"In that case, I shall not upset Mrs. Watley's arrangements. You may plan on serving at the usual time." Baron Bardstow began to ascend the stairs. "However, when my brother returns, please inform me at once."

Hours later after a solitary meal consumed in his small but pleasant dining parlour, Baron Bardstow requested that Watley, who was removing the last dishes from the mahogany table, follow him to his study and bring a salver with the port decanter and a glass.

After Watley had poured the Baron a measure of the dark purple wine and handed it to him, the Baron asked bluntly,

"Does my brother often give you no notice of an absence for a meal?"

"Not too often," related Watley. "Most of the time he'll send a note to let us know he's dining elsewhere."

"Young scoundrel," muttered Bardstow under his breath. He strode to his desk and grabbed a piece of paper. "Probably at that damned club of his."

Scrawling hastily, he wrote, "Have returned to town. Must speak to you immediately. Bardstow."

"See that this is delivered at once. And tell whomever you send to wait for Mr. Hamilton-Smythe to enter a hackney before returning here." Baron Bardstow downed his port without tasting it.

The servant was at the door when the baron's voice stopped him. "Watley, have you heard whether Lord Rossbury has returned to town?"

"No, m'lord, I've heard nothing. Mrs. Watley and I have been turning the rooms over, as it were, polishing and the like in preparation for –"

Bardstow cut short Watley's apology by saying, "Of course, you have." Bardstow remembered that the couple always gave the London house a top-to-bottom cleaning before the family's visit in the spring. "Of course, you have," he repeated while wondering if Rossbury had received the letter he had sent to Earl's Wood Park.

"Will there be anything else, m'lord?"

"Please return in half an hour. I shall have another note which requires delivery tonight," informed the Baron.

"Very good, m'lord."

The rest of the Baron's evening hours were a blur of waiting and worrying, pacing and planning. First, he wrote a shorter version of the letter he'd sent to Earl's Wood Park, adding that he was in London and wished to speak to Rossbury as soon as possible. But the messenger sent to deliver this note to Rossbury House returned empty-handed. Lord Rossbury, Harris had said, was still in Shropshire and not expected until the following Thursday.

The note Bardstow had written to Tyler was brought back to the house unopened. Those at Tyler's club had not seen him that day, and none of his cronies there knew where the young Mr. Hamilton-Smythe might be found.

At eleven o'clock Baron Bardstow toyed briefly with the idea of sending a note to Farnsworth Place but discarded it. *There is no reason to alarm the Dowager Marchioness so late at night with worries about her companion*, he thought.

At midnight Bardstow retired to bed, bone tired from the journey and his vigil. Watley had been notified that, if Tyler returned, the servant was to awaken the Baron no matter what the hour.

*If I have not spoken to Tyler by tomorrow morning, I'll have to visit Lady Farnsworth. With Rossbury at Earl's Wood, I have no choice.* It was not a visit he looked forward to. Bardstow sighed heavily, reached over to snuff the bedside candle, adjusted the coverlet, and stared into the darkness, knowing sleep would elude him for some hours.

## CHAPTER 21

# FRIDAY, MARCH 15, 1793

"Gideon!" Elizabeth rose from her seat at the writing table after Dunhill had announced her brother and closed the morning room door behind him.

"Good morning, Elizabeth. I am happy to find you here," Gideon's indeterminate gesture encompassed the entire room, "rather than upstairs. It appears that you have taken no harm from, from…" His sentence floundered.

"As you can see, I am well," said Elizabeth quietly. "It was good of you to come to inquire."

"I wanted to see for myself that, that…" Gideon stared at the floor, unable to meet the placid gray eyes of his sister. "To see that you were well and thank you for helping me select those volumes for Felicity."

"I hope she, and perhaps Emma and Marianne as well, enjoys them."

"I also wanted to tell you that I realize things have been difficult between us in the past fortnight." The words rushed from Gideon's mouth, and he swallowed twice before continuing. "And that I wish things were different."

"I also, Gideon."

Gideon's face brightened at Elizabeth's words. "I am glad to hear it. Because I'd like to invite you and Lady Farnsworth..." He paused while his eyes searched the room as if he expected to find the Marchioness seated in a corner. "...to invite you to accompany me back to my townhouse for, for..."

"Lady Farnsworth is not at home this morning, Gideon," related Elizabeth.

"Perhaps you..." Gideon put a finger into his stock to loosen it. "I need your advice, Elizabeth. My son, your nephew Peter. Well, he is ten now, and it is more than time to consider his future, his connections."

"Yes, I remember your saying last week that you had received Felicity's anxious letter about Peter, but we –"

Before Elizabeth could suggest that they remain at Farnsworth House, Gideon hastened on. "I should like you to read Felicity's letter for yourself and to speak to you about a few other matters. I have ordered a fire laid in the drawing room and a nuncheon to be served after our talk. And..." Gideon walked to one of the morning room's windows, which looked out onto Carlington Square, and pointed invitingly. "And you can see that I have hired a phaeton and a patient old cob incapable of a pace faster than a walk." He turned from the view of the vehicle, its horse being held by the Farnsworth boot boy. "The house is only a short distance from here. Though the streets are still wet from last night's rain, there's enough sun to warm us a bit. The drive will do you good, Elizabeth, after so many days indoors since your, since you..." Gideon recalled his part in the accident that had sent his sister to her bed and reddened. "Say you'll come," he pleaded.

Elizabeth glanced at the half-finished letter to Lord Somerville lying on the writing table and then at her brother's face.

"Of course, I will, Gideon," decided Elizabeth. "I only need a moment to fetch my bonnet and pelisse."

Gideon hurried to open the door for his sister. "Thank you, Elizabeth," he replied as they both passed into the hall. "I promise to give you a pleasant morning, one that I hope is the beginning of an easier relationship between us."

Elizabeth impulsively touched her brother's arm before she mounted the stairs. "That is my hope, too, Gideon."

Thirty minutes later Dunhill found himself responding to a knock at the front door of Farnsworth Place for the second time that morning. The caller announced himself as Baron Bardstow and inquired whether Lady Farnsworth or Miss Elizabeth Laurence was at home.

"Both ladies are out, m'lord," stated Dunhill politely.

"Please give Lady Farnsworth my card," said Bardstow after scribbling a few words on its back, "as soon as she returns."

"I shall, m'lord." After Dunhill closed the street door, he laid Bardstow's visiting card on a silver salver placed on the hall table.

Meanwhile, Bardstow walked rapidly across Carlington Square. Rossbury House first, he told himself, though I am certain Rossbury has not yet returned to London. Then to Tyler's club. I shall roust out the Secretary, no matter where he is, and demand some answers. Someone at that hellhole must know where Tyler is.

Determined to find his brother, Bardstow continued resolutely on his mission.

"How could Elizabeth have become ill so quickly?" anguished Gideon Laurence for the third time later that morning. "She was well during the drive here." He paced restlessly in Sir Augustus Tremaine's drawing room, every turn prompting a glance first at the door as if staring at it could cause the doctor who had been called to materialize and then at the clock whose hands seemed unwilling to pass the twelve o'clock hour.

From a spot near the fireplace, Tremaine watched him but said nothing.

"It couldn't have been anything she ate." Gideon shook his head in confusion. "We never had our meal. There was only the chocolate Inchcomb served to warm us after our drive." He stopped pacing and looked at Sir Augustus, his face creased with worry. "But I drank it also, and I'm..." As Elizabeth's hasty departure from the drawing room and the sudden onset of her bout of lightheadedness and nausea were recalled, Gideon left the rest of his wonderings unfinished.

"Inexplicable, Laurence," soothed Sir Augustus. "Fortunately, Inchcomb had asked the Carter woman to assist him today with the preparations and serving. She seems to be an adequate nurse."

"Yes, she does," admitted Gideon. "Though she reminds me of our nursery governess. Wouldn't let me near Elizabeth. Said I'd be no good in a sickroom. Don't know how she could have known that. Perhaps Elizabeth told her," he said with some animation. "And if she did, that would be a good sign."

"Yes, it would," replied Sir Augustus. "And as soon as the doctor comes--"

"Where is he? Inchcomb has been an age!" complained Gideon with yet another look at both door and clock. "Perhaps we should send for Patterson who attends Lady Farnsworth?"

"I am certain sending for a second physician is unnecessary," Sir Augustus commented quickly. "In fact, perhaps Inchcomb has already returned and is awaiting the doctor's knock in the hall." He moved to Gideon's side and briefly laid a hand on the other man's shoulder. "In fact, I believe I heard a knock just now," he stated in convincing tones before walking towards the door. "I shall return with news in a moment."

Once outside the drawing room, Sir Augustus hastened not to the entry hall but to his own study. There he found both Tyler Hamilton-Smythe and Inchcomb.

"You must make your visit to Miss Laurence immediately," ordered Sir Augustus. He strode to where Tyler was standing and regarded the younger man's changed appearance critically. The silver streaking the temples of Tyler's conservatively styled blond locks, the spectacles perched on his nose, and the somber coat and waistcoat gave Tyler the look of a staid medical professional.

"If he had arrived in Miss Laurence's room too quickly after her illness, Carter might –" Inchcomb began to explain while thrusting a doctor's black bag into Tyler's hand.

"I realize we must do nothing to arouse either lady's suspicions," interrupted Sir Augustus with an imperious wave of his hand. "But we must also do nothing to arouse Laurence's." His scorn was like a whiplash across the faces of the others in the room. "And Laurence is anxious enough to go upstairs at any moment to see how his sister fares!" He paused for a moment, head cocked attentively as he listened for any sounds that would indicate that Gideon had left the drawing room. "Having the two of you meet at Miss Laurence's bedside," he hissed as he whirled to face Tyler again, "might spell disaster for my plans. And that I will not have."

Tyler and Inchcomb moved toward the door. "You have the vial?" asked Sir Augustus.

"I put it into the bag myself," noted Inchcomb. "He cannot mistake it, for it is the only one with any fluid in it. And when I prepared the guest room earlier, I placed a decanter of water and glass on the small table near the bed as well as the usual ewer, bowl, and towels."

"Excellent!" approved Sir Augustus. "The emetic added to Miss Laurence's chocolate did its job well. I doubt not that Doctor Adam's," he nodded at Tyler and curved his thin lips into the semblance of a smile, "laudanum will prove equally effective."

Harriet Carter dipped a small towel in a basin of water and wrung it out. Then she lifted a damp cloth from Elizabeth's forehead and replaced it with the one she had just moistened.

"That's right, Miss Laurence," Harriet cooed encouragingly while pushing away some of the springy red curls escaping from her white mobcap. "Eyes closed, head still. You're feeling a little better already, I think." Harriet based her last statement on the return of a hint of color to her patient's pale cheeks.

"I am," replied Elizabeth in a voice that sounded weak even to her own ears. "In fact, I feel well enough to..." Elizabeth attempted to rise. But the movement of her head brought on another wave of nausea. "Oh!"

"You lie there quietly, Miss, 'til the doctor comes. Mr. Inchcomb'll be back with him in a minute, I expect." Harriet's narrow face with its pointed chin puckered in concentration as she readjusted the wet cloth and smoothed back a few damp tendrils from Elizabeth's brow.

"Thank you again..." Elizabeth could not recall the name of the woman who tended her.

"Carter, Miss Laurence, Harriet Carter," supplied the sturdy nurse.

"Thank you, Harriet." Elizabeth sighed. Her queasy stomach still felt as it had aboard *L' Oiseau Vite.* "I am sorry to have been the cause of so much unpleasantness." The mere recollection of her own retching made Elizabeth's stomach heave in rebellion.

"Don't be sorry, Miss Laurence. I've dealt with much worse," Harriet chirped brightly as she prepared for another towel exchange. Keep talkin', Harriet told herself. Better for her to hear me rattlin' on 'bout nothin' than to think about her insides ready to revolt. "When Mr. Inchcomb asked Mr. Paine, he's butler at Number Two up the Crescent where I'm housemaid, if one of us'd be free to help him Friday morning, Mr. Paine recommended me. He knows I send as much as I can to Mum and Dad.

He reckoned I'd jump at the chance to earn a bit extra. And with both master and mistress from home this week and next, Mr. Paine knew I'd not be missed."

Harriet laid a newly moistened cloth on Elizabeth's head. "Mr. Inchcomb told me that his gentleman wanted everything to be perfect for his sister's visit and that he could use some help with the preparations and serving. Seemed an easy way to earn two shillings."

"I don't think most people would think it was easy," Elizabeth said, her eyes still closed.

"You may be right, Miss Laurence, but helping does make you feel…". Harriet adjusted the wet cloth before finishing the sentence. "Well, feel useful. Like you have a purpose even if it's not a very important one." She grinned. "That sounds daft, doesn't it?"

Without waiting for Elizabeth to reply, Harriet continued, "Earlier this morning, I'd done so little that I was beginning to think I should only accept a shilling. But after you…" Suddenly embarrassed by her own words, Harriet stopped. "Oh, Miss Laurence," she gasped as she put a hand to her cheek, "I never meant, I mean I…"

"Taking care of anyone who has been revoltingly ill is definitely worth two shillings," Elizabeth said, while wishing she were in her own bed.

"But you've been ever so good, Miss, and really I'm glad to be here 'coz I don't think Mr. Inchcomb'd be much use. And Mr. Laurence, well, he looked a little green himself after he looked in. I think he was happy I turned him out." As Harriet reviewed these facts, she wondered if Inchcomb had known Elizabeth might be ill that morning,

"You're not," Harriet began, unsure of how to frame the question forming in her mind. "You're not – increasing, are you, Miss Laurence?"

In spite of her queasiness, Elizabeth smiled. "No, Harriet, I am not. But God willing, in a year, perhaps the answer will be different."

"Oh, Miss Laurence, are you to be wed then?"

"On the third of April at St Etheldreda's near Carlington Square," Elizabeth recounted the time like a talisman against the illness she was experiencing.

"Less than three weeks away!" breathed Harriet, hands clasped, eyes gleaming. To that Richard whose name she moaned when she was sick earlier, thought Harriet. "Don't worry, Miss Laurence. You're bound to be right as rain by then."

But before Elizabeth could answer, Inchcomb opened the door and announced, "Doctor Adams, Miss Laurence." Then Inchcomb asked, "Is there anything you need, Doctor?"

"I think not. If I do, I shall ring or send..." Tyler, who had followed Inchcomb into the room, looked at Harriet.

"Carter, Doctor Adams," informed Inchcomb.

"If I need anything, I'll send Carter to find you." Tyler walked toward the bed. Harriet rose from her chair and stepped aside.

"Inchcomb's told me you have been ill this morning, Miss Laurence." Fearing that Elizabeth might recognize him from the encounter in Eastons, Tyler did not to move the wet cloth covering Elizabeth's forehead and eyes. He laid a perfunctory hand against one cheek, briefly held her wrist, and hoped she would not feel the racing of his own pulse. "Feeling better now, are you?"

"Yes, I am, Doctor Adams," replied Elizabeth. "In fact, I believe that if I could simply lie quietly for an hour or two, I should be fine."

"She's been quite ill, Doctor," inserted Harriet. "But she's..."

"Yes, yes," interrupted Tyler, hurrying towards the black bag he had placed on top of a small table. Beads of perspiration prickled his hairline. Damme, he thought, this is harder than

I thought it would be. He quickly took out the vial of dark liquid Inchcomb had packed and returned to the bedside. "But a soothing draught will speed the process and insure that another episode will not occur. Carter, please pour some water into that tumbler." Tyler gestured with his free hand towards the glass on the nearby table. And as Harriet did as she was bid, Tyler mopped his brow and added, "Half full will be sufficient."

With the water glass in one hand and the vial in the other, Tyler paused, the number of drops he had been told to add a blur in his memory. Better too much than too little, Tyler told himself before dumping a fifth of the contents of the vial into the glass. "If you would drink this now, Miss Laurence." With a nod, he indicated that Harriet should assist Elizabeth to drink the draught he had prepared.

With her arm behind Elizabeth's shoulders, Harriet helped Elizabeth into an upright position and then put the glass to her lips. When it was empty, Harriet lowered Elizabeth back onto the bed and replaced the glass on the table.

"You may feel a trifle sleepy," noted Tyler, shoving the vial into the bag and preparing to leave, "but rest is what you need now."

"Thank you, Doctor," said Elizabeth. "I am sure you're right."

A quarter of an hour later, Inchcomb summoned Harriet Carter from her place by Elizabeth's bedside, put two shillings into her hand, and dismissed her.

"She is sleeping now, and that's probably all to the good," noted Harriet. "But you will let me know how she feels later?"

"Of course, I will," lied Inchcomb blandly.

Shortly after Harriet's departure, two carriages left Hanover Crescent. The first was the coach that had brought Sir Augustus to London. On its box were Moss and Inchcomb, both returning to Throck Manor. Inside Inchcomb's pocket was Sir Augustus' note ordering The Reverend Jeremiah Cuthbertson to be at St Mark's the next day at five o'clock. The other was the traveling coach refurbished during Gideon's stay at Hanover Crescent. On its box sat Tyler Hamilton-Smythe. Inside, Gideon Laurence hunched in one corner, angry over how he had been tricked and blackmailed, frightened by his neighbor's refusal to tell him anything about where they were going, and concerned about his sister curled up asleep on the facing banquette. Next to him, Sir Augustus Tremaine triumphantly eyed Elizabeth, determined to make her his that very night.

Even as Dunhill opened the front door of Farnsworth Place, Rossbury and Grantleigh clattered through.

Rossbury stripped off his riding gloves. "I should like to see Miss Laurence at once, Dunhill. I trust she is at home."

"I am afraid she is not, milord," replied Dunhill while masking his amazement at the sight of the two mud-splattered travelers in the spotless entry and their drooping mounts in the square outside.

At the negative reply, Rossbury's eyes locked briefly with those of Viscount Grantleigh and then settled on Dunhill's face. "And Lady Farnsworth?" Rossbury's voice was low and urgent.

"She has just returned with Lady Dalrymple and is –" Dunhill began.

After Dunhill's fourth word, Rossbury hastened towards the stairs, Grantleigh hard on his heels.

"The horse outside, milord?" called Dunhill.

"Have them taken across the square. Private Compton will see to them." The order was given crisply without so much as a backward glance over the shoulder, the ascent of the stairs uninterrupted. "And have two saddles placed on whichever of my godmother's horses are best suited to riding. They should be at the door in five minutes."

"Yes, milord. Very good, milord."

Silence greeted Dunhill's words. The butler stared up the stairs, but both men had already disappeared.

Having pushed open the door to Lady Farnsworth's boudoir, Rossbury limped rapidly in. "Lady Dalrymple, Godmother, I believe you know Andrew Beresford, Viscount Grantleigh." Over the murmured assents and Grantleigh's abbreviated bow, he continued, "Miss Laurence, Dunhill has informed us, is not at home." His eyes scanned the room while he spoke as if he hoped to find Elizabeth in one of its chairs.

"That is correct," asserted Lady Beatrice. "Shortly after I left this morning to attend to some business, her brother arrived and..."

These words startled Rossbury into a stumbling step forward on his right leg that momentarily buckled under his weight. He grabbed the back of a chair and repeated hoarsely, "Her brother. And is she with him now?"

Lady Beatrice rose, her distress at Rossbury's pain evident. "Yes, she is. And I am certain all is well, Richard. Dunhill said that Laurence was driving a phaeton and that its single horse seemed ready for retirement to the pasture." The hint of desperation that tinged her voice hinted of an attempt to convince herself, not Rossbury, that no cause for concern existed. "In fact, Dolly and I..." She glanced over her shoulder at Lady Dalrymple who nodded and then felt compelled to rise herself. "We were saying before you arrived that Elizabeth..." At that moment, the clock on the mantle chimed the hour. "Elizabeth should have returned a half hour ago."

Rossbury's face, pale with fatigue and the ache of his old injury, grew shuttered and hard. "And Gideon Laurence's London residence is..." He and Grantleigh turned toward the door, both prepared to leave at once.

"Neither of us knows, Richard." The admission sounded weak even to Lady Beatrice's ears.

Rossbury rounded on his godmother, the pain that shot its way up his right leg from his swiveling movement thrust to the back of his mind. "Neither of you?" He searched the faces of both dowagers for confirmation.

"I have cudgeled my brain for the past quarter hour, Rossbury, but the name Gideon Laurence elicits nothing." Lady Dalrymple, whose knowledge of those in the upper circles of society was wide and whose memory was almost legendary, added, "I am sorry."

Rossbury clenched his fists and opened them again, his mind straining to find a course of action.

"I know I wrote you a rather overwrought letter last Saturday, Richard," stated Lady Beatrice, believing that this note was the sole cause of the two men's desperate journey, obvious from the mud caking their boots and breeches. "But surely Gideon Laurence will do Elizabeth no harm while she is presiding over his own tea table."

"I pray he will not, Lady Farnsworth," interjected Grantleigh. "But I must tell you that it was not your letter only that has brought us to London." Before giving any more details, he glanced at Rossbury who nodded his agreement although he appeared to be deep in thought of his own. "Catherine Calvert, a neighbor of ours at Brookfields, recently died. She left both the estate of Rosemont and the sum of £5000 to her grandniece Elizabeth Laurence."

Lady Beatrice immediately exclaimed, "But that's wonderful!"

"However," Grantleigh continued in a flat tone, "Gideon Laurence's reply to the solicitor's letter stated unreservedly that Miss Laurence had died."

Both Lady Farnsworth and Lady Dalrymple gasped. The final word of Grantleigh's statement underscored the danger that Elizabeth's brother posed to her. "And Laurence himself?"

"Laurence is the secondary heir." Rossbury's words dropped like a black cloud, shadowing all those in the room with even darker thoughts.

"Tremaine," said Grantleigh into the silence that followed, his sense that a possible answer to their dilemma might lie in this man.

Lady Dalrymple's lips moved soundlessly as she sorted through the address book lodged in her memory. The others were too engrossed in their own musings to remark her reverie.

"Laurence's friend," recalled Rossbury.

"Not long ago, Sir Augustus Tremaine came to Rosemont looking for Gideon Laurence," Grantleigh informed a confused Lady Beatrice.

"Sir Augustus Tremaine has a residence on Hanover Crescent!" announced Lady Dalrymple. "Number Six."

No sooner had the last word left her mouth than Rossbury and Grantleigh turned as one towards the door.

"Richard!" Lady Beatrice's frightened voice halted Rossbury in mid-stride. Grantleigh, his fingers grasping the door handle, also looked back at the dowager marchioness who now clasped a small white visiting card.

"Baron Bardstow called this morning while I was out." Lady Beatrice hurried forward as she spoke and gave the card to Rossbury.

Its message – *I have a confidential matter to relate. Urgent. You must contact me today* – sounded an alarm in Rossbury's head.

Wordlessly he returned the card to Lady Beatrice's hand. "You have sent for Baron Bardstow," he stated. At her nod, he added, "His may be another matter altogether."

Grantleigh, knowing the problems Rossbury's family by marriage had caused in the past, asked, "Do we wait then for Bardstow's arrival?"

"No." The syllable sounded more like an order than a reply. "We do not. When he arrives here, tell him," Rossbury directed Lady Beatrice, "whatever you deem prudent. But say nothing of what has happened to any of the servants." Both women nodded. "Pray that when we return to hear what Bardstow wishes to communicate, Elizabeth is with us," Rossbury continued, his calm voice an effort to maintain while his throat tightened painfully.

Grantleigh once again placed his hand on the door handle as Rossbury concluded, "For if Elizabeth is at Tremaine's house in Hanover Crescent, we shall find her."

Hearing the if and Rossbury's use of Elizabeth's name as measures of his disquiet, Lady Beatrice found her own fear growing as the door closed behind the two men.

At the sound of horses entering the stable mews, Jim Compton looked up from the harness he was polishing.

"Jim? You there?" called Ben Tolliver, one of the stablemen employed at Farnsworth Place. Two muddy animals trailed dejectedly behind him.

"Be right there, Ben," replied Jim, having recognized the other man's voice. After hanging the harness on a peg, Jim marched quickly towards the wide stable doors.

"What's this then?" he asked after one look at the horses Tolliver led. "These don't belong to us."

"According t' Lor' Rossb'ry, they do," announced Tolliver, a hatchet-faced man with the wiry frame of a jockey. He put the reins of the two animals into Compton's unwilling hands. "Leastways he told our Mr. Dunhill t' have 'em brought over 'ere."

"Capt'n Verinder, that is, the Colonel said to..." began Compton in confusion. "But he's up north!" Compton stared first at the weary horses and then at Ben Tolliver. "How could..."

"Rode up to our front door with Lor' Grantleigh no more 'n a quarter hour ago," answered Tolliver. "From the looks of these here," he patted the neck of the horse nearer him, "we all reckon that as it's more 'n three weeks since he seen Miss Laurence last, his lor'ship was in a bit of a hurry t' get 'imself back t' London." He grinned broadly.

While Tolliver spoke, Compton cast a critical eye over the two sorry-looking horses. Shaking his head, he unsaddled one of the pair, opened an empty stall, and led the animal inside. By the time he turned around, Tolliver was already unsaddling the other horse. "Thanks, Ben." Compton forked some straw into the stalls.

The two stablemen worked together for the next few minutes, each fetching water and feed for the animal in his stall. Then the bridles were removed and replaced by simple halters. Tolliver carried the tack to the area where Jim polished and repaired equipment while Compton found a couple of blankets. He put these over the well-lathered animals to prevent them from cooling down too rapidly.

"Brushes, Jim?"

But Tolliver's question remained unheard, for Compton was thinking about the state of the horses and Rossbury's usual care for any animal in his keeping.

Tolliver touched Jim's arm and repeated, "Brushes, Jim?"

"Oh yes, brushes, Ben," replied Compton vaguely. The words sank into Jim's consciousness only after Tolliver placed a brush in his hand and then walked into one of the stalls to begin grooming the mud-splattered horse inside.

"Ben, you needn't stay. Must be plenty for you t' do 'cross the square." Compton began the tedious process of removing the caked mud from the animal now nosing with some interest at its manger.

"That's all right, Jim," observed Tolliver, his voice muffled by the stall separating him from Compton as he brushed the matted hair of his horse's chest. "Looks t' me like you need a bit of help t'day." He chortled – a short, amused guffaw. "You n' yer Capt'n." He paused in case Compton had missed his small joke. He often teased Compton about his forgetful use of Rossbury's former name and rank. "Yer Capt'n n' his Private Compton!"

"What?" Surprised, Compton stopped brushing and stuck his head over the stall to peer at Tolliver. "What's that you say?"

"That's what Lor' Rossb'ry called you, Jim! Private Compton!" Tolliver laughed again. He straightened and swiped playfully at Compton with the brush. "He's smitten for sure, he is."

When Compton said nothing in reply, Tolliver resumed both his brushing and his teasing. "Our Mr. Dunhill said that his lor'ship ordered these two beasts taken 'cross the square. 'Private Compton, 'e says, 'll see to 'em!'" Another chortle escaped his throat. "Private Compton – that's you, Jim," he added for emphasis. "Then soon's 'e n' 'is friend th' Viscount find out from 'er ladyship that Miss Laurence's with 'er brother, off they go, quick as a wink, on two of our horses. What'd you say 'bout that, Private Compton?"

"T'isn't like the Capt'n, er, Lor' Rossb'ry," corrected Compton hastily in reply. "That's what I say; t'isn't like him at all." He brushed the patient animal standing before him, an animal quite unused to the attention it was receiving. "First of all, these two we're working on were never from his lordship's stable. Any nodkin can see they're a couple o' hacks, post horses hired from some coaching inn." He walked to the other side of the stall and ran a practiced hand over the animal's legs. "Second, they've been ridden hard n' –"

"'e's been away near a month, Jim!" interrupted Tolliver. "May be an earl now, but 'e's still a man with red blood in 'im just like rest o' us. 'Course he come harin' back. What you'd 'spect?" Tolliver snorted derisively.

"I tell you, Ben, usin' horses this hard t'ain't like the Capt'n," insisted Compton. "He's, he's..." The words he needed to describe the officer he had served under escaped him. "You'd have t' have been there, t' have seen him when things were bad." He heaved a frustrated sigh. "He'd not treat animals this bad 'less he had a good reason."

"Well, 'e's got a good reason. The best reason, Jim," argued Tolliver. "He's gettin' married next month."

"That's not…" Compton broke off his rebuttal as the memory of Baron Bardstow's letter – marked 'Urgent' according to Harris and placed on the entry hall table at Rossbury House the previous night – struck him. Servants' gossip about the late Lady Sarah, Bardstow's relationship to both Patience's secret admirer and Rossbury's late wife, and Rossbury's apparent breakneck journey to London all added to Compton's unease.

"Not what, Jim? 'Nuff t' send a man runnin'? Mind you, Miss Laurence is not much to look at, but she's kindness itself. Everyone at Farnsworth Place says so. N' she's got bottom to 'er. Look at 'ow she 'andled all these accidents. N' soon she'll be your mistress, Jim. Don't you forget that."

"Accidents? What about the accidents?" demanded Compton. The word had been like a musket shot round Jim's ear and only increased his anxiety.

"I know you musta heard 'bout 'em!" Tolliver looked up to see Compton's nod. "They was terrible. Both o' 'em."

"Mr. Harris didn't say…" Compton began, while trying to remember exactly what the butler had said.

"Mr. Harris! He never says much 'bout anythin' does he?" Tolliver huffed before relating, "Well, it were like this…"

Thirty minutes later when the two horses were groomed and Tolliver had returned to his own duties, Compton left the mews stable.

I'll find Mr. Harris, he told himself as he ran to the back entrance of Rossbury House, n' ask him t' let me take that letter from Baron Bardstow 'cross the square. I'll tell him the Capt'n's there t' see Miss Laurence, tell him it's important I be th' one t' take the letter. I've earned his trust. He'll know there's somethin' I'm not saying. He's no green recruit, our Mr. Harris. He'll let me go. Then I've got t' find a way t' speak t' Patience private-like. That's goin' t' be hard. But I'll think of somethin'. I got to.

"No one appears to be here, Richard," stated Grantleigh after a third round of rapping upon the brass doorknocker had brought no response from Number Six, Hanover Crescent.

Rossbury took a step backward and quickly scanned the windows of the elegant town house. Drawn curtains in each one, he noted while trying to quell the fear rising within him.

He turned his back on the front door and limped down the steps. "Perhaps Tremaine's servants are about."

Without comment, Grantleigh followed him to the half flight of stairs leading down to the area and the outside door to the servants' hall and kitchen.

Yet once again Rossbury's knocking brought no one to the door.

As Rossbury raised his hand to knock again, a boy's voice said, "They's all gone away at Number Six."

"Are you certain?" Rossbury's question, almost a demand, came even as he and Grantleigh turned from the door.

"Course I am." The lad – his big cap set a jaunty angle, his dark eyes flashing with the anger of offended youth – put the parcel he carried under his left arm and his right fist on his hip. "Seen 'em two carriages leaving meself, din't I. Think I knowed Number Six's..."

The knocking on the areaway door had led him to believe he was speaking to a fellow servant or perhaps a deliveryman. However, the two men who emerged from the area were obviously gentlemen. No amount of mud splashed on clothes could disguise excellent tailoring.

"Ooh sirs," the boy yelped, suddenly aware that the men standing before him could land him in trouble with his employer.

"Can you tell us anything about the carriage's departure?" Rossbury asked at once.

Mouth gaping, the frightened lad hesitated, unsure of what to do.

Hoping to coax an answer from him, Rossbury relayed solemnly, "A lady may be in danger."

"The lady they carried int' one o' 'em carriages!" exclaimed the boy.

Rossbury choked back Elizabeth's name and said, "Could you describe this lady or tell us anything about her?"

"Looked ter me like she was kinda small. With dark brown hair. And it seemed like she was asleep. Coz Sir Augustus, dressed all in black just like always, he carries her inter th' carriage, n' this other older gent is fussing 'round both o' 'em. I was bringing down some slops and..." The tide of words halted briefly as the boy realized he should not be mentioning slop jars to a couple of gentlemen.

"Well," he continued, "that Mr. Inchcomb – he works at Number Six – and Sir Augustus too when he's 'ere, they ain't got no use fer me. N' I might add th' feelin's mutual. So's I stays outta sight n' just watch. Some other gent gets on th' box o' th' carriage th' lady's in, n' Mr. Inchcomb, he climbs onter th'other one. N' they both leave. The one with th' lady goes that way," the lad pointed east. "N' th' other one goes there." His hand swept towards the west as he finished.

The boy looked at Rossbury and then at Grantleigh. "Is the lady I seen really in danger?"

"I fear she is," Rossbury replied with a sinking heart. "Is there anything at all you can tell us that might help us to find her?"

The boy's eyes screwed shut for a moment and then flashed open. "Harriet! Harriet Carter!" he exclaimed suddenly. "She can tell you everythin'." Knowing the name meant nothing to his listeners, the lad explained, "She was asked t' work at Number Six this mornin'. I knows coz Jenny Mason, she works at Number Four same as me, she was like an old wet cat. Flouncin' and fussin' coz Mr. Inchcomb, th' one I tol' you works at Number Six, he asked Harriet t' help this mornin'. N' Jenny, well, she thought Mr. Inchcomb shoulda asked her, you see." The boy threw Rossbury and Grantleigh a satisfied smile and a sharp head bob for emphasis.

"And Harriet Carter works at...?" Rossbury inquired.

"Number Two." The boy's finger pointed behind them to a house at the end of the crescent.

Rossbury dug into a pocket and offered two of the coins he found there to the lad. "Thank you," said Rossbury.

The boy's eyes widened at the sight of more money than he had ever held at one time in all his nine years. Then Rossbury put out his hand. Seeing it surprised the lad even more than the unexpected coins. Quickly transferring the coins into his own pocket, he carefully put his own rough hand into Rossbury's larger one. Before he could speak his gratitude, Rossbury had turned and begun striding in the direction of Number Two, Hanover Crescent, Grantleigh having already gathered the reins of the two horses and headed down the road.

"Thank you, sir!" called the boy after he found his voice. "Thank you! And if them at Number Two needs to know, you can say Jemmy Baxter sent you!"

"Who is it, Floss?" asked Mr. Paine after Flossie Oates, the scullery maid he had sent to answer the knocking on the areaway door, neither spoke nor allowed the callers into the servants' hall.

Flossie, completely dumbfounded by the sight of two gentlemen standing in the area, simply moved aside so that Paine, the butler at Number Two, could see the visitors for himself.

Both Rossbury and Grantleigh removed their high crowned hats.

"We should like to speak with Harriet Carter. We understand that she is employed here," Rossbury requested politely

Unseen by either man, Harriet Carter rose. She had been sitting at the large scrubbed deal table near the centre of the room and telling her fellow servants about the events of her morning. Mrs. Cole, the cook, also heaved her ample frame from her seat at Harriet's side and advanced towards the door, menace in her step.

"Up to no good, Mr. Paine," the cook muttered enigmatically. In her opinion any man who dressed as Rossbury and Grantleigh did and knocked on the areaway door could only spell trouble.

"I'll take care of this, Mrs. Cole," ordered Mr. Paine, a man with a prizefighter's physique, an intelligent-looking face, and educated enunciation.

Even as the butler strode to the door, from which Flossie Oates now slunk away, Grantleigh's hand sought his visiting card case. Meanwhile, Rossbury, whose leg was aching abominably, straightened imperceptibly.

"What business have two gentlemen, like yourselves, with our Harriet?" The butler's tone clearly reflected his belief that, while their clothes might proclaim otherwise, neither Rossbury nor Grantleigh was really who he appeared to be.

Though using his own and Grantleigh's titles to gain access to Harriet Carter seemed a little unfair, Rossbury felt the danger to Elizabeth increasing with every minute. Thus, he disregarded the butler's question and staked everything on a formal introduction.

"Allow me to introduce my friend." Rossbury ignored the skepticism in the butler's face and the balled fists of Mrs. Cole who had taken three more steps towards the door. "Mr. Paine, may I present Andrew St John Beresford, Viscount Grantleigh."

Grantleigh thrust one of his visiting cards into Paine's hand and smoothly continued the introduction. "And may I, Mr. Paine, introduce my friend, the Earl of Rossbury –"

"Richard!" Harriet softly exclaimed. Her interruption and use of the visitor's Christian name caused Mr. Paine and Mrs. Cole to turn. Both looked with astonishment at the housemaid. Their shifted positions put Harriet into Rossbury's line of sight for the first time.

"That's right, Miss Carter. I am Richard Verinder..." began Rossbury,

"And you're to be wed on April the third at St Etheldreda's near Carlington Square!" interrupted Harriet again in a breathless rush. She clasped her hands. Oh, she thought, he has come for her. Just like a knight in a story. Her eyes gleamed.

"We are, indeed, Miss Carter," confirmed Rossbury, grateful to have found someone who had spoken to Elizabeth. "But now, I believe Miss Laurence requires my assistance." He limped forward, his eyes focused on Harriet Carter's face while willing her to speak.

Mr. Paine, looking somewhat abashed at his former suspicions, wordlessly offered the titled guests two chairs that were silently but courteously declined.

"The doctor's been to see her and all," remembered Harriet blithely unaware of the effect her words had on Rossbury and Grantleigh. "I'm sure she'll be right as rain in the morning. You ask Mr. Inchcomb yourself or..." Suddenly she stopped. She stared at Rossbury and wondered, Why is Lord Rossbury here speaking to me when he could be in Miss Laurence's room at Number Six?

The same question had also crossed the minds of Mr. Paine and Mrs. Cole. They exchanged a puzzled look as Harriet's last sentence hung uncompleted in the still kitchen.

"We have just come from the house of Sir Augustus Tremaine, but our knocks on the front door and the area door remained unanswered."

"But they were all there this morning!" protested Harriet.

"They were to be sure, milord," affirmed Mr. Paine.

In one corner of the hall, Flossie put her apron over her head and began to wail. "We're all gonna be turned out when master n' missus comes 'ome. Then what'll I do?" Flossie rocked back and forth in her chair, her hysterical sobs growing more intense.

"Hush, Flossie," ordered Mrs. Cole. "No one's going to be turned out. Not you, not me, not Mr. Paine, not Harriet." Mrs. Cole put a motherly arm around the girl's narrow shoulders. "These gentlemen are just as confused as the rest of us and need our Harriet to put 'em right. Isn't that so, Lord Rossbury?" Her hand made a comforting circling motion across Flossie's back as her eyes appealed to Rossbury.

"It is, Mrs. Cole." Rossbury voice was polite, but his anxious glance at the large clock holding pride of place atop a Welsh dresser told its own story.

Before either Mrs. Cole or Mr. Paine could reply, Flossie lowered her apron, hiccupped, and asked, "But why are they 'ere 'stead o' up th' Crescent?"

"A lad named Jemmy Baxter heard us knocking and informed us that he had seen two carriages leave Number Six earlier today." Grantleigh felt Rossbury's warning touch on his arm and omitted any mention of what else Jemmy Baxter had seen. "He told us that Miss Carter had worked there this morning and directed us here to gain information."

"There! That's easy enough to understand, isn't it, Floss?" exclaimed Miss Cole. "Young Jemmy sent their lor'ships her sos Harriet could tell 'em what she's just been tellin' us."

While Flossie nodded her understanding, Rossbury asked, "Your account of this morning's events is what we have come for, Miss Carter. Hearing it may enable us to help Miss Laurence."

Harriet needed no further prompting. "Mr. Inchcomb, he's Sir Augustus Tremaine's man and keeps Number Six single handed when Sir Augustus is not in town and sometimes even when he is, he asked me to help him with a nuncheon. It was for the sister of a gentleman Sir Augustus had lent the house to, Mr. Inchcomb said. Since the master and mistress are staying with Mr. John's family – he's their son – I could oblige. When I arrived this morning, Mr. Inchcomb asked me to take water and towels to the bedroom nearest the top of the stairs. Told me Miss Laurence might want to wash after her arrival. Then he set me to work in the kitchen. Though I must say that the food we were preparing looked more like a working man's midday meal than a nuncheon for a lady."

Harriet paused for a minute as the scene in the kitchen unfolded in her memory.

Rossbury nodded his understanding of what Harriet had recounted thus far. "And then?" he prompted.

"Then the guests arrived, and Mr. Inchcomb told me to stay in the kitchen and continue with the nuncheon. I assumed he went off to take their coats and perhaps to stoke up the fire in the drawing room. Anyway, he was soon back again and busy pouring out some chocolate he'd prepared earlier. I helped him arrange the tray, and he carried it out."

Once again Harriet paused to search her memory. Have I forgotten anything? she asked herself. No, she thought, everything happened just as I said.

"Go on, Harriet. Tell their lordships what happened next," advised Mr. Paine who had noted Rossbury's anxiety and concern with time.

"Next thing I know, Mr. Inchcomb's flying back into the kitchen and tellin' me to go at once to the bedroom I set up earlier. He says, Miss Laurence's been taken ill and I'm to see to her while he goes for the doctor."

Grantleigh saw Rossbury stiffen as soon as Harriet said the word ill. Grantleigh also realized that the thought that had leapt into his mind must also be in Rossbury's. Poison! Dear God, don't let them have poisoned Miss Laurence. "And what form did this illness take, Miss Carter?"

Harriet reddened. Illness was not a topic suitable for mixed company, and its symptoms were usually discussed in whispers by mothers or those caring for invalids. "Well, Miss Laurence was quite ill, if you know what I mean," she hedged., not daring to look at anyone. "She, well, that is, I held the basin and she…" Harriet decided that she had said quite enough to be understood. "And considering that she'd only had one cup of chocolate, she…" Harriet struggled again with her sentence. "Well, considering that, Miss Laurence was ill for a long time, I'd say." Harriet halted. She looked up and saw both Rossbury and Grantleigh nod their understanding.

"And then?" Rossbury prompted.

"Then I helped her to the bed so she could rest. She was feeling more n' a bit weak, and dizzy, too as you might imagine after… Well, after being so ill as she was." Harriet paused, remembering the paleness of Elizabeth's face. "That's when she spoke to me. Treated me like…" Harriet wondered briefly whether to include her impression of the woman she had nursed. "She treated me like I was the same as her. She's a real lady, milord."

Harriet addressed these last words directly to Rossbury, and what she saw in his face before he erased his expression with studied attention caused a quiet intake of breath. Although what she had glimpsed was indescribable, it plunged her into the end of her account.

"Then Mr. Inchcomb returned with Doctor Adams. Our Doctor Quincy must have been away so it a real bit of luck that he found this Doctor Adams. He knew just what to do, for he no more n' glanced at Miss Laurence before he told me to bring him half a tumbler of water. Then he poured a dose of medicine into the water, and Miss Laurence drank it. He said it'd soothe her and maybe make her drowsy. And he was right. It did. Bit later Mr. Inchcomb called me into the hall, gave me the two shillings promised me, and sent me home. And he said he'd come 'round later to tell me how Miss Laurence was."

As Harriet completed the recounting of her morning, a conclusion she had not seen before struck her. "But Mr. Inchcomb's not at Number Six, is he? So he can't tell me anything about Miss Laurence, can he?"

"Can he, milord, Harriet," whispered Mr. Paine.

"No, he cannot, Miss Carter." For a moment Rossbury considered telling Harriet and the other servants at Number Two, Hanover Crescent that Elizabeth's brother had probably taken her home. Instead he added, "But I am certain that Miss Laurence shall soon send you her thanks for the help you were able to give her."

No one spoke. Even Flossie, somewhat dazed by her second hearing of Harriet's story, remained silent. Without being asked to do so, Mr. Paine brought Rossbury and Grantleigh the hats he had placed on the Welsh dresser.

"Thank you, Mr. Paine." Rossbury moved stiffly from his position near the table. "And thank you, Miss Carter. Your account of the events of this morning has proved most helpful."

Harriet rose from her seat, hastened towards the two men heading towards the door, and impulsively laid a hand on Rossbury's arm. "You will let us know, Lord Rossbury," she began before the stern voice of the butler interrupted her.

"Harriet," Mr. Paine rebuked, "mind who you are!"

The housemaid instantly withdrew her hand and lowered her eyes in shame.

However, to put her at ease and to assure Mr. Paine that Harriet's gesture had not offended him, Rossbury replied simply as Mr. Paine opened the door into the areaway to usher them out, "I shall do whatever I am able."

*And that*, thought Grantleigh, *will be to move heaven and earth to find Miss Laurence and to scourge those who have used her so cruelly, no matter who they are or where we find them.*

Rossbury looked at those assembled in the Farnsworth morning room without seeing any of them. He and Grantleigh had returned from Hanover Crescent to find Baron Bardstow closeted with Lady Farnsworth and Lady Dalrymple. After the Baron had recounted the contents of the letter Watley had sent him to him at Stowe Manor, they all knew that Tyler Hamilton-Smythe had played a major role in the two accidents involving Elizabeth.

"Let's go over everything we know. Perhaps something we haven't seen before will strike one of us." Yet even as he made this suggestion, Rossbury feared the review of information was a mere clutching at straws.

"First, Catherine Calvert dies and leaves her estate and the sum of £5000 to Miss Laurence in her will," Rossbury began. "When notified of this inheritance, Gideon Laurence informs Mrs. Calvert's solicitor that his sister has died in France. Meanwhile, Miss Laurence returns to England and takes a position here at Farnsworth Place." As he spoke, Rossbury envisioned his last visit to this very room – the place of his proposal of marriage to Elizabeth. *I gave her the protection of my name that day*, he thought. *And what good has that name done her?* The question flayed his conscience.

"Then my letter to Laurence at Hopeden Hall arrived and informed him of Miss Laurence's presence here in London." *Had I waited to write to Laurence until my return to town, none of this would have happened!* The lines of Rossbury's face grew grimmer, his eyes bleak, as he recognized that, in many ways, his actions had brought danger into Elizabeth's life.

"Laurence arrived in London and came here. There were disagreements between him and Miss Laurence. And somehow during Laurence's time in the city, he met Tyler Hamilton-Smythe."

Silently, Bardstow thanked Rossbury for not telling the others about the watch Tyler had kept on Rossbury House. All my work to pull my family away from financial disaster will be for nothing, Bardstow despaired. This time Tyler's ruined us all for certain. And Rossbury will never forgive me.

"They arranged the first accident; and when it did not have the desired effect, they carried out the second one in front of Stanfield's Bookshop."

Lady Beatrice closed her eyes briefly. Her godson, she knew, would be castigating himself unmercifully for his absence at a time when Elizabeth needed him. Dear God, she prayed, let him find her safe.

"Then Gideon Laurence invited his sister to Sir Augustus Tremaine's townhouse on Hanover Crescent. There it sounds as if Miss Laurence was given an emetic followed by a dose of laudanum administered by someone who called himself Doctor Adams." Speaking about this deliberate plot to make Elizabeth ill filled Rossbury with cold rage.

While Rossbury spoke, Grantleigh recalled what Jemmy Baxter and Harriet Carter had said. Suddenly some of Jemmy's words took on additional meaning as Grantleigh connected them with what they had learned from Baron Bardstow. "Tyler Hamilton-Smythe is the driver of the carriage," Grantleigh stated. "Jemmy said, 'Some other gent gets on the box.'"

No one needed further explanation. The boy would not have called a servant a gent, and Tyler's driving expertise had been all too well proven by his part in Elizabeth's accidents involving carriages.

Bardstow put his head in his hands, and Rossbury nodded before voicing the question he could not answer. "But what is Sir Augustus Tremaine's part in all this? He visits Rosemont at a time when he knew Laurence was in London. And today he carried Miss Laurence from his house to the carriage waiting outside."

Tremaine was a shadowy figure. No one in the room had met him. His role in all that had occurred pricked Rossbury's instinct for danger.

"I still think that Tremaine's coach was bound for Laurence's home in Hampshire." Grantleigh recalled the conversation he and Rossbury had had during their return to Carlington Square. "And if not Hopeden Hall, then to Tremaine's home."

"Throck Manor," related Lady Dalrymple succinctly. "Near Little Throckton, I believe."

"As is Hopeden Hall." Rossbury scanned the faces before him. Lady Beatrice and Lady Dorothy were side by side on the small sofa where he had sat with Elizabeth less than a month earlier. Bardstow and Grantleigh stood behind, the baron obviously agitated while Grantleigh's features gave no hint of his feelings. "To Hopeden Hall and then Throck Manor," Rossbury began before a knock at the door made him turn.

Looking somewhat abashed, Dunhill appeared in the now open doorway. "Pardon the interruption, milady, but Lord Rossbury's Compton insists that he be allowed to speak to you." His eyes took in the assembled company, only Rossbury showing any recognition of the former soldier's name. "He says that it's about Miss Laurence."

"Show him in," ordered Rossbury without a moment's hesitation.

Dunhill then ushered Jim Compton, trailed by Patience Downes, into the morning room. Jim, looking serious but calm, took a stance facing Rossbury. Patience clung to his side, her hands ceaselessly pleating and unpleating a corner of her apron, her head hanging low.

"That will be all, Dunhill," said Lady Beatrice.

Her command forced the reluctant butler to say, "Very good, milady" and to leave the morning room with one backward glance which no one observed.

When the door had closed, Compton said, "Patience has somethin' important t' tell you 'bout Miss Laurence."

Patience's head rose at the mention of her name. She cast her eyes wildly about the room before fixing them on Compton. She opened her mouth and then closed it again.

Then Lady Beatrice said, "You may tell us what you know, Patience." Noting the girl's fear, she added, "No one here wants to hurt you."

"Go on, Patience," prompted Compton. "Just tell 'em what you tol' me."

However, Patience found the effort beyond her. After another despairing glance at the five titled people in the room, she clutched Compton's arm and began to cry quietly. "I can't, Jim. I can't."

"First let's help Patience to a chair." Rossbury fit deeds to words, and in moments he and Compton had Patience seated. He next turned to Compton. "Time may be precious so whatever information about Miss Laurence Patience has relayed to you may be given to us, particularly as Patience herself is present."

"Yes, sir," replied Compton while trying to order his jumbled thoughts. "Well, Cap't Verinder, er Lor' Rossb'ry, it's like this. Patience's been seein' a gennelmun every Thursday afternoon. He tol' her his name was Viscount Geoffrey Armbruster, but I learned – and it don't matter why I did, sir, or how I figured out that you had to hear 'bout it today, sir – I learned that his name is Tyler Hamilton-Smythe."

Baron Bardstow groaned aloud. "Are you certain? Could you not…?" The unfinished question was a plea.

"I am, milord." Compton guessed that this man was the Baron Bardstow the Watleys had told him about and that Dunhill had said was with Lord Rossbury in the morning room.

"You see," Compton explained, "I followed him to his townhouse. Your house, milord. N' then, well, I'm 'fraid I lied t' Mr. n' Mrs. Watley. Got 'em t' think I was a lost delivery man n' well, th' rest isn't important, but–"

"Why?" interrupted Bardstow, pounding his right fist into his left palm. "Why would Tyler pretend to be a viscount and walk out with a servant?"

"When did these meetings begin, Compton?" Rossbury asked.

"'Bout the same time, 'parently, as word came from Sergeant Craddock that you'd returned t' England, sir," replied Compton.

The answer to Bardstow's question was now obvious. "Winkling information out of this poor girl. Spying on you. Hoping to harm…" Bardstow walked to the fireplace, leaned his head against the mantle, and muttered, "You must rue the day you ever met the Hamilton-Smythes." Then realizing that Compton had said nothing yet of Miss Laurence, Bardstow whirled and demanded, "What else has my brother done, Compton?"

"Well, m'lord, I can't rightly answer that, but Patience did say that after Cap't Rossb'ry here went up to Earl's Wood Park, he was alwa's askin' 'bout Miss Laurence n' all her outings n' things."

"They knew I'd not be at home this morning!" The conclusion hit Lady Beatrice with the force of a pugilist's jab to his opponent's jaw. "They knew and that beastly brother of Elizabeth's took advantage and –"

"And it's all my fault!" wailed Patience suddenly. "It's all my fault." She folded her arms across her chest, her hands pressed tight to each side, and hid her face in her lap.

"No, Patience," soothed Compton. "T'weren't your fault. How was you t' know it was wrong."

"No," gulped Patience between sobs. "It was wrong to take one of Miss Laurence's handkerchiefs. To take it without askin'. But I went back to get it. I did, sir, n' washed it myself n' put it back 'n all." Her eyes pleaded for Rossbury's forgiveness.

Immediately Compton explained, "That handkerchief, sir, well, it is a good thing Patience did borrow it. 'Coz she left it at the Hare and Hounds by accident 'coz she was upset. Then she missed it n' went back for it. That's when she heard two men in the private parlour she'd just left. One was Mr. Hamilton-Smythe. T'other was a man she never seen before. N' she heard a few words here n' there. She heard 'im say, "Th' 'King's Arms' n' 'Surrey.'"

Before anyone could ask about the name, Compton continued, "It's part of the trade, sir, if you take my meaning. My friend Jack Harper – you 'member Jack, sir. You met him on th' beach when you n' Miss Laurence came off that French–" Rossbury's frown cut off the rest of the sentence.

Compton plunged on. "Well, Jack, sir, he once told me he was part of a crew shiftin' some, some, ah, barrels at th' King's Arms in Surrey. He said t'was east o' Thornfield on the Guildford road. Funny sort of place for a couple o' gennelmun t' be speakin' 'bout."

"Did you ever see this other man, Patience?" Rossbury asked.

Patience finally lifted her head from her lap. "He was tall and dressed all in black, n' he…" She shivered and then struggled for words. "He looked at me like I was street sweepin's. Tol' Geoffrey," she hesitated. "Tol' the… I don't know what to call him now," Patience stammered, "Told him t' get rid o' me. I was scared o' him." She shuddered again. "Scared he'd come after me, find me somehow."

However, Patience's reaction to the man who fit Jemmy Baxter's description of Sir Augustus Tremaine brought Rossbury different but equally disturbing recollections. Elizabeth's fear of a pursuer before the confrontation with Henri LeBeau. And her failure to discuss why she had gone to France or why she did not want to return to Little Throckton for their wedding.

Meanwhile, Grantleigh noted, "From Guildford, the Portsmouth road joins Surrey with Hampshire."

"And since Hopeden Hall is the first place anyone trying to find Miss Laurence would search, going to some place in another county makes a devilish kind of sense," added Bardstow.

Especially, thought Rossbury, if the plan includes a deed that must be performed away from the eyes and ears of sharp-witted servants, nosy neighbors, and gossipy acquaintances. His lips compressed and his fists clenched as hatred for a man he had never met began to grow. "I must leave at once," he stated almost to himself. "I shall need a horse."

Lady Beatrice apologized, "You know my stable. The two you and Grantleigh took earlier are doubtless the best of the lot, but they're not riding horses."

At the same time, Lady Dalrymple rose and crossed to the small escritoire where she knew Lady Beatrice kept writing materials. Drawing a sheet of paper towards her, she began to write. "I've riding horses eating their heads off at Camden Close. Bellamy can have one of them here in thirty minutes."

"Two," stated Grantleigh without hesitation.

"Three," amended Bardstow. "If Tyler..." He found the thought impossible to voice. "I owe you whatever help I can give, Rossbury."

"Four," added Compton, "if you'll pardon my putting myself forward like, sir." Swiftly he explained, "There's three o' 'em at least. Don't know who's at the King's Arms. N' Jack did give me an idea o' where th' place is." Seeing Rossbury's nod of agreement, Compton was prompted to remind, "Can't be a tighter corner than Yorktown, sir."

Lady Dalrymple had not waited for Rossbury's assent before changing the number of horses required to four. As Compton finished speaking, she handed the folded note to Lady Beatrice. "If you ring for Dunhill, this can be delivered at once."

"The door, Compton," Lady Beatrice suggested. "If I know Dunhill, his curiosity has kept him hovering in the corridor."

The stableman hastened to obey and jerked the door inward so quickly that a rather flabbergasted Dunhill almost stumbled into the morning room.

Ignoring the butler's embarrassment, Lady Beatrice ordered as she held the note out, "Send someone to Camden Close with this immediately. Speed is essential."

"If you'll pardon me again, milady," interrupted Compton. "Ben Tolliver in your stable be a good 'un to send." Dunhill goggled, Compton's boldness astonishing him. "Extra pair of hands," the former private explained.

"Send Tolliver," revised Lady Beatrice; and when Dunhill continued to gape, she added, "Thank you, Dunhill. That will be all."

"Very good, milady," Dunhill finally gulped before finding his way to the door and scuttling off.

When the door had closed once again, Lady Beatrice rounded on her godson. "When did you last eat, Richard?" Deliberately she put a sharp edge on her voice, for she knew Rossbury hated to be fussed over.

Grantleigh answered, "Last evening, Lady Beatrice." Like the dowager marchioness, he was worried about how hard Rossbury was driving himself.

Before Rossbury could utter a word of protest, Lady Beatrice continued, "Mrs. Featherstone can have the contents of the larder on the sideboard in the dining room in five minutes. Doubtless, there's bread, cheese, some meat pie – plenty for all of you." Her gaze included the four men in the room. "Falling out of the saddle or rushing in muddle-headed because you were too stubborn to eat won't do Elizabeth any good at all."

"We'll use the interim to cross the Square and arm ourselves," said Rossbury, his mind already scanning the rooms of Rossbury House for weapons.

Lady Beatrice exchanged an anxious glance with Lady Dalrymple but said nothing.

"I have a musket I know Private Compton can shoulder well," Rossbury stated with the briefest of smiles for the man who had served under him twelve years earlier. "We shall return here for our meal. By the time we've eaten, Lady Dalrymple's four horses should have arrived."

Unbeknownst to Rossbury, the plan conceived for Elizabeth's rescue had thrown the mantle of leadership upon him as clearly as his old uniform. And while Compton saw the officer he knew taking charge, the others saw a man who was almost a stranger to them.

"Godmother," Rossbury continued as his brain ticked off items that had automatically appeared on an internal list, "have someone find a saddlebag and see that Patience puts a change of clothes for Elizabeth in it. Old ones might be best." At the sound of her name, Patience's eyes flew to Rossbury's face. Though he wasn't looking at her, Patience bobbed a curtsy in assent, glad to be given a task to do after all the harm she had caused.

Rossbury moved to the door, the trio of men following. "And you must go to Lady Dalrymple's musicale soiree this evening." Seeing Lady Beatrice's crestfallen expression, Rossbury explained with evident bitterness in his voice, "We cannot possibly send you word about anything tonight. And if another scandal-plagued marriage is to be avoided, Elizabeth must be thought to have accompanied her brother back to Hampshire for a visit."

Lady Dalrymple nodded sagely. "And, of course, when you, the ardent bridegroom, returned to London some days earlier than anticipated, you journeyed post haste to Hampshire to join her." She grinned. "Beatrice and I are old hands at this sort of thing. We shall make certain that everyone present tonight knows about Miss Laurence's visit to her brother's home and your journey south. We have played tougher roles before skeptical audiences more than a few times, haven't we, Bea?"

"We have," agreed Lady Beatrice, determined to give Rossbury no more to fret over. "And our toughest audience now will be our servants. We'd best be about it."

Without another word, Rossbury opened the door, his mind already pondering how to arm his small band, probing how to enter the King's Arms, wondering why Sir Augustus Tremaine had allied himself with Gideon Laurence and Tyler Hamilton-Smythe. And, he told himself, I must ask Compton to share anything he knows about the King's Arms.

"Five minutes," Lady Beatrice called as the men entered the hall, but Rossbury never heard her. Instead he heard Elizabeth's nightmare shrieks of "Don't" and saw a shadowy figure behind her, a figure around whose throat he longed to put his hands.

Consciousness returned gradually to Elizabeth. Somehow she knew that safety lay in remaining asleep for as long as possible. Thus, when arguing voices, one her brother's, the other disturbingly familiar – "...gave her too much," "...wouldn't come willingly...no fuss" – intruded briefly, she willed herself to sink into the lassitude that had gripped her body and made it feel heavy and inert.

Hours later, she finally awakened. An attempt to move her arms, which lay above her head, met with resistance. She felt ropes about her wrists. Her eyes flashed open. "Harriet," she croaked, her voice a hoarse whisper, her throat dust dry.

"Harriet Carter is not here to attend you, my dear." Sir Augustus Tremaine stepped into Elizabeth's view from his place at the head of the bed. "I fear you must make do with me." Although his words were courteous, the obviously appraising look with which the baronet raked Elizabeth's body was anything but gentlemanly.

Elizabeth found herself both hot and cold at once. Beneath the thin sheet that covered her, she was naked. She could not prevent the heat of her shame and anger from reaching her face, her cheeks reddening, her grey eyes flashing fire at the familiar figure, elegantly attired, looking down at her with hooded, reptilian eyes.

"Yes, in the absence of a tiring woman, I fear I had to perform the offices of your maid myself," Sir Augustus apologized insincerely. "The next time I do so, I trust you will be able to enjoy the experience with me." He picked up a lock of Elizabeth's loosened hair, lying upon the pillow like a dark cloud, and then ran a forefinger slowly down her cheek. "There will be no laudanum then to dull your senses ... or mine."

Laudanum! echoed Elizabeth's brain, understanding at last the cotton wool sensation that made thinking difficult.

Forgetting the ropes that bound her, Elizabeth immediately jerked her head to the side and wrenched her shoulder. An involuntary spasm of pain crossed her face. "Gideon, help!" she screamed as loudly as she could before Sir Augustus slapped her face hard and then grabbed her jaw in a crushing, two-handed grip.

"You, my dear," intoned Sir Augustus smoothly, while increasing the pressure on Elizabeth's jaw, "will remain silent. There is no help for you in this place. And your loving brother has sold you to me for just a bit more than the Biblical 'mess of pottage.'"

Sir Augustus squeezed harder yet and moved his face close to Elizabeth's. She tasted blood in her mouth. "If you think cooperation is impossible this evening, perhaps you may reconsider your decision once we examine the choices together." Suddenly the hands holding her jaw released their grip. Elizabeth gasped when the pressure was momentarily relaxed and then cried out as Tremaine's left hand spanned her face, his thumb digging painfully into her cheekbone. Her eyes closed with pain. Then with one quick movement, Sir Augustus pulled back his hand and, as Elizabeth gulped for air, pushed a thick rope into her mouth, each end held tight against the bed by one of his hands. Tremaine stretched the rope tighter, its coarse fibers cutting cruelly into Elizabeth lips.

"There is only one choice, Elizabeth – soon to be my dear Lady Tremaine."

Elizabeth's eyes widened. No! her mind shouted silently. Richard!

"That choice I have made for you since your own ability to choose was proven quite deficient almost five years ago." His face inches from hers, Sir Augustus stated, "Your cooperation I shall have. You may select its manner of delivery. Either this," he offered while he drove the rope deeper into her flesh, "or your promise to refrain from futile screams for help. Which is it to be?" Tremaine twisted the rope that cut Elizabeth's mouth.

I must have time to think. I must make him believe that he has cowed me into submission, Elizabeth told herself. Her mind fended off pain as she grappled with terror. The terror of learning that her intuitive fears of Sir Augustus were real. The terror of knowing that beneath the baronet's polite façade lay something vile and sinister. The terror of finding herself in nightmarish circumstances that did not make sense.

I need to know more, Elizabeth thought. Then perhaps... Elizabeth stifled notions of escape, no inkling of which, she immediately understood, should be reflected on her face. Realizing that tension betokened resistance, Elizabeth let her body go limp. She let fear dim her eyes.

Tremaine smiled with satisfaction as he surveyed Elizabeth, recumbent and motionless except for the rise and fall of her breathing. He leaned his left arm upon her, moved it slightly so that it touched her breast. "Shall I remove the rope?"

Elizabeth nodded, carefully keeping the shake of her head small.

"A pity, my dear," remarked Tremaine conversationally as he observed the blood darkening the rope he had taken from Elizabeth's mouth. He stood and walked away from the bed.

When he had done so, Elizabeth asked quietly, "Where are we? At Throck Manor?"

"No, my dear," answered Tremaine returning with a cloth and a basin of water. He dipped the cloth into the water and began dabbing at Elizabeth's lips. "This may hurt."

Elizabeth steeled herself to avoid flinching at Tremaine's touch, his very nearness making her feel sick. "If not Throck, then where?"

"The King's Arms. A public house with an avocation which is a bit, shall we say, disreputable. Not the sort of place anyone we know would frequent. Not the sort of place to want to draw attention to itself." Sir Augustus wrung the blood-flecked cloth out into the basin. "Quite a way from Throck and Hopeden," he added. "And help."

The baronet dabbed again at Elizabeth's mouth. "The bed chamber you will occupy at Throck Manor is much more commodious than this one." Lips wrinkled disparagingly, distaste stamped clearly on his features, Tremaine sneered. He turned his attention to the small room that he had coerced Micah Whitbread to prepare for him. A pair of branched candlesticks and a crackling fire in the hearth at its other end provided light.

This glanced off the dark wood of furnishings – a testered bed with a low side table where the basin rested and a massive chest of drawers near the solitary window. A crude table and single chair had been placed before the fire and looked as if they were not part of the room's ordinary furniture. Atop the table was a ewer of water, a bottle of wine, and two glasses. "More tastefully decorated as well as cleaner."

Sir Augustus returned his attention to Elizabeth and smiled coldly. "At Throck you shall, no doubt, find the conjugal bed firm under your back. A fitting place for marital embraces." He dabbed once more at the corner of her lip and returned the cloth to the bowl. "And sport, my dear, for which I believe you are, if my preliminary investigations are correct and I trust they are, eminently suitable."

Elizabeth fought the urge to scream or cry. Tremaine's implications were clear, and her unbound hair and unclothed state bore testimony to what he had done while she was unconscious. The lack of other aches and pains assured her that he had reserved the final ignominy for a time when she would be aware of exactly what he was doing.

Hysteria, Elizabeth knew, would not save her. Reason might. The glimmer of a plan began to form. She needed more information and determined how best to coax it from Tremaine.

"However, the King's Arms will do – for tonight." Tremaine rose and carried the basin back to the table. While he did so, Elizabeth's eyes flicked quickly to the door. Almost as if he were reading her mind, Tremaine, with his back to the bed, said, "By the way, the door's locked from the inside, my dear."

Tremaine removed his coat and hung it over the back of the chair. Then he strolled back to the bed and seated himself. Leaning over Elizabeth so that she could feel his breath on her face, he noted, "The key is here." He patted his waistcoat pocket. "And besides..." Sir Augustus tugged once at the ropes that bound Elizabeth's wrists to the left bedpost, the movement wrenching her shoulders again and causing another spasm of pain to cross her face.

"This time you will not elude me by going to France or anywhere else for that matter." Sir Augustus scowled at the memory. No woman refuses me, he thought. No woman. I shall make her pay for that refusal. Later. A vision of how he would exact his revenge made him smile.

"In fact, before this time tomorrow, you will be my Lady Tremaine and will require my permission to do anything. And my permission shall only be given if you prove yourself amenable to your conjugal duties." Sir Augustus put his left hand possessively over her breast and squeezed

Elizabeth found herself trembling. No, she told herself, no. Fear will numb me, paralyze me. God help me to think! Think! she ordered herself.

"You are trembling, my dear," noted Sir Augustus with satisfaction. His finger absently circled her breast covered only by the sheet.

"If I am to be Lady Tremaine…" Elizabeth paused, willing herself to stop shaking, willing Tremaine to continue speaking.

"When, not if, my dear," Sir Augustus corrected. "The when is tomorrow at Little Throckton. The ceremony will be short so doubtless the Reverend Mr. Jeremiah Cuthbertson will have no difficulties fitting it on his calendar." He moved his hand lower, glanced at the place where it lay, and then said, "He may remonstrate with us for yielding to our mutual passion and celebrating our marriage night before the ceremony, but his disapproval will only make him more adamant that the rite must be performed at once."

Meanwhile, Elizabeth had been thinking, If I can escape this room, what then? Are there others here – servants perhaps – who will aid him? she wondered. Then feeling as if a net were tightening around her, she encouraged Tremaine to reveal more of his plan and answer her question. "A marriage, even a hasty one, requires witnesses."

"You are right, my dear. Clever as well as..." Sir Augustus' hand slid to her inner thigh and began to stroke it through the sheet.

Gritting her teeth, Elizabeth was unable to suppress a shudder. Feeling it gave Tremaine a sense of power and satisfaction. Good, he thought. She is fighting me in her own way.

"I always knew we would be well-matched. Well-mated." Tremaine's hooded eyes lingered over Elizabeth's body before returning to her face.

"And you are perhaps wondering who these witnesses are and whether either might be convinced to gainsay me?"

Although this information was not what she hoped to learn, Elizabeth forced herself to appear abashed, her small gasp of surprise and downcast expression seemingly giving credence to the idea that she had been outwitted. Silently she prayed, Let him tell me who is aiding him and whether they are here.

"First, my dear Elizabeth, let me warn you that if you have any ideas about refusing to sign the register yourself, you should forget them." Sir Augustus touched her right hand and then jerked the rope that tied it to the bedpost. After Elizabeth's short mew of pain, he remarked softly, "T'would be a pity if this lovely hand were to suffer a broken finger or two, would it not?"

Elizabeth knew that no answer was required and remained silent, waiting for him to tell her the names of those he had compelled to witness the mockery he would call a wedding the next day.

"Your dear brother Gideon will be even more happy to write his name in the register now than he would have been in '88." The baronet again recalled Elizabeth's refusal and abrupt departure from England while he had gone north on business. The memory angered him afresh. To hide his anger, Sir Augustus rose and walked to the table where he poured a glass of wine for himself. He raised it in a mocking salute to Elizabeth, took a sip, and continued. "If you are wondering why this should be so, the reason is, oddly enough, a letter received from one William Clewett, solicitor, announcing that while you were enjoying your French sojourn, a Mrs. Calvert died."

"Great Aunt Catherine?" gasped Elizabeth as images of garden walks with a woman she had loved and admired surfaced.

Sir Augustus nodded in acknowledgement. "Of Rosemont, near Ashcoombe in Gloucestershire. A pretty place." He sipped meditatively at the wine. When Elizabeth said nothing, he explained, "Yes, I have been there. Quite recently in fact. It will be a pleasant addition to my holdings. A dowry perhaps for our daughter." His lips curled in a smile, but the eyes visible over the glass once again raised to her appeared merely appraising. "Our son will, of course, inherit Throck." He allowed his eyes to leave her face and travel downward while taking another sip from his glass.

Elizabeth willed back the stomach churning loathing his crude assessment of her body evoked in her and concentrated instead on the astonishing and unexpected inheritance. "But why," she questioned, "should Aunt Catherine's leaving Rosemont to me make Gideon eager for us..." Hearing the plural pronoun made Elizabeth hesitate. Any word that suggested a relationship between herself and the abhorrent Tremaine was anathema. Before she could rephrase the end of her question, Tremaine interrupted.

"How glad I am to hear you say <u>us</u>. It shows, I believe, your willingness to bow to the inevitable." Refilling the empty glass, Sir Augustus observed, "When Clewett's letter arrived, your brother hadn't heard from you in some time. Laurence simply wrote what he believed and hoped to be true – that you were dead."

Tremaine whirled around so that he could catch the dismay he knew would be on Elizabeth's face after hearing about her brother's action.

"Why so disappointed, my dear?" Sir Augustus asked sardonically. "£5000 is a rather powerful inducement. Jacob acquired his brother's birthright for far less, and the Good Book is kind in its assessment of the deceiver while poor Esau is treated as an oafish lout. Quite inexplicable in my opinion." He returned to the bed and reseated himself, the wine glass in his right hand. "Let's not be too hard on dear brother Gideon. After all, his greed has allowed us to be together – though, I must admit, I had to keep him in the dark about my plans for tonight."

Tremaine pushed a stray tendril of hair from Elizabeth's face. "I believe he was prepared to tell you all at that little tête-à-tête arranged earlier today at my house on Hanover Crescent."

"£5000!" stammered Elizabeth, coaxing a tone of wonderment into her voice. "Your house?" Keep him talking, she told herself. Her mind had registered every item in the room while his back was turned and now considered how each might be used against Sir Augustus.

"Surely you didn't think that Laurence had been able to purchase a London townhouse while you were in France? Or that I'd allow him to go up to London to fetch you without some way of monitoring his progress?" Sir Augustus drained the wineglass in his hand and placed it on the low table near the bed. Then slowly he lowered the sheet covering Elizabeth until her shoulders and the tops of her breasts were revealed. "Not so clever as you thought, are you, my dear?"

Despite the look of fear she knew must be in her eyes and the increased rate of her breathing, Elizabeth refused to rise to Tremaine's baiting and stated as calmly as she could, "The money. It's still there."

"Very good, my dear. Very good." Sir Augustus' praise was hollow. He leaned over Elizabeth, supporting himself on his left hand while one finger of his right hand swept slowly back and forth upon Elizabeth's body just above the edge of the sheet. "Old Mrs. Calvert was wise. Your £5000 is still safe in the Bank of England – or should I say our £5000 since, as your husband, all you have is mine."

Sir Augustus paused deliberately. His right hand cupped Elizabeth's breast and squeezed it suddenly, painfully. Hearing her involuntary moan, he smiled coldly and repeated emphatically, "All you have is mine. And because of this undeniable fact, I shall, of course, recover your inheritance."

His finger resumed its motion at the sheet edge. "Without, of course, endangering Gideon. Having a brother-in-law in Newgate would not do. Gideon is far more valuable to me outside prison walls. His gratitude for my silence about certain matters connected with Mrs. Calvert's will should insure his current and future cooperation. And two letters to Clewett should easily rectify the situation. Gideon's letter to announce your surprising resurrection from the dead and joyful marriage to a neighbor who has long held you in the highest esteem. Then our letter to assure him that the funds already transferred to Gideon Laurence are now in the proper hands. All's well that ends well, as the Bard said. Wouldn't you agree, my dear?"

"Current cooperation," repeated Elizabeth, riveting her concentration on Sir Augustus' words rather than his hands. Is Gideon here? she wondered. Sir Augustus had already hinted that Gideon had not agreed to the forced abduction and had been, in a sense, blackmailed into consenting after the fact. Perhaps, she thought, if I can escape from this room, Gideon will aid me in spite of what Sir Augustus told me after I screamed earlier.

"Insured, at this moment, by the presence of Tyler Hamilton-Smythe in a room not far from ours," related the baronet idly, his inadvertent half-glance at the fireplace telling Elizabeth where her brother was lodged. However, Sir Augustus himself was unaware of the slip, for his fingers drew lazy patterns on Elizabeth's flesh as his mind reviewed the various possibilities for the hours that lay ahead.

Elizabeth allowed recognition of Tyler's name to enter her eyes. And Gideon, she guessed, would have told Sir Augustus about their conversation.

"You have not had the pleasure of Hamilton-Smythe's acquaintance, have you, my dear? Not officially at least." Sir Augustus rose and lifted the sheet at the right side of the bed. He carefully folded a large triangle of it back so that Elizabeth's side lay open to his gaze.

"No." Elizabeth expelled the syllable on a long, shaking breath. Wondering why he had added officially, she ordered her body to lie still and awaited his reply.

"Doctor Adams?" Sir Augustus suggested. When Elizabeth said nothing, he simply smiled. Then he resumed his seat and began running his right hand over Elizabeth's rib cage, hip, and thigh with sweeping perpendicular strokes, each one at the crease in the sheet.

"I fear I cannot spare you his further acquaintance. Hamilton-Smythe will be our other witness at Little Throckton tomorrow. However, I doubt that we shall be forced to endure his company after the ceremony. You would soon find his lack of personal responsibility as tiresome as I do. He has a veritable litany of grievances which he recites at length to anyone who will listen, and he lays them all at the door of his former brother-in-law Richard Verinder, Lord Rossbury."

Elizabeth could not prevent the longing Rossbury's name elicited from being mirrored in her face. She extinguished it quickly as allowing Sir Augustus even to glimpse her feelings for Rossbury seemed a profanation of that love and respect.

Sir Augustus observed Elizabeth's unmasked emotions with a brief hiss of displeasure. He moved his hand under the sheet, found the crescent of the lower half of Elizabeth's right breast and began to outline its shape. "And I fear that you will never be a countess." His eyes narrowed, and he leaned closer, his weight crushing her as he whispered, "An hour from now neither Rossbury nor any other of his ilk will want you." He sat back and smiled smugly. "But you will be my Lady Tremaine, Elizabeth. A title that will have to content you."

Elizabeth felt his hand move down to the inverted vee below her breastbone and remain there. Without thinking, she held her breath, unsure of what to say or do, waiting as long as possible to put the plan she had formulated into action. Lord, help me! she prayed again silently. Then taking a deep breath, she said as calmly as she could, "I am thirsty, Sir Augustus."

Her words erased the displeasure that had tightened Tremaine's features. "Of course, my dear. Would a little wine suit you?" Sir Augustus asked, his courtesy somehow more disgusting to Elizabeth than his earlier cruelty.

"Yes, please," Elizabeth replied quietly. And with great relief she felt him remove his hand and flick the sheet back into place.

Moments later Sir Augustus was back at her side, his right arm beneath her head, his left holding the glass to her lips. After Elizabeth had swallowed two small mouthfuls, she said, "Thank you." Then, as soon as the glass was withdrawn, she added evenly, "I am surprised you would consort with one such as Tyler Hamilton-Smythe."

When Sir Augustus had looked searchingly at her face and seen no trace of sarcasm there, he laughed mirthlessly and agreed. "As well you should be. Hamilton-Smythe has been most useful to me, my dear Elizabeth. And that is all he is good for – being used by his betters, who, I assure you, are legion. But were you to speak to him, you would be thankful, my dear, that you are to wed me and not Rossbury. I have saved you from the ignominy both of being the relation by marriage to Hamilton-Smythe and of being the wife of a man whose late wife died in scandalous circumstances."

Elizabeth allowed her eyes to widen.

Tremaine smiled as he prepared to shock her with revelations he felt certain she had not heard. His hand stroked her shoulder. Rossbury may appear quite different to her after she hears what I have to say, he considered. Yet he guessed that she was attempting to persuade him to speak simply to forestall another kind of communication.

Sir Augustus remarked nonchalantly, "Delaying the inevitable, my dear, does not make it any less inevitable." Suddenly his fingers pinched the soft flesh of her upper breast, and Elizabeth cried out in pain. "Tonight, you will know who is master. You will feel my flesh within you; nothing can prevent our union, my dear. And if Hamilton-Smythe has his way, Rossbury will soon be but a memory. You don't need him. Besides Rossbury is not the man for you. You need a firm hand, just as an unbroken steed must feel the bit and spur to know who is in control."

Tremaine's fingers explored the spot he had pinched. "There'll be a bruise, I'm afraid." He sighed. "Tyler Hamilton-Smythe," he began reflectively. "What a sniveling cur he is. Since you wanted to know, let me tell you not only what he has related to me but also what Inchcomb has unearthed as well."

Meanwhile, Elizabeth, her eyes glued to Tremaine's face, her body quivering with fear and revulsion, reviewed each step of her plan to escape from the trap Sir Augustus had lured her into.

## CHAPTER 22

# EVENING, FRIDAY, MARCH 15, 1793

"There's a gennelmun's traveling coach outside th' stable. N' th' horses inside, well, they's no posting hacks," Jim Compton whispered as he slipped back under the trees outside the King's Arms

Rossbury nodded. He stared at the King's Arms, light reflecting like squares of gold from the two windows on either side of the front door.

Grantleigh and Bardstow stood nearby. Each held two horses from Lady Dalrymple's stables.

Pale slivers of moonlight dappled the ground in the small copse where the four men waited. Drops of water from the recent rain splashed onto them from the tree branches overhead.

"What's at the back?" asked Rossbury quietly.

"One door. Prob'ly to th' kitchen," replied Compton. "Two windows lighted upstairs."

"Two," repeated Rossbury, a plan for how to use the three men under the trees taking shape.

"Bardstow, go with Compton. Take the horses with you. We may be forced to make a hasty departure."

"Some old blankets in th' stable, Capt'n," Compton suggested, knowing they had ridden their horses hard and the night was cold.

"Use them," agreed Rossbury. "Leave the horses behind the stable. Then stay close to the back entrance. Stop anyone coming out."

The steel in his voice told them resistance was not to be tolerated.

"Keep a watch on those lighted windows as well. Load your weapons after you are in position," added Rossbury grimly. "You may need them."

Without thinking, Compton put his hand on the leather strap of the Brown Bess lying across his back. The familiar feel steadied him.

Bardstow's hand sought the large pocket of his heavy coat. The pistol inside was one of Rossbury's, but its similarity to a brace he owned made him sure he could load it quickly. However, never in his life had he fired on another human being. The thought made him feel slightly sick.

Rossbury recognized the fear coming from his brother-in-law and said, "Bardstow, I trust you have your watch with you."

Turning his head sharply at the sound of his name, Bardstow stammered, "Yes, yes, I do."

"Grantleigh and I will give you and Compton five minutes to hide the horses, reach your places, and ready yourselves."

Bardstow fumbled his hand into his waistcoat pocket. He flicked the watch cover back and squinted at the black hands just visible in the fitful moonlight.

"Then Grantleigh and I shall enter. You may hear us singing that song we rehearsed over our meal at Farnsworth Place."

Three heads shook in understanding.

"If Tyler is in the tap room, you'll probably hear warning shouts. If you do, come through the back door immediately. Don't let anyone catch you from the rear."

"Understood, Capt'n." Compton remembered Yorktown where their retreat had been cut off and a company of rebels had moved between them and the rest of their regiment. "Camden, not Yorktown," he added.

"If only locals and the innkeeper are downstairs, Grantleigh and I shall order a pint, survey the taproom, and perhaps ask about a room for the night. With any luck the stairs will be in view and the landlord will tell us something about his paying guests." As Rossbury spoke, phrases that would neither alarm nor rouse the landlord's suspicions began to form.

"If, at any time, you hear shots or any indications of a struggle, enter at once. I'm hoping there's no resistance; but if there is, we'll need to move quickly."

Rossbury looked at the three men he now considered his command. Grantleigh wore the empty expression Rossbury had often seen on his face ever since the death of his wife Louise. Compton stamped his feet and flexed his fingers, well remembered habits designed to insure physical readiness. Bardstow cleared his throat and then swallowed, his hand still cradling his pocket watch.

"Compton's an expert skirmisher, Bardstow. Take your cues from him."

Bardstow cast a look at the stableman and touched the other man's arm. "Just tell me what to do, Compton."

"Yes, sir," Compton replied.

"Miss Laurence's safety is paramount," began Rossbury. He decided not to say more. They all understood what must be done, and he feared he wouldn't be able to control his voice if he used Elizabeth's name again. "It's time," he said instead. "Five minutes, gentlemen. God speed."

Compton immediately slid off into the darkness with the horses, Bardstow trailing behind him.

Grantleigh put a hand on Rossbury's shoulder. "We'll find her. Safe," he stated more positively than he felt. And it must be so, Grantleigh thought as he huddled deeper into his coat.

Minutes passed as Elizabeth listened to the poison dripping from Sir Augustus' lips. Whenever his tales – first about the brilliance of his plan for spiriting her away from London and later about the hatred motivating Tyler Hamilton-Smythe, the stupidity and greed of her brother Gideon, and the scandal surrounding Rossbury – had flagged, she asked another question. Sir Augustus' smile and patronizing tone showed that he knew her ploy for what it was – a delaying tactic.

He is like a cat toying with a mouse, considered Elizabeth, determined to keep Sir Augustus talking.

Suddenly a familiar melody crept under the door. Customers in the taproom below were bawling out the words of a song. Sir Augustus looked at the door, shrugged, and continued talking.

"England rules the waves forever.
She will never be enslaved..."

Elizabeth strained to hear. *La Marseillaise*, she thought, recalling the inn at Caudebec. But the song is not well known in England and the words… Richard! Elizabeth's heart beat out the syllables of his name. He's here!

The song ended just as Sir Augustus finished telling her about his visit to Rosemont. Hoping her face did not betray her, Elizabeth said nothing.

"No more questions, my dear?" asked Sir Augustus, moderate surprise in his voice.

Elizabeth remained silent.

"Good. I am weary of speaking and feel it's time we enjoyed a taste of connubial closeness, don't you?"

"Before, before..." Elizabeth stammered, her nervousness very real now that the time had come to set her plan in motion and to speak about a subject no lady ever mentioned to a man. "I must relieve myself," she blurted out.

"Oh, must you really, Elizabeth?"

Elizabeth ignored Sir Augustus' skeptical smile. "Yes, I must, before, before you, we..." Elizabeth broke off in what she prayed Sir Augustus would interpret as embarrassed confusion.

"Or is this just another of your delaying tactics?" Sir Augustus' tone lifted in disbelief. "Or an attempt to reach the door?"

"Which is locked."

"It is. But, I think your ..." Sir Augustus paused and said condescendingly, "Relief must be put aside until after we have enjoyed some bed sport."

"Then I must relieve myself where I am." As Elizabeth stated the lie, she knew her face was reddening in convincing shame. "Don't force me to soil both myself and the linen."

"Setting conditions for me, are you? A hint of fire still. I like that. A woman who gives as good as she gets – not like my late, unlamented wife Edith." Sir Augustus' hands began to unknot the cords that bound Elizabeth's hands to the bed-posts. "But," he added as he pulled maliciously on the ropes and drew a gasp of pain from Elizabeth before loosening her wrists, "I warn you, Elizabeth, neither to scream nor to pound on the door." Sir Augustus stood at the side of the bed and looked down upon Elizabeth, a smug smile playing about his thin lips.

Elizabeth pulled the sheet up to her chin and chafed her wrists.

"The chamber pot is there." Sir Augustus pointed to a spot by the room's chest of drawers.

Elizabeth sat up, her fingers clutching the sheet. "A robe or a gown, Sir Augustus, if you please."

"Is either necessary? In a few minutes, you must remove any garment or give me the pleasure of removing it for you." The sight of Elizabeth grasping the sheet and firing off commands increased the baronet's desire to force himself upon her. Definitely worth taming, Sir Augustus thought with anticipated pleasure.

"True as that may be," Elizabeth retorted, "a husband must surely permit his wife the dignity of a *robe de chambre* in their own apartments."

Sir Augustus walked to the bottom of the bed, stooped, and then tossed Elizabeth a filmy peignoir from inside a small traveling trunk placed there.

"Thank you." Elizabeth pulled the garment behind her back and then gripped the edge of the sheet in her teeth.

"Your modesty comes a bit too late, does it not, my dear?" With amusement Sir Augustus observed Elizabeth's struggles under the sheet.

"My mother taught me that modesty lends grace to all a lady's accomplishments. Perhaps you think her wrong." Elizabeth pushed her arms through the peignoir's sleeves and moved her legs so that they hung over the side of the bed.

"Far be it from me to question your dear departed mother, Elizabeth." Sir Augustus watched Elizabeth tie the peignoir's belt and then take a few unsteady steps towards him.

Sir Augustus moved aside as Elizabeth approached him. "Although, very shortly, I'll show you that your mother's teaching is definitely not always applicable."

"But until you do so, perhaps you would be good enough to give me some privacy while I…" Elizabeth hesitated before adding, "Surely you do not wish to…"

"In this instance, you are right. But be warned that I shall regard any attempt to inconvenience me in the slightest with great displeasure."

"The door is locked, and Gideon has already sold me to you." Elizabeth allowed her head to droop.

"It is good that you recognize your position so clearly, my dear," Sir Augustus said as he leaned against the door and half-turned.

Elizabeth immediately used the brief lull in Sir Augustus' scrutiny. I must convince him that my illness is real. And only a well-placed finger can do that, she told herself still crouching and already a bit sick as she thought about what she had to do.

Sir Augustus wheeled abruptly at the sound of Elizabeth's retching.

Cannoning into the table, Elizabeth grabbed it with both hands as if to steady herself and knocked both the ewer and the basin from it. While broken pottery and water fell at her feet, she stumbled backwards, the hearthside poker jostled from its stand. Clutching her side, she bent over and with her foot pushed one end of the poker into the fire.

"What's wrong? If this is a trick..." Sir Augustus stepped towards the table, his eyes on Elizabeth's face.

"My head's spinning, and I feel dizzy, faint," gasped Elizabeth. "Never had laudanum before..." She doubled over again while inching forward. "Must lie down."

"That idiot gave you the whole dose!" Sir Augustus ground his teeth in anger. Holding Elizabeth's head over a basin was not his plan for the evening. "I told him... Damn!"

As Elizabeth stumbled back towards the bed, she forced her breath to come in shallow pants.

"Get back to bed. Lie perfectly still. I am certain you shall feel better shortly," Sir Augustus said, as he bent down near the shattered pottery. The landlord's wife, he'd decided earlier, was an interfering busybody, someone whose help he'd require only after he'd made Elizabeth his. That door remains shut, he thought, until then. For ill or not, Elizabeth shall learn what it is to be a wife tonight.

Seeing Sir Augustus gathering the pieces of the broken ewer and basin, Elizabeth padded quickly to the bed and lifted the candle burning in a pewter stand nearby. Without hesitation, she touched the flame to the bed curtains.

After two areas were burning brightly, Elizabeth applied the flame to the bed sheet. As it caught, Sir Augustus smelled smoke behind him. Still hunched on the floor, he crooked his neck, saw the bed flaming, roared, "What the devil?" and stood.

Elizabeth tossed the candlestick onto the bed as Sir Augustus ran at her. Grabbing the arm that moments before had held the candle, he wrenched her off her feet and dragged her from the bedside. "You little hellcat! You'll pay for this!"

Elizabeth did not resist as the baronet pulled her farther away from the bed and dumped her unceremoniously into the corner she had left only minutes earlier.

Then Sir Augustus reached towards the table before remembering that the pitcher and bowl lay in pieces.

"Clever, my dear, but not clever enough." Sir Augustus glared at Elizabeth through the smoke beginning to billow from the flaming bed. "There's no help for you on the other side of the door. And should you so much as attempt to move anywhere near it, I shall not be answerable for the consequences that will make you very sorry, indeed."

Sir Augustus paused; but Elizabeth said nothing. Instead she gathered her breath for the single syllable that she knew would draw help to her.

"A few buckets of water will take care of this mess; and then, my dear, I shall give you all that you deserve and more," choked Sir Augustus, one hand on the door, the other fitting key to hole.

"Fire!" screamed Elizabeth as loudly as she could the moment the door was wide.

In the room below, Rossbury slammed his tankard onto the table he shared with Grantleigh, rose, and whirled instantly, his eyes searching past the angle in the staircase at the back of the room for Elizabeth.

"Whitbread, we need a few buckets of water here," Sir Augustus ordered from above, without a trace of alarm in his tone. "Step lively now, before there's any real danger."

Two men cradling pints of ale at a table near the hearth looked apprehensively at one another and stood. Sally Whitbread bent over from her spot behind the long counter at one side of the main room of the King's Arms and set two buckets of dirty water on the bar. Rossbury, with Grantleigh close behind him, strode to the counter. Micah Whitbread hustled from behind it while carrying two buckets.

"Looks like you could use some help." Without another word, Rossbury grabbed the two buckets on the counter.

"Thanks." Micah threw the word over his shoulder as he ran towards the stairs. Water slopped out of the buckets, a slick trail marking his path.

Rossbury limped along in Whitbread's wake, his thoughts not on the fire but on Elizabeth.

"Are there any more buckets?" Grantleigh asked Sally Whitbread who was retreating through a door he guessed led to a kitchen or scullery.

"Pump's in here," the publican's wife stated without slowing her steps. Grantleigh hurried after her, anxious to fill a couple of buckets and join Rossbury upstairs.

"That's Elizabeth's voice!" Gideon Laurence jumped out of his chair in a small upstairs bedchamber.

"Sit down!" Tyler Hamilton-Smythe, a pistol in his hand, pushed himself up from an uncomfortable chair near the door.

He listened for sounds of panic and only heard Sir Augustus' calm demand for buckets of water.

Gideon began walking toward the door. "Elizabeth said, 'Fire.'"

"Sit down, Laurence," ordered Tyler, pointing the pistol directly at Gideon.

"But..."

"I don't care what your sister said. It's nothing I tell you. Sir Augustus wants us both to remain here until morning and remain we shall." Tyler took a step forward and growled, "Sit down. Now!"

Gideon dropped back into his chair and whimpered, "But if there's a fire..."

Tyler heard the thud of feet pounding up the stairs. "The Whitbreads," he announced confidently, "are bringing up water now."

Gideon put his head in his hands. Oh God, he groaned to himself, what have I done? The small room seemed to close in on him. Like the prison cell he feared was waiting for him,

"I'd lie down if I were you," suggested Tyler. "One of you Laurences may as well sleep for it seems that your sister will be getting precious little rest if Sir Augustus has his way."

Tyler's laugh brought Gideon's head up with a jerk. He balled his fists and half-rose from his seat.

"Move over to the bed," Tyler demanded, the pistol again aimed at Gideon. "You will need your energy to witness the wedding tomorrow." The wedding, he thought with relish as he watched Gideon slump disconsolately towards the bed. And when Rossbury hears of it and of my part in it! Ah, Sarah, revenge will be sweet!

Once inside the upstairs bedchamber, Rossbury surveyed the room, his gaze fastening upon Elizabeth. She stood defensively in the corner farthest from the door, a poker in her hand.

For an instant their eyes locked, and in the exchange of glances, Rossbury read that he'd arrived in time. Then he saw the bruising around Elizabeth's mouth; and a murderous cold rage settled upon him.

Richard! Richard! Elizabeth wanted to shout, to feel Rossbury's name on her lips. But she said nothing. It's not over yet, she reminded herself as she noted that Sir Augustus stood between her and the door. Elizabeth gripped the poker more tightly.

Meanwhile, Micah Whitbread's only thought was to save his hostelry's best bedchamber from destruction. He emptied his two buckets on the flaming bed covers and then reached behind him. Rossbury put the first of the buckets he carried and then the second into the innkeeper's outstretched hands. The dousing of the four buckets all but extinguished the blaze on the bed, only the hangings on the side opposite still alight.

"What happened?" Micah Whitbread asked as he put down the fourth bucket and pulled a sleeve across his face.

"I started it." Elizabeth's calm assertion made Whitbread's head turn in her direction.

Sir Augustus scowled. "She is overwrought. T'was an accident, no more. But Whitbread we require another room tonight. We can wait in our friends' room until…"

"I shall go nowhere – with you," Elizabeth interrupted as Grantleigh, carrying two more buckets of water, came into the room.

Micah Whitbread grabbed one and tossed its contents on the remaining flames. Scanning the charred but sodden bedding with a critical eye, he poured the water in the last bucket over the last two smoldering spots.

While Whitbread extinguished the fire, Sir Augustus looked first at Elizabeth defiantly holding the poker like a weapon, and then at the man who had followed Micah Whitbread into the room. Tremaine saw a tall man in travel-stained clothes, a man whose blue eyes, full of icy anger, stared at him as Rossbury stepped from his position behind Whitbread.

Sir Augustus stared back, his lip curling with disdain as his appraisal meandered slowly from Rossbury's face to his muddy boots and back again.

"Rossbury, I presume," he said, his tone laden with scorn. "And an assistant – to lean upon." His eyes flashed dismissively over Grantleigh, who moved purposefully to Rossbury's side.

Rossbury's face hardened, but his voice was composed as he replied, "Viscount Grantleigh, Miss Elizabeth Laurence. I believe the two of you are already acquainted."

Grantleigh, taking his cue from Rossbury, bowed and murmured, "We are, and I remain Your servant, Miss Laurence."

"Lord Grantleigh." Elizabeth said with some surprise, though her eyes never left Sir Augustus. "It is good to see you again after so many years though I wish we were at one of Aunt Catherine's parties as we were when we first met."

"Bravo. Very well done, indeed. Wonderful theatre." Sir Augustus inched toward the corner where Elizabeth stood.

Micah Whitbread had watched the scene playing out before him with trepidation. Knew he'd only be trouble soon as tha' man o' his come wi' his bloody letter. Gawd, o' all the places he coulda come, why'd he come 'ere! Whitbread thought as he sidled towards the door behind Rossbury and Grantleigh. "If none o' yew gennelmun 'ave nothink more yew want or need, I'll..."

"You shall be readying a decent room for both me <u>and</u> my companion," stated Sir Augustus nonchalantly while shifting his position to the left again.

Whitbread, seeing the set jaws of the two men who had helped him put out the fire, simply nodded. That one's goin' to get his comeuppance and no mistake. And I'd best be downstairs when it 'appens, he told himself before he scuttled out the door.

"I fear you are mistaken, Tremaine," Rossbury noted after the innkeeper had departed.

Stung by Rossbury's deliberate omission of his title, Sir Augustus, flung back, "And I fear you shall find your merchandise a trifle," he paused and smiled secretively, "shopworn." He glanced at Elizabeth for a moment before looking with cool condescension at Rossbury.

Elizabeth gasped at the slur on her reputation, the syllable "No" framed on her lips as Grantleigh burst out, "Cad!"

Unflinching Rossbury cut across them both and said simply, "That is, of course, a lie. If it were true, Miss Laurence would not be so courageously defending herself in the corner where your crude cruelty has driven her. And even if it were true, one cannot be robbed of honour by another. One can only forfeit his honour by his own villainy."

"Richard," Elizabeth breathed softly while continuing to watch Sir Augustus' movements.

"And this is the man, my dear," Sir Augustus sneered in retaliation, "you have accepted? Your taste is in sad need of refinement. A cripple who looks decidedly like a rag picker."

"Perhaps Miss Laurence feels there is greater honour in being wed to a ragman than in being connected to a man whose reputation is in rags," replied Rossbury evenly.

"It is your reputation that will be in tatters after Gideon Laurence's theft of his sister's inheritance is bruited about. But then you are accustomed to scandal, are you not, Rossbury?" Sir Augustus spat out.

"Accustomed enough to know that only those enamored of gossip," Rossbury paused briefly before adding with slight emphasis, "or of extortion, tar the innocent with the same brush they've already sullied themselves with."

Sensing a slight relaxation of Elizabeth's guard, Sir Augustus suddenly sidestepped. Immediately Elizabeth lashed out with the still hot poker.

"Aargh!" the baronet yelled as the glowing metal connected with his flesh. "Bitch!" He backed away and nursed his left hand, a vivid weal already rising across his palm.

Sensing that Sir Augustus would offer no further resistance, Rossbury requested, "Drew, would you escort Miss Laurence downstairs?"

Sir Augustus watched sullenly as Grantleigh crossed the room to the corner where Elizabeth stood. "That's right. Let the troops do the real work. From what I've heard, Rossbury, you are not much good of taking care of problems on your own. Or women either." He laughed derisively. "You shall need your talent for dealing with other men's leavings with this she devil."

Seeing Elizabeth safe at Grantleigh's side, Rossbury ordered, "Get out, Tremaine."

"Gladly." Sir Augustus gazed casually around the room. "Whitbread can send my trunk on later. And," he turned to Elizabeth, "you, my dear, may keep my robe. Removing your own garments and touching what lay underneath was..."

"Enough, Tremaine." Rossbury's words whiplashed across those of Sir Augustus. "You..." He stopped to gain more control of his emotions and voice. "Leave. At once." His hands remained relaxed at his side though the desire to clamp them around Sir Augustus' throat was strong. Not now. Later, he told himself.

Rossbury's intent, though, was plain to Sir Augustus; for as the baronet took his first step towards the door, he remarked, "Perhaps we should dispense with the delay. Your second calling upon mine?" Sir Augustus waved a hand towards Grantleigh. Then standing only five feet from Rossbury, he added, "But my being seconded by either your former brother-in-law or your prospective brother-in-law might be something of an embarrassment, might it not, Rossbury?"

"To whom?" inquired Rossbury quietly. "The truth has a way of becoming known, and shame adheres to those who have behaved as no true gentleman would. Society can judge which of us that is."

"Frightened to act now?" Sir Augustus threw back as he moved closer to the door. "Perhaps you are more eager to take the little hellcat yourself. Or shall I say retake as, no doubt, during your sojourn in France you have already sampled–"

"Have you no decency?" Grantleigh interrupted.

"Has he promised to share her with you, Grantleigh?" Sir Augustus replied sardonically without so much as a glance at the Viscount. He took two more steps forward, Rossbury now within inches.

"Only someone without an ounce of personal integrity would invent such a slander," Rossbury said, his contempt evident. "And only someone completely devoid of honour would voice it."

Instantly Sir Augustus right hand arced toward Rossbury's cheek as he shouted, "No one impugns my honour, Rossbury!"

But before Sir Augustus' hand could deliver the blow, Rossbury grabbed the baronet's wrist and wrested his arm down. "You have no honour, Tremaine."

"Why you…" Sir Augustus, infuriated to the point of utter recklessness, lunged at Rossbury, his hands reaching for Rossbury's neck.

Tyler heard Sir Augustus' shouted "...my honour, Rossbury!" and leapt to his feet. "Rossbury!" he exclaimed as he turned towards the door. "How the devil…"

Gideon Laurence heard the shouts, too, and saw that Tyler's attention had been distracted. Seizing the opportunity, he scrambled from the bed and ran at Tyler's back. But the sound of feet on the floorboards alerted Tyler, who whirled to face Gideon.

"He'll ruin everything!" Tyler wailed as he slammed the pistol he still held against the side of Gideon's head. With a groan, the older man collapsed in a heap, momentarily stunned. Then Tyler darted out the door, muttering, "I'll stop him this time, Sarah."

Gideon, his left hand cupping the side of his face, tottered to his feet. "Must get away," he told himself. "Must get away. Downstairs. Horses in the stable."

Gideon stumbled to the door, his only thought being to flee from the King's Arms as quickly as possible.

Meanwhile, Tyler had bolted down the hall and stood gaping at the scene in the bedchamber. There two men were locked in a desperate struggle. Rossbury's hands circled Sir Augustus Tremaine's throat while the baronet fought to tear those hands away. Tyler did not see Grantleigh and Elizabeth, her eyes wide with apprehension, in the corner to his right. Nor did he sense Gideon Laurence's presence behind him as Elizabeth's brother scurried down the hall towards the stairs. The only object Tyler saw was Rossbury's back, a tantalizing target that faced him and offered no resistance. He raised the loaded pistol he still carried.

Rossbury concentrated on the face of the man he wanted to kill. His hands tightened. The desire to squeeze the life from this inhuman monster who had hurt Elizabeth was a kind of madness, and he wanted to yield to it. But another part of his brain said, No. He does not deserve to die so easily. To be scorned, ostracized, known for what he is, called to account – this is a more fitting punishment. Killing him now will make you what he is. Gradually Rossbury's hands loosened their grip.

Feeling the pressure on his neck lessen, Sir Augustus sought to gain the advantage over the man who had charged him with dishonour. Having seen Rossbury's limp, he kicked out at his opponent's right side.

Immediately, searing pain knifed through Rossbury's leg, and it began to buckle beneath him.

Tyler cocked the pistol. Hatred for the man he deemed responsible for his sister's death and for his own reverses overwhelmed him. He pointed the weapon and aimed it carefully.

With anger-fueled effort, Rossbury torqued his body to the left so that his weight was not on his injured limb, his sudden shift simultaneously causing Sir Augustus to stumble in the same direction. At that very moment, Tyler fired.

The roar of the shot sounded unnaturally loud in the confined bedchamber. Elizabeth screamed, "Richard!" and darted forward.

As the two grappling men fell towards the floor, Tyler turned and fled down the hall.

Tyler, still holding his fired pistol, ran down the stairs, then through the taproom towards the main door, and into the arms of a large man in a fur collared greatcoat. Behind the newcomer were two burly men.

"Let go of me!" Tyler demanded, wriggling unsuccessfully to free himself from the pinioning arms of the stranger dragging him back into the room.

"Not before I take this." The self-assured man wrested the pistol from Tyler's hand. "Huckaby." He thrust Tyler towards one of the men behind him. Immediately Tyler's arm was grabbed, expertly twisted behind his back, and held in a grip that nothing could break.

"Is he...?" The well-booted man jerked his head in Tyler's direction while he looked at Micah Whitbread standing nervously near the counter of the taproom.

"One o' 'em wi' 'im, sir." Whitbread wiped his hands continuously on a grubby towel he held.

Despite the vagueness of Whitbread's reply, his questioner nodded. Then he looked past Whitbread to the doorway that led to the kitchen. "And them?"

Following the direction of the other man's gaze, Whitbread saw three men. Baron Bardstow firmly grasped the arm of Gideon Laurence. At their side stood Jim Compton, musket in hand.

"Never seen 'em two afore, sir." Whitbread's head moved sharply from right to left. "But 'e woz wi' yer, yer..."

"I see."

"Killed him, Geoff," remarked Tyler in tones verging on the hysterical, once he saw his brother. "Rossbury's dead."

The customers, who had risen in alarm at the sound of the pistol shot and been silenced by the sudden and unexpected arrival of the commanding man who seemed to be in charge of the situation, looked gape-jawed at Tyler as if he were a member of a species never seen before.

Upstairs Rossbury extricated himself from Tremaine's clasp and laid the other man's body on the floor while taking care to keep his head and shoulders slightly elevated.

"Damned fool shot me," grimaced Sir Augustus, a red flood flowing rapidly from the wound in his back. The pistol ball had penetrated his left lung, which was filling with his life's blood.

Elizabeth, huddled on the floor at Rossbury's side, reached out to grasp his hand. When their eyes met, Rossbury shook his head slightly. Stationed near the door, Grantleigh intercepted the glance and the head movement, and his face grew somber.

"Killed me," Sir Augustus gasped. He could taste blood in his mouth. "That's what comes of allying yourself to idiots," he thought aloud.

"Tremaine, is there anything, anyone we can…" began Rossbury.

"No, damn you." Sir Augustus struggled to rise. "Damn the lot of you," he shouted before blood poured from his mouth and he fell back, his angry eyes staring at nothing.

Rossbury levered Sir Augustus gently to the floor and closed the dead man's eyes. No one spoke.

Rossbury stood slowly, his leg protesting anew at the additional strain; and Elizabeth, still clinging to his left hand, rose with him. Wordlessly she stepped into his embrace. "Richard," Elizabeth sobbed, "I thought you were dead." She began to shiver uncontrollably.

His left arm about Elizabeth's shoulders, his right cradling her head against his chest, Rossbury murmured, "And I thought I had lost you forever. I thought…" Putting his fears into words threatened the steadiness of his voice so he left his sentence unfinished. "Beth, my dearest Beth," he whispered into her hair.

Grantleigh shifted his feet quietly. His back to the bedchamber, his face towards the hallway, he considered, They deserve more privacy than this but… Then his reflection was cut short by the commotion at the foot of the stairs.

"Dead, I tell you, Geoff. Sarah's…" Tyler reiterated before he realized that the others were staring over his head.

Tyler lifted his eyes and saw Rossbury standing at the top of the stairs, the front of his clothes daubed with blood.

"Rossbury! Thank God, you're alive!" blurted out Baron Bardstow.

"But, but," Tyler stammered, "you should be, I fired, and, and…"

The man called Huckaby who had pinioned Tyler's arms shook him roughly. "I'd shut my face if I woz you."

Unseen by anyone else in the taproom, the shock of recognition passed through both Rossbury and the man now standing at the foot of the stairs. The latter's lips curved in a brief smile. My stretch of beach at midnight and now here! Tangled in my affairs again. "We meet," he began before deciding that referring to their previous meeting near *L' Oiseau Vite* was unwise. "We seem," he restated, "to have a small crisis on our hands."

Rossbury, noting that the taproom still contained a few local customers, replied simply, "We have. But as you can plainly see – despite evidence to the contrary," his right hand motioned towards his bloodied clothes, "I remain uninjured."

The unnatural steadiness of both Rossbury's voice and gaze together with the almost imperceptible stress laid upon the word I relayed a silent message to the man below. Only a mere flicker of the man's eyelids told Rossbury that the smugglers' leader knew what he would find upstairs. "That's well then," he remarked mildly.

"Don't know 'bout that," interjected the oldest man amongst the customers. "He's," the gray-bearded fellow continued, a finger pointed at Tyler Hamilton-Smythe, "as good as admitted he tried to murder 'im." His head jerked in Rossbury's direction. "Seems ter me a magistrate–"

A loud guffaw from Huckaby interrupted this statement. "He is a magistrate." No one asked to whom he referred.

"Be that true?" demanded the greybeard suspiciously.

"It is," asserted the nameless man. "In fact, I shall need to question all of you here," he let his eyes move slowly over the faces of all those who were not with either Rossbury or himself, "and take your statements about this attack."

"T'all started with the fire," offered a young man whose thatch of badly trimmed hair, weathered face, and coarse clothing proclaimed him someone who spent his days outdoors. "Him," the labourer pointed to Rossbury, "'n Micah 'ere went upstairs to put her out. Then – Oof!" The elbow of the man standing next to him dug into his ribs.

"Hsst, Sam," the elbow's wielder whispered before stating loudly, "None o' us 'ere seen nothin'. We's jist havin' a quiet pint when all this to do begun. It's they furriners," two sharp motions of his head indicated Rossbury above and Bardstow and Compton near the kitchen door, "started all th' trouble. Ask 'em what 'appened. We knows nowt 'bout it, right?" He looked at his drinking friends fiercely. All of them nodded in agreement.

"I see," the man in the fur-collared greatcoat stated gravely. "None of you," he said, while looking at each of the local men in turn, "has been upstairs at all."

"No, we's been down here all evening." The graybeard answered for the others.

"And..."

But before the smuggler could say more, the self-appointed spokesman for the locals interrupted, "And Micah's been 'ere, and all. The whole evening. Only went upstairs to throw couple o' buckets o' water on t' some fire. Couldn't have been much o' one coz he come back quick enough."

"He's telling the truth," Rossbury put in quickly.

"Seems I won't require your statements after all," remarked the smuggler's leader to the nervous men facing him. "You're all free to leave."

As soon as he had spoken, the regulars headed for the door. All of them went silently except the gray-bearded spokesman. "And Micah?"

"This appears to be some kind of dispute between outsiders to me," replied the well-booted man sagely. "And Whitbread here has had the misfortune to see his fine inn used as the scene for their altercation."

Though the crusty elder had never heard the word alterca-tion before, he understood that the trouble at the inn would not rub off onto his friends the Whitbreads. Satisfied, he nodded.

"In fact," the smuggler added, "I expect to have this matter cleared up shortly and those responsible brought before a court of law this very night. And to make up for the unfortunate interruption to your evening, here's..." He tossed a sovereign to Micah Whitbread who caught it and slid it immediately into a pocket. "More than enough for a pint for each of you tomorrow evening."

"Thank 'e, your worship," said Sam. "We'll drink t' yer–" His remarks were again cut short by his gray-bearded friend.

"'e's got work t' do, Sam. Leave 'im to it." An emphatic shove sent Sam stumbling out the door. The other regulars, eager to quit the scene of trouble, followed while muttering their thanks for the smuggler's generosity and their promises to see Micah Whitbread the next day.

After Whitbread closed the door behind his departing customers, the nameless smuggler asked, "Tremaine upstairs?"

"He is," replied Rossbury. Without saying more, he moved towards the room where the baronet's body lay. Near its open door, Grantleigh and Elizabeth stood. Her peignoir now covered by the matching robe she had found on the top of Sir Augustus' trunk, her disheveled waist length brown tresses flowing over her shoulders, Elizabeth watched Rossbury limp towards her.

"The worst is behind us," Rossbury said softly as he reached Elizabeth's side. He reached for her hand and squeezed it warmly.

"I know it is," Elizabeth agreed, her eyes scanning his face and marking the evidence of fatigue.

"Can you bear up for a bit longer? We must all leave here soon." Rossbury tightened his grip on Elizabeth's hand.

"I'll be fine," noted Elizabeth. "It is..." She hesitated, remembering Rossbury's dislike of having anyone call attention to a physical weakness. "I'll be fine," she repeated, "especially – "

"Miss Laurence." The smuggler's greeting halted Elizabeth in mid-sentence.

All those who had been below, save Sally Whitbread, now crowded behind the unnamed man in the narrow hallway. He nodded politely while his eyes noted Elizabeth's unorthodox apparel, the bruises around her mouth, and her hand still enclosed in Rossbury's.

Why damn me, he considered, if this whole mess Tremaine's left me isn't about her! His thoughts strayed to his own sensible wife Kate – a wide-hipped, big-bosomed woman whose fervent church attendance, numerous charitable committees, and unblinking lies about his absences were the perfect cover for his clandestine activities. "Remarkable," he noted finally before amplifying, "you are – once again – simply remarkable, Miss Laurence."

Elizabeth's response was to move even closer to Rossbury's side as he confirmed, "She is, indeed."

"And unfortunately," continued the smuggler, once again the canny businessman, "I must make further calls upon that remarkable ability of yours this very night."

"Lord Rossbury has already told me that we must leave soon," Elizabeth observed calmly, wondering how the man she had last seen on a Sussex beach came to be at the King's Arms.

"Perhaps Whitbread here has a room where you might…"

"Room at end o' hall should be…" Micah Whitbread replied hurriedly before recalling who had last occupied the room.

"Where Gideon…?" Elizabeth stopped.

At the sound of his name Gideon's head came up, and for an instant his eyes looked into Elizabeth's. Shamed by the pain he saw there, Gideon lowered his head and stared at the floor.

Gideon Laurence here as well, considered the smuggler silently. He shook his head. Right mess this is going to be.

Meanwhile, in answer to Elizabeth's unfinished question, Whitbread swallowed hard and nodded. "Should be a nice fire in there still," he offered hopefully.

At the mention of the fire, Elizabeth shivered.

"Compton, my saddle bag contains some items Miss Laurence has need of." Rossbury drew Elizabeth's arm up so that he could tuck it under his own while still holding her hand.

"Yes sir, Capt'n." Jim Compton relinquished his grip on Gideon Laurence's arm and clattered down the stairs, his musket still in his hand.

"Items fit only to be given to the rag man, I'm afraid," added Rossbury with a look that was anything but apologetic.

"If that is so, I must give them to him myself." Elizabeth pressed closer to Rossbury and tightened her grip on his hand.

"N' p'rhaps some water for, for…?" Whitbread's question trailed off discreetly.

"Yes, both hot and cold water." Elizabeth intended to scrub every inch of herself to remove the taint of Sir Augustus' touch. "And some soap if you have it."

"Missus has a kettle on the hob right now if I knows 'er. I'll have 'er bring 'er up right away." Whitbread bobbed his head, cast a furtive glance at the smuggler, and scurried off.

"Half an hour, gentlemen?" Reluctantly Elizabeth withdrew her arm from Rossbury's.

Before Elizabeth moved away, Rossbury caught up her hand and raised it to his lips. As the sleeve of the robe fell back from her wrist, he saw a thin red line braceleting Elizabeth's arm. Loathing directed at the man who lay dead only a few feet from where they stood rose within him. He pushed it aside and said, "Downstairs in half an hour then. We shall find the time to speak later, I promise. All will be well yet."

"All is well," Elizabeth insisted quietly. "You are here."

Seven men gazed down upon the body of Sir Augustus Tremaine. The free trader's henchmen had taken up positions at the door. Both stood, arms folded across their chests, unblinking and apparently unmoved by the corpse on the floor.

Upon seeing the dead man, Tyler gasped and then blanched before backing into the solid bulk of Huckaby. He gaped about as if looking for an avenue of escape and, when he realized there was none, settled into a slack-jawed stare.

The sight of the blood seeping from beneath Sir Augustus' body made Gideon Laurence moan and stagger. Grantleigh righted the chair overturned earlier and guided Elizabeth's brother to it. There Gideon put his head in his hands, closed his eyes, and prayed for a way out of the disaster looming over him.

Meanwhile the well-booted smuggling leader eyed the bedchamber, each detail noted – the charred linen covering the bed, the shards of broken pottery lying amidst a puddle of water, the fireplace poker dropped some feet from the grate, the livid burn marking Sir Augustus' hand.

"Remarkable," he repeated more to himself than to the others in the room. He added the cruel weal on Elizabeth's wrist and the bruises on her face to the tale told by debris in the bedchamber. "Remarkable." He glanced at Rossbury, whose shoulders leaned against the mantle, and then back at the body at his feet.

"A business acquaintance perhaps." Rossbury's assumption was more a statement than a question. Whatever brought him here tonight, he expected to find trouble, Rossbury realized.

"Yes, Sir Augustus Tremaine, Baronet of Throck Manor, was, as you say, a business acquaintance." The unnamed man shifted his gaze to Tyler. "And now he is dead." His tone became more solemn, his mouth set in a judgmental line. "Murdered."

"I never meant to, to…" Tyler stammered frantically. The faces he saw all seemed to condemn him. "I, I meant, that is, not him, not…"

"No, of course not." The smuggler's tone was genial for a few seconds. Suddenly his right arm lifted, the index finger pointing directly at Rossbury. "You meant to murder him, Richard Verinder, the Earl of Rossbury, did you not? T'was only Tremaine's misfortune that he came between the ball you fired from this pistol," from a capacious pocket he took the weapon he had wrested from Tyler's grip earlier, "and Rossbury."

"Oh, Tyler," muttered Baron Bardstow, tearing his eyes from the murdered man on the floor, "what were you thinking? I had hoped to..." Bardstow shook his head sadly. "Too late now. You've put yourself beyond my help."

"And you are...?" The smuggler asked. "Rossbury, perhaps you'd be good enough to introduce me to your friends here." His hand gestured towards Bardstow and Grantleigh. "Compton," he said as the stableman along with Micah Whitbread appeared at the entrance of the room behind his two henchmen, "I know already. But these gentlemen..."

"Baron Bardstow, brother of Tyler Hamilton-Smythe to whom you have been speaking." Rossbury paused long enough to allow the smuggler to murmur, "Lord Bardstow" and the two men to exchange nods. Then he concluded, "And Viscount Grantleigh."

As the smuggler repeated, "Lord Grantleigh" and nodded in the viscount's direction, he noted the set face and the steadiness of Grantleigh's gaze. Good man to have at your back, I'd warrant. Then turning back to Bardstow, he said, "You implied a that you'd hoped to help your brother here, Lord Bardstow. Might I ask what that hope was?"

"Our father's youngest brother left England some years ago to seek fortune and a new life, first in the American colonies and then in Canada. He has done quite well. And I thought, before all this happened..." Bardstow explained while making an indeterminate gesture that encompassed Tremaine's body and all those presently occupying the room. "I thought that... Well, it's impossible now."

As soon as Bardstow said Canada, Rossbury and the nameless smuggler exchanged looks. The smuggler mentally reviewed the list of ships stored in his brain. "Ship sailing to Halifax and then St. John's in three days. Captain's another acquaintance of mine."

"You're not sending me off to some God-forsaken wilderness," yelled Tyler enraged upon hearing his future discussed by a man whom he had never even seen until that evening and whose name no one seemed to know. "Canada may as well be the end of the earth, and Uncle Josiah's in trade!" He stared defiantly at the men he viewed as the architects of this proposed exile – Rossbury, his brother, and the smuggler – and snarled, "You'll not be rid of me so easily!"

"Canada or the hangman's noose – makes no difference to me," replied the smuggler calmly. "Yet I'd have thought Canada preferable to a short trip to New Drop. Appears my tastes are quite unlike yours." He returned his gaze to Tremaine's body and shook his head. "Murder's a capital offense. And this is as clear a case of murder as ever I've seen in all my years as a magistrate."

"I, I didn't, I didn't mean..." gulped Tyler wildly. One hand moved to his neck as if he already felt the noose tightening about it. "Geoff, can't you...?" As Tyler spoke, he backed away from Tremaine's corpse. When he thudded again against the unyielding bulk of Huckaby, he turned and peered into the other man's merciless eyes. "Canada!" Tyler whispered despairingly.

"Seems your brother's changed his mind," noted the smuggler.

"Can you really...? That is, the ship to St. John's, that's where..." began Bardstow uncertainly.

The smuggler interrupted. "Better not to say too much," he advised. "As long as Lord Rossbury is agreeable, I see no reason why Mr. Smith here," he pointed to Tyler, "shouldn't be on his way across the Atlantic in a couple of days." He looked at Rossbury,

The smuggler's words gave Rossbury a chance to rethink the decision he had made earlier. On one side was the law. And on the other was the future of two families. Families who would not have a future if Tyler were hanged for murder.

"My only quarrel with Tyler," answered Rossbury at last, "lies with the harm he tried to do Miss Laurence." Turning to Bardstow, he added, "But with your help, Bardstow, that has been prevented. And no one here desires you to suffer for a folly not of your own making."

Bardstow found himself unable to reply.

The smuggler nodded twice before putting a hand to his chin and rubbing it thoughtfully. That decision'll cost him dear, he considered after a surreptitious glance at Rossbury. Doesn't matter that what he's about to do will prevent innocent people from being hurt. He's breaking the law. A novel experience for him. And doing so'll make him think about the difference between law and justice. Poor devil. He shrugged. In the smuggler's business, conscience was an expense he could not afford. He felt no desire to avenge Tremaine's death, only contempt for a man who had endangered a business arrangement for personal gain. For tonight, he and Rossbury were partners; but men with principles had no permanent place in his world.

"I suggest we discuss the details downstairs," the nameless smuggler remarked. "We should leave in a quarter of an hour. Huckaby, Barton, move him," a jerk of his head towards Tremaine's body indicated his intentions, "into his carriage. Keep it clean."

As the men began to obey, Micah Whitbread offered, "Got some sacks in th' stable."

"Good." The smuggler barked out orders. "You two go with Whitbread. Bring up plenty of those sacks. Whitbread, harness the horses to his coach while you're down there. Then I'm afraid…" His gaze took in the state of the bedchamber with its overturned furniture, broken china, and charred bed linen.

"Me 'n Sal'll have her right side up 'fore we sleeps t'night. I'll put this lot," he pointed to the burned material on the bed, "onto th' fire. But don't know 'bout that." He waved a hand at Sir Augustus' trunk, standing open against the wall. Clearly visible at the top were a woman's clothes, apparently hastily folded.

"Ask your wife to go through the trunk and take out everything not belonging to Tremaine." Rossbury fought to keep his voice steady. Whatever the smuggler had in mind, whoever eventually opened Tremaine's trunk must not find any woman's clothing there. "She can do whatever she likes with them. Then the two of you can carry the trunk downstairs. Compton can help harness the horses."

"Good plan," the smuggler agreed. Without another word, Huckaby, Barton, Compton, and Whitbread left the bedchamber, each intent on doing the tasks appointed to him as quickly as possible.

Moments later, the other men assembled in the taproom. The smuggler whispered a few words to Bardstow who then drew his brother aside and began speaking to him in low tones.

"We shall remain here until," the Baron paused, realizing that he did not know the smuggler's name. "Until he returns tonight. Then we shall travel to the coast."

"Canada, Geoff. I shall never see…" Tyler's voice broke.

"Uncle Josiah's a good man. He has no sons and will be glad to have a trusted nephew help him with his business."

"Trusted!" Tyler's laughter was edged with hysteria. "He'll never trust me, not after…" His eyes desperately searched his brother's face for signs of mercy.

"I shall write him, of course, but only to say that England holds no opportunities for you and that you want to make a new life for yourself."

Tyler gawped in disbelief. "You won't, you won't write about…" He dashed an arm across his eyes. "You'd do that for me," he finished almost inaudibly.

"You are my brother, Tyler." The two men locked eyes for a moment before Tyler looked away in incomprehension and embarrassment. "Uncle Josiah's home in St John's is one of the town's finer residences, I understand." Bardstow paused as he sought another positive comment. "And we shall have time to outfit you properly since your ship does not leave until Tuesday."

However, Bardstow's last word and the realization that in three days the gulf represented by thousands of miles of ocean would lie between them silenced both men. As Tyler stared ahead without seeing anything, Bardstow put a hand on his brother's shoulder.

Meanwhile, Rossbury and the unnamed smuggler stood in a corner deep in their own plans. "Leave the accident to my men and me. When we reach the site, go west to the first house you see – the vicarage at Thornfield. The vicar is well known for his rather odd habits: retires early, rises before dawn to write. And his only servants are a couple of local lasses who don't live at the vicarage. The time of your arrival will make reporting an accident impossible until tomorrow. And those who do come out will not look too closely at anything."

Rossbury pictured what he must do and recalled the explanation he and Lady Beatrice had already worked out. "When I returned to London with Grantleigh and found Miss Laurence had left with her brother and a neighbor to visit her family at Hopeden Hall, we followed."

Even now Godmother and Lady Dalrymple are spreading the tale of my impatient pursuit of Elizabeth into the Hampshire countryside, Rossbury thought. He could imagine the indulgent tones and amused glances the two would employ.

Excellent, the smuggler thought. "And next, of course, you happened upon the scene of the unfortunate accident involving the coach Miss Laurence and her companions were traveling in." Then seeing Huckaby, Barton, and Compton reenter the taproom, he asked, "And Compton?"

"Compton can remain here for the rest of the night and depart for London at first light with Bardstow's horse."

Before the smuggler could voice his approval, Gideon Laurence rose suddenly from a chair in the taproom's inglenook and knocked it backward. The crack as it hit the floor caused the others in the room to turn.

Gideon rushed at Rossbury and grabbed his arm. "This was all Sir Augustus' doing. And when Clewett's letter arrived. £5000 in Bank of England investments – enough to, enough to... And then there was Rosemont. And Sir Augustus said... You do see, don't you?"

Gideon's eyes were wide as they scanned Rossbury's face for understanding. Gideon did not even feel Grantleigh pull him away. "I thought Elizabeth had died in France. And then when your letter arrived... Marriage to an earl. Announcement in the papers. Clewett'd know and then... What was I to do?"

"You could have told the truth." Grantleigh's stern advice brought Gideon's head around. He shrank from the censure he saw in the Viscount's expression.

"How could I? How could I?" Gideon whimpered. "Newgate, I'd, I'd, and my family... Peter, my daughters. I couldn't, could I?" he turned back to Rossbury.

"And what happened in London?" Rossbury asked evenly.

"It was all his idea." Gideon's voice sank to a whisper as his eyes rolled towards the table where Bardstow and Tyler spoke. "He said you were a mur…"

Gideon saw the anger on Rossbury's face replaced by a shuttered look and decided not to finish his sentence. "I did not believe him, of course. Elizabeth was only to be frightened into coming home. Never hurt, I swear. I never meant to…"

Once again Gideon scanned the faces of the three before him before plummeting on. "She should have married Sir Augustus in '88. If she had, none of this would have happened. As her brother, it was up to me, to, to… Elizabeth could have handled him. She's not at all like Edith Norwood. Edith was, she was…"

The woman Sir Augustus had wed shortly after Elizabeth had gone to Rouen rose before Gideon. He saw her bruised and stiff as she was on his last visit to Throck Manor before her death.

"She, she," Gideon broke off, unable to think of anything to say about the late Lady Edith Tremaine. "Sir Augustus wouldn't have, he only wanted, he wouldn't, not Elizabeth." His voice stumbled on, its tone frantic, pleading. "Besides now," he reached out to grasp Rossbury's arm and then pulled back as he thought better of the familiarity, "you are to marry Elizabeth."

As the smuggler grasped this fact, Gideon added, "My sister. You're practically a member of the–"

"Family. Elizabeth's family." Rossbury's voice cut across Gideon's like the clash of swords. He continued in a flat tone, "And it is only care for her that…" Rossbury left his sentence unfinished for his mouth tasted foul, his thoughts about Elizabeth's brother like bile on his tongue.

Gideon's lips moved soundlessly, and he shrank from Rossbury's disgust.

"Tomorrow," ordered Rossbury, "you will write to William Clewett. Your letter will tell him about your sister's surprising return from France."

"The investments. I've borrowed on them," Gideon babbled while taking another step backward. "My creditors..."

"Say nothing about that to Clewett. And prepare a list for me."

"A list?"

"Of your debts."

"Yes, yes, of course." Gideon gulped. I'm safe, he thought before recalling Sir Augustus' body. He put a hand to his head and felt the bump made by Tyler's pistol. "I am not well," Gideon whimpered. "I feel quite ill, quite unable to..."

"Of course, you are." The smuggler smiled without warmth. "You've been in a terrible carriage accident. You and your sister were badly bruised and dazed. Your neighbor Sir Augustus Tremaine, unfortunately, was also injured. Fatally."

Gideon's mouth worked as his eyes grew wider. "But, but, how can, he was..."

"Your own head injury has left you with no memory of events before the timely arrival of two good Samaritans, Lords Rossbury and Grantleigh." Although the smuggler spoke slowly as if repeating information for a child, he was watching Rossbury rather than Gideon Laurence.

"Timely, indeed, for travelers in need of assistance," Rossbury noted.

The smuggler approved. "Chance meeting. No need for explanations tonight or tomorrow. The less said, the better." He ticked off the advantages, his mind looking for flaws and finding none. "Better for everyone here," he concluded.

"The city, however, is another matter," stated Rossbury answering the smuggler's unspoken thought. "Compton, a word."

"Yes, sir," replied the stableman without hesitation, almost saluting.

The smuggler, pleased with the way plans were working out, turned back to Gideon and reiterated, "There has been an accident, Laurence, that you know nothing about."

But Gideon's eyes were drawn to a movement on the stairs. Elizabeth descended the flight carefully, Rossbury's saddlebag in her arms. Her hair had obviously been braided in haste, and damp tendrils framed her pale face with its livid remainders of Sir Augustus' cruelty. Her crumpled dress was one of those she had worn as Madame Verinder.

"Elizabeth," wailed Gideon upon seeing her, "I want to go home. Felicity, the children…" He crumpled into the nearest chair, his soft sobs making his shoulders shake.

"Remarkable," breathed the smuggler. And whether his comment concerned Elizabeth's composure or her brother's lack of it, no one knew.

Rossbury met Elizabeth at the bottom of the stairs. After transferring the saddlebag to his right arm, he wordlessly offered his left.

Elizabeth grasped his arm tightly, and Rossbury covered her hand with his. Rossbury's touch steadied her. With her eyes on Rossbury's face, Elizabeth said, "A satchel and a small trunk are in the room at the end of the hall. I believe the trunk is my brother's."

Before Elizabeth finished speaking, Huckaby and Barton began to mount the stairs.

"The satchel's mine," croaked Tyler. Bardstow laid a hand on his brother's shoulder. At the same time, Grantleigh moved to Gideon Laurence's side. With a firm hand under the older man's elbow, he helped Elizabeth's brother to his feet.

Then Huckaby with Gideon's trunk balanced on his shoulder and Barton with Tyler's satchel clutched in his hand appeared at the top of the stairs.

"It's late, and we've much to do." The smuggler's words were unnecessary. The others – Elizabeth bolstered by the presence of Rossbury at her side, Grantleigh supporting Gideon Laurence – were leaving the well-lit taproom of the King's Arms for the darkness of the March night beyond the door.

Less than an hour later the party of seven stopped at a sharp bend in the road. Immediately Huckaby and Barton jumped down from the driver's box of Sir Augustus' carriage and unharnessed the horses.

"This'll do nicely." The smuggler looked at the muddy embankment to the right of the carriage as rain dripped from his wide-brimmed hat onto his greatcoat. He turned to Rossbury, who had dismounted, and stood nearby, "Leave the rest to us."

Moments later the smuggler watched as four riders splashed west. He looked down at his muddy boots and shrugged. Then turning to his men, he said, "A job to do here. Let's be about it."

Pounding at the front door of the vicarage at Thornfield awakened the Reverend Mr. Timothy Arbuthnot from sleep. Unable to find his slippers, he lit a candle at his bedside, pulled a dressing gown about his slight nightshirted figure, and started, barefooted, for the door. His old-fashioned nightcap barely clung to his bald head befringed with wisps of snow-white hair as he called, "I'm coming!"

Rossbury, shielding Elizabeth from the worst of the rain, and Gideon, leaning heavily on Grantleigh's arm, stood before the door, four mud-covered horses behind them.

As soon as the Thornfield vicar pulled open the door, Rossbury said simply, "We came upon an accident."

Even as he was speaking, Arbuthnot stepped aside and invited them in with a sweeping motion of his arm. "And these good people," he concluded peering at the bruised faces of Elizabeth and her brother, "have been injured."

"An accident," moaned Gideon. "It's all been a terrible accident." He stumbled towards a chair in the entry hall and sank into it.

"Carriage horses," noted the kindly reverend aloud as he observed the two animals still in harness before he closed the door. "Was anyone else...?" He addressed Rossbury who seemed to be in charge of the small group of people now dripping water onto the vicarage floorboards and wished he had found his slippers before leaving his small ground floor bedchamber. The cold was already making his rheumatic bones ache.

Rossbury edged a step closer and replied quietly, "I fear so."

"Dear me," murmured Arbuthnot. Doubtless, he considered, these two men have done all that can be done tonight. "Dear me." He set the candle he carried on a long table, half-covered in books. God have mercy on the poor soul, he prayed silently.

"Is there anywhere we can put the horses?" asked Rossbury, aware that Elizabeth was shivering at his side. "And rooms where Miss Laurence and her brother may rest for the night?"

"Where are my manners?" cried the reverend. "Of course, whatever I have is yours to command. You will find my small stable behind the house. My mare occupies but one of its stalls."

Grantleigh said, "I shall see to the horses then."

"Take whatever you need," offered Mr. Arbuthnot as Grantleigh left. Then seeing the sagging shoulders and weary faces of the three still in his hall, he continued quickly, "There are four rooms upstairs though I don't what state they are in." He spread his hands in a self-deprecatory gesture. "These old bones have refused to fight the stairs for the past three years. However, there's a blanket chest and wardrobe in the first room to the right of the stairs. You'll find linens and some old night-shirts there." He added apologetically, "I am afraid I keep no servants. Jane and Nancy Potter shall be here in the morning, but tonight…" He broke off as Elizabeth crossed to where her brother still slumped in a chair.

"Come, Gideon." Elizabeth helped her brother to rise.

"It was all a mistake, an accident. I…" In confusion, Gideon looked about the dark hallway, lit only by the single candle Arbuthnot had carried with him. "My head aches. I want to go home."

Elizabeth guided her brother to the stairs, his steps shambling and halting. "Tomorrow, Gideon." She looked at Rossbury for reassurance on this point.

"You'll be home tomorrow."

Elizabeth knew Rossbury's statement was meant for her as well as Gideon, and suddenly she was near tears. She bent her head so that Rossbury could not see her face and whispered, "Thank you."

"You will need my candle, Miss Laurence," offered the vicar as he thrust it into Elizabeth's left hand. "And you, sir," he turned to Rossbury, "need candles, water, and..." He shivered, wishing once again he had been able to locate his slippers. "It is all in the kitchen," Arbuthnot added before padding through a door to the right of the stairs.

An hour later, Grantleigh and Rossbury trudged up the vicarage stairs, each carrying a lighted candle stub. Between them, they'd seen to four horses, now crowded into two stalls in Arbuthnot's small stables. Both were entirely spent. They separated without a word, Grantleigh going to the room at the far end of the hallway, Rossbury taking the one in the middle.

As Rossbury entered, he saw the linens, blankets, and nightshirt placed at the foot of the cot in the middle of the room and a basin of water on a nearby table.

Elizabeth, he breathed soundlessly. She's done just what she said she would when I brought up that bucket of water from the kitchen earlier. As he laid sheet and then blankets atop the bed, he knew without question that Grantleigh and Gideon had found the same items in their rooms.

Rain still fell, drumming against the room's single window as Rossbury finally lowered himself wearily onto the cot and tried to empty his mind of all the next day would bring.

He turned restlessly and then suddenly lay still. A faint cry came from the next room. He raised himself on one elbow and stared at the door connecting the small dressing room where he lay with the room next to it. Yes, he told himself, there it is again.

Rossbury rose despite the protest from his aching leg, threw a blanket around his shoulders, and padded to the door. There he hesitated, but the next muffled sob made him open the door.

Elizabeth sat on a large bed with an ornately carved but ugly headboard, dark with age. Her body was enveloped in a man's nightshirt several sizes too big for her. On a low chest near the bed, a single candle guttered in the draft the open door created. Seeing the flickering flame, Elizabeth turned her head.

"Richard!" Elizabeth gasped in surprise. She slid to her feet as Rossbury limped to the foot of the bed. Wiping her eyes with the heel of one hand, she apologized. "I'm sorry to be so stupid. I know there is nothing to fear now, but I thought that…" Tears began to run freely down her cheeks.

Rossbury moved forward, enfolding Elizabeth in his arms. "Beth," he whispered, "Beth, don't be sorry."

Elizabeth continued to cry quietly, her terror releasing itself. Rossbury used one hand to wrap his blanket about both their shoulders while stroking her head and reveling in the feel of her cheek pressed against his chest and her arms circling him.

When some of her emotion had spent itself, Elizabeth shivered.

"You're cold." Rossbury sighed. He let the blanket that he clutched with one hand fall. Then he scooped Elizabeth up in his arms and placed her gently onto the bed. As he did, her hands clasped about his neck descended to his arms, then his hands, her fingers entwining with his, refusing to let go.

Elizabeth struggled to voice the fear that chilled her far more than the cold of the room. "I need to know, to know that you don't, that you don't…" Tears once more sprang to her eyes.

Rossbury sat on the edge of the bed and gathered Elizabeth up so that once again she was cradled in his arms, her head resting under his chin. "Beth, Beth, dearer to me already than life itself." Rossbury lifted her face with one gentle hand and forced her to look at him. "He was the man in your nightmare."

Elizabeth nodded once and dropped her eyes, her body burrowing closer to his.

"While we were in France," Rossbury continued, "you had already become a part of me without my even being aware of how it all happened. And during these past weeks at Earl's Wood, every time I entered a room, I saw you there; every time I considered a problem, I wondered how we should solve it together. Being there without you..." He recalled the busy but lonely days. "Life without you would be unendurable," he concluded simply. "And then Grantleigh with his concerns about Rosemont arrived...."

Rossbury reluctantly loosened his hold on Elizabeth. "It's a long story." After lowering her head to a pillow, he tugged the bed covers into place. "And we have much to do tomorrow." Though he now stood at the side of the bed, he kept one of her hands enclosed within his.

"I wish," Elizabeth began, "I wish we were..." She bit her lip, fearing to speak her thought aloud and yet desiring to drown in the blue of Rossbury's eyes.

For a moment Rossbury felt neither the ache of his leg nor the cold floor under his feet as in a startling flash, he knew what Elizabeth wished. "In the Martin's barn," he finished, the words uttered so softly that had her eyes not been on his face, Elizabeth would not have known he had spoken.

"Yes." Elizabeth breathed out her assent and felt his grip on her hand tighten.

Not wanting to reconsider her decision, Elizabeth immediately slid to the right and threw back a corner of the blankets with her left hand. When Rossbury remained unmoving at the side of the bed, she stammered, "I did not mean..."

Rossbury bent over and laid a finger across her lips. "I know what you meant." Secrets from their pasts, things unsaid and buried under pain and shame about both Sir Augustus and Lady Sarah, lay between them. Like ground fog, he told himself. And unless the pain of the past is shared, it will not disperse. But the time for sharing is not now. Not now, but soon. Soon. Rossbury took a deep breath. Then with a grimace, he lowered himself gingerly to the bed and then eased his right leg into a horizontal position. "My hesitation was caused by this damnable leg of mine, and that alone."

This acknowledgement of pain, of vulnerability, Elizabeth knew, was, in a sense, a gift, a trust. Without a word, Elizabeth turned her head to watch Rossbury draw the covers into place over them both.

After shifting his weight onto an elbow, Rossbury looked down at Elizabeth and found her watching him. "Love," he noted quietly, "reveals itself in many ways. Discovering all of them together shall provide us with a lifetime of joy."

His words erased Elizabeth's last doubt. Her heart was so full that she could only whisper, "Richard!"

A lamp appears to have been lit behind her face, Rossbury thought. And despite the bruises, he marveled, she has never looked more beautiful. "And one special kind of love we shall anticipate as a gift to be shared on the third of April."

Rossbury turned to extinguish the candle. Then he lay on his side and reached behind him to draw Elizabeth's arm around his chest. "Rest now. Tomorrow..." He sighed again, thinking of what the day would bring. "We'll face it tomorrow. And all our tomorrows together."

Elizabeth moved closer to his warmth, her head touching his back.

"Together."

## CHAPTER 23

# SATURDAY, MARCH 16, 1793

"Lemuel Archer's found a body!" Nancy Potter burst into Mr. Arbuthnot's library as soon as she and her sister Jane arrived at the vicarage early Saturday morning. "Under an overturned carriage," she panted. "By the side of the Guildford road!" Nancy stood in the doorway, her square face alight with excitement, her breath coming in gasps after she had dashed from the village to the vicarage with the news.

The clergyman looked up from his study of Cruden's *Concordance.* "Yes," Mr. Arbuthnot nodded slowly. "It was a terrible business."

"But..." Nancy frowned, her square shoulders still heaving. "But Lemuel just come back. To tell Mary. Just as we were comin' away. Tol' her that he was goin' to get some of the men. Wants 'em to go back with him. To set the carriage back on its wheels." Nancy stared at her employer, not understanding his lack of surprise.

"And to recover the poor soul who died." The vicar turned from Cruden to Nancy. "Thank God, Miss Laurence and her brother were not more seriously injured."

"Miss Laurence?" Nancy repeated. "And her brother? Injured?"

"Yes, I believe they are bruised from the accident, but otherwise well, thanks be to God." The vicar smiled at Nancy, whose walnut eyes were blinking rapidly and whose stubby fingers were clasped tightly together. "They and the two gentlemen who rescued them. I'm afraid I didn't ask their names last night. It was late, and they were wet and tired. But all of them will need some hot water shortly and breakfast a bit later."

"Hot water upstairs?" As Nancy pieced the story together, she could scarcely believe her good fortune. The people in the coach came here! Wait 'til I tell Mary Archer that! Nancy bustled from the room, eager to join her sister Jane in the kitchen and then to see to the vicarage's four guests.

The sound of hurrying footsteps below and the chatter of high-pitched voices awoke those upstairs. And so when Nancy and Jane, each carrying two cans of steaming water, rapped on the bedroom doors, every knock was answered by a voice calling out, "Enter."

Ten minutes later Rossbury and Grantleigh met Mr. Arbuthnot at the foot of the stairs. Rossbury performed the introductions that had not occurred the previous evening.

"One of the men from Thornfield already came upon the carriage accident this morning, Lord Rossbury." Mr. Arbuthnot made this announcement as he pointed the way towards his small dining parlor. "He returned to the village with the news; and, I believe that he and some of the other men have gone out to the Guildford road to right the carriage and to recover the unfortunate traveler who died so tragically." The vicar entered the dining parlor and nodded appreciatively at the neatly set table and the steaming dishes Nancy and Jane Potter were placing on the sideboard.

Behind the vicar, Rossbury and Grantleigh exchanged a concerned look. "We should join them there as soon as possible,"

Rossbury said. "The Laurences' trunks will need to be located, and Miss Laurence and her brother..." He let his sentence trail off.

"No, of course not," Mr. Arbuthnot agreed. "It would be far too distressing for them to return to the coach. Especially...." He thought of the man he did not even know lying dead in the road all night. "You'll have to make arrangements for the... For their friend," he amended. "Lemuel Archer, he's a carter and the one who came upon the accident this morning. He should be able to help you."

"Lemuel Archer." Rossbury wondered if he was one of 'those' the smuggler had referred to at the King's Arms. "We'll ask for him."

The vicar shook his head. "A sad business. But before you go, you must eat. Nancy and Jane have prepared..." He walked to the sideboard and lifted one covered dish after another. Then turning to beam at his titled guests, he said, "A morning feast."

By the time Elizabeth, Gideon leaning heavily on her arm, descended the stairs, Rossbury and Grantleigh had eaten and were ready to leave.

"A man from the village came upon the coach early this morning," Rossbury related at once. "Grantleigh and I will go to do what we can to assist."

The hastily given explanation caused Elizabeth's face to pale and Gideon to mutter, "An accident, a terrible accident." And after Rossbury and Grantleigh made their excuses and departed, he continued to repeat the phrase as Mr. Arbuthnot escorted them into the dining parlor.

The clergyman pointed to the variety of dishes on the sideboard and said, "You must eat." He seated Elizabeth at the warmest side of the table, in a chair where the sunlight from an east-facing window fell across her shoulders.

"What can we tempt you with, Miss Laurence?" Mr. Arbuthnot then asked as he sank into his own chair. Immediately the Potter sisters began to flutter about the table, serving dishes in their hands.

"An accident. A terrible accident," Gideon Laurence said around bites of toast. "And my neighbor." His hand reached for his teacup. "My best friend and neighbor. It's terrible." He gulped some tea and said, "Sir Augustus Tremaine of Throck Manor. A good neighbor and a good friend. A good man." He stared at Elizabeth for a moment, and she lowered her head over her plate.

"A neighbor, you say?" Mr. Arbuthnot tutted soothingly. "He will be missed by many, I am sure, God rest his soul."

As Gideon rambled on, his reminiscences haltingly given in sentences that were seldom complete, the eyes of the Potter sisters met. Gentry! their excited faces confirmed.

"And the driver?" Nancy blurted out before covering her mouth with her hands.

Mr. Arbuthnot looked reprovingly at the girl as Gideon choked on a piece of toast.

"I don't know," inserted Elizabeth who had said nothing at all during Gideon's monologue. "He was gone by the time Lords Rossbury and Grantleigh arrived, wasn't he, Gideon?"

"Yes, yes." Gideon swallowed some tea and then dabbed at his mouth with a napkin. "Gone. I don't know where. He…"

The vicar and his servants visualized the driver on the box of the coach, the unfamiliar road, the darkness, and rain.

"Trying to reach The Crown at Guildford, no doubt," supplied Mr. Arbuthnot. "Tsk, tsk. Thrown clear or jumped from the box perhaps. And after the accident, took fright and fled, no doubt. A natural reaction. Feared he would be blamed." He nodded his head and awaited Gideon's confirmation of his opinion.

But instead, Gideon stated, "Sir Augustus' cousin must be notified." Putting down his napkin, he rose from the table. "I must do so at once."

Two miles away Rossbury and Grantleigh stood silently as Lemuel Archer eased a tarpaulin under the body of Sir Augustus Tremaine. Rossbury's fear – that the body might be turned over – was never realized. The body was so horribly crushed that it was almost unrecognizable. Ben Potter, younger brother of Jane and Nancy, took one look and stumbled backwards into two other men, his face a sickly greenish color. After that, no one even offered to help Archer with the tarpaulin.

After Archer finished folding the heavy material around the body, Grantleigh stepped forward to help the carter lift it into his wagon. Meanwhile, the other men loaded the luggage that had spilled from the coach.

"We'll get this," Archer jerked his head towards the broken vehicle now listing to one side at the edge of the road, "back to the vicarage somehow. Then that wheel'll need some work. Mr. Arbuthnot can send word to his family when it's ready."

Archer looked at Rossbury, who nodded his agreement. Then the carter climbed onto the driver's bench of his wagon and gathered up the lines.

With nothing more to be done, Rossbury and Grantleigh mounted their horses. Soon wagon and horses, trailed by the villagers in a ramshackle dogcart, were making their way back to Thornfield vicarage.

By midday, the wagon had carried its load – as well as Gideon Laurence and Elizabeth – to Guildford, Tremaine's coach horses tied behind it, Rossbury and Grantleigh riding beside it.

Once in Guildford, the carter stopped the wagon outside of a shop on a side street. Above the door, a sign read Tanner and

Sons, Joiner and Undertaker. As Rossbury and Grantleigh dismounted, Archer entered the shop, returning some moments later with a man brushing sawdust from his sleeves, a boy of twelve by his side. Neither spoke as they lifted the tarpaulin-covered body from the back of the wagon and carried it inside.

"Tanner'll see he's coffined. Tol' him just to leave the tarpaulin be, given what happened in the accident and all. He understands what to do," Archer explained tersely after the undertaker had gone. "Said he'll see to it right away, and send him and this lot," he began to untie the two carriage horses now standing patiently behind his cart, "back to Little Throckton today."

"Thank you for your help, Archer. I'd like to..." Rossbury began, his hand moving towards his pocket.

Archer touched his hand to the brim of his hat and muttered, "No thanks needed. Been taken care of. Coroner, too. Late already. 'Nother delivery to make." He scrambled back onto the wagon and turned his team east back down the road they had traveled that morning.

A word with Tanner told Rossbury that the nearest place to hire a private post chaise was three streets west. There he and Grantleigh quickly made the necessary arrangements for Laurence's return to Hampshire and their own journey to London. Throughout, Gideon clung to Elizabeth's arm while continuing to murmur, "A terrible accident. Terrible. My head aches. I should be abed. I want to go home."

Then as the post chaise Rossbury had hired to go to Hopeden Hall pulled up, Gideon withdrew two letters from his coat and offered them wordlessly to Rossbury. One was addressed to William Clewett, the other to The Reverend William Dean.

"You said..." Gideon stared at Rossbury's chin, unable to meet his future brother-in-law's eyes. "Still at the bank of England...

And Elizabeth's return... I told him Farnsworth Place," he stammered before deciding he had said enough.

"Clewett will send you his thanks, and that will be the end of the matter." Rossbury put the letters in his coat pocket.

"The end of..." Gideon breathed out in relief. "I need do nothing else to, to..."

"No." Rossbury thought, You've done more than enough already. "Nothing more."

"Good." Gideon turned to climb into the chaise, and then swung back to face Rossbury again. "That list you asked for. Will you...? I mean, you said, you said last night ..." Embarrassed by the question he wanted to ask and the number of his debts, Gideon did not know how to continue.

However, Rossbury understood and confirmed what he had told Gideon the previous evening. "A list sent to Rossbury House will suffice," he stated succinctly. He hoped that escaping as cheaply as Gideon had from his unholy bargain with Sir Augustus and Tyler would mark a turning point in Laurence's life, but he believed that hope was vain. Not one work of apology to Elizabeth. And only concern for himself, he thought with disgust.

Seeing from Rossbury's set face that he should say no more on the subject, Gideon instead shifted his gaze to Elizabeth. "My apologies, Sister, for being unable to attend your wedding. I have written to Cousin William." He glanced at Rossbury's pocket. "He will represent me, I trust. The journey to London would be beyond me. The accident and... It was terrible."

At these words, Elizabeth edged closer to Rossbury who instantly drew her arm through his. "It has been a terrible experience for us all, Gideon."

"Yes. Terrible. I feel quite unwell. I should be in bed." Gideon put a hand to his head and heaved himself into the chaise.

After Grantleigh closed the door, Gideon leaned out of the window. Ignoring the three who still stood by the side of the chaise, he called out impatiently, "Drive on. I must reach Little Throckton today."

A quarter hour later yet another post chaise prepared to leave Guildford, this one heading north to London. As Rossbury handed Elizabeth inside, Grantleigh mounted one of the horses borrowed from Lady Dalrymple and grabbed the reins of the other with his right hand.

When Rossbury turned around, the Viscount was already in the saddle and Grantleigh's sidestepping horse blocked Rossbury's path.

Grantleigh leaned over and ordered softly, "Into the coach you go." Over the start of Rossbury's protest, the Viscount continued, "I am perfectly capable of handling both horses." He kneed his mount to move it farther away from Rossbury. "And you will have much to do in town."

"Thank you," said Rossbury, grateful both for Grantleigh's offer and his tact. "Without the information about Rosemont you brought to Earl's Wood, Drew..." Rossbury took a deep breath, realized with some surprise that his fists were clenched, relaxed his hands, and focused his gaze once more on his friend. "Because of you, all is well."

"It was no more than any friend would do, Richard," Grantleigh replied. He sat motionless in the saddle, both horses quiet under his control.

No further words were needed. A small movement of Grantleigh's leg sent his mount forward. Meanwhile, Rossbury climbed carefully into the post chaise, the ache in his leg a constant he could not will away.

"Richard," asked Elizabeth in alarm, seeing Rossbury enter the coach and take a seat across from her, "is anything wrong, are you...?"

"Nothing is amiss, Beth. I thought..." Rossbury paused and added more truthfully, "Grantleigh thought my place was here." A sweeping gesture of his right hand indicated that here was the interior of the coach. He smiled ruefully as the vehicle lurched forward.

Elizabeth said nothing but simply looked at Rossbury, her grey eyes wide with concern, the cuts and bruises across her face vivid reminders of yesterday's terrors.

"Here with you, Beth." Rossbury rose awkwardly in the rocking chaise and shifted to the seat next to Elizabeth. She leaned into his left shoulder and closed her eyes, her nearness making Rossbury yearn to crush her in a long embrace and assure her that never again would anyone hurt her

Then remembering that Elizabeth did not know about the story that would explain both her absence from London and her bruises, he continued, "And tonight we shall be in Carlington Square. And much of London will be agog with the tale Godmother and Lady Dalrymple spread about me at her party last evening." Rossbury took Elizabeth's arm and drew it through his as he attempted to find the position that would put the least stress on his right leg.

"Lady Dalrymple's musical soiree!" Elizabeth recalled the event that seemed to belong to another life. "I was invited to attend with Lady Farnsworth!"

"You were. And all who did attend were told of your decision yesterday to take a flying trip to Hopeden Hall, Hampshire in the company of your brother and his neighbor who were returning there after a visit to town. Then I came back from Shropshire sooner than expected. Eager to see the woman I had been parted from for over three long weeks, I followed you to Hampshire." Rossbury paused and added, "Unfortunately we never reached Hopeden." The lie they would all be forced to live with grated.

Elizabeth was silent as she absorbed the elaborateness of the deception and the number of people involved. Because of

Ladies Farnsworth and Dalrymple, the story will be believed, she told herself. People will think Richard and Viscount Grantleigh stumbled upon our overturned coach. And after hearing the tale, others will congratulate Richard and fête him as a hero. He will hate the whole business, Elizabeth realized with a flash of understanding.

"Thank you," Elizabeth said simply. And seeing that Rossbury was about to speak, she laid a gentle finger across his lips. She saw not only Rossbury's face but those of several others. Baron Bardstow whose family would remain untainted by Tyler's trial and execution. Her brother Gideon whose children would never know the shame of their father's dishonesty. The shadowy figure of Throck Manor's new owner whose inheritance would remain untinged by scandal. And finally mirrored in Rossbury's eyes, Elizabeth saw herself, her marriage to Rossbury unsullied by the gossip that would have trailed public knowledge of the previous day's events and her time alone with Sir Augustus at the King's Arms. "Thank you for all of us whose honour you have preserved." And, Elizabeth thought, at the sacrifice of some of your own.

Rossbury searched her face and found on it gratitude and understanding. That she knew him so well, that what he believed to be safely locked away from prying minds was visible to her both frightened and comforted him. From Beth, I can keep no secrets. With Beth, I can be myself. These thoughts touched him in a way he had not considered possible. His face relaxed, and he drew Elizabeth's arm more tightly through his and put his right hand over hers.

Elizabeth sighed. She edged closer to Rossbury's side and put her left hand on his arm as the coach rattled forward.

For some time, neither spoke. The past and its 'what-ifs' and 'should haves' were solemn company for both.

Finally, Elizabeth broke the silence. "Tell me about Earl's Wood Park, the land, the house, the people." Beneath her side, she felt the easing of Rossbury's tension as soon as she had named the place she knew he loved best.

"Earl's Wood Park?" Rossbury repeated as if uncertain of her words.

"Yes. I want to see it as you do, especially as we shall be traveling there in a little over a fortnight." Elizabeth moved her head into the hollow of Rossbury's shoulder before adding softly, "Though eighteen days seems an eternity."

"Eternity is what we shall have after those eighteen days." Rossbury's reply sounded more than a trifle hoarse even to his own ears, and he forced himself to take two deep breaths before continuing. "Earl's Wood Park is quite the loveliest estate in Shropshire," he began.

Thus, while each turn of the post chaise's wheels brought them nearer to London and the safety Carlington Square represented, Rossbury's increasingly enthusiastic words walked Elizabeth through the estate that would soon be their home, their future.

## CHAPTER 24

# WEDNESDAY, APRIL 3, 1793

While pulling his surplice over his head, the Reverend Mr. David Michael Souther of St Etheldreda's heard the vestry door open. Only one person would disturb him in the middle of his preparations for Morning Prayer, Desmond Montgomery, his weekday sidesman.

"Yes, Mr. Montgomery," Souther acknowledged without turning around.

Montgomery, a portly man with a shiny bald pate, came straight to the point. "I think you should delay the start of the service, Mr. Souther."

The vicar adjusted one sleeve of his surplice and swiveled to face the sidesman. "Is Mrs. Croft late?" he asked. Mrs. Croft, along with Montgomery, were the only parishioners who came daily to St Etheldreda's

"Mrs. Croft is in her pew," related Mr. Montgomery. "But the church is nearly full, and more carriages are arriving all the time, and..." He paused as the first notes of a magnificent John Stanley prelude burst forth from the organ.

"Martyn Ballard didn't tell me he could play today!" exclaimed the Reverend Mr. Souther, hastening towards the vestry door and opening it slightly. The sight that met his astonished eyes told him that Desmond Montgomery had not exaggerated. The nave was filling rapidly, but not with St Etheldreda's normal parishioners. Soldiers resplendent in military uniforms, working class couples clad in their Sunday best, members of the peerage – the women beruffled and bejeweled, the men decked out in snowy cravats and well-tailored coats, prosperous merchants correct in black and white, and servants wearing the habitual costume of those in service – all sat in St Etheldreda's box pews or waited in the aisles to take a seat.

A quick glance into the balcony gave the Reverend Mr. Souther another surprise, for Martyn Ballard sat turning pages next to an unfamiliar man whose hands were bringing joyous sounds from St Etheldreda's pipe organ. Before Mr. Souther asked, Desmond Montgomery said, "That's another thing. Our Mr. Ballard said to tell you that Mr. John Marsh from Chichester would play this morning."

"Marsh of Chichester," repeated Mr. Souther incredulously. He closed the vestry door and rapidly considered what hymns might be appropriate. Not to take advantage of a musician of Marsh's considerable talents would be a sin, he thought.

"Did Mr. Ballard say why Mr. Marsh came to St Etheldreda's today, Mr. Montgomery." Souther found a scrap of paper on the vestry's untidy writing table and scrawled the names of three hymns on it.

"It seems Mr. Marsh is acquainted with Miss Laurence."

"Our bride." And as Souther said the words, he realized that he had seen neither of those in the wedding party. He folded the note he had written, moved to the vestry door, and opened it again. Glorious patterns of rippling eighth notes flooded the room. Another look at the church showed Mr. Souther not only that the prospective bride and groom had not yet arrived but also that the front pew on the left side remained empty.

After closing the door, he handed the note to Montgomery. "Please see that Mr. Marsh receives this. And thank you, Mr. Montgomery, for telling me about the need for a slight delay of the service. I propose we wait until the arrival of Lord Rossbury and Miss Laurence, who are to be wed after Matins. You might relay that information to Mr. Marsh as well."

"Very well, Mr. Souther," replied Montgomery. He turned to go but then wondered again about the crush of people in the pews. "Am I correct in recalling your saying that this wedding after Morning Prayer is to be a small private ceremony, Mr. Souther?"

"Yes, it is, Mr. Montgomery." Mr. Souther paused as his sidesman opened the vestry door and John Stanley's cascading flow of notes danced joyfully through the room. Thinking of the couple to be married and the nave full of people, he smiled broadly and amended, "It was."

Sitting near the end of a back pew, Mrs. Ballantyne also smiled. A few of the servants at Rossbury House had thought her preparations for the wedding breakfast were extravagant. But during the last fortnight, first Rossbury, and then Elizabeth had visited the kitchen. Each had spoken about the other's friends who might come to the church uninvited. Then when Lady Farnsworth appeared and mentioned that the new Rossburys' reputation would rest, in a sense, in the hands of their staff, Mrs. Ballantyne redoubled her efforts. The crowd in St Etheldreda's now proved her preparations were wise. The cook nudged Mr. Harris seated to her left.

After the Rossbury House butler bent his head slightly, the cook whispered, "We've enough for all."

Harris looked about the church and nodded. His eyes gleamed with pride. "You were right, Mrs. B. Lord Rossbury has more friends than he knows," he whispered. "A buffet then?"

Mrs. Ballantyne's bobbed in agreement. Already she was visualizing how all those who filled the church could be accommodated.

"I'll just go and tell Lord Grantleigh, shall I?" Harris rose from the pew.

"Yes," urged Mrs. Ballantyne quietly. "And be sure to have him tell our Dickon we won't disappoint him. Not on his wedding day!"

Grantleigh watched the steady procession of people walking into St Etheldreda's. Wasn't the count for the wedding breakfast a dozen? Grantleigh frowned slightly as four more people walked into St Etheldreda's.

A discreet 'ahem' interrupted Grantleigh's thoughts and turned his head towards Harris, now standing beside him.

"Lord Grantleigh, please tell his lordship all the guests can be invited to the wedding breakfast at Rossbury House."

"All?" Grantleigh could scarcely credit his ears. Had the servants known something Rossbury and he had not? he considered. "Are you certain, Harris?"

"Mrs. Ballantyne and I are both certain, sir." Harris recalled the cook's parting words and added, "We'll need a bit of time to change the table arrangements, but we shan't disappoint our, er," he fumbled over the name, "Lord Rossbury." Harris paused momentarily before finishing, "Especially not on his wedding day."

Grantleigh grinned broadly. He wondered what private name for Harris' employer had almost slipped from the butler's lips. "I'll tell Lord Rossbury, Harris. And I know he will be very pleased."

Harris gave a slight bow and then hurried away. Still smiling, Grantleigh strolled towards Rossbury.

"Richard," Grantleigh began and then paused to allow Rossbury to turn his attention, but not his gaze, from the street to the presence of his friend. "Harris has informed me that you can extend the wedding breakfast invitation to all of your guests."

"All?" repeated Rossbury exactly as Grantleigh had moments earlier. "Harris made no stipulations?" As the bridegroom spoke, he spotted the Farnsworth carriage. His face relaxed into a smile.

"None," replied Grantleigh while moving forward with Rossbury to the place where the carriage would deposit its passengers.

"And St Etheldreda's?" Rossbury asked while still walking towards the approaching Farnsworth carriage.

"Filling rapidly when I looked a few minutes ago," answered Grantleigh.

Mrs. Ballantyne's preparations must have been prodigious, thought Rossbury as he wondered how society would perceive the increased size of the wedding party. Concern began to erase the gladness that had wreathed his face after he had seen that Elizabeth was safely arrived. After all their efforts to bury the sins of Tyler Hamilton-Smythe and Gideon Laurence, to have another marriage beset by scandal – all because he sought to safeguard Elizabeth from Tyler's rumors by offering her not only his love, but also the protection of his name – seemed bitterly ironic.

What was passing through Rossbury's mind was perfectly legible to Grantleigh as he scanned his friend's face. "Edward would not feel his memory demeaned by those who have come to wish you and Miss Laurence every happiness today. Besides," he added in a less serious tone, "some of those tempted to criticize can scarcely do so when they or their friends have come today uninvited, can they?"

"No, they can't," responded Rossbury, the tension draining from him as rapidly as it had surfaced. "Harris said all could be invited, Drew?"

Both men watched as the Farnsworth carriage rolled to a stop. Before a footman could jump down to do so, Rossbury stepped forward to open the door.

"He most emphatically did," answered Grantleigh.

"Then all will be." Rossbury moved aside as a footman, anxious to complete at least part of his job, lowered the steps.

Down them bounced the Reverend Mr. William Dean, an elderly man whose unlined face belied his years.

"Good morning, Lord Rossbury," Dean greeted warmly. "A lovely day, is it not?" He turned back and handed Elizabeth out as he spoke.

Elizabeth stood radiantly while the clergyman helped his wife Honoria to exit the carriage. The older woman straightened the folds of Elizabeth's pale blue gown, beautiful in its simplicity. "Blame me and not your bride for our tardiness, Lord Rossbury," said Mrs. Dean without preamble, her hands still busy with Elizabeth's dress. "I offered to be Elizabeth's tiring woman this morning, and I fear my fingers are not as nimble as they once were."

"It is of no consequence, Mrs. Dean," replied Rossbury politely as the soon to be married pair clasped hands and devoured each other with their eyes.

Elizabeth's gaze caught on the pin she had purchased from Danforths now nestled in Rossbury's snowy cravat, and the light in her eyes brightened.

Then the Reverend Mr. Dean moved to Elizabeth's right side, coughed once, and stated in his usual hearty tone, "It's after the time. And though your Mr. Souther may have delayed Morning Prayer somewhat, no doubt he dislikes keeping our Lord waiting as much as I do." After offering his left arm to Elizabeth who immediately put her hand on it, the Reverend Mr. William Dean marched towards the double doors fronting St Etheldreda's.

Without a word, Rossbury offered his own left arm to Honoria Dean and followed. Grantleigh, with no lady to escort, outpaced the four and opened one door. As he did so, the magnificent slow preface to John Travers' Trumpet Voluntary in C ended and the dancing rhythms of sixteenth notes skipped joyously about all of them.

At the end of Morning Prayer, the chords of Old Hundredth rang forth from the organ. Everyone rose to sing William Kethe's sublime words "All People That on Earth Do Dwell." Elizabeth raised her voice with the rest, Rossbury's passable baritone strong at her side.

After the final "amen" boomed through the nave, the vicar of St Etheldreda's waited in front of the altar as Elizabeth, escorted by William Dean, and Rossbury, flanked by Viscount Grantleigh, stepped forward. The ceremony with its prayers, readings, vows, and exchange of rings was soon over, and the bridal party retreated to the vestry to sign the register. When they returned to the nave, the newlywed couple faced the congregation, all agleam with delighted approval, and walked down the aisle together.

Marsh immediately began Jeremiah Clarke's *Prince of Denmark's March*. Its celebratory rhythms wrapped the departing couple with brilliant harmonies and flowed beautifully about the guests as people left their pews and followed the bridal pair into the soft April sunshine.

"Our congratulations, Lady Rossbury, on this happy occasion." Major Gresham, his uniform bright with gold epaulets and braid, its buttons gleaming, bowed over Elizabeth's hand. Then Gresham took his wife's arm and headed for the buffet table.

"Lady Rossbury!" whispered Elizabeth to Rossbury in awe.

Rossbury, whose arm circled Elizabeth's waist, asked, "Would Madame Verinder content you better?"

"Any name linked with yours contents me. Goodwife would do very well, I think." Elizabeth gazed at Rossbury with such adoration that for a moment he felt his throat close with emotion. Then she turned her gaze back to their guests.

All, upon exiting the nave at St Etheldreda's, had been invited to join Lord and Lady Rossbury for the wedding breakfast at Rossbury House, its drawing room doors opened wide so that it and the dining room beyond became one large room. Now at one side of the room, Elizabeth and Rossbury stood side by side, surveying the crowd that filled the space almost to overflowing.

"That was very bad of me, was it not, Richard?" continued Elizabeth while inching closer to Rossbury. "I have heard that a married couple is supposed to maintain a certain distance from one another in public?" Her rising inflection invited a return sally.

Rossbury pressed her more tightly to his side and replied, "I believe you are correct. Society dictates that husbands and wives remain aloof while in company and give their attention to everyone except each other."

Both smiled and nodded as Lord Ashburton passed them on his way to the buffet table.

"However," Rossbury added with mock seriousness, "I feel that a wife's duty is to obey her husband in all things."

"I await such instruction with eagerness, my Lord Rossbury," murmured Elizabeth reveling both in their word play and Rossbury's nearness.

"Rule number one." Rossbury's voice held the sternness of command. "One you must never forget, Lady Rossbury, if you wish to please me."

"Oh, I do wish to please you, my lord." Elizabeth worked the fingers of her left hand beneath Rossbury's hand at her waist.

"To disregard society's dictates on the public behaviour of married couples!"

"A difficult task, you must admit."

"But one I command you to obey."

Elizabeth edged still nearer into the warm, protective circle of Rossbury's arm. "Have I not made a good beginning, Richard?" she asked quietly. Although their banter had been playful, beneath the words lay a subject she knew Rossbury felt deeply about.

"Far, far better than good, Beth," Rossbury replied, his tone now matching hers. A host of scenes crowded his memory – her singing of the *Marseillaise* which appeased Jacques Rovault at Caudebec, her diving rush which sealed Henri LeBeau's fate in the barn near Tancarville, her calm assertion after Tyler's false accusation in Eastons, her poker wielding defiance of Sir Augustus Tremaine at the King's Arms. "Both here in England and in France."

His confirmation that all their marriage was founded upon had begun on that journey from Rouen to Le Havre touched her so deeply that Elizabeth felt tears of joy spring to her eyes. For a moment neither spoke, each watching the guests partaking of Mrs. Ballantyne's excellent buffet and speaking animatedly in small groups.

"And rule number two?" Elizabeth said at last, her words a return to their previous bantering.

"Prepare to be instructed, Beth." Rossbury paused and then turned upon her a gaze alight with a mesmerizing blue fire she had never seen before. "Tonight."

A glass of wine in one hand, William Clewett assessed the crowded rooms even while making the appropriate responses to Robert Danforth and Philip Stanfield's recounting of the new Countess of Rossbury's first visits to their shops. Two weeks earlier, Clewett had received Gideon Laurence's letter relating his sister's return from France and her imminent wedding. The news had prompted him to journey to London to meet the 'resurrected heiress' as he privately named Elizabeth to himself.

During a morning spent with Elizabeth at Farnsworth Place, Clewett had read the terms of Catherine Calvert's will. And when he had gently probed for information about the report of her death in France, Elizabeth had replied, "Gideon mistakenly thought that Aunt Claire and I had succumbed to the same ailment." Clewett wondered whether that was the whole truth of the matter and left Farnsworth thinking that his client had chosen her beneficiary well. The crowd at St Etheldreda's – expected apparently by no one except the servants – and all that he had heard about both bride and groom reinforced that opinion.

Gathered around the spinet in one corner of the drawing room, John Marsh and Martyn Ballard stood on either side of the bench where John Naismith sat. In the trio's animated conversation about Mozart, and in the tutor's simultaneous playing of the minuet from *Don Giovanni,* Naismith forgot his disfigurement.

On a nearby sofa sat Lady Eleanor Bardstow flanked by Baron Bardstow and Simon Verinder. Simon grinned as his cousin James emptied his plate for the second time that morning.

Conversing in hushed tones, the Villiers family perched on Hepplewhite chairs next to Faith and Charity Plover and studied the clothing of those at the wedding breakfast with a professional eye. Meanwhile, Alain eyed the plates of Mary, Betty, and Kate as they returned from the buffet table. "*Maman*?" Emìlie nodded and, taking her son's hand, felt him pulling her toward a three-tiered cake plate heaped with sweets.

The first guests the mother and son passed were the Craddocks and Smallwoods. Having found themselves in the same pew at the church, they soon traded particulars. As they feasted on Mrs. Ballantyne's delicacies, Sergeant Craddock regaled the drayman and his wife with tales of his former commanding officer's heroism. Then Smallwood countered with his own story about how Elizabeth's escape from a mad hackney driver had led to their Nan being offered a position with Mrs. Braithwaite.

Meanwhile, in a far corner on two straight-backed chairs angled towards each other, Winifred Braithwaite and Lord Somerville spoke quietly. Her seated posture as properly erect as it had been forty years earlier, Mrs. Braithwaite listened as Somerville talked about the nearly completed ground floor renovation of Hillgrove, his home in Buckinghamshire.

Standing with Lord Grantleigh, Nigel Farquhar glanced at the chairs where his uncle contentedly engaged in conversation with the sweetheart of his youth. He nodded in satisfaction and remarked, "A happy occasion."

"That it is," replied Grantleigh, looking in a different direction and thinking that he had never seen Rossbury appear more at ease.

Across the room from where the men stood, a trio of dowagers watched Lady Ashburton approach the sofa where they sat. "A pity," said Lady Farnsworth, "that Gideon Laurence has yet to recover from that unfortunate carriage accident last month. Simply too unwell to attend his sister's wedding."

Lady Ashburton, an angular woman with a nose for gossip, joined the conversation. "Yes, that's what I heard." She turned her head towards the bridal couple standing near the buffet table. "Quite remarkable that Lady Rossbury was not badly injured."

"I doubt that Doctor Patterson would agree with that statement," offered Lady Beatrice.

Lady Ashburton's eyebrows lifted marginally. "Oh?"

Lady Dalrymple patted her lips delicately with a handkerchief to hide her smile. That one'll get nothing from Bea, Dolly told herself.

"Fortunately, Mr. Laurence deputized the Reverend Mr. William Dean to stand in for him." Lady Farnsworth adroitly turned the conversation.

"And he is Lady Rossbury's…?"

"Her father's cousin," supplied Lady Dorothy as if the fact were well known by all of London.

"A cousin," repeated Lady Ashburton. Her eyes narrowed as they sought out William Dean. Quite ordinary, she thought as she saw the Gloucestershire vicar engaged in conversation with the Reverend Mr. Souther. Looking at the older man's clothes, she reflected, No money there. "But Lady Rossbury, I'm told, comes well dowered."

"Indeed, she does," supplied Lady Grantleigh. "Her great aunt, my dear friend Catherine Calvert, bequeathed Rosemont to Lady Rossbury. The house is as lovely as its name and lies not far from Brookfields." Lady Cecily paused and, seeing the surprise on Lady Ashburton's face, concluded, "It will be good to see Elizabeth there again."

Before Lady Ashburton could speak, Lady Beatrice stated, "A beautiful ceremony, don't you agree?"

"Beautiful, yes, it was," agreed Lady Ashburton, a trifle nonplused by the new direction of the conversation.

"And good of so many of those who know my godson and his bride to come to wish them well." Lady Beatrice smiled broadly while the other two dowagers murmured their assent.

Walter Cholmondeley-Musgrove handed a plate laden with delicacies to his wife who was seated next to Honoria Dean. Seeing the plate topped with the items she enjoyed most,

Mrs. Cholmondeley-Musgrove smiled at her husband whose attention was obviously elsewhere. In a corner of the room, she saw a much-decorated military gentleman surrounded by a group of officers. He seemed to be making pronouncements about something, and many of the room's other male occupants were drifting towards him.

"Thank you, Walter," Mrs. Cholmondeley-Musgrove said. "I believe Miss Dean and I both have all that we require."

While Mrs. Cholmondeley-Musgrove watched her husband make his way towards the General, Honoria Dean enjoyed the sight of her husband deep in conversation with the Reverend Mr. Souther, regaling him, no doubt, with Lord Rossbury's generous offer of a coach to take them to Steventon to see his university friend George Austen on their way home to Cranford.

Then Kenneth Weatherholt, Miss Henrietta Danforth on his arm, strolled across both women's line of sight. The young couple was oblivious to all around them.

"Those two will be another pair before the altar soon, I'll warrant." Honoria Dean's words echoed Mrs. Cholmondeley-Musgrove's thought.

"They will to be sure," agreed Mrs. Cholmondeley-Musgrove.

A quarter of an hour later a well-booted man detached himself from the group about the General. He glanced casually around the room to where the bridal couple stood near a doorway, for the moment alone. Smiling and nodding at those he had spoken to earlier, he crossed the floor.

"Lord Rossbury, Lady Rossbury," began the smuggler, "I could not leave without offering my sincere congratulations on this most happy occasion." His laughing eyes invited them to share the joke of his presence in a London drawing room.

"Lady Rossbury and I are honoured by your presence," Rossbury replied.

And by God, he means it, thought the smuggler wishing now that he had brought his wife to London with him.

"And it gives me the opportunity," Elizabeth added, "to thank you for arranging to bring my trunk to London. All I have left of my mother was in it."

Without thinking, Elizabeth had put her right hand on the smuggler's arm as she spoke. The gesture touched the man in a way he would have sworn was impossible. Feeling a trifle embarrassed, he shook off Elizabeth's thanks with an indeterminate wave of his hand. "No thanks needed, Lady Rossbury. Your note was more than ample."

"Sent with Mr. Abel Black," added Elizabeth.

"Mr. Black, it was!" agreed the smuggler as the three pairs of eyes gleamed with their shared knowledge of the false name. "This time I thought I'd make the delivery myself." He pulled a square of folded paper from his coat pocket. Then with a small bow he had not even intended to make, he handed it to Elizabeth. "Unfortunately, this will be the last delivery."

A letter from Uncle Léon! Elizabeth's inner voice sang. On our wedding day! For a moment, her heart was too full for words.

Taking the letter from Elizabeth's hand and tucking it securely into his own coat pocket, Rossbury spoke for them both. "What you have given Lady Rossbury is priceless."

The small tableau near the doorway had attracted the attention of Lady Beatrice who could not put a name to the man commanding so much of her godson's time. When she saw a square of paper transferred from the unknown man's pocket to Elizabeth's hand and thence to Rossbury's pocket, she rose from her seat at Lady Dorothy's side and moved towards the newly wedded pair and the nameless guest.

Her lips smiling politely, eyes bright with curiosity, Lady Beatrice asked, "Rossbury, be good enough to introduce me to…"

"Mr. Beecher, Lady Farnsworth." The smuggler erased the impoliteness of his interruption by taking the dowager marchioness' hand and bowing low over it. "Mr. Hiram Beecher, at your service, milady." Releasing her hand, the smuggler nodded his farewell, turned on his heel, and walked away, a rather surprised Lady Beatrice staring intently after him.

"Godmother," said Rossbury before Lady Beatrice could even organize a question, "it is more than time that Elizabeth and I made the rounds of all of our guests, don't you agree?"

More secrets, sighed Lady Beatrice with a forced smile, before adding with what she considered justifiable asperity, "Indeed, I do. Unless it is your intent to have a houseful staying overnight!"

By midafternoon, all those employed in the houses facing each other across Carlington Square sat shoulder to shoulder around the table in the servants' hall at Rossbury House, as satisfied with the meal they'd just eaten as the guests who'd left earlier.

With Dunhill sitting at his right, Harris scraped back his chair and raised his class. "A toast," the butler announced.

Harris looked upon the familiar faces as all rose. Mrs. Ballantyne and Mrs. Featherstone – for once in harmony about the quality of the food set before them. Mrs. Green and Martha Pearson – eying the younger servants like Edith without a word of criticism to mar the happy occasion. James Oak and John Black – teasing one another over who had eaten more of Mrs. Ballantyne's wonderful cake. Betty Kemp and Jake Porter – obviously enjoying the unanticipated opportunity to be together. Mallory and Weaver – two ex-soldiers pleased that the officer they had known for so long seemed destined for happiness at last. Patience Downes keeping close to the side of Jim Compton who had been telling Ben Tolliver about his own impending marriage and move to a position as stableman at Stowe Manor.

"To Lord and Lady Rossbury," Harris stated. "May they have all the happiness they deserve."

Everyone in the half-basement room immediately rose and sincerely echoed his sentiments. "Lord and Lady Rossbury."

That evening, Elizabeth sat contentedly at her dressing table. The fingers of one hand toyed with the small Sèvres bowl placed there, its tell-tale thumb shaped chip a reminder that beauty can exist within imperfection.

Slowly her eyes drank in the quiet of the candle-lit bedroom. Elizabeth could not quite believe it was now both hers and Rossbury's to share. Thinking that Rossbury, who had helped her with her buttons and then retired to his dressing room to give her some moments of privacy, would return soon, she quickly unplaited her long brown hair. Then she picked up a brush. Soon she was counting the strokes as she would have on any other night.

"Here." Rossbury took the brush from Elizabeth's hand. "Let me." Keeping his attention on his wife's head, he ran the brush gently through Elizabeth's hair.

Elizabeth watched him in the mirror. A lock of black hair fallen across his forehead gave him a boyish, vulnerable look. However, the triangle of pale skin at the top of his dressing gown and the shadows highlighting his cheekbones made her shiver in anticipation. A slight scent of soap, clean and homely, told her that while Rossbury had been away from the room, Mallory had shaved him. That knowledge and Rossbury's concentration on her hair touched her.

Unbidden, a remark made privately to her by Lady Ashburton returned. Apparently somehow details of Lord and Lady Rossbury's unorthodox bedchamber arrangements had circulated – beginning, no doubt, with an innocent remark by one of the staff to a servant from another house.

Consequently, Lady Ashburton had believed it "a kindness" to advise Elizabeth that "it is always wise to keep a little mystery in marriage." Fortunately, Lady Ashburton had expected no reply to her unsought piece of advice and had soon drifted away.

Mystery, Elizabeth mused, as the hair brushing continued, and saw Diana Holroyd, this season's most desirable catch. The sultry temptress, her parents, and her coterie of admirers had all appeared at St Etheldreda's. There's a young woman who can put mystery into any relationship.

But, Elizabeth reflected, marriage should be founded upon something far more solid than mystery. As she watched Rossbury plying her brush, she recognized that this something was epitomized by everything the man standing behind her represented. And sleeping anywhere but against his warm, strong back was unthinkable, for this was the joy for which she had guiltily longed ever since returning from France. Would Lady Ashburton be scandalized? Elizabeth wondered with a smile that made her gray eyes gleam and the corners of her mouth twitch. Probably, but nevertheless she would say a firm "No to mystery."

The smile and the words Elizabeth did not know she had spoken aloud prompted Rossbury to lay the brush on the dressing table and repeat, "Mystery?"

"Lady Ashburton's recipe for a happy marriage." Elizabeth turned and rose to face her husband.

"We have had more than enough of that already." Rossbury's quiet rejoinder and unfathomable look sent Elizabeth into the arms ready to enfold her. The thoughts of both flew to a long conversation they'd had on their third day in London after the events at Micah Whitbread's inn in Surrey, each having related at that time details from the past not shared previously with one another, secrets that – had they been known – might have prevented the near disaster at the King's Arms. Mystery, both thought, did not serve us well.

For a long moment, neither spoke. Elizabeth rested her head against Rossbury's chest and felt calmed by his reassuring, regular heartbeat.

Then in a tone of amused speculation, Rossbury broke both the silence and the serious mood. "Perhaps we should ask my godmother to introduce Lady Ashburton to Hiram Beecher."

"Or Captain Bird?" Elizabeth giggled while picturing the gossipy Lady Ashburton attempting to ferret out information from either of these men and her scandalized reaction if successful.

Still locked in Rossbury's embrace, Elizabeth lifted her head and saw his blue eyes brimming with laughter, eyes that told her whatever mysteries they left others to unravel, none would exist between them.

Then Rossbury's eyes darkened, and a look that quickened Elizabeth's pulse replaced the smile. His left hand tightened its grasp on Elizabeth even as his right extinguished the candle on the dressing table. Her lips parted as the blue flame of his eyes threatened to devour her. His kiss – possessive and lingering – left them both breathless.

"The mystery," Elizabeth whispered, her heart ready to burst with pure joy, "is that you love me."

"I propose that the reverse has as much, if not more, truth, Beth." Rossbury's hand caressed his wife's face, his fingertips tracing eyebrows, cheekbones, chin, and then mouth before his lips trailed over the same territory. By the time their mouths met, Elizabeth felt he had lit a fire within her that only he could assuage.

Rossbury clasped her close once again, felt her slim body press into his, and shuddered with longing. "It is with profound thanks I note that we have the rest of our lives to plumb this mystery," he murmured into her hair, his voice husky with emotion.

"And the two shall become one flesh." Elizabeth recalled the words the Reverend Mr. Souther had recited during the wedding ceremony earlier that day. How this can be, she thought, is the true mystery of marriage.

And as if reading her mind, Rossbury agreed. "Yes, Beth, that is the crux of the mystery of a true marriage."

"And one with which I have no experience."

Elizabeth's admission was made in an almost inaudible voice. In fact, had not Rossbury, who had suspected that his bride might be harboring some anxiety on this point, been keenly aware of every nuance of Elizabeth's behaviour, he might not have heard this quiet plea for reassurance.

With one finger beneath her chin, Rossbury tilted Elizabeth's head up. As his gaze locked with hers, he noted, "Nor have I – with you. We are both in an uncharted land, one we shall explore together, Beth."

"Together." The fear that had flickered briefly behind her eyes died and was replaced by something warmer, hungry for release.

"One of the most beautiful words on our language, I think." Rossbury smiled tenderly at the woman who had renewed his belief – dead for so many years – in the words he had just spoken.

In answer, Elizabeth moved quickly from his side to the only remaining bracket of candles lighting the room. After snuffing them, she returned, guided only by the gleam of the fire on the hearth, to face Rossbury. Without giving herself a chance for second thoughts, she grasped Rossbury's hands and placed them on the neatly tied white ribbon drawn through the neckline of her nightshift.

She heard his intake of breath as he understood what she wanted him to do; and while his fingers unloosed the bow at her neck, hers fumbled with the sash fastening his dressing gown in place. When the knot was undone, she dropped her arms and looked up at Rossbury as her nightgown slid from her shoulders and pooled around her bare feet.

Wordlessly, he shrugged out of his robe and then lifted her in arms that shook ever so slightly. A few strides brought them both to the great canopied bed, its rosy dome almost invisible in the shadows.

A moment later, she was reaching out to him, pulling him near, using her mouth to rain butterfly kisses all over his face while his hands glided gently over her curves – always moving, touching, circling – and fanned the fire within her.

With a shiver, she sighed, "Richard, make me yours."

"Together, Beth," he replied huskily, his body drawn ever closer to hers.

And together, two became one, love and trust wed in their embrace.

# AUTHOR BIOGRAPHY

Dianna Louise Lund spent thirty-four years sharing her love of British literature with her students. In the thirteen summers she passed in England, she reveled in traveling to historic residences and imagining the adventures and romances of times gone by. For Lund, these storied environs were the inspiration for the Rossbury saga.

Lund, a resident of California, enjoys hiking, flying right seat in a Cessna 172, and assisting her husband in ministry. She is hard at work on the next installment of Elizabeth and Verinder's story.

Printed in Great Britain
by Amazon

79075690R00251